The Soulkind Awakening

Book 1

Steve Davala

For Laurie
For her tireless efforts reading and rereading this story.

Chapter 1: The Beginning

Freezing water dripped from Jace's nose and chin. He shivered despite the blanket wrapped around his shoulders. The last thing he remembered before being swallowed by the icy waters of the Soulwash was racing that girl. He smiled.

Technically he beat her.

An old man wiped Jace's brow with a cloth. "When I said I might see you inside, I did not mean like this." The man's long frazzled ponytail hung over his brown Healer robes.

"Your first time in the Library and you see something no one else has."

"Turic, right?" Jace said.

"Well, your memory is working fine. At least part of your mind is still functional. Welcome to the Hall of Healing."

A dome, its color a pale mix of blue and green, curved upwards above his bed. The voices of people talking replaced the previous quiet. Turic stood a little taller as they looked over at the boy.

A stern voice interrupted the murmuring. "Let me see him."

Turic stepped aside.

Jace looked up into the sharp features of a tall man in deep purple robes. "Who is he?" Jace whispered to Turic.

"The Guard Master. He accompanied me from Myraton."

"The leader of *all* the king's guards?" Jace said.

"That is correct," the man said. "I am Huron Caldre. What happened?"

"Thought I'd go for a swim." Several of the onlookers chuckled, but were silenced by Caldre's look.

"From the roof of the Library?"

Jace nodded.

"The waters of the Soulwash are icy, and you were under for several minutes."

"Minutes?" Jace said.

"Several guards swam in after you," Turic said. "But it was too cold and they did not stay long. I have no idea how you survived."

"I… don't remember a thing."

"If you remember *anything*, you will tell me." The Guard Master's hand tightened on Jace's arm.

"Jace."

Jace winced as he heard Karanne call to him. Her voice lacked its usual sting, but he knew it was there, somewhere. He saw her red hair a head above the others bobbing as she weaved through the crowd towards him. Thoughts of how she would punish him for this one flooded his mind. She reached his side and knelt down.

One look from Karanne and the Guard Master finally let go of Jace's arm. But then she fixed that look onto Jace. He braced himself.

"I'm glad you're all right."

Jace shrugged and rolled up the edge of his blanket. He let out a sigh.

"But I am going to kill you later for this."

There she was.

Straeten pushed his way to Jace's side. "I can't believe I missed it." With his height and stout build, only his round face gave away his twelve years.

"It wasn't that good," Jace said, but Straeten still frowned knowing that not every day somebody did that.

The girl from the race stood beside him, as well. Cathlyn? She closed her eyes and shook her head. What was she worried about? It's not like she pushed him over the edge of the library roof.

"You were fast," Jace said.

She smiled a bit.

"But I was first."

Her smile fell. "More like *lucky*."

Huron Caldre spoke again. "Whatever happened to you under those waters, you have Turic to thank for your recovery."

Jace nodded at Turic, who gave him a squeeze on the shoulder before walking away with the Guard Master. The two spoke low and fast.

"Hey, what's in your hand?" Straeten said.

Jace looked down at his hand, red and shaking from holding something tightly. The funny thing was he didn't know what it could be. With some effort, he pried his fingers back. And there he saw it: a cloudy green stone with three white lines across it, smooth as if washed by many waters. He rubbed its cool surface between his fingers.

"Turic!"

Jace looked up from the green stone as he peered into Turic's house. He dropped it into his pouch at his side and the clarity of his memory of that day ten years ago faded, like a dream after waking suddenly. He pulled the drawstrings tight and then once again to be sure and he heard the stones inside click against each other.

Turic had to be all right.

"He goes up into the hills to the west sometimes. Maybe he left us a note," Cathlyn said, still on her horse.

"Do you really think he'd be out in the hills this late?"

Cathlyn dismounted, and Jace watched her long brown hair trail behind her as she jumped. "Are you going in or what?"

Jace fumbled for the flint on the lantern before it lit. The lantern cast flickering shadows on the darkening walls as they walked into the empty house. The two paused for a moment when they saw a chest ajar and papers and books strewn about. Cathlyn quickly started thumbing through the piles.

"It seems like he was actually looking at his research again." She moved a book, exposing some maps of the Hall and the valley below.

"Someone's coming," Jace said.

"I don't know how you do that. I can't hear a thing."

Jace shrugged. "Check your ears. It's not Straeten, his horse doesn't step that way."

"All right, I get it, I'm impressed."

Jace smiled until Allar, Cathlyn's older brother, appeared outside the doorway on his horse. "Greetings, lovebirds..." Even Jace couldn't hear his next words. But he could guess what they were.

His hand instinctively went to his knife, but Cathlyn put her hand on his forearm.

"What are you doing here?" Cathlyn asked.

Allar shifted on his horse and straightened his fine clothes. "Mother and Father sent me out to look for you. Influential members of the Hall Council are staying at our estate tonight and you're to be there, as well."

"Allar, I can't come back now. Turic is missing."

"Isn't he always missing? It's a wonder he's still alive." Allar was cut off by another horse galloping through the trees into the clearing. Allar stood straighter and kept quiet when he saw the rider.

"I thought I smelled something," Straeten said with a glance at Allar. "No luck down by the river. Did you find anything here?"

"Well, his maps and research were scattered all about. He went through his old notes, Straeten." Cathlyn smiled for a moment. "The maps were of the west side of the valley and, like Jace said, he's been known to explore around there. I say we head up into those hills."

"Cathlyn, you must not have heard me the first time." Allar shot a glance at Straeten and then in a slightly softer voice, "Mother and Father want you home, now!"

"Well then you go home and tell them I'm going to be a bit late." Cathlyn leapt up into her saddle and more than just nudged the side of her horse with her heels.

Jace shrugged his shoulders at Allar and walked over to his ride, Straeten's oldest horse, Blue.

"Better do as she says," he said and jumped on the horse. "I always do."

Blue neighed back in response, making Jace laugh. The old horse looked young and sleek in the dark as she sprang to catch the leader.

Straeten led his mount beside Allar and he just stared at him. Straeten's black horse shot off after the others, leaving Allar grimacing in the clearing and his horse itching to follow them.

Darkness settled in and the trees seemed to swallow the light from Cathlyn's lamp bobbing up ahead. Soon, Cathlyn slowed her horse as the slope of the hill increased and the sky opened above the thinning trees. Jace urged his horse alongside her to gaze out upon the valley and down on the Hall. Across the river, their town of Beldan looked alive with all the lights twinkling in the dark. Carts crossed the bridge, vendors packed up booths, and smoke curled upwards from nearly every building.

"I see you brought your friend along, Straet," Jace said when Allar broke into the clearing. Jace scanned the hills looking for any sign of Turic. Blue snorted and the mist from her breath curled upwards.

"It wasn't my idea, but another set of eyes wouldn't hurt, I guess." Straeten peered downward at the Hall. "Do you really think Turic would go this far up into the mountains?"

"The maps are all we have. Let's go," Cathlyn said, preparing to start her horse up the steep hill before them.

Jace shook his head and Blue snorted again. "I don't think the horses will make it in the dark. It looks pretty rocky up there."

4

"He's right, Cath, maybe we should leave them here and go on foot." Allar dismounted, untied the lamp from his saddle, and strapped his horse's reins to a tree. He walked over to Cathlyn's horse and helped her down. Strange enough, she didn't argue with him.

Straeten and Jace exchanged looks and shrugged, and then both secured their horses, as well. "Don't worry, Blue, we'll be back." Jace patted the old mare's nose and she playfully nipped at him.

"The old man better be up here," Allar said. He stood close to Cathlyn and walked fast with her away from Jace. He knew he was talking about him, and he only heard a few words, but they were enough.

"I can't believe you're here with *him*."

He scowled back at Jace, but Cathlyn didn't turn around. Jace's heart twisted in his chest.

She took three faster strides to get away from her brother. She led the way and kept a fast pace on the winding path, even as it grew rockier. The chill in the air deepened and Jace pulled his cloak out of his pack to throw around his shoulders. Allar tried to put his cloak around Cathlyn, with little success. She pushed him away without words and with such determination that he gave up. Jace smiled.

"Don't even know your own sister, do you?"

"Like she knows you?"

Jace's step faltered a moment. Before he could do anything else Cathlyn put her hand gently on Allar's arm and gave Jace a silent look with a small smile. She turned forward again towards the waxing moon rising well above the western peaks and lighting the path and hills. The light reflected off Cathlyn's long brown hair and made her breath visible in the cold air as she walked on the path. The waterfall plummeting into the Soulwash behind the Hall sparkled in the moonlight and the group could faintly hear the roar of the falls as they gazed out upon the valley.

"What's that over there, Cath?" Straeten said and pointed northeast into the night sky to where a mix of red and yellow lights rose above the horizon and then faded away. "You're always watching the stars…what was that?"

"I…don't know. It seemed to happen right over the town," Cathlyn said. "Let's remember to ask Turic later, when we find him. Come on." She started to walk again, when Straeten, munching on a twig, called for her to stop.

"He's probably just out for a stroll somewhere. When we head back down later, he'll be waiting for his supper. Here, have one of these. You'll feel better." Straeten handed everyone a twig off of a low bush.

"No thanks," Allar said with one eyebrow raised. Straeten shrugged his shoulders.

Jace bit into the plant and its minty taste cleared his mind. "Let's go to the top of the falls tonight and see what we can see. He couldn't have gotten all that far." He shouldered his pack again while looking cautiously down the steep cliff and at Cathlyn as well. She didn't look back.

After an hour of scrambling around on the rocks in the dark, the group reached the top of the path where the water first leapt from the cliff to the valley floor. The dark eye of a cave peered out from the hill and water swept from its mouth, plunging to the Soulwash hundreds of feet below.

"Watch your step, Cathlyn," Allar said.

Glaring at him over her shoulder, she slipped and sent a loose rock bouncing down the cliff wall. Allar caught the back of her robes and shook his head. As she leaned over to see the falls, she gasped, seeing the top of the Tower of Law glisten in the moonlight so far below. She waved everybody closer.

Jace looked down again at the waterfall plunging into the waters he had fallen into some ten years ago, and brushed his hand across the pouch at his side. The others joined him to stare at the sight.

"You going to jump in there again?" Straeten said with a smile. "I missed it the first time."

"Nice," Jace said with a look to Cathlyn. Jace was sure, even after these many years, she still felt bad for racing him through the Library, even though he was the idiot who fell off the roof. "Come on, we're here. Let's just hope he's in there."

"Hello! Turic?" Straeten yelled into the cave. He felt the wet moss clinging to the cliff wall, and the ivy hanging over the opening brushed his face. Holding his lantern in front of him, he stepped into the darkness.

"Watch the rocks, Straet," Jace said. "I'm right behind you and I'd rather stay dry." He pushed back the ivy and stared at the stone carvings lining the entrance, among them foreign words and strange creatures. He saw some familiar animals; the most prominent being a scruffy wolf with a bird poised on its shoulders, followed closely by a noble-looking steed. There was also a dragon.

"Who made these?"

"I don't know," Cathlyn said, gracefully watching her step and the carvings at the same time. "I've never heard of this place before."

The water rushed past, trying to grab their feet as they walked along the narrow path beside the flow. Jace nimbly balanced upon the rocks without getting his feet wet, while Straeten just trudged through the water, making an effort to splash the water back at Jace. Fifty paces into the cave, the path widened and the lamplight cast great shadows on the walls around them. All four stopped and gazed at the stories told on the walls. Cathlyn held her lantern higher to see the whole room, when her light fell upon a still form sprawled on the floor.

"Turic!"

She rushed to kneel beside him. "He's freezing! We need to warm him up. Quickly! Build a fire!"

"Is he dead?" Allar asked. Straeten and Jace, on the way out to look for wood, slowed a step.

"He's barely breathing. Hurry, please!"

Allar looked around at the cave. "What should I do?" He paced back and forth.

"Find his things; they should be lying around here somewhere."

Jace and Straeten ran out while Cathlyn grabbed Allar's cloak to wrap the old man. Cathlyn wiped the cold water from his lined face while Allar scrambled about. He came back soon after with Turic's pack just as Straeten and Jace returned with some dry wood.

"This will have to do for now," Jace said. "There's not much out there."

He quickly stacked some tinder and pulled out his flint, scraping it with his blade to get the fire going. "Straeten, check his pack to see if he has anything to get him warmed up."

Straeten pulled out a small pouch of herbs and a pot. "Glad he came prepared." He glanced over at Jace, who was still working at building the fire. "I sure could use something to dry off my boots here. You going to get that started or what?"

Jace laughed nervously and shook his head. "If you could ever do better, I'd let you try."

"Good point," Straeten said.

Soon, a blaze started and Cathlyn had warm tea to pour into Turic's mouth. The pungent liquid had a strong medicinal odor. It took five of the longest minutes Jace had ever waited, but Turic's eyes fluttered. He looked up at the four sets of smiles and coughed.

"It's all going to begin soon, if it hasn't already," he said and coughed again. He tried to stand.

Cathlyn placed her hand on Turic's forehead. "Shh. You don't have the energy to talk much less move. Now rest until morning and then we'll see about getting you home."

Turic tried to sit, but he slumped back down.

"What are you doing up here anyway, old man?" Allar said.

"Hey, enough." Jace said. "You can head home now if you want and tell your parents everything is all right. We'll let him rest and then maybe talk to him. Right now, I'm thinking of the supper we brought with us. Anyone else?"

Straeten's stomach rumbled an answer. Jace handed out food and everyone ate his or her small portions, realizing how long of a climb they had really made. After a few minutes, Allar sat down and stared at the food. "Well, do I have to beg?"

Jace tossed him a chunk of bread and cheese and he gnawed on it hungrily.

"Mother and Father will worry when we don't show up tonight, Cath. We should head down first thing in the morning."

Cathlyn nodded reluctantly, continuing to cradle Turic's head in her lap while Straeten and Jace hung the old man's soaked clothes beside the fire. Jace watched Cathlyn trace symbols on Turic's forehead. It was just a show, he thought. She always had a soft spot for anything Turic could teach her, even if her parents and a few others in the Hall dismissed his research as foolishness. But Cathlyn always held true to his words. Jace smiled at her; he probably did, too.

After the fire crackled for an hour or so, Straeten lay down to sleep on his rolled up cloak. "See you in the morning, everyone. Enjoy your rocky beds."

"Goodnight, Straet." Jace walked over to Turic and saw some color struggling to return to his pale checks. "You'd better get some sleep, Cath. I'll tend him for a while." He paused and took a deep breath. "Cathlyn…"

She smiled and yawned. "It's all right Jace."

"But…"

"You lied to me, and Straet. I'm sure you had your reasons."

"I did," he said and reached unconsciously for the pouch of stones at his side. "Friends shouldn't do that, though. I know you wouldn't."

8

"You're right. And don't forget it!" she said with a sharp punch to his arm.

After Jace smiled she continued.

"It's not like that's who you are anymore. Karanne is helping you out now. And you're working with Straeten," she tried to stifle a laugh. "Cleaning out his horse stalls."

"Don't remind me." He watched her face in the soft flickering firelight. She laid Turic's head on his pack and traded places with Jace.

"What is this cave? It feels old, and...alive." She yawned again and tried to find a comfortable spot on the cold, rock floor.

"Hopefully we can get some answers in the morning." Jace put his back against the wall and placed his hand on Turic's forehead. Seeing Cathlyn struggling to get comfortable, he rolled up his cloak and handed it to her for a pillow.

"Good night, Jace."

She rested her head upon the cloak.

In his efforts to stay awake, Jace flicked out a knife and began twirling it in the air. Spinning on his palms, flipping it end over end; it was as if the blade was alive. With a sudden snakelike motion, he threw the dagger firmly into a drying log by the fire.

Turic appeared to be resting soundly, so Jace put the rest of the wood on. While slipping the knife away, his hand brushed past the pouch at his side. He pulled out his green stone from the Soulwash, feeling its smoothness between his fingers.

The memory flooded into his mind and senses. He wasn't in the cave anymore; there he was, running on the roof of the Library, staring at Cathlyn's blue robes, and not at the ever-approaching roof ledge. Off the tower he plummeted to the waters below, watching Cathlyn's horrified face spin quickly away. He felt the water as he crashed into the surface of the Soulwash.

In the next instant, he lay on the table with Turic watching over him.

No matter how many times he relived this memory, he could not remember what happened below the icy depths. It was almost within reach, but somehow not close enough.

"Are you just going to lie awake all night over there?" Jace asked without looking up, while turning the stone in his hand.

"You just stay away from my sister," Allar said across the fire. "We all know what you are."

Jace closed his eyes. "Not anymore."

"You'll always be one of them." Allar turned around to fall asleep.

Jace sat thinking of what Allar said for a long time until he reached into the pouch for a particular stone. Memories flitted across his mind as he sifted through them, and then he found it.

He was in the marketplace of Beldan, no more than ten years old, with nondescript, gray clothing hanging from his shoulders. The sights and sounds of the peddlers, dancers, and animals moving in every direction at once surrounded him. After each quick scan across the crowd, he looked back down to the ground. People would remember his bright green eyes, his boss told him. Not a good trait to have. His short-cropped, curly brown hair bobbed up and down above his blank expression as he threaded his way through the maze in a seemingly aimless fashion, never once bumping into anyone unintentionally.

"You look a little light," Jervis Redferr said as he walked beside him. "I'll be top man today, huh?"

Greasy red hair hung over his eyes as he looked straight down on Jace. His brown teeth sat crookedly in his mouth. Jace resisted the urge to say something about his breath, but just barely.

A thin whistle sounded over the crowd, hardly noticeable to anyone not listening for it. Jervis turned his head sharply at the warning and Jace saw a man across the crowd slipping a whistle under his black cloak before blending into the background. Jervis bumped forcefully into Jace's shoulder, knocking him backwards. Patting down his coat, he knew he already had at least twice as much as Jervis. Probably one of the reasons Jervis hated him so much.

The unfamiliar sound of a foreigner's accent drew Jace out of his thoughts and he edged closer to hear the rotund merchant speak. Exotic daggers glittering with bright gems lined his booth.

"Yes, I just came from Myraton with these knives. They came from the island of Gorahda. They're the sharpest blades you'll ever see."

"What's Myraton like?"

Jace stepped closer while the merchant held a curved knife in the air for the people to see.

The merchant looked down at Jace and smiled. "Towers many times higher than your own here! Ships filling the harbor, foreigners walking about...and the castle!"

He waved his arms into the air. After winking at the boy, he returned to selling his wares.

Jace pulled himself away from the merchant's stand and stories. An awful pit in his stomach accompanied the extra weight under his cloak. The dagger he lifted from the merchant's table poked into his side, and once again, he cursed his boss. He cursed being a thief. He pried out one of the stones from the hilt of the blade. Not to sell, not to barter with in the Thief Guild, but to remember. He gripped the gem so tightly it cut his palm.

And with that thought, Jace put the stone into the pouch and pulled the drawstrings shut and then rechecked it. He fell asleep with fitful dreams of his past.

Chapter 2: The Cave

Jace woke the next morning when the sun's first rays fell upon his face. And when the sharp rocks bit into his neck. He squinted and tried to move out of the light, but could not avoid the glare. When his eyes adjusted to the brightness, he saw through his curly hair that Turic was not only awake, but also walking about, staring at the carvings on the walls and writing down the words written beneath them.

"Turic!"

"Shhhhh, boy!" Turic said. "You'll wake the others. Now, do me a favor. Go to the entrance of the cave and cut down the rest of those vines so we can let a little sun in here."

"It's good to see you back to your old self," Jace said and clasped his arms around Turic. "And what do you mean, 'a little sun?' What do you call this?"

Turic patted the boy on his shoulder. "All right, now we have work to do."

Jace smiled and looked around at the cave while stretching his back, sore from last night's rocky bed. When he reached the cave's entrance, he saw the sun rising in the east over the mountains. With his knife, he sliced through the vines around the perfectly round entrance and splashed a little cold water on his face. It was as if the cave was here to greet the sun each morning.

"When we first saw you last night, you said something about a beginning?"

"Let me show you what I mean," Turic said. The sun pierced the cave entrance and lit up the walls, which were covered in elaborate carvings.

Jace just gaped at them as the light filled the room. With this much light, even Straeten would have trouble sleeping. Sure enough, as he walked further back to where they slept, he found the three others in various states of awakening.

"Remind me to never do that again," Straeten said, rubbing his neck.

"Turic!" Cathlyn said and rushed over to him, throwing her arms around him. "How do you feel?"

"I knew you had skill, but who knew it would manifest itself in such healing arts?"

Cathlyn blushed.

"How did you get up here?" Straeten asked.

"Well, I may be old, but I still have something left in these bones, yet. Now, look at all these carvings. They appear as if they grew right out of the walls." Turic stepped back, taking in the twenty-foot long wall covered with scenes and symbols.

"What does it all say?" Cathlyn said. "I don't understand any of it." Turic placed his arm on her shoulder and rested his head on hers, still facing the walls.

"You will not believe me when I tell you."

"I've seen something like this before."

Everyone looked back at Jace.

"Under the Soulwash. Seeing the walls more clearly triggered it. I don't remember exactly. A small cave with a pool...."

Turic's eyes widened. "Something like this under those waters? Do you know what this means? There must be hidden pathways beneath the Library further below the catacombs than I have ever been. I don't know how I could have missed them...."

He trailed off, reaching for the quill he dropped. Without warning, he stumbled and Jace rushed to his side.

"I'll be all right," he said, as Jace helped him to his feet. "We must explore the Library as soon as we get back."

On his tablet of paper, he resumed copying down the strange lettering and the carvings with a shaking hand and a smile across his face.

"Why did you come up here in the first place?" Jace asked.

Turic, once again concentrating on his drawings, managed to say, "Yesterday, I just began to climb up this path, I do not know why."

"We saw your research on the bed and desk in your house," Cathlyn said.

No one dared mention the research to him for the past ten years. Jace held his breath.

"Yes...yes. Something called me to look at my maps and papers. Then, I climbed up that hill for hours. I needed to reach the top."

Cathlyn let out a sigh and Turic continued to scrawl everything down while he spoke.

"When I finally got to this cave, I knew this wall had not been seen for hundreds of years, or I would have heard of it. I stepped backwards to view the whole wall and fell into the water. 'Old fool,' I thought. 'You'll freeze for sure now.' Luckily, I had enough left to pull myself out, if nothing else. But without you kids...."

Straeten bent over the rushing water to get a drink. "Well, we had to find you. Who else would tell us all those stories?" He splashed Cathlyn and she jumped.

"This is why I came here," Turic said, and handed the notes to Jace.

Jace read over Turic's writing. He looked up at the Healer with a questioning look and then read it again.

Turic walked over to the wall and put his hands on the first carving.

"This says the Soulkind will awaken."

Allar rolled his eyes and finished packing. "Soulkind? All right, I've had enough. We came all the way to hear him tell his stories of *magic?* Isn't that the reason he got kicked out of the Hall in the first place? Someone else was chosen to study those things back in Myraton because he wasn't good enough, or he was just plain crazy.

"We're going home now, Cathlyn."

Cathlyn slapped her brother in the face.

"How dare you?" Cathlyn said as Allar rubbed his cheek. The only sound in the cave was the running of the water. "Turic is a great man, and this will show the Hall how foolish they were to lose him."

Jace slipped the knife back into his sleeve after he listened to Cathlyn. Lucky for Allar this time she was faster.

She placed her hand on Turic's shoulder and looked into his eyes. "Is this for real, Turic? I mean, you've always taught they would awaken, but..."

The faint sound of a bell resounded through the cave. Its ringing snapped Cathlyn out of her thoughts.

"I have to verify the rest of the carvings to be sure, but I know in my heart the Soulkind will awaken. Now, your parents will be worrying..."

"I'm sorry Turic, for my brother. I want to help with all this. Will you be all right?"

"Straeten and I will help Turic down the hill when he's finished, right, Straet?" Jace said.

Straeten nodded and Jace folded the paper he was writing on and put it in Turic's pouch. "Just tell Blue I'll be right there. We'll see you at the Library when the third bell rings with the rest of the notes. Be careful on that hill."

He smiled at Cathlyn as she bid farewell to Turic and walked to the cave entrance. Allar glared at Jace before he, too, turned to leave.

"My, that Allar has never grown up, has he?" Turic said.

Straeten threw his arm around Jace's shoulder. "Don't worry. I'll protect you from him."

"Aw, get on. Turic, how's the sketching?" Jace turned and elbowed Straeten in the gut. "We'd better think about heading down soon, too; the sun is shifting from the tunnel."

"Patience, boy, patience. I do not want to trudge up here again if I can help it. Plus, the Hall will want to hear about this right away." Turic paused for a second. "Did you say the Hall has changed quite a bit since... I left?"

"More different than the same, I'm afraid, from what we've heard. Few old Healers remain, and the new tell stories about a crazy old hermit who lives out in the woods. Sorry."

"No worries. But, if I am to make a convincing presentation on this to the Council, I must be prepared. Now, just be patient." Turic seemed to stand a hair taller than he had before.

Jace and Straeten looked closely at the walls. From what Jace could make out, the scene depicted two groups of people marching out onto the plains of a valley, preparing for a battle. One side was backed by countless hideous beasts, while the other was greatly outnumbered, yet confident. The old man cursed and repeatedly adjusted his spectacles.

"Do you need any books from the Library to help you, Turic?" Jace said.

"Not now, thank you. I have some books in my house that may help. However, it appears you may be able to assist me with the translating. You were always good with..." Turic faltered and stumbled again. Before Straeten could move to help, Turic stopped himself with his arm against the wall and waved him off. "Maybe we should leave..."

"I'm sure you have enough material to get started on a translation," Jace said. The sunlight slowly crept to the bottom of the walls. "And if not, Straet and I can come back up here and finish it."

Turic nodded and packed his things.

The hike down the hill proved even more difficult than the ascent, and with the addition of caring for the seventy-year-old man, the two boys were soon out of breath.

"You know," Turic said, "I probably could have stayed up there all day."

"Yes, but who would've brought you food tonight?" Straeten replied. Turic nodded and tilted his head.

An hour later, they reached the clearing where the horses grazed on what was left of the late summer grasses. Blue pricked up her ears and whinnied into the cool morning air. Jace returned her cry and laughed.

"What's so funny?" Straeten asked.

"I think she said we're late. Look, Cathlyn must've left her horse for us," Jace said pointing to a third horse. Walking over to Blue, he saw a note under the saddle. He opened the small piece of paper and read the note with his back turned to the other two.

Jace,

I left a horse for Turic. I didn't want Straeten to cry about having to walk down the mountain. Let me know when you make it down all right.

Cathlyn

PS. Tell Straeten I think he scares my brother a bit.

Jace looked back at Turic and Straeten and smiled. "Hey Straet, whatever you're doing to Allar, it's working. Now let's go." He and Straeten then lifted the Healer onto Cathlyn's horse and the three of them started down the path.

"Later when you come to the cottage, I would like you to try to remember more of what you saw that reminded you of those carvings. Then, we can explore beneath the Hall Library."

Jace grinned. Yes, he was definitely back to the old Turic.

After reaching Turic's cottage in the woods and making certain he would be fine by himself, Straeten and Jace headed back towards town.

"Shouldn't you go tell Karanne where you've been?"

"Karanne, great. I forgot. Yeah, she's going to kill me," Jace said. "I'll see you later. Blue, you ready for a morning run?"

The horse reared back, whinnying before bolting into the woods.

The cool morning air blew onto Jace's face as Blue galloped across the Lower Bridge, south of NorBridge, to the other side of the Crescent River. The open country called to him; the woods, the hills, the

16

skies. As if in response to his thoughts, the solemn cry of a hawk pierced the air. Sighing deeply with a breath of the cold mountain air, he continued on. His hand strayed to the pouch at his side as he thought of Karanne and he sorted through the stones again. Another memory flashed into his eyes.

Jace was crossing NorBridge with Straeten. They were heading to the Library for the very first time. River birds called and swooped over and around the people crossing. Jace stared at everything. He had only seen this from afar, and never thought he would be on it. Halfway across, Karanne snuck out from behind a statue and playfully grabbed him around his neck.

"You're getting slow, kid."

Jace shook his head. This was getting old. He'd have to get even someday.

She quickly stood up when Straeten stared at the knife she held to Jace's neck. "Uh, this is a little game we play."

"This is Karanne."

Straeten lowered his eyebrows. "Your, mom?"

"Yeah, sort of." He looked up at her. A couple of strands of her red hair fell across her face. There was an expression there Jace seldom saw, but he knew it when he saw it.

She would always be there to look out for him.

He reached down and picked up a stone to remember.

Jace stopped his horse in front of Karanne's cottage and the memory slipped from his mind as quickly as he dropped the stone into the pouch.

"Karanne! Karanne?"

He walked in and looked around, but saw no one. She must have already gone to Mathes' school today: her new *job*. Well, it wasn't really new, but it always felt new to her, she told him. Mounting Blue, he looked up at the city walls to the north and noticed a lot of people gathering on the bridge. Something was going on there, something different than normal. He nudged Blue into a gallop.

Jace hurried Blue to her stall so he could join the crowd. Vendors' booths lay empty in the streets, leaving only a few remaining stragglers hurrying off to join the others. He quickened his pace to a run and tried to listen to the hum of the crowd. He could only hear a few snatches of conversation, among them garbled ramblings of "magic."

His eyes opened wide and he sprinted the rest of the way, slowing only to dodge and dart around the dawdling pedestrians. Along the streets, sure enough, he heard that Brannon Co'lere, the researcher who replaced Turic, had returned from his eight year stay at the castle in Myraton with results from his studies.

Turic had been right.

One of the Soulkind was Awakened.

Chapter 3: Awakened

Jace darted around the corner near the center of town. It appeared that the entire town was crowding the streets, blocking the way to the Hall. He struggled to fight his way through the onlookers but finally gave up when the crowd refused to yield, and after they shot him many nasty looks. If the Soulkind had been awakened, he needed to see with his own eyes.

Jace turned and sprinted away. Long ago, thieves strung rope under the bridge to help them sneak across. Hopefully, no one was using the rope now or he might accidentally toss off a few old friends in his excitement. He felt pretty certain they would be elsewhere exploiting the desertion of the townsfolk. His mind spun and his breath quickened.

Fortunately, the makeshift bridge was vacant.

Halfway over, his right foot slipped off the rope and he stared into the churning white water. Taking a deep breath, he tried to focus. Slightly shaken, he grabbed onto the ropes and watched his steps more carefully. Sure, when he was a new thief and had to scale walls, or walk along a narrow, high rooftop he did feel a few loops turned in his stomach; but not like this.

Once safely across the rope bridge and up the steep rocky bank, he encountered a crowd again. From this point, he could see directly into the courtyard where Brannon stood. Brilliant glowing reflected off the sides of the buildings.

Jace still couldn't see anything, and he could stand it no longer. He vaulted off the back of a surprised man and pulled himself onto the rooftop of a short building. Just at that moment, a great stream of fire burst from Brannon's fists and dispersed with a *boom* a hundred feet into the air. Jace nearly fell back off into the crowd but held on and cheered along with everyone else. Undoubtedly, the rumors held truth and the power of the Soulkind had awakened. Some townsfolk stumbled backwards over the bridge; others stood and shook their heads; others merely stood motionless. Whispers of doubts also filtered through the air, mirroring the awed townsfolk with disbelief.

"Looks like a good fireworks display," a short, fat man said just below Jace.

Jace risked shooting him a look. This *was* magic. A place within his heart began to burn and he quickly looked back to Brannon. Just when the crowd appeared on the verge of a riot, Brannon stepped upon the stage and raised his hands, silencing the crowd. Jace strained to hear every word he spoke.

"Today, we will begin recruiting for a school in Myraton. The school was set up years ago, awaiting the return of the Soulkind magic, and King Camas Reldrich anticipates our coming. However, not everyone will be able to join as thorough testing will take place for several days to see who will become Followers."

The crowd was silent for a moment, and Jace could only imagine they were as dumbfounded as he with the news they would all be able to take that test. Before they could say a word, Brannon reached around his neck and held aloft an amulet, golden and glittering in the morning sunlight. Some of the crowd dropped to their knees.

So, *that* is a Soulkind. Jace smiled. Having learned from Turic, he thought he might know which one Brannon possessed, but he could not be certain. With a somersault off the roof, he landed perfectly on the ground. Before he realized it, he was standing at the front of the crowd, trying to get a better look. Someone grabbed his shoulder before he walked upon the stage.

"Jace!" a voice said. "Can you believe this is happening?"

Taking a second to realize someone spoke to him, Jace tore his eyes from the Soulkind. It was Cathlyn.

"How long have you been here?" he said, half hugging her and half looking up at the Soulkind. Her hair still smelled of last night's campfire.

Brannon still held his amulet aloft and paced back and forth. Jace could not stop staring at the Soulkind with its gold glinting from the sun, nor its bearer, who boasted a smile. A strange black mark, like a scar or tattoo, wound around Brannon's neck.

"When the second bell rang, I was waiting at the Library. Then he came out."

Like Jace, Cathlyn's eyes kept shifting to the golden amulet. Before they could manage a closer look, Brannon tucked the Soulkind under his cloak and walked away with his head held high.

"Remember those flashes in the night sky last night, Cath?"

Cathlyn nodded slowly. "I guess Turic was wrong about him, after all."

20

"Turic! He was right! We've got to go tell him."

As the crowd started to disperse and plan for the testing, they hurried away to tell their old friend and teacher the news he had foretold, yet suspecting he would be distraught over who made the discovery.

He took it poorly.

Turic paced across the wooden floor, his hands clasped behind his back. The floor creaked every time he spun around to head in the opposite direction.

"Awakened? Brannon? How could *he* have done that? The man is an imbecile! No conjuror, no sorcerer, and definitely not the image I had of the one who would awaken the Soulkind. I thought the Soulkind choose who becomes a Master. How could this have happened?"

He walked to the wall with his back to Jace and Cathlyn.

"Was it——?"

"It was amazing——" Jace said.

"Fire sprang from his fingertips," Cathlyn said. "The crowd was staggered."

Turic nodded with a smile. His face seemed to grow younger as they continued spilling out their excitement. When they stopped, he shook his head and threw himself down at his desk. His arms drooped over the desktop, knocking a stack of papers to the floor. Jace rushed over to pick them up.

"You've made a big discovery, too, Turic! Look at these drawings of the cave...."

As Jace straightened the papers, he noticed some scribbled notes along the margins of Turic's intricate drawings.

"You expect my scribbling to contend with the Awakening?" Turic sighed and his shoulders sank. The lines on his face seemed to grow deeper again.

"There's more here than just the Awakening, Turic."

"What do you mean?"

"Here it looks like some sort of warning."

Turic reread the part Jace was looking at but sat down in a chair and slung his arms over the sides.

"It does not matter now. Can you at least describe to me what the Soulkind looked like?"

"Gold and shining in the sun," Cathlyn said. "More beautiful than even I——"

"There was a fiery red gem in the middle——"

"…and golden wings across the front…"

Nodding slowly, Turic closed his eyes. "Marathas. I can imagine you will be the first in line for the testing, Cathlyn?"

She smiled and her lip quivered. "At the third bell after noon, the doors open at the Hall of Guard's barracks room. That leaves us five more hours. They're setting up a makeshift classroom there. I wonder what they will do to test us."

Her eyes focused on a faraway place and then back on Turic.

"You *will* be coming to test…right Turic?"

Turic continued to stare at his desk.

Jace tried to think of something that would rekindle the spirit that resurfaced earlier this morning. "Remember you wanted to help me recall what I saw beneath the Library? I could try now…" He opened his pouch and began to look for his green stone.

Turic's eyes opened wider. "Well, of course I do. Let's see if your curious memory can help figure this out. Now sit down and we shall begin."

He stood up and busied himself to gather more paper and a quill and ink.

Cathlyn smiled at Jace and he winked in return. When he took the green stone out from his pouch, he rubbed its smooth edges. Flashes of the memory brushed past his mind and he nodded to Turic. These memories had never been clear.

"Try to focus on the stone wall. Let your mind go back, let it drift…."

Jace held the stone and closed his eyes as Turic repeated those words in soothing tones.

With a jolt, Jace dropped off the tower, and plummeted to the icy waters below. After he crashed through the glassy surface, he found himself on the table, waking to Turic, Straeten, Karanne, and Cathlyn.

And then he was back in Turic's house.

Again, he tried to remember what happened, and yet again, he plummeted off the roof into the Soulwash and then immediately lay on the table. Jace thought of the stone wall and his faint memories of something similar under the water.

Under the water….

Suddenly, he saw quite vividly the surface from the depths and felt himself straining to reach the top. Something moved on the other side! What was it? He was so close now that he could almost make out the shifting shape above. His head broke through and he gasped for air.

He emerged into a small room lined with flickering torches and a carved wall surrounding the pool. The water glowed softly and cast odd shadows onto the carving-covered wall; indeed like the one up in the mountains above the waterfall. Among the drawings were a king on a throne engulfed in a shadow and a dragon soaring through the air.

A hooded man, who previously stood quietly in the room, spun around at the sound of Jace coming through the water. The man raced to the water's edge and his eyes narrowed. The man grasped his hair and forced him back below the water.

Jace sat up with a start and threw his stone across the room.

Only Turic's hasty writing was heard over the minutes of silence following Jace's tale. Jace stared at the wall. Cathlyn kept her eyes on him.

"Did you get a good look at the man's face?" she placed her hand on his shoulder and shot a glance towards the still scribbling Turic.

Jace held his throbbing head in his hands.

"I don't remember. His eyes. I…just don't remember."

The man's face was a cloudy vision in his mind, but he would never forget the burning, rage-filled eyes. How could someone have that much hate? He rubbed his temples with the heels of his hands.

"I remember that day well," Turic said. "I had just returned from Myraton. Many others came back with me. Do you remember seeing any of those people?"

"I only remember seeing the Guard Master that day, but I don't think it was him." Jace stood up to get some air from the open window. He flinched when he mentioned that man. He was the one who had asked permission from Turic to send Brannon to be the head researcher of the Soulkind that day. Probably something Turic didn't want to be reminded of.

"Perhaps it was someone from Beldan? Maybe you could try the stone again…."

Jace grimaced as he remembered his aching head. At least Turic wasn't fazed by what he had said. "No thanks."

Blue looked at Jace through the window. Jace smiled and patted her nose. Somehow he knew he would see those eyes again, whether he wanted to or not.

"The man is not from the Hall, nor is he from Beldan."

Cathlyn carried the green stone over to where Jace stood by the window. "After we pass the testing, we'll find this person, right?"

Her breath quickened after she mentioned the test.

"When we leave for Myraton, we'll find him."

Jace continued to stare out the window at the Khalad Mountains beyond the cliffs of the valley. He opened his pouch, motioning for Cathlyn to put the stone inside. When it hit the bottom, he pulled the drawstrings shut and tied a fast knot.

Turic finally stopped writing. "First let's find the room you ended up in below the waters. I know of some walled up areas beneath the Library that no one has ventured into for centuries. Oh, don't worry. Of course we will finish before our testing starts."

Jace smiled. "I'm not worried about missing the test, it's just…well, it's just good to see you…."

"What? Back to my old self? Well, don't just stand there…come on!"

On their way to the Hall, they took a slight detour to Straeten's family's stables. Straeten, standing beside his shovel, greeted them with a broad smile, speechless after the events of the day. He had seen it too, but not quite as close as his two friends had. When Jace told him about his memory of the Library and their plan, Straeten jumped out of the stables and went to clean up and change clothes. After a few minutes, he raced out of the house to meet up with the three others.

Wrinkling his nose, Jace said, "Straet, you could have used a few more minutes cleaning up."

"Get on. I didn't have time to dolly myself up like you did." Straeten chomped down on an apple and grinned at his friends. "Thanks for stopping by, I hoped I'd find something better to do until the test than cleaning the stalls."

Turic walked away from the stalls and back again. "Come now, the day will not wait for us. We have a lot to do in the hours ahead." He wound his way through the crowd, apparently not caring anymore if the others followed.

"I'm not dolled up, am I?" Jace whispered to Cathlyn.

With a laugh she ran to catch up to Turic.

NorBridge bustled with excitement. Nervous talk of those who planned to take the test left lips furiously. The four friends heading to the

Hall were silent, having exhausted their words earlier over what possibilities lay ahead. Now, they had to focus on finding Jace's room beneath the Hall, though their thoughts strayed to learning magic and their unspoken fears of failing the test.

"Turic should go first," Jace said.

"I agree," Cathlyn said. "Our teacher deserves the honor."

Straeten nodded and Turic bowed his head. "I thought I was going to have to beat Jace to the front for certain."

After what seemed like ages of wading through swirling crowds, they finally crossed NorBridge and the great Hall opened before them.

"We shall head directly to the Library to look for that room. If we happen to run into Co'lere, well, I will congratulate him and then show him our research from the cave." Smiling, Turic continued to lead.

Peering into the Hall, the group saw people assembling desks and makeshift rooms for the testing and quickened their pace. Turic kept his head under his hood, but could not escape a few welcome shouts from old friends.

"I have been investigating some ancient carvings I need to research and interpret," Turic told them.

Although he told them not to speak a word to any others, he saw them scurry off to no doubt find more of his friends. Straeten turned to Jace.

"I thought people would barely remember him."

"I guess he meant a lot to them. Maybe they're his former students."

Turic rejoined the others. "I have been through this building countless times and have seen almost every room," he said. "The lower levels contain the catacombs, which hold bodies buried hundreds of years ago. Somehow, the records of the inhabitants have been either misplaced or destroyed. A shame, to be sure. But I digress. There are many twisting tunnels and possibly secret passages throughout."

"Secret passages, huh?" Straeten said.

The three young ones grinned at each other and began to look for switches or hollow paneled walls. Their method of knocking on everything soon caused other people to stop what they were doing and stare.

"I am quite certain there are no secret doors on this level," Turic said. "Come, young Ver Straeten, we will seek out the original design prints of this Library. I know exactly where they should be. I see no need for all of us to go. Jace and Cathlyn, you may continue to the lowest level and wait for us by the book lift. You will know it when you see it. Take this key; you will need it to get through the door to that area. We shall meet you there, momentarily."

Turic lifted a scaly-looking, claw-shaped key from around his neck with great care and reverence and handed it to Cathlyn. Jace and Cathlyn then ran over to the spiraling stairs with only a brief glance at Turic and Straeten, the latter looking back at them longingly as Turic pulled him by the sleeves.

"Remember where running got you last time, Jace," Turic said, but they kept running down the staircase two steps at a time.

"That was up on the roof. We can't get any closer to the ground here," Jace said from around a corner of the staircase.

The light from the Library began to fade. Jace lit the torches set in ornate sconces every eighth step to prevent them from being engulfed in darkness. Soon, he lost track of how many stairs they had descended and their speedy steps soon slowed to a walk. The twists of the narrow stairway towards the catacombs made them dizzy but they eventually arrived at a circular room containing a large, gilded stone door. The door bore no handle, only an elaborate keyhole resembling a dragon's grinning visage, which seemed to move and laugh with the shadows.

"Well, this must be the door he meant. Have you ever been down here, Cathlyn?"

After removing the chain from her neck, Cathlyn carefully inserted the claw-shaped key and turned it until a loud *click* emanated from within.

"Never."

The doorway gaped open upon a large and silent room. Only the flicker of the single torch in the stairwell reminded them that time continued, as shadows leapt about shelves and carvings on the walls. No dust or cobwebs had accumulated and the air felt fresh and cool. A breeze blew across their faces.

From beside the doorway, Jace picked up a small, brass lamp and lit it from the torch he brought, filling the air with the oil's aromatic fragrance. He lifted the lamp high to scan the room for other openings and headed off towards the wall to look at some carvings.

"Wait for me." Cathlyn hurried to catch up while taking in her surroundings. "Don't touch anything you shouldn't."

"Too late. Come over here! Look at this. It looks like a tomb."

When she caught up, he motioned to a stone coffin set in the wall.

"There's no name plate on it. Probably no one important."

Cathlyn shook her head, as she looked further down the wall at other similar coffins. "For them to be buried here, they must have been important. Whoever they are, they've been here a long time."

Nearly thirty other coffins lined the walls, not one with inscriptions on them. Cathlyn reached for the lid to a casket, then shook her head and scanned the rest of the room instead.

They walked to the shelves in the center of the room and soon they found themselves poring over the leather-bound volumes.

"Look at these books," Cathlyn said. "They have a script I've never seen before."

"Well, this one isn't very interesting. Sort of a log of finances and purchases. And this is about the purchase of farm land. Come on. Let's look for the lift and see if Turic and Straet are back."

Jace put the book down with a start when Straeten appeared with Turic, who began walking along the coffin-lined walls.

"Hello, you two," Turic said. "Come now, there is little time to spare before the testing."

Straeten held a lamp above the old man's head while Turic looked over a folded piece of paper.

"According to these plans, a passage lies this way. Come along!"

Abandoning the books, Jace ran to catch up. "Is the room under the Soulwash in the plans?"

He bumped into the shelf as he hurried, knocking several books to the floor. He started to pick them up, but only toppled more in the attempt, and so he left the mess to follow Turic down the passageway.

"I think I can see where the room should be, Jace," Turic said. "These plans are vague in several areas, so I cannot be totally sure."

He wiped his hand over a coffin in one of the recesses in the wall.

"Now, notice how there is no dust in here? I have heard tales that the people buried here were great Followers. You can feel the power in this place, yes? Are you not in complete awe of what surrounds us? Take a second to feel it."

He looked around and smiled. "These walls were built using magic and still resonate with that power; a remnant of another time."

After a moment of silence, Turic said, "You must have proper respect if you desire to become Followers. Those without respect will not be chosen to follow. And maybe one of us will be chosen to master a Soulkind, for there are other Soulkind awaiting their awakening."

"Turic, why are all those books down here instead of upstairs in the Library? You'd think someone would be interested in them."

"Those books are written in an unfamiliar language. No one in this town can read them and I do not know of a person alive that can. Me? I've tried to find the cipher for that script, but unfortunately, all records appear to have vanished."

"They can't all be like that, there was at least one I could read," Jace said.

Raising one eyebrow, Turic responded, "Well then, we will have to get a clerk down here to bring them upstairs."

In the several minutes that followed, the party walked through the narrow hallway in silence; that is, until a gray brick wall awaited them.

"Great. Now what?" Straeten said.

From the pouch on his back, Turic removed a hammer and chisel and handed them to Straeten.

"What happened to having the 'proper respect for the magic resonating within these walls?'"

"We will find out on the other side of these bricks. Now, get going!"

Turic settled down on the steps and held the plans in front of his face. Jace and Straeten exchanged shrugs and soon the halls echoed with the clanging of metal upon stone.

Minutes passed like hours and the well-placed bricks did not feel like being moved, even under Straeten's continuous hammering. Cathlyn and Jace sat on the steps next to Turic staring at the blank walls.

"Do you want me to take a hand, Straet?"

"No. I'm definitely going to finish this." The muscular boy caused everyone to wince with every pound.

Cathlyn grabbed Jace's sleeve and spoke into his ear. "Let's head back to the lift room. I want to look around some more and maybe you could clean up the mess you left behind."

Without looking up from his plans, Turic said, "A grand idea."

Jace looked at Cathlyn and rolled his eyes. "Yes, a grand idea. Straeten, you don't mind if we go, do you?"

Straeten kept pounding.

"Okay," Jace said. "We'll be back soon to see if you get anywhere." Jace and Cathlyn got up and walked down the hall with their lamps held high to light their way.

When the *chink, chink* nearly faded, Jace asked, "Cathlyn, what do you want to do when you're a Follower?"

Cathlyn responded without pause. "Last night, when I revived Turic, I felt so wonderful. I actually felt like magic moved my hands. Of course, that was all in my mind. What about you?"

After a few steps in thought, Jace responded, "Ever since I was a kid I wanted to fly. And see dragons. And…"

He stopped when he noticed Cathlyn no longer walked beside him. When he turned around, he saw her standing behind, staring at him.

"That sounded stupid. I know dragons don't exist, but—"

"Don't back away from your words. All that can happen." Cathlyn smiled and ran to catch up.

"When we get back, let's ask Straeten what he's going to do. My guess is he'll want to use magic to knock down walls."

"Or to clean out the stalls," Cathlyn said. The two laughed on their way down the hall.

After reaching the entrance to the catacombs, Jace looked into the book lift and saw a sliding door and a pulley system on the side.

"Where do you think the lift goes?"

Pausing a second, Cathlyn responded, "I'm not sure. Probably up or down, what do you think?"

Shaking his head and smiling, Jace tried activating the contraption by turning the switch and pulling the rope. Nothing. He turned the switch again. Still no luck.

"I think I see the problem; it's the pulley cord along the side here and the switch. They're not attached to the lift anymore."

Cathlyn looked in the door with her lantern above her head and examined the inside of the lift. "It looks like we can both fit inside. Let's give it a try."

Jace boosted himself into the lift, then held Cathlyn's hand to help her in.

"Thank you, sir," she said and curtsied in the small compartment.

Jace held her warm hand for a moment. He opened his mouth to say something but the lift suddenly creaked and dropped a couple of inches and he let go.

Cathlyn smiled and pulled the gate downward. Jace pulled on the rope and they began to descend slowly.

"Whatever you did, it must've helped," Cathlyn said.

Jace shrugged his shoulders. "Maybe all it needed was some weight…"

"Hey!" Cathlyn said.

"Nice. And for that gate to be shut. I thought this was the lowest level."

"Jace? Maybe we shouldn't be going this quickly," Cathlyn said when they began to drop a little faster.

"I think you're right, but I'm not moving us anymore," he said, trying to grab the rope. "Ow!" He pulled his hands back, blowing on his palms.

"We better hold onto something, I don't think this is going to be gentle."

They continued to accelerate downwards and smelled smoke. Jace mouthed the words, "I'm sorry." Cathlyn managed a smile and reached over to hold his hand. Jace felt his face turn red.

The walls began to shake, dust filled the air, and just when they thought the walls would burst apart, they hit the bottom with a resounding crash. All Jace heard was Cathlyn's quick breathing.

"That wasn't so—"

Jace was cut off as the floor creaked abruptly underneath the lift and then cracked open. The lift plunged into darkness as it dove further through the foundations of the Library.

When Jace opened his eyes, he feared he had gone blind. Total darkness surrounded them and he heard nothing but his breath amidst the settling dust. A musty smell hung heavily in the air. He sat up to search for Cathlyn, wincing as his head spun. Shaking off the pain, he reached out and felt her back and then her head. He quickly leaned over to make sure she still breathed. He would never forgive himself if he let her die.

He placed his ear by her mouth. If only he knew as much about healing as she did. Like the faintest whisper, her warm breath touched his ear and he exhaled his long-held breath. He could have waited forever feeling that warmth on his cheek.

A few minutes later, Cathlyn's breathing deepened and he felt her move.

"I can't see," she said.

"Really? I can see just fine!"

She inhaled sharply.

Jace laughed. "The lamps are out. I can't see either. Let's try to go back up," Jace said. "Ow! Hey, I thought you couldn't see."

Cathlyn laughed as he pulled on the rope. It pulled straight through the ceiling and coiled onto the floor.

"We're stuck here."

Cathlyn scrambled to reach the gate of the lift.

"All right, we have to get out of here," Cathlyn said, her voice quivering. She bumped her head trying to stand.

Jace grasped the gate and grunted while trying to lift the bent metal. "Together!" An inch at a time, the gate creaked upwards, but when it fully opened, they found that the entrance outside the gate was blocked. They both started to kick the barrier.

"Maybe...Straeten...is on...the other side."

"Be serious, Jace." Cathlyn quickened her kicking, but snickered nonetheless.

After several futile efforts to knock in the obstruction, Jace heard Cathlyn's breath quickening. Suddenly, they felt a brick shift. With a shout, they kicked faster and harder and soon the wall tumbled over, leaving the two coughing on the dust. Whatever room they came to, they could not see.

"Let's not get separated," Jace said. "I've got a wall here."

"Ouch!" Cathlyn, not four feet away, rubbed her nose. "Over here, too."

The hallway they walked through seemed to be carved right into the bedrock of the Library's foundation. The air dripped with moisture, yet was not musty. The walls felt slick when they slid their hands across the surface. Jace tripped over a rock jutting out of the ground. "Watch your step. It doesn't look like anyone's been here for a while."

"Where are we?" Cathlyn said. "This isn't on any map I remember."

Before Jace got to his feet again, he felt something else on the ground, a small box about the size of his fist. "I got something here, it's locked, though." He fumbled in the dark with it and brushed off the bits of dust and dirt that was crusted on it. "I can get into this later when we can..."

At that moment Jace froze.

"Something's on my hand." He brushed at it with his other hand and tried not to panic.

"What is it?" Cathlyn said.

"I don't know, probably just some bug." He brushed at it again.

"Bugs." His voice raised a bit as he felt them crawling on his hand. He swatted and hit his hand against the wall and felt a small pinch like a bite.

Suddenly, they were gone.

Jace let out a breath and put the small box in a pouch at his belt. "It's all right. Sorry about that."

The two continued in silence, listening to the other's breath. Each held one hand out in front and the other on the wall. Their feet hit an obstruction after a few hundred feet. Thinking she had reached the end of the tunnel, Cathlyn swung her fist, but hit empty air.

"Steps!"

"Cath, is it getting lighter in here?" Jace hastened his steps upwards. Indeed, he could see the texture on the walls, now. With each passing step, the light grew brighter and he turned and saw Cathlyn smile as she climbed.

When he reached the top of the stairs, they saw that another wall blocked the path, however this one had holes through it that let in some light from a room on the other side. Jace's jaw dropped when he looked through a hole. This had to be the room from his memory. Inside, he could see stairs spiraling downward to a pool of water. Straeten and Turic were there staring into the depths.

"I guess I could manage to fall again," Jace shouted out to them with a smile.

His smile fell from his face when he saw Straeten's and Turic's worried expressions. Straeten ran up the steps around the pool to the wall. "Are you okay?" he said and pounded on the wall with his fist.

"Yeah, we're all right, other than being stuck on the other side of this wall," Jace said and began kicking. Straeten was pulling bricks down almost in a frenzy and it soon toppled down.

Without a word, Straeten enveloped them both in a monstrous hug. Almost silently, he said, "I thought you two were dead."

"We're okay," Jace said. "We fell, but nothing big."

"Nothing big?" Straeten said. "We *felt* something hit rock about an hour ago. We ran back to the catacombs entrance and guessed that you two went into the lift."

"We couldn't resist," Cathlyn said.

"That was foolish," Turic said from the pool's edge, "but I am extremely relieved you are both okay. When we pulled up on the rope, we felt no resistance. Like it snapped off the lift. Now imagine if you were hurt and could not get out, we would never have known where to-"

"We're fine," Jace said. "Really. Let's get back to what we're here for. The test is going to start soon."

He took a few steps towards the pool and then slowed. For the first time in eight years he would see into the waters that almost took his life.

Turic turned around to look at the walls and pillars lining the circular room. "Does this look familiar to you, Jace?"

"Yes."

Jace turned to look on his way down to the pool. The light from Turic's and Straeten's torches cast shadows on the walls and glittered brightly upon the surface of the water. He ran his hand along the short carved rim around the water until he came to a crack in one carved section.

"And no. The steps and the pool look familiar, but not the carvings. Maybe there is another pool somewhere. Or maybe I just can't remember."

"You have always recalled events precisely before. Perhaps it was the shock. Maybe if—"

"I'm not going to try the stone," Jace said. "Besides, how many more rooms could there be like this in the Library?"

Straeten scratched his head as he looked at a carving of a man holding a talisman above a mass of people. "How old do you think these are?"

"Seems like these are from the same time as the ones in the cave above the waterfall," Cathlyn said. "Possibly by the same person, or at least in the same style." She ran her hands over the cool, stone surface.

"Oh yeah. I almost forgot," Jace said as he took the box from the passageway out of his pouch and looked at it for the first time.

Turic walked over. "What is that?"

Jace shook the black box and heard something rattle. "I don't even see how to open it, much less pick the lock."

"No I mean what's on your hand!"

Jace held his hand up to the light and saw something underneath his skin shifting around.

Jace looked at the cut in his wrist. He backed up and tripped on a small stone step while he stared at his hand.

Turic grabbed Jace by the wrist.

"I once read about these things," he said and held the boy's arm up to the light. "But I did not think they still existed."

"Just get it out of me!" Jace said. Whatever was in there began to wrap around his wrist under the skin. His hand began to twitch uncontrollably.

"I think heat was used to remove them, or even …" With a sudden motion he thrust Jace's hand under the water inside the pool.

"That's freezing!" Jace shouted and tried to yank his arm out, but Turic kept it there with an intensity that Jace couldn't resist.

His hand twitched stronger than ever. He watched with morbid fascination as the thing uncoiled and burrowed its way back through the skin. As soon as its head touched the water, it seemed to realize its mistake and tried to go back in. The water, however, slowed its movements and in that moment, Turic's hand shot through the water and grabbed its head with a pincer-like grasp. He slowly drew out a long, black colored creature. The thing's mouth opened and closed, revealing tiny but razor sharp teeth. Its tail wrapped around Turic's wrist, but soon it stopped moving as the coldness of the water took it.

Jace pulled his arm out of the water, his skin red from the cold.

"What was that thing?" Jace said and looked at the tiny holes in his wrist and then back at the creature, to make certain it wasn't moving under the water.

"I'm not sure," Turic said. "But the important question is why did it attack you?"

"What do you mean? It was just sitting there in the dark and it just bit me. Right?"

Turic looked at the small box lying on the ground and then picked it up. He traced his fingers along the edges of the material.

"What, you mean it was protecting the box?"

"Perhaps."

"How did I not even feel that going in my hand?"

"It must have a strong anesthesia in its mouth. Fascinating creature," Turic said.

Jace looked at it floating in the water and then at Turic, who was also watching it. "You're leaving it in there."

34

"I suppose I should," Turic said, and sighed. "Now this box of yours, I don't know what it is made out of. It feels like stone but it is as light as wood. I have a feeling that you couldn't open this even if Straeten were hammering on it."

"Maybe you should hold onto it, to record for the Library," Jace said.

"Perhaps," Turic said. "But for now, you keep it. It came to you for a reason."

"Admit it; you just don't want to hold it in case there are more of those... things on it."

With a smile, Turic turned around and examined the carvings on the walls and copied them down into a journal. Straeten came over cautiously and sat next to Jace. Cathlyn, too, came over to talk quietly while Turic walked around the room.

It was then at that moment Brannon Co'lere appeared.

He crossed his arms and watched them with a half-smile.

"Well, hello!" Brannon said. "When the others told me old Turic returned to the Hall, I had no idea what you would be up to. I have spent some time trying to track you down.... Welcome back, old friend."

He bowed to Turic, the Soulkind dangling for all to see.

Turic stood up straight and bowed his head, but his eyes kept drifting to the amulet. The Soulkind sparkled in the torchlight, beckoning to everyone. Three golden wings seemed to grow from its backside and nearly covered the brilliant red gemstone they encircled.

"Indeed, it is Marathas."

Brannon's smile wavered and then he responded. "Yes, I forgot you spent some time studying the Soulkind before I did. This one, Marathas, is proving very exciting to explore. And the new magic we have created with it..."

He paused and looked sideways at his audience as he caressed the amulet.

"May I see it?" Turic asked.

Brannon walked past him, looking at the carvings as he spoke, "Perhaps later. Now, Cathlyn, will you be at the testing? I hear you are our top student in the Hall. No doubt you will be first in line."

Cathlyn blushed. "We'll *all* be there today."

"What— even Turic?" Brannon laughed, but when no one else joined in, his smile faded. "I will have a lot of people to test. We are looking for apt *young* pupils to begin a lifetime of research in Myraton."

Turic took a deep breath. "Brannon, I wish to show you a discovery I made that will help explain why the Soulkind were dormant. And how they may have been awoken improperly."

Brannon continued to admire the walls for several seconds before turning around. When he finally did, he stroked the golden wings of the amulet and pulled down his high-necked collar to scratch a marking around his throat. The pattern looked like a ring of twisting flames.

"Well that really doesn't matter too much now that I've awoken one, does it?"

Turic stared at the mark around Brannon's throat for a second then continued. "I'm sure you had little to do with it." He opened his pouch to examine his notes. "A cave exists in this valley that no eyes have seen in many, many years. Therein lies the history of the Soulkind, of sorts. I have yet to translate all the carvings, though they are very similar to these in this room. I think its discovery will be a great help in figuring out how and why magic ended."

He brought out his partially translated manuscript and showed it to Brannon.

Brannon laughed. "Those are truly lovely pictures. Have you been practicing for the past eight years?"

"Here, Jace and I discovered a battle where it seems the Followers of Light and Darkness met for the last time," Turic said. "Of course, it is incomplete, but when I finish, I will bring it to the Hall—"

"If we haven't left yet with the new students. Indeed, I must be on my way back up to the testing room; we will be starting soon. Best of luck to you all." He looked at the three young ones and exited the room.

They waited several minutes until Brannon was well out of earshot before they unleashed a barrage of curses in his direction. After a minute they addressed Turic.

"I thought for sure you were going to tell him about the box I found."

"He's not the one you want looking at that, I'm sure."

"What was that mark around his neck?" Straeten said.

"I have read in ancient writings that a Master Follower bore a marking created by his or her Soulkind," Turic said. "When a Master passed on magic to a student, the student gained a small marking similar to that of the teacher. I am confused by his mark, though. It's probably just my imagination. So, are you three ready to become that man's Followers?"

36

"We've seen him teach," Cathlyn said. "He has such a 'logical' approach to it."

"He takes the fun out of everything," Straeten said. "We'd rather just learn from you."

Turic looked up, pausing a moment, his frazzled ponytail hanging in his face and his spectacles resting at the end of his nose. He smiled. "Thank you. Thank you all. Now, let's see how well I actually taught you and go show him how to be a *true* Follower."

Just after noon, with nearly two hours left, Turic, Jace, Straeten, and Cathlyn paced in front of the closed doors of the testing chambers. Occasionally, someone walked out from inside the barracks, causing the doors to open briefly, and Jace pushed the others aside and looked in. However, he never saw more than just hastily constructed walls covered in purple sheets before the doors shut again. Talking to any of those people was useless, too. Both Jace and Cathlyn backed off when two guards were placed on either side of the door.

The guards here were fitted differently from those in the Hall. Stout leather armor covered their chests, gray cloaks flowed over their shoulders, and tall black boots protected their feet and legs. A circular silver clasp held their cloaks in place. They scanned the courtyard from beneath their helmets, warning everyone not to move a step closer.

Straeten spoke up. "Who are you? We've never seen guards dressed like you...."

The two guards were tight-lipped, yet after some prodding, one did respond.

"We are members of the Soulkind Guardians. We came from Myraton to protect the Soulkind, and soon, the Followers."

After that, Straeten could get no more out of them.

People from every walk of life—from beggar to merchant to noble—formed a line stretching within the courtyard. One's status made no difference in this test, only the ability to learn magic. Not that any of the well dressed people looked at the beggars or said anything. Jace recognized a few faces; one in particular stood out: Jervis Redferr. The older boy cut in line behind Jace.

"Jace Lorefeld." Jervis sneered through long, stringy red hair. "It's been a long time, hasn't it?"

"Not nearly long enough."

Jace turned back to the others but Jervis walked in front of the group and put his arm around Jace's shoulder. He bowed to them all, but his eyes strayed to Cathlyn and he smiled.

"Introduce me to your friends."

Cathlyn tilted her head slightly. Straeten and Turic, too, nodded, then turned away.

"Maybe not," Jervis mumbled. "This thief was pretty good, I have to admit, even scared me a little."

He pushed his hair out from his eyes and looked over at the attentive guards. When they looked away, he brandished a small blade with a flick of his wrist, and within a breath, Jace had his drawn. Straeten glared and Jervis laughed and stepped back.

"Bet you didn't know how good a thief he really was. All the things he used to do."

"What are you doing here?" Jace asked and slid his knife back under cover. Although his friends knew about his past, he tried not to draw attention to it. He eyed Cathlyn to see some of her reaction, but there didn't appear to be one.

"I'm here for the test, what do you think? I'm going to become a Follower, or whatever they'll call me. Just think of the things I'll be able to do with magic."

"Yes, that's what I am afraid of," Turic said under his breath. "But not to worry."

"What did you say, old man?" Jervis walked forward until he stood less than a foot away from his face. Jace stepped towards them both.

"Just that the Soulkind will choose those who follow," Turic replied, not backing down, and held a finger up to Jace, who stopped and slowly nodded. He knew better to cross the old man when he looked that way. Turic pushed his spectacles up from the end of his nose.

"I believe most of the Soulkind embody goodness, and I am quite sure a pure heart is needed to follow."

For a second, Jervis stared at Turic and then over at Cathlyn. "What is he talking about? No one's used these things for thousands of years. Pure heart, huh? I suppose you've got one?" He raised his knife towards Turic's chest.

Just then, Karanne appeared and grabbed a tuft of Jervis' hair from behind his ears. With a clenched fist, she yanked him up and away from Turic's face. His knife clattered on the ground.

"You never learned your manners, did you? Cutting in line is quite rude, young Redferr. Good day, Cathlyn, Straeten, Turic." She gave a smile to Jace and said, "I'm glad you're all right."

Jace smiled weakly at her until her smile dropped.

"We'll talk about where you went last night later."

She yanked upwards again with her fingers full of hair. Jervis squawked and she released him. He glanced at his blade but she returned a look that resounded, "I wouldn't." He started backing away to the end of the long line.

"You're not one of us anymore," Jervis said. "You can't order me around."

Karanne feinted in his direction and Jervis tripped over his own feet trying to get away.

Mathes Spier caught up to her. "I never knew you were so good with children. I'll have to remember that when I leave you alone with my students again. Good morning, everyone." He bowed with his hands folded in the cowls of his robe.

"Greetings, Mathes Spier. Are you here for the test?" Turic asked.

Mathes' eyes widened, but he then replied with a laugh, "Me? Never. It's a dangerous tool I don't think we're ready to handle again." He folded his arms tightly and looked at Jace, Cathlyn, and Straeten. "And that's something you should all think of."

After a moment of awkward silence, Jace walked to Karanne and put his arm around her shoulder. He still had to reach up to do so. "Are you going to take the test, Karanne?"

At first, Karanne scoffed at Jace's question, then she looked to the side and shrugged. "I actually came looking for you, but...why not?"

Mathes laughed, then his smile slid into a frown when Karanne stared at him.

"I thought for certain that you more than anyone would see how foolish this is."

He gave a short bow and left. Karanne stuttered, then peered over the top of the crowd to see where he headed.

The group stood without speaking until Jace pulled out the small black box. "Take a look at this, Karanne." And in a whisper to the others, said, "She's really good at opening things."

She raised her eyebrow at him and then turned her attention again to the box. Slowly she turned it over, inspecting each side carefully.

"What is this? I've never seen anything like it."

Jace explained where he got it, glossing over the part where that thing was in his arm.

"Well, I don't think I can open this thing," she said, handing it back. "It's locked, but I can't even see how it would open in the first place. Pretty crafty. Too bad Picks isn't around."

"'Picks?'" Cathlyn said.

"Someone we both knew a long time ago. He's the best at... what he does," Jace said.

Just because she knew the truth about his past didn't mean she had to know all the details.

"Good luck with the test," he said uneasily to Karanne.

"And to you all, and who knows? Maybe I'll return to Myraton to go to the school with you."

She frowned, then smiled a brief good-bye to Jace and walked back to the end of the line. Jace watched her leave and saw her eyes stray to where Mathes departed. He wondered what she meant by "return to Myraton." Karanne never left the valley here. He was sure of it. He turned around to see the line of people wrapped around the Tower of Law and out into the Hall of Guards. Before anyone could say a word about the encounter between Mathes and Karanne, a trumpet blast sounded and a man announced the beginning of the testing. Jace smiled at his friends while they stood awaiting the opening of the door.

Chapter 4: The Testing

The two Guardians watching the entrance unlatched the door and presented Brannon Co'lere. He wore purple robes and the Soulkind around his neck, exposed for everyone to see. He held his head up high as he surveyed the many people in line waiting to learn from him. He scanned the crowd with a smile and a slow nod, but his smile faltered when he recognized the first man in line.

Turic returned his look with confidence.

"Each of you will have the opportunity to test," Brannon said, his smile returning, "to see if you have the innate ability to work the magic of Marathas. But if you fail, all is not lost. You will also have the honor of attempting to awaken other Soulkind."

He held his amulet aloft and it began to glow with a reddish light. The crowd grew silent, and with a start, Brannon let go of the Soulkind.

"We will bring ten of you in at a time."

"How do you know if you can actually teach anyone?" a person shouted from the line.

"We do not know," Brannon answered.

"You mean you have not tried yet?" Turic asked.

"I have, but with no success. Hopefully, today will be more successful and those who are chosen as Followers will test others so we can all leave soon to begin studying the Soulkind in Myraton. Now, let us begin."

He swept his robes around himself and walked through the doorway. Two men and a woman, robed like Brannon, hurried out of the testing area and ushered in the first ten in line, including Jace. Jace held his breath. The two Guardians shut the massive doors and returned to their posts, holding back the enthusiastic crowd.

Jace had never seen such security in the barracks before. Guards stood everywhere; some guarded the perimeter of the room, others never left Brannon's side.

"I suppose they're here to make sure nothing is stolen," Straeten answered Jace's unspoken question in a whisper. "They sure are being careful about this."

"They should be," Turic whispered. "Brannon and his people brought every Soulkind from the castle in Myraton. I suppose your little friend, Jervis Redferr, will have second thoughts if he came to lift any."

Still in a single file line with Turic at the lead, the first ten testers arrived at a long table surrounded by men and women wearing the purple robes. When the robed individuals parted, Jace's jaw dropped, as did everyone's. He stared at the different forms set before them—fifteen Soulkind in all and no two alike.

A few in particular caught Jace's eye—an ornate sword, a shield shaped to wrap around an arm, a fist-sized metal bird, and a belt with a leaf for a buckle and a root-like strap. Brannon stepped in front of the table and began speaking, but Jace heard nothing as he tried to see past him.

Turic leaned close to his students, "According to rumor, more Soulkind exist, but they were used for dark purposes. I wonder if they were brought here, as well."

Jace looked at him and mouthed the word, "Dark?"

"...and each of you will be in a separate room waiting for me, or possibly someone who just passed, to test you," Brannon said, speaking loudly. "You will all get a chance to learn from Marathas, the Flame. However, if you fail to do so, that does not mean you cannot become Master Follower of another Soulkind. We will bring in these still dormant Soulkind to see if you can awaken them. If you succeed, they will be yours to use for your training and for teaching others—under my guidance, of course."

Those about to test turned to each other and all began whispering at once. Turic turned to Cathlyn.

"He must believe the others will awaken, too. Perhaps now is the time."

Cathlyn stared ahead in silence.

Amidst the murmuring, Brannon continued, "Either way, if you pass, you will be briefed on what will happen next. Otherwise, you will be escorted out through the barracks and to NorBridge. Best of luck to you all."

Brannon's eyes settled on Cathlyn and he came to her side. "I expect you will be a strong Follower. Good luck."

He walked away, leaving her flushed. She turned to thank him when a woman wearing dark robes, standing upon the walkway above the room, caught her attention. The lady smiled at her, nodded, and then walked to a narrow stairwell spiraling down to the ground floor. Cathlyn's eyes followed her for a moment until she disappeared around a corner. She turned to ask Turic who that was, but Brannon got to him first.

"Turic, I will test you. Come with me." Brannon did not look up from the ground as they walked. "Don't worry. I cannot cheat. The Soulkind will decide whether or not you are worthy."

Turic followed Brannon with his head raised high and back straight, but not before giving a smile to the three others. Jace nodded his head.

Cathlyn took both Straeten's and Jace's hands and gave them a strong squeeze. "Here we go!"

Three purple-robed people came to escort them into separate rooms. The three friends let out deep breaths.

"Good luck, you two," Straeten said, waving.

Jace looked at his shaking hands and laughed. "I can't believe this is actually happening."

The young man escorting Jace never made eye contact and only beckoned for Jace to follow. He walked towards a corner of the room away from anyone else while keeping his hands hidden in the folds of his robe.

Jace looked around and noticed Straeten trying to speak a few words to his non-responsive escort. Shrugging his shoulders, Straeten walked behind a curtain and into his testing chambers. Turic and Cathlyn passed behind their curtains without a glance back. Jace closed his eyes, let out another great breath, and followed his young guide to his own testing area.

The room had space enough only for the table, two chairs, and two or three people. The guide exited and pulled shut the curtains. Jace began to sweat. Several minutes passed before another young man walked into the room and sat down across from him. He opened a leather-bound book and prepared his pen for writing.

"What is your name?" he said, not looking up and poised to write.

"I am Jace. Jace Lorefeld. What is yours?"

He scrawled down Jace's name, the second upon the otherwise blank pages but didn't respond. Jace leaned closer to the book, but the man's arm covered the writing.

"What do you do for money?"

"I work in the stables," Jace replied which was followed by the scribbling of a pen on paper.

"Jace, are you prepared to spend a lifetime studying magic?"

Jace laughed and the man finally stopped scribbling and looked up from his book.

"Are you serious? I mean, I can't imagine anyone not dropping their shovels, or whatever, to follow. Can you?"

The man returned his eyes to the script. "No, I suppose not. I, too, am here to be tested, although being one of Master Co'lere's students, I'll be among the last." He muttered something under his breath.

"I imagine scribes from the Hall will be writing down the details of the next few days for months." Jace shifted in his seat.

"That's my job," the man said, looking up. "My name is Kal. I'm a scribe for the Library. Perhaps you've read some of my work. Today and the next few days, I'm to help keep track of who passes and who fails. Although I'm supposed to stay here in the Library for more schooling, I hope to travel to Myraton, even if I don't pass the test, to record all this for future generations."

Jace continued to squirm and Kal said, "I don't know how long he'll be testing others, so I can't say he'll be right here. Just try to relax and maybe he'll arrive soon."

The minutes that followed were perhaps the longest Jace experienced in his life. He ran out of pleasantries to exchange with Kal to try to pass the time; he could think of nothing but the test. He tapped his fingers on the table and resisted the urge to pull out his knife to throw at something.

Barely.

Just when he thought his heart could race no faster, Brannon Co'lere pulled back the curtains and stepped inside. Jace sensed Brannon was upset about something. Brannon greeted Kal with a curt nod and motioned for him to stand up, while glancing in the record book. Kal gathered his book and pen and moved to the side of the table, ready to write. Brannon flourished his robe, sat in the chair, and looked Jace directly in the eyes.

"Welcome, Jace Lorefeld." He reached out across the table to hold Jace's wrists. Closing his eyes, he bowed his head.

Jace took a deep breath and opened his mind to welcome the magic. He smiled, waiting to be filled with the magic of Marathas. A minute passed and nothing happened. He thought he could sense something in the distance, but it would come no closer. Looking up, he saw Brannon still bowing his head in deep concentration. Several moments later, Brannon brought his head up and opened his eyes, his expression blank. Jace began to breathe quicker and started to shake.

"Now, just because you cannot learn from Marathas does not necessarily mean you cannot learn from another Soulkind."

Brannon opened the curtain and motioned to Kal, who scribbled something and left the room. And with that, Jace's world began to spin until a guard appeared carrying the falcon-shaped Soulkind he saw earlier on the table. The guard placed the relic into Jace's hands. The silver wings, stretching above the falcon's black head and emerald eyes, made the bird appear ready to swoop downwards. Hope welled up inside him as he thought about awakening the dormant Soulkind.

Catching his breath he asked, "What do I do with it?"

"Perhaps you should try to feel the magic. Try to awaken it," Brannon said, sounding not quite sure himself.

Jace turned the Soulkind over in his hands and placed it against his head and chest, all the time concentrating on reaching the magic within the bird. The Soulkind remained cold to his touch. Not able to admit defeat, he would not let go of the Soulkind. Only when the guard brought forth a different Soulkind did he relinquish the relic to try another.

And another.

And another.

Until none were left to try.

The guard whispered to Brannon, "How do you know you did not do something wrong?"

"I know because I taught someone before I came in here," Brannon answered as he stood up. "Now, who is next?"

His eyes never met Jace's and he callously pushed back the curtains and left. Jace felt exposed to the world, felt the eyes of others. Felt their pity as they looked in on him and shook their heads. The room grew even smaller as panic gripped Jace's mind. *How could this be happening?* He stood up, knocking the chair over, and ran out of the room, trying to escape from the enveloping madness. *I cannot learn magic...I cannot learn magic...*

Chapter 5: After

Empty. Jace was… empty. He sat on the railing of NorBridge and rested his head against one of the statues. With listless eyes he looked out across the pounding Crescent River. The waters looked so inviting. He was coming out of his shock and denial, and grief settled into his bones. He tossed a small gray stone up in the air and wondered if he should keep this memory or just toss it into the waters below with the rest of his dreams. After rolling the pebble around his palm several times, he set it down on the bridge.

What seemed like hours later to Jace, Straeten found him sitting on the side of the bridge. A line filled with nervous townsfolk waiting for their turn at the test still wound itself out of the Hall. Straeten put his hand on his shoulder.

Jace finally spoke quietly. "I was happier when I could *imagine* using magic. Now that it is alive and I can never touch it…."

A silence stretched for many minutes while each boy gazed at the churning water below.

"So what happened with you, Straeten? Are you a *Follower* now?"

Straeten continued to stare into the waters for a moment before answering. Taking a deep breath and shaking his head, he said, "I'm not going with them to Myraton, either. You know, I never really cared to go away like that anyway. I guess we're stuck here in Beldan."

He closed his eyes and slumped down on the railing beside Jace. Jace laughed, realizing how much he had been looking forward to actually leaving the town.

"Whatever happens, Jace—if Cathlyn and Turic make it and we end up staying here for the rest of our lives—we'll still be best friends. I know you probably want to jump into those rocks about as much as I do, but…"

Straeten shook his head and climbed up on the wide railing of the bridge to sit beside Jace.

As the sun set over Beldan, the townsfolk still remaining in line were told to return the next day and the newly initiated Followers exited the Hall. Out of the several hundred that were tested that day, only eight were chosen to be Followers. Turic, Cathlyn, and Karanne walked out side by side, but instead of the happy expressions Jace expected, each looked exhausted and depressed.

Straeten and Jace had not moved from their spots on the bridge and stood up slowly to stretch out their sore backs as the others approached. Karanne looked up at the two and mixed emotions crossed her face. At first, she started to rush over to Jace, but then she stopped while Turic and Cathlyn walked on in silence. Jace took a deep breath and forced a smile.

"Congratulations."

Straeten walked over and hugged Turic and then put his arms around Karanne and Cathlyn. Karanne then walked towards Jace and he looked back at her with a smile. He opened his mouth to speak, but she stopped him.

"I'm so sorry, Jace. I'm so very sorry."

His façade started to fade and he went to his knees. Karanne rushed to catch him as he fell, helping him back onto his feet. Straeten and the others joined her to support him on his way back home.

Karanne lit a lamp while Straeten helped Jace down onto a cot in the living area of the house. Kneeling beside it, Cathlyn placed her hand on Jace's arm and looked down. The summer day turned into a cool evening yet the mood itself could have cast any remaining warmth out of the room. Turic busied himself building a fire and Karanne fetched a red bottle from a cabinet and poured a glass for everyone.

"Your parents would consent," she said when Straeten and Cathlyn looked at each other after smelling the strong liquor.

Taking their cups, they all sat in front of the growing fire. Jace explained his test and how he felt the magic resist him. The others listened as he lamented, shaking their heads without a word. No one asked to try to teach him the spell again—not after Turic's failed attempt on the bridge. On their way home, Turic had taken Jace's hands and the boy pulled away, his eyes alive with pain.

He now sat on the cot and fiddled with the locked black box. When Jace finished his tale, the only sounds in the house were the roaring flames, the wind gusting through the chimney, and the creak of Turic's rocking chair.

"Karanne, what about your test?"

Karanne downed her remaining drink and furrowed her eyebrows at Jace. With a heaving sigh, she slowly began. "At first, I almost turned around while still waiting in line. Mathes' words lingered in my mind and I stood thinking…doubting, but something drew me through those doors. On the other side, I met a scribe named Kal who guided me to my room."

She stopped and looked at Jace, who stared into the fire.

"A long time passed after I went into the room before Brannon arrived. When he finally did, he took my wrists, and that's when it happened. A flood of light poured into my body and I could feel the fire, feel it coursing through my veins."

As if in response, the fire before them blazed higher for a moment. She looked into her empty glass then up at the ceiling. "I have been asked to go within three days time. The group leaves and heads to the new Follower training school at Myraton…. Jace?"

Without looking away from the blaze, Jace said, "Of course you're going."

Karanne nodded. "I haven't told Mathes, yet. I don't know what he will say about all of this.

"They gave us marks, too." She gazed into the flames and at her hand, showing Jace the fiery pattern running the length of her right index finger. "Hurt like fire when they put the needle to it."

Flames crackled in the following silence.

"What about you, Turic? What was your test like?" Jace asked. Again, his expression showed no emotion.

Taking off his spectacles, Turic rubbed his eyes and temples.

"Brannon did not want to teach me anything. He asked me about the seriousness of my desire to follow and told me I was far too old to begin now. All the while, he tried to impress me with his spells. Quite frankly, I said I did not feel like following if it meant learning his silly parlor tricks."

Straeten nearly launched the liquor in his mouth into the air with a cough.

"No, I am serious. I realize I could have been more respectful, but he is behaving much like a street performer. After that, I told him he should direct the Soulkind's magic towards more beneficial purposes, like healing, or building, or growing." He took a sip of his drink.

"What did he say to that?" Straeten asked.

"Well, I could tell he wanted me out of the room. He looked as if he were about to call one of the Guardians in, but stopped himself. He thought I had no chance of learning from him, but when he held my wrists, magic burned through my arms, although I am quite sure he tried to prevent it."

He prodded the flames with a metal poker, causing sparks to swirl through the air.

"'You can summon a bolt of flame,' he told me. I asked him what I could do with it, how long would it last, how powerful it was. He had no answers, though. He only looked irritated. Especially after I asked him why I would want to know that spell."

After filling a long pipe with aromatic tobacco, he reached over to the fire and picked up an ember with tongs. As he touched it to his pipe, silver smoke curled around his lips and through his short beard, and then flitted through the room in a gray cloud. He looked at the mark on his hand and shook his head.

"What is it, Turic?" Straeten asked.

"These marks. From what I read, the marks were never tattooed, but rather appeared on their own after a spell was learned. Maybe I have been reading all the wrong books, eh? And there seems to be something…missing. I cannot quite place it, but this magic, through the fault of Brannon or my own misperception, seems almost…wrong."

After a minute of silence, he said, "Mathes Spier was certainly uncomfortable today. Do you know what caused his strange behavior, Karanne?"

Karanne shifted in her chair. "I can't say. I've never seen him like that. I thought he'd be quite excited about the Soulkind awakening, but…well, you saw him. I'll try to find out what he meant."

"He's never gone for Soulkind research, has he? Not even once did he attend one of my lectures. When I've spoken about them and he was in the same room, he always found some reason for leaving."

Karanne stared into the fire and tapped her finger against the arm of the chair.

"Cathlyn, what about you?" Straeten said after the silence continued. Everyone looked up, just now noticing that Cathlyn was sitting nowhere near the fire.

"I'm tired, Straeten. I'd rather not talk about it." She gave a look to Jace.

"Don't hold back on my account," Jace said. "It doesn't matter now."

Cathlyn just sat in silence regardless.

"Well, we all had a busy day," Turic said, looking at Cathlyn.

"I've got to go now," she said, standing up from her corner and walking to the door, shadows flickering across her blue robes.

"I'll walk you home, Cath," Straeten said.

"I'd rather be alone now," she said. "Goodnight."

And with that, she opened the door and left the others in silence. Straeten sat back down.

For many minutes, the four sat staring into the fire sipping their drinks. Finally, Turic stood up and stretched, downed the rest of his liquor, and bid farewell. After he departed, Straeten got up to leave, as well.

"Tomorrow, let's ride into the woods," Straeten said to Jace. "I'll get Blue ready for an early run."

Jace looked into the fire and laughed quietly. "You don't get it, do you? We just lost our one chance at magic and you just want to go for a ride in the woods?"

"Do you have any better ideas?" Straeten asked. He stood facing the door and said, "Make sure he's up and at the stalls tomorrow morning, okay Karanne?"

Karanne slowly nodded, said goodnight to Straeten, and closed the door behind him, leaving just her and the empty boy.

"What's that in your hands, Jace?" she asked, seeing him fiddling with something.

"Something to remember the day by." He placed the gray stone from the bridge into a chest from under his bed, but left it unlocked.

The sun rose the next morning, despite Jace's doubts. Karanne gently shook his shoulder and he slowly opened his eyelids to the new world.

"I have to go now. Brannon wants us to return to the Hall so we can continue helping him with the tests. If you need me, that's where I'll be."

Jace covered his eyes with his arm and opened his hand, the small gray stone falling onto the bed covers.

"I dreamt last night, a dream I've had before, where I walk the hills wandering the countryside… alone. That dream is looking just fine to me now."

"Maybe you could become a Guardian and protect the Followers."

"Being around the Soulkind like that would drive me crazy. All that magic so close… Forget it."

"I'm sorry I can't be here today. But Straeten said you two should go for a ride. Why don't you get up and go see Blue?"

"I'll think about it. If I'm not around, I've decided to go away for a while." He turned over and faced the wall.

She bent over him. "I'll see you when I get back late tonight."

"Do you want me to speak to Mathes for you?"

She paused after she stood up and sighed. "No. I'm on my way over right now to tell him."

The walk to Mathes Spier's house dragged on. *Why didn't he want to test? And what will he say now that I'm a Follower?* Karanne kicked several rocks out of her way and followed them as they bounded down the street.

When the fire first coursed through her, her dreams from youth were awakened; she once longed for magic to be real. The experience was exhilarating, yet she felt like the magic wasn't listening to her, like the power she had was being held back. She wanted to summon the fire right now, but remembered what Brannon said in the Hall: "Do not cast the spell outside the realm of your fellow Followers and do not use magic without purpose." Despite his warning, she had used magic to light the fireplace at her home.

Of course, she made sure Jace was sleeping when she did so.

Even though she dragged her feet, her path along the cobbled roadway of Beldan eventually ended up at Mathes' doorstop. She knocked loudly. Mathes opened the door while her arm was outstretched. He glanced at the mark on her hand, then walked back inside, leaving the door partially open. She took one step through the door and into the living area where Mathes sat facing a cold, empty fireplace. With his folded hands, he propped up his chin.

"Good morning," she said. "How are you today?" She felt like leaving.

"You may have a seat, Karanne." He sipped a cup of tea. Now she really felt like leaving.

"Tell me what's wrong," she said and almost touched his shoulder, but drew back when she saw the look on his hard face. "How come you've never spoken of this before?"

He stared at the ashes from last night's fire. "I cannot believe you did this. What possessed you to want to learn something so dangerous?

That crazy old teacher convinced you to go, didn't he? I have had to put up with his nonsense for years and have worked hard to undo much of his damage."

"What are you talking about?" she asked. "Turic is a well-learned Healer. Maybe he is a little eccentric and maybe he has told some stories that are a little crazy, but he knows his history, and he also saved Jace's life. Furthermore, *he* did not convince me to go, I chose to test on my own." She straightened her back.

Mathes swirled his drink. "Regardless, I also have studied the history of the Soulkind and this awakening is a terrible sign of dangers to come. The Soulkind's magic was locked for a reason, and I believe it was meant to stay locked."

"Maybe some will abuse magic. You could join us and help make rules; help give us direction. And the school in Myraton, people will make sure it is used for good."

His voice rose as he answered. "What people? Brannon Co'lere? I've watched him *grow up* and I've seen how eager he is. He is not nearly responsible enough for the power he possesses. He will only use it for his own purposes. Someone else may awaken another Soulkind and abuse it, likewise."

"But Turic says the Soulkind are essentially good, and that they choose, somehow, who will awaken them."

"*They* choose? Then what were they thinking when they chose Brannon? And who else was chosen to be a Follower yesterday? Why would it even choose you?"

She backed away from him.

"You could do something, and yet, you choose to sit back and do nothing."

Before she reached the door, she turned around to see if Mathes was watching her, but he still faced the fireplace. She shook her head and reached for the handle.

Mathes, still staring straight ahead, said, "The path has been set for the Followers, and I fear it is a dark one. You need not be lead down a dangerous road if you do not wish it, Karanne Lorefeld. You have a strong will. Mind your steps along the way and try to use what you have learned for good."

She closed the door behind her.

The sun shone through Jace's window onto his face. Although he tried to turn away, he couldn't ignore the warmth on his neck.

A knock on his door broke him out of his efforts to sleep the day away. He stayed quiet until the pounding began again. He stumbled out of bed and opened the door.

"Good morning," Turic said, and walked quickly past Jace into the house. "I have a favor to ask you."

Jace closed the door, yawned, and fell into the chair in front of the fire. "Come on in."

Turic placed his pouch on the table and took out a manuscript. "I would like you to go back to the cave and finish what we started. I believe there are more to the stories on that wall than any of us suspected."

Jace stared into the crackling flames. "Maybe tomorrow. Shouldn't you be training new recruits now?"

"It would do you well to go out there."

"Well, I don't really feel like it."

Turic thumbed through the pages of his notes and stopped at one of Jace's drawings. "I know that no matter what I say, you are going to be unhappy right now, but look at this. Your drawings are like none I have ever seen, and you have such a skill in languages.... You could very well be a royal ambassador in Myraton someday."

"But never a Follower."

"You do not know that for sure. Perhaps when another is awoken—"

"What then? Another failure? Forget it."

Turic closed up his pouch and put it over his shoulder. "I am sorry, Jace. But perhaps you were meant for even greater things. Not all paths are clear."

He walked out the door and shut it while Jace sat in the chair.

When Jace finally roused himself an hour later, he found a new, leather-bound journal on the table. He opened it and saw his name inscribed in Turic's handwriting inside the front cover and a full pad of paper for notes and drawings. With a sigh, he sat down at the table and buried his head in his hands.

Friends shouldn't do that.

Cathlyn barely slept that night, as Jace's words kept repeating in her mind. She had lied to everyone and hated herself for it. She had lied to Jace. She had been rejected by the Soulkind, as well. How could this be happening…to her?

Despite the wall she sensed between her and the magic, the ancient relics felt warm to her touch, which seemed odd. Jace told her on NorBridge they all felt icy. She never once considered failure as a possibility. She begged Brannon Co'lere not to tell others of her failure and somehow he agreed. And on top of that, insisted she, the Library's top student, be his aide in Myraton. Ignoring her pride, she accepted. Or maybe it was her pride that made her accept. How could she face her friends who passed the test? She could not bear their pity. Later, when she saw Jace and Straeten sitting on the bridge rejected, as well, she felt even guiltier, yet could not confess.

After Cathlyn left the testing room, the woman whom she had seen in the dark hallway earlier stood waiting for her outside the curtain with her arms folded and her hands hidden in her robes. The front half of her long, black hair twisted into a tight bun and the rest hung over one shoulder in a thick braid. The woman's striking brown eyes pierced unblinkingly into Cathlyn's.

"My name is Aeril," she said. "I am a Soulkind researcher sent from Myraton. I will be working with you now that you are accepted into the study of the Soulkind."

Cathlyn wiped tears from her eyes. "But I did not pass the test."

Once again smiling, the woman continued. "I know what happened. I did not pass the test of Marathas either. This is all the fault of Brannon Co'lere and his new Followers, something is not right with the magic."

That has to be it! There's a mistake in the testing. Cathlyn's eyes glowed. Aeril placed one delicately gloved hand on Cathlyn's shoulder.

"I encouraged Brannon to bring you along," Aeril said.

"You did?"

Aeril nodded. "I know of your potential. When we reach Myraton, we will learn together."

Cathlyn believed her.

Now, she sat in her house with her family, proud of her for passing the test. Allar, actually in a good mood, smiled at his sister.

"I am going to train to become a Guardian."

Their parents beamed.

Cathlyn sank in her chair, rubbing her guilt-stained hands together as she smiled with her mouth only. How could she keep this from them? How could she keep this from Jace? And why didn't she try to get him to come along with her?

Because, she answered herself, she might ruin her own lies.

Plus, she was embarrassed, although she did tell Turic. He heard her cry and her face betrayed her, but she begged him not to tell anyone else. Reluctantly, he promised.

After finishing their morning meal, Cathlyn and Allar walked to the Hall together.

"Why are you so quiet? Don't let your friends failing bring you down. You finally have what you always wanted. And now, I'll be able to watch out for you, too."

Allar put his arm around her shoulder.

"Good luck today, Allar," she said when she and her brother parted inside the Hall. He was going to the forest to train to be a Guardian.

Allar smiled. "I'll see you at the end of the day, Cath."

He ran off to join a gathering in the Hall Courtyard near some of the Guardians who had already been selected.

Cathlyn needed to leave this place. How could she stay here and live as a student when she knew she was worth so much more to the world? Her dreams had not changed since yesterday, and she vowed to find a way to use magic, without Marathas.

Chapter 6: The Thieves' Guild

The forest was quiet this morning as Jace stepped lightly amongst the underbrush. The fog still clung to the ferns and felt cold against his cheek. He had gotten sick of the town and all the talk of the Soulkind, how it was all-powerful or all just sleight of hand. He knew the truth. He looked at the strange black box he was absently carrying and let his thoughts wander from the magic of the Soulkind to its contents. If only he could forget about the magic.

And if Karanne knew where he was heading this morning to do his forgetting, she would give him an earful for an hour or two.

The thieves would let him live.

Probably.

He felt eyes on him as he passed the old watch posts. Felt the arrows trained on him. Despite the fact he made no noise as he crept through this part of the woods, he knew they were watching him, and had been for awhile. Yet, if they wanted him dead, he supposed he would be so already. Still, it wouldn't hurt to move quicker.

The woods became mixed with giant boulders strewn about the steep hills. He remembered the way through them with his eyes closed. He smiled as he thought about the hours he spent with a blindfold over his eyes wandering through the woods to get to the cave where the Guild lay hidden.

The morning sunlight cast long shadows across a small valley between towering rocks. When he finally reached the entrance, he met two thieves he didn't recognize. They sat hidden behind rocks and shrubs guarding a narrow opening in a craggy rock wall. One had an arrow pointed at Jace's heart and the other stood tensed. Jace knew that thief was ready to throw the knives he held clutched within his sleeves.

"Dral says you may enter."

Just like that? He wondered what his old boss, Caspan Dral, was thinking.

"Well, are you going to let me 'enter?'" he said when they didn't budge from the entrance.

They scowled at him, but finally stepped aside. They didn't appear any less tense though.

Better find a different way out.

He looked around at the old guild built into the hillside. Memories floated through his mind; memories he never collected any stones for. He had not wanted to remember anything. The darkness of it all. That was what he remembered most. He felt the hopelessness of his youth again, but for some reason, felt almost comforted.

He felt eyes watching him, eyes of the few thieves who were still awake. Gaffie, the man who checked in wares after raids, sat behind his caged counter and stared at Jace.

"It is you, Jace! Bring anything for old Gaffie?"

"Don't you ever sleep, old man?" Jace said and tossed a chunk of cheese through the bars. Gaffie grabbed it and smiled a toothless smile.

"Beauty sleep never done me any good," he said and began gnawing on the cheese. "Dral will be wanting to see you now, see what you're here for. See what he can offer you."

"I see," Jace said. "It's good to see you again."

Gaffie laughed and continued to eat. "You too, boy. You too. Now go on, before you send Dral on a rampage."

Jace worked his way past the mess hall, the bunks, and finally to the darkest part of the guild: Dral's meeting room. In it, three men huddled around a table with a single, small, almost burnt out candle. They seemed to be in a heated argument.

Offer me? Why would he want to offer me something?

Jace coughed.

The three stood quickly and looked up. He recognized them all, and memories of their training burned in his mind, and his backside. Caspan Dral stood, but Jace still looked down on him. He hadn't changed. Jace would know that jet black hair anywhere. Still slicked back. He always had a way of disappearing from your view, though. Even if he were in the room alone you somehow wouldn't notice him. That always used to get Jace into trouble. And his fingers; never still. They always seemed to be grasping for something to steal.

"Jace! Welcome back. It is good to see you. We always knew you'd be back, didn't we?" Dral did have his charm, though. Jace almost felt comfortable. Almost.

The two others stood silently and stared at him. Almost appraisingly; like they would towards something they were getting ready to steal.

"I just need to ask Picks a few questions," Jace said. "If that's all right."

"Not here to stay, huh?" Caspan said. "What've you got for Picks?"

His fingers twitched.

"Just a question," Jace said, trying not to back up a step.

Caspan stopped and smiled. "Sure, sure. Anything for our returning son. He's in the back with some trainees. Nothin' like you, though, the lousy bunch."

Jace nodded his thanks and stepped backwards out of the room while he could see Caspan eyeing his pack. Same old same old. Once out of the room, he wound his way through the familiar darkness of the guild to Picks' Place, as he and the other thieves called it. Well, back when he was a thief anyway. Picks ran the classes on opening pretty much everything from doors, locks... and hopefully antique boxes.

Seven kids sat on the floor in one of the nicer rooms in the guild. The trainees were fiddling with the locks and doors built into the walls and dark wooden floors and having a time with them. Picks sat at the head of the room talking with a young girl with freckles across her face, apparently about a lock she was working on.

"That's a tough one, Evvy," he said. "The Taran. You don't see many of these around, only in the really rich part of Beldan. Not too many people can get into these..."

Jace walked into the room, smiling at the kids who all seemed so safe here, and a sense of that safety flooded into his mind. This was one of the few places he actually remembered fondly. Probably because of the eye-patched old man who taught there.

"Well speak of the devil, kids," Picks said. "Everybody, look at who just walked in."

Jace heard whispers from the little kids as he walked up to Picks. They looked up at him with their grubby faces and one pointed at him. Jace thought that he heard his name whispered between several kids. Jace smiled at Picks as he patted him on the shoulder.

"It's good to see you, boy," Picks said. "Now will you show these kids why I keep talking about you?"

He tossed him the Taran lock.

Jace laughed. "Is he still scaring you with his eye patch?"

The kids laughed, but they stopped when the lock popped right open in Jace's nimble hands. He gave it to Evvy who stood with her mouth gaping.

58

"Once a thief..." Picks said. "Keep working kids, I'll be talking with our guest."

He led Jace over to a table but instead of working, the kids couldn't keep their eyes off him.

"You're lucky to be alive. You must be on Caspan's list, or you've got something he wants."

"Yeah, well I don't really know which and I don't want to, but I thought you could help me out with something."

He handed Picks the black box and explained where he got it.

"Well I'll be," he said and turned it over and traced the edges. "Never actually seen one of these. Hold on a minute, and look after the kids while I get something."

He handed the box back to Jace and walked out of the room. When Picks left, all the kids brought what they had in their hands and stood around Jace, asking him to show them how to open their locks.

"Can you really open anything?"

"Why did you leave? Are you coming back?"

"Can you do magic?"

Jace's smile dropped.

"All right kids, back to work," Picks said walking in with a big locked book. "Some teacher you'd make," he said with a wink and set the book down on a table in the middle of the room. The kids gathered around him.

"Now where's my key?" he said, patting his shirt and pockets.

Jace and the kids laughed. "Once a bad joke teller..." Jace said.

With a raised eyebrow, Picks deftly and effortlessly picked the lock and opened the book. He flipped through the pages.

"Remember this book?"

"Of course I do. I think everyone wanted it. To see every lock ever made. In fact, we were pretty sure that if you let anyone else have this book, you'd be out of a job."

"What would I do with my life then? Be one of those 'Followers?' Speaking of that, what are you doing nowadays?"

"Just looking for something." Jace flipped through the pages without looking at them. "This looks like it came from the Library."

"Well, I sure didn't write it. Ah, here it is," Picks said and pointed to a yellowed page with some intricate drawings. "This box looks a bit like yours."

"They're both black, but other than that..."

"Come on, and you've got two good eyes, jeesh," Picks said and pointed to almost invisible feather-like lines on the box in the picture.

"A couple of lines?" Jace said, squinting.

Picks turned the box so Jace could see it from an angle. Both the box and the picture had the same unfamiliar symbol.

"It's too bad I can't read everything in this book. Never went to 'school' like you did. Whatever good it did you."

Jace smiled and shook his head. "Knew I missed this place for some reason."

"And what reason is that? My good looks?" Picks said and turned around for the kids to see his smile with more than a few missing teeth. They all laughed again.

"It says that this box is some kind of relic of the magic days, from what I can make of this," Jace said.

The kids moved in closer.

"It's not a Soulkind, but it says someone created the box from a Soulkind to contain something important, maybe something powerful..." he trailed off when he looked up and saw Caspan standing in the shadows.

When Jace saw Caspan watching him, the leader slowly disappeared in the dark hallway.

"Can you open it?" a little boy asked and Jace looked down at him.

"The book doesn't say how to open it. It doesn't have a keyhole or anything."

Jace handed it to Picks who turned it over in his hands several times.

"I don't think you could even bust this open."

Picks turned it over several times, trying to locate a weak spot or a latch, Jace thought. With a shrug, he handed it back to Jace.

Jace sighed and dropped it into his pouch. "Thanks for your help."

"Did I do anything?"

"If anyone could've opened it, it would've been you. At least I found out something about it." Jace smiled. "It was really good to see this place again."

"Did you hit your head somewhere? Well, we'll see you again...?"

"Who knows?"

"Please don't go!" the children said.

60

They gathered around Jace and he laughed and patted a few on the head.

"You better check your pockets before you go. These kids are pretty good."

Jace looked back at the young thieves and felt his sleeves. Evvy sheepishly walked up to him and handed him one of his knives. Picks shrugged and smiled as the little girl scurried behind him with a huge grin on her face.

"Oh yeah, thank Karanne for last week."

Jace stopped.

"What?"

"Thank her for the…"

"She's been here?"

"You didn't know?" Picks faltered. "Wait, wait, wait. You think she really could become a teacher? Hah! You and I both know there's only one thing she can teach, and what that is ain't gonna happen in one of them schools out there."

With a slow nod Jace left the room.

And after all she told him. Fortunately he had other things to think of now. Like leaving the guild quietly. Knowing Caspan Dral, making it out with the box would be tough.

Karanne had taught him many things, including knowing every exit.

Karanne.

There was an old exit through the climbing room out back. It wouldn't be easy, but it was the only one that might not be guarded. Jace kept to the shadows the best he could.

Not much had changed since he'd been here in the cave last. Still the dank air and sallow lights, same practice sessions and gambling going on, some sleeping waiting for the night. With his hood pulled down over his face, he hoped the climbing room was as unchanged.

With every step of his own, he could hear another echoing it. He quickly scanned the room and saw no one, but he could sense the eyes of a few who sat in carved out sections of the cave. He quickened his pace slightly, but when he saw the entrance to the climbing room, he couldn't stand it anymore and ran.

Not much had changed about the guild; except the climbing room. And it changed a lot.

He skidded to a halt and gaped. The simple rungs that had once been fastened to the wall were replaced by a multitude of ladders, ropes, and rickety looking bridges spanning from wall to wall. Posts, poles, and swings littered the floor up to the ceiling. Thieves filled the room like flies in a suffering spider web. With a sigh, Jace looked at the ceiling and saw the exit: a small skylight nearly fifty feet above the ground.

Before he could even think of finding a clear route, he looked back at three thieves dressed in black pointing and running straight for him. He ran for a rope ladder to his right and quickly scaled it to a platform halfway to the ceiling. One thief got to the ladder and then the race began.

Jace pulled out a knife and it made quick work of the ladder below him. The ladder and thief toppled to the floor. Jace looked at the other two thieves, both climbing up ladders across the room and almost to the top. He jumped onto a chain beam in the center of the room. It swayed back and forth as the other trainees climbed and swung, although most now had stopped to watch him. Some began to cheer Jace on as he raced up another ladder, apparently getting caught up in the race.

The two thieves chasing him were well up on the structure, heading as straight to him as they could through crossovers and looped ropes. Jace got to the top of the ladder and saw two ways to go, the closest one was three barrels attached to the ceiling and also laden with three trainees. Jace jumped onto the barrels as the young thieves on it clung tightly.

He scrambled over the barrels and stepped on a young boy as he did. The boy yelped and slid over the edge. Jace knelt quickly to grab the boy's wrist. The weight pulled his legs off the barrel but he kept on the ropes until he could swing the boy up to another one. Jace looked back to see one pursuer jump onto the first barrel. He scrambled up and kept on.

Up ahead a narrow plank bridge hung across a gap that lead to the last ladder to the ceiling. However, the second pursuer was heading straight towards him from across the room. Without a thought, Jace sprinted out onto the shaky bridge well above the floor.

By now, everyone was cheering, including the kids who came into the room led by Picks. They stood in a circle around him and he was pointing up and smiling. Jace saluted him quickly and kept climbing. Always quick with a bet, some thieves were laying down money. Jace reached the post at the end and climbed onto another bridge just in front of the other thief. At the end, he jumped onto a ladder, but a few rungs up the thief grabbed his ankles. Jace kicked wildly and struck him in the face with the heel of his boot. He stumbled backwards for a moment while Jace was able to scramble up a few more rungs. At the top, he looked out at a long plank stretching towards the middle of the room under the skylight. A rope with a weight hung suspended from the ceiling, fifteen or so feet out from the plank. The second thief who was chasing him had climbed up onto that side, facing him.

They both broke out into a sprint along the plank and leapt for the rope. Jace's heart beat in his ears loudly as time seemed to slow in the middle of the jump, but he snagged the rope with one hand just as the other thief grabbed it below him. They both spun around for a moment and the cheers of the bystanders silenced.

The thief below clutched the rope with both arms and glanced down at the floor spinning fifty feet below. Sweat rolled down his face when he looked back up at Jace who had pulled out his knife again and began to cut the rope.

"Don't!"

But it was too late. The weight pulled the severed rope down. The thief waved his arms as he fell to a safety net about twenty feet down. The weight plummeted to the floor with a crash. Jace climbed up the rope and rang the bell at the very top. The thieves cheered his name wildly as one.

He smiled and saluted them all and climbed out on the rocks supporting the rope. The bright sunlight and a blast of wind greeted him.

As did Caspan Dral.

And two others.

"You're kidding," Jace said, panting, down on one knee.

"They certainly love you, huh?" Caspan said coming over to Jace and put his hand on his shoulder.

Jace backed away and sat down on the rocky ground. He leaned against a scraggly tree.

"And, if you haven't noticed, we've been watching you since you came in."

"You made it by most of the lookouts," one of the men behind him said.

"And did exceptionally better than our three best climbers," the other man said.

Maybe he wasn't after the box after all.

"Indeed," Caspan said. "You're lucky Jervis is no longer one of us. He would have been…at least a little of a challenge."

"What?" Jace said. "What happened to him?"

Caspan looked at the men behind him and they all laughed.

"You haven't heard? He left us now that he's a Follower…"

All of a sudden Jace's vision closed to a single point and his hand went numb.

"Whoa! Don't go punching rocks. You're going to need that hand if you're going to come back to us."

Jace felt his body shake as he held back a scream. Come back to them?

"You know you're the best, Jace. You belong with us…"

Jace didn't hear anything else as he got up and started his way through the forest. Caspan exchanged looks with the two other men as he left.

"You know where we are."

Chapter 7: Valor

Jace ran when he got his breath back. He made his way through the woods as fast as he could and finally stopped where he and Straeten often went to get away after working the stalls. It was a quiet place away from the town; tall trees surrounding a little glade. Just quiet enough to not hear about magic. Straeten was already there with Blue and his own horse. Jace told him about his morning in the Guild.

"You've got to be kidding," Straeten said. "I get that you wanted to find out something about the box, which you didn't, by the way. But I didn't know you wanted to get killed. For the suffering, Jace, they could've—"

"They want me back."

Straeten laughed. When Jace didn't respond, he stopped.

"You're actually thinking about it? You've talked your whole life about getting away from that world and now you're thinking about it."

"But it felt really good to be good at *something*."

Straeten cuffed him upside his head. "Wake up, idiot. You're good at plenty of things."

Jace scoffed.

"You know Turic wasn't putting you on about your drawings. They're pretty good. Hey, we haven't gone back to the cave to finish up like he asked and you promised we would. With him leaving and all, it might set his mind at ease."

The journal Turic gave him sat uncomfortably in the pouch by his side; reminding him daily.

"Yeah, I've been thinking about that," Jace said.

"Why don't we go now, then we could give him a going away present," Straeten said and headed to his horse. "Anything to keep your mind off the Guild."

Jace nodded and reluctantly strapped his pack to Blue and they began their trek up the hills to the west.

Not long after they began the arduous climb, Jace heard the cries of many crows. Amidst the cawing he heard another call, but he couldn't quite hear it well enough to know what it was; their raucous laughter drowned it out. He patted Blue's neck and whispered to her to watch for the birds. The urgency of the singular cry intensified and he nudged Blue to pick up her pace. The calls spoke to him... Was the animal hurt? Scared? He glanced around under the thick cover of trees.

"What's wrong, Jace?"

"Something's in trouble."

Jace looked up and saw nearly twenty black birds circling furiously above a patch of trees. They were cawing loudly, almost painfully, and suddenly two of them flew upwards, holding something that was struggling in between their talons. Thirty feet up, forty, and suddenly a hawk's cry sounded up over the crows'. A chill ran up Jace's back, as it did whenever he heard that call. What were they doing to it?

The two crows bearing the hawk then let go, and then it was clear to Jace that the bird was injured. It spiraled downward, flapping one wing, but unable to do so with the other. With a sickening sound, the hawk crashed into the branches of a tree and the crows all wheeled and dove.

Even before Jace could kick Blue into a run, she raced up the hill on her own towards the group of carrion hunters. When they reached a clearing, they were just in time to see the swarm of crows surround the flapping hawk on the ground. Black feathers flew as the hawk fought back, but even it couldn't hold off the horde of birds and again two crows held it between their dark talons.

In an instant Jace and Straeten jumped off their horses and yelled, waving their arms at the crows, and looked for something to scare them off. The black-feathered birds cawed loudly, but did not abandon their prey. The young red-tail screeched loudly as it reached the tops of the trees, perhaps realizing it wasn't alone.

Straeten swung a broken tree limb at the crows, but they only flew a few feet away and then returned. They even began to peck wildly at the branch and flap towards Straeten. Only when Jace started hitting the crows with rocks and planted a dagger in one of their oily, feathered chests, did some start to disperse. With one last effort, the hawk clawed at its captors with both beak and talon. Surprised by the attack, the crows left and the hawk spun again to the ground.

Using the reaction and dexterity honed after a lifetime of thief training, Jace grabbed a blanket off Blue and stood with it held open. The hawk circled erratically downward and Jace ran to get under it. With luck, the bird avoided the trees and landed in the blanket. Jace quickly set the bird on the ground.

"It's all right, it's…"

Jace reached towards the bird and suddenly it clawed and bit at Jace's arm, drawing blood. "Well that's going to leave a mark…"

Straeten rushed forward but Jace waved him away. The pain in his arm burned and blood dripped through the slashes in his shirt. The hawk stared back and forth between him and Straeten with its beak open. Taking a deep breath, Jace slowed his movements and stared into its eyes. Soon after, the bird's crippled flapping settled, allowing Jace to come closer.

"Don't worry, friend. We're here to help."

"Here you go Jace," Straeten said. He handed him a white piece of cloth.

"Thanks," he said.

He folded it into a makeshift hood for the bird. He remembered reading somewhere to block off the animals sight and it would be easier to work with.

"No, it's for your arm. Look at the blood!"

"I'll be all right if you'll be all right with it," Jace said as the blood dripped off his elbow.

He continued to stare in the bird's eyes and soon the hawk's feathers seemed to settle.

"How did you run into such a nasty bunch of birds?"

He spoke quietly while draping the hood over the hawk's head to try to cover his sharp, golden eyes. A small cry escaped the hawk's beak and it looked past Jace.

Jace looked behind and saw amongst several dead black birds and piles of their feathers another hawk, its brown feathers stained heavily with blood. The hawk in front of Jace hopped pitifully over to the other bird and called out to it.

It did not respond.

Jace and Straeten stood quietly as they watched the hawk stand over the other for what seemed like forever. The dead hawk was about the same size as the other, perhaps they were brother and sister. Jace didn't know, but he knew not to disturb him.

It felt like a he.

Finally the hawk turned away and Jace walked over to it,

"It took a lot of valor to keep fighting, my friend. Valor. How about that?"

The hawk's head twisted at the question in an almost quizzical manner.

"Too bad Turic's not here. Here's some water, though. Let's try to patch up his wing." Straeten handed Jace some more torn cloth and a flask of water.

Jace was able to sit beside him and he poured some water on the cloth and cleaned up the oozing wounds. Valor was uncertain at first, but soon let Jace finish.

"Okay, now will you patch up your own arm please?"

Jace finished applying the bandage to the bird's wing and stood up.

"I didn't know you were afraid of a little blood."

"A little I don't mind, but wasn't part of that shirt white earlier?"

"All right, I'll do it. But why don't you do something else, you look like you're going to pass out."

"I wonder if we should bury this bird's friend?"

Jace looked at Valor. "I think that would be best, but don't let him see you. I don't think he'd understand."

Valor turned around and hopped about. "Well, my friend, are you coming with us? I don't think you'll make it on your own right now. Those crows might come back and you're in no condition for it."

Jace offered his arm and Valor crept onto his sleeve.

"I'll keep him busy, Straet."

Straeten hurriedly began to dig a patch of earth away for the hawk. He also cleared away the dead crows into the trees before laying the hawk in the ground. He even said a few words before covering it.

"Okay Jace, we're good here."

As Jace walked back to the clearing, Valor stared at the crows lying among the trees, and mostly at the one with the dagger hilt sticking out of its chest. Jace removed his blade and wiped the foul blood on the grass. Valor let out a screech.

"Ow! Watch it!"

The hawk loosened his grip on Jace's shoulder. Taking a closer look at the crow, Jace said, "Look at the size of that thing. It's huge."

"It's about as big as a vulture."

"You're a very lucky bird, Valor. Just be careful if you run into that bunch again."

The tiny red-tail glanced from side to side.

"Let's get going before the day runs out of sunshine," Straeten said.

68

Jace nodded and mounted Blue with Valor on his arm. Once on their horses, Straeten and Jace continued heading westward up into the hills.

Jace and Straeten tied the horses off in the same place they did last time they climbed the hill. Blue shook her head and whinnied. Jace patted her nose and fed her a fat carrot from Straeten's garden. As she munched loudly, she kept an eye on Valor, who returned the look.

"Fast friends, I'd say," Jace said. "Let's go."

Straeten and Jace played games to see who could climb a hill or a fallen tree faster. Sometimes the person behind even pulled at the other's legs to take the lead. The journey took half as long as the last time.

Out of breath, but laughing over their speedy climb, the two boys stood with their hands on their knees and surveyed the view over the valley. Valor's head moved quickly as he scanned the scenery. Jace wondered what Beldan would look like while circling hundreds of feet in the air. Valor attempted to move his wing and made quiet screeches from his throat.

"Someday, friend, but not now," Jace said.

After catching their breath, the two boys walked into the cave. What they found took away more breath than the climb. The late afternoon sun shone in on bare walls; not a carving in sight.

"Turic's not going to believe this…"

Inside Karanne's house, Turic held his breath and lifted the cloth away from Valor's wing. The bird twitched his head rapidly, but after a few words of encouragement from Jace, Valor accepted the Healer's help. Turic made certain Jace always stood close enough for the hawk to know he was near.

"What type of sorcery is afoot, friends?" Turic said. "This turn of events is quite…well, I cannot think of what it is. By the way, Jace, very nicely done."

Jace smiled as Turic tied off Valor's bandage.

"Could someone have chipped it all off?" Karanne asked.

"Not unless they were really busy," Jace said. "Especially at cleaning up."

The room filled with the soft gray smoke of Turic's pipe as speculations ran rampant.

Straeten knelt in front of the fireplace and started a roaring blaze that filled the room with light and warmth. He stood up and a thick cloud of smoke settled upon his head.

"Could this be related to the Awakening somehow?

"Unlikely," Turic said.

"Magic was highly unlikely, too, only a few days ago."

Turic nodded. "We know that waterfall feeds the Soulwash, a once magical pool. And from under its depths, Jace saw another wall, similar to the one in the cave. Do you suppose the walls could also have changed under the Library...?"

Reaching into his pouch, Jace fished around for his smooth, green stone.

"I'll try."

"Are you certain?" Turic asked, noticing Karanne's frown.

Shutting his eyes and closing his fingers around the cool rock, Jace attempted to call forth his memories. First, thoughts of water—cold, yet inviting—filled his mind. He plummeted downwards, splashing into the depths. The memory flashed by, like pieces of an almost forgotten dream. Concentrating on something sometimes helped him focus while dreaming, so he looked at his hands. He turned them over, and soon his vision became clearer. Suddenly, he was gazing at the walls, which appeared as clear as if he were there now.

Indeed, the carvings *were* different than when he saw them the other day! The rooms were identical, except for the man standing with his back to him, looking down at something in his hands. He tried to stop remembering, to slow down his thoughts, fearing what lay ahead. But he could not let go of the stone and remained stuck in the memory. The man turned around, his face blurry...except for his eyes. Hate filled, they pierced into his.

"You're still alive?"

He ran towards him with his black gloves opened. The man locked his fists in his hair and pushed him beneath the water, holding him down. He waved his arms, reaching for the man, but to no avail. Finally, Jace snapped out of the memory when Straeten pried the stone from his fingertips.

"You were yelling," Straeten said. "I don't like this thing."

He held the green stone between two fingers and placed it back into Jace's pouch. Valor gripped the head of the bed and opened his beak, as if about to cry out.

70

"The carvings were different, but… He tried to kill me. I don't know why, but he tried to kill me."

He looked at his shaking hands and forced a laugh. "I must've been under the water for a long time, or else the waters of the Soulwash really wrinkle up your skin pretty quick. I never looked at my hands in my memory before."

"You're alive, and that's what matters. Did you get to see his face this time?"

"No. Just his eyes." Jace shivered, as if he just emerged from the frigid Soulwash behind the Library.

Silence fell and soon he sat back in his chair and let out a deep breath.

"So have you seen Picks lately?" Jace said.

Karanne shifted in her seat. "What do you mean?"

"I went to see him today about the box."

Karanne dropped the knife she was twirling in her hands. "You what?"

"It's all right, it's all right," Jace said standing up.

Karanne picked up the knife and looked at him.

"Turic, Straet, leave."

They left quickly without even looking at Jace.

"Sit," Karanne said, and stuck the knife into the kitchen table. Jace slunk into the chair and looked to Valor, who wasn't offering any help.

"I didn't—"

"Stop."

"They said—"

"I'm sure they said a lot of things."

Jace took a deep breath. "But you should've seen me in the new climbing room."

"I'm sure you were great. And don't think I don't know why you're thinking this."

"But the kids in there," Jace said. "I could help."

"What, are you going to get back in and free them all? Is that it?"

"You went back, why can't I?"

Karanne stopped and slowly tugged the knife out of the table.

"I spent my whole life there. Made a lot of friends that are still in. And I was pretty good myself. It's been hard out here on my own with you. I can't find work anywhere, and Mathes is only pitying me by taking me on at the school. I'm too old to start finding something new. But you, you're young. You can make the right decisions from the beginning. "

"Yeah but look who's the Follower now. Like Jervis. I guess it takes a real liar to be one."

Karanne cringed.

"It's not right, Jace. It's just not right he became one."

Jace scoffed, then shook his head. "You weren't going to tell me that one either?"

Karanne just stared at the knife in her hands.

"Well I'm going back to the guild, and you'll be gone so you can't do anything about it."

"Don't think I won't stay and make sure you don't."

Jace did know. And now that he spilled it, he was sure she'd tell someone else to watch him even if he did promise to not go. Suffering.

He'd have to go behind her back.

Good one. Behind her back. Nothing ever got past Karanne, and he was sure even from hundreds of miles away she'd know.

"You need help packing for the trip?"

"No, I'll be all right."

She slumped into a chair across from him for a silent minute and sighed.

"Were you really good in that room?"

Jace smiled at her and she laughed.

"Maybe you should go say goodbye to Cathlyn?"

The thought of not seeing her for, well, for a long time, dropped his heart into his stomach. He nodded and walked to the door but Valor called out.

"Come on," Jace said, and the hawk climbed onto his arm. "Want to show you to a friend of mine. I'll be back later, and no, I probably won't stop at the Guild."

Karanne smiled but fidgeted with her knife as he left.

Jace took a few steps towards the lights of town when Turic and Straeten surprised him.

"Everything okay in there?" Straeten said.

"We're good," Jace said and kept walking.

"You know, maybe you two should keep an eye on the cave while we are gone," Turic said. "Keep a record to see if anything changes. Also, if you want to see the lower levels in the Library again, I can get you cleared."

He stared a second at his two students with a small smile. "I am glad you went up there, Jace."

With a nod, he headed south away to his house.

When Jace and Straeten arrived at Cathlyn's, Jace knocked on the door and waited. The door opened and Allar appeared.

Allar puffed up his chest and folded his arms across his new tunic from the Soulkind Guardians.

"I heard about you two. Only the best made it as Followers, I guess. A thief and a stable boy. Seems like they knew what they were doing."

He grinned, but faltered when he met their eyes. Valor began to pace on Jace's shoulder. Jace grimaced. A thicker glove or a tougher shirt would help with those things. He glanced at Straeten, whose expression seemed to match Valor's intentions, but only shook his head.

"Hey, birdie!" Allar said and reached towards Valor.

"Go ahead. He won't bite," Jace said, but fortunately for Allar, Cathlyn came to the door.

"Bye, Allar," she said.

Allar lingered for a moment. "At least I won't have to worry about protecting her from you two now," he said over his shoulder as he walked away.

"He's been gloating." Cathlyn gestured inside towards a set of armor and a winged helm sitting on the kitchen table.

"Come on in, I'm just packing for tomorrow," she said. "Introduce me to your friend."

"This," Jace said, "is a very brave young hawk. Valor, meet Cathlyn."

Cathlyn smiled and greeted the hawk, who cried a greeting of his own. They all laughed and walked inside.

"We're going to miss you," Jace said.

Cathlyn stood at the kitchen table with her back to the two and gripped a chair with clenched fists. Jace looked at Straeten. Her strange mood suddenly left like a cloud after passing over the sun.

"As soon as I can, I'll find a way for everyone to use the Soulkind."

Tears came to her eyes and she placed her hand upon Jace's. It felt warm on his.

Straeten coughed and Jace put his hand in his pocket and looked away. Straeten quickly told Cathlyn about the missing carvings.

"This is amazing," she said. "You two should research this while we're gone. For the suffering, I wish I could stay with you."

"Cath, we want you to know we're happy for you," Jace said. "And I'm sorry I acted the way I did. I should've been there for you."

Cathlyn smiled, and then stared at the wall, biting her lip.

The three stayed up for hours telling stories, reminiscing about their past, and sharing hopes for their futures. As a clock chimed in another room, Straeten stretched and yawned.

"Well, I'm going to head home and let you two say goodbye," Straeten said with a grin as he walked out of the room.

Jace's face went scarlet and he stood up quickly, knocking over a cup on the table. "Cathlyn, I…"

Cathlyn smiled and stood to help him.

"Yes?"

"I—"

Cathlyn's parents walked in. "It is really getting late, you need to get some sleep. Time to say goodbye."

They stood there with their arms crossed, looked around the room, and then eyed Jace's pack.

"Um, I'll be sure to see you off in the morning," Jace said as he walked after Straeten with Valor on his arm.

Cathlyn watched them walk away into the night until they disappeared from sight.

Chapter 8: Partings

Karanne busied about the house early the next morning in her brown Follower robes, going over her bags carefully. Jace laughed and shook his head as they headed outside towards town.

"You in robes. They look really...nice."

She scoffed. "Not my choice."

"Have you spoken with Mathes, lately?"

"We spoke a little bit a few days ago," she said, shaking her head, "and he was the same as he was at the testing."

Before reaching the gates of Beldan, they stopped.

"You've always been a good kid, Jace. You'll be fine. Just listen to Straeten."

Karanne half turned her head towards him and raised her eyebrow when he walked in silence. "And I've got people watching you. Stay out of that Guild."

Jace reached down to the ground, picked up a stone, and caressed it with his thumb and forefinger.

"You need a stone to remember me?"

"Nah. I just don't want to forget how you look in those robes."

She laughed and together they walked into the city.

NorBridge was crowded as everyone gathered to see the departing Followers. Wispy trails of fog from the Crescent River curled around the statues lining the stone bridge. As Jace and Karanne crossed over and entered the Hall, the Soulkind Guardians sat upon their steeds in a delta formation facing the bridge. The horses shaking their heads and expelling clouds of misty breath into the cold, morning air made the only movement. Jace counted fifty Guardians—some bearing spears, some swords, and all with plain, yet solid, shields beside their saddles. They were dressed in dark gray cloaks with sturdy leather armor underneath and winged helms atop their heads. Some appeared to have the skill of veteran soldiers, but most appeared quite green. The land had been in a state of peace for many years, after all.

Jace saw Turic and Cathlyn already atop their horses. Straeten stood beside them, speaking to the animals and petting their noses. Jace waved a greeting as he approached carrying Karanne's pack. Several people, both Guardian and Follower, gave Valor wide-eyed glances.

"Well you three, best of luck on your journey. Don't forget about Straet and me here."

Jace leaned in close to Turic. "Now, will there be someone to cook your meals?"

The Healer scratched his head. A second later, he smiled and clasped Jace's arm.

"Well, I certainly hope so!"

Cathlyn smiled at Jace and the two held the glance for a moment. Jace patted her horse.

"She looks like a good one. Stick close to her and she'll take good care of you."

Cathlyn opened her mouth but just then a horse moved in between them. Jervis stared straight down on Jace.

"Never had a chance to tell you how sorry I am that you won't be joining us," he said, straightening his brown robes and eyeing Cathlyn with a disgusting grin. "Maybe if I come back, I'll be able to teach you something."

Jace's blood boiled and his fists clenched. Straeten placed his hand on Jace's shoulder.

"You don't really want to have Cathlyn see that, do you?"

Jace prayed Jervis would not use magic to hurt anyone, especially anyone he knew. Jervis rode away and Jace looked up at Cathlyn. Probably for the last time in a long while. Her horse started to stomp in excitement and moved away from Jace as the Followers prepared to depart.

"Take care, Cathlyn," Jace said with a wave.

"You too," she said and clenched her reins trying to steer back towards Jace.

He grasped the horse's bridle and stroked its nose. He was never very good at goodbyes. Goodbye. He never fully realized how final this goodbye felt now. He felt for a stone in his pouch as he watched Cathlyn up on that horse.

Jace squinted as he looked down a long row of bookcases.

"I think I hear them over there." Jace started running down an aisle.

When the shelf ended and he rounded the corner, he found the class he was supposed to meet standing around a dark-haired man in brown scholar's robes. As he came into the open, the teacher stopped instructing and looked at him. Behind, Jace heard Straeten yelling.

"Where are they?"

Straeten ran around the corner and straight into Jace, leaving them both on the ground in front of the laughing children. While the robed teacher tried to hush the students, a girl knelt down and helped the two boys to their feet.

"Are you all right?" she asked, smiling.

Jace stared for a moment up at her long brown hair and into her blue eyes before speaking.

"Uh, I think so…"

"Welcome lads, I was told of at least one of your attendance. You must be Jace."

Jace whirled around while the teacher addressed him in front of the students. His face turned red and he stammered for a moment.

"I'm Jace Lorefeld. And this is my graceful friend, Straet."

Straeten looked around and waved, his face, too, turning a deep crimson. The children snickered. While Jace looked over his shoulder at Straeten, he saw the girl's blue robes out of the corner of his eye. She was talking to an older boy in a red velvet robe.

"Lorefeld? I did not realize you were related to Karanne," the teacher said when Jace turned back around. "I am Mathes Spier, teacher, Hall Council member, and your guide through the Library. Class, we have *two* visitors today. Please make them feel welcome."

Sweeping his long, brown robes around himself, Mathes nodded to Jace and Straeten then continued his lecture. As Mathes spoke, Straeten pulled Jace to the side.

"That's the girl from the stables. And look who she's with! Let's get out of here."

"We're not going anywhere," Jace replied, turning around. He was cut off when the girl's brother grabbed his collar and dragged him into an aisle.

"Allar, don't!"

In the instant Allar glanced sideways, Jace spun out of his grasp like a snake and pulled a knife up to his throat.

"Don't move."

Allar was several years older and at least a foot taller than Jace, yet he did not move.

"No!" the girl yelled again, this time at Jace.

Jace, caught off guard, fell backwards when Allar pushed him. He felt shocked, but not by the push.

Straeten jumped between the two of them. He held his hands up, and both boys started, then Jace cracked a smile. Allar shook his head and headed off to join the other students.

"Nice cloak," Jace said.

Allar glared back for a second but saw his sister staring at him.

"Just ignore Allar. He once told me about an older boy threatening him with a knife or two, but I think he overestimated your age. I am Cathlyn," the girl bowed a greeting, but eyed Jace's knife.

Jace finished dusting off his pants, hid his blade in a single movement, and then returned her greeting with a sweeping bow.

"Nice, to meet you, I'm Jace. I'm, uh, sorry for...."

"Well, he is my brother, but he probably deserves something like that; perhaps not that dire, though. Where did you learn to do that?" Cathlyn then looked over at Straeten and smiled. "I remember you from the stables."

Straeten stood up straighter.

Jace shifted his weight. "I've wanted to come here forever. Do you know much about it?"

"You've never been here? I love the Library." Cathlyn started walking down the aisle towards the class and motioned for the two boys to follow her. "I come here whenever I can, usually by myself. I know a Healer who spends a lot of time in these rows of books. He's teaching me to be a Soulkind Follower. But don't mention Soulkind to Mathes, or he'll have your ear the rest of the day."

Jace reached down to pick something up from under a bookshelf.

"What is it?" the girl asked.

"It's just a stone."

He held up a small red rock with rough edges. "I remember things that are important to me this way. I can hold it later and then see it all over again."

She smiled. "What's so important about right now?"

Again Jace was left without words.

"You really want to remember me beating you to the tower?"

Jace paused. "Huh?"

But she was already gone, and he darted off after her trailing blue robes. Her laughing echoed and floated back to him. Up stairs and around bookcases they raced up to the roof of the Hall Library.

Brannon led his horse in front of the party on the bridge. He stood out among their bland colors with the bright gold of his Soulkind glinting in the rising sun.

"Good citizens of Beldan, we bid you farewell. We hope to spread magic throughout the world and awaken new Soulkind to bring back to you. Expect some of us back in the spring to begin the school in Beldan, as well. Farewell!"

Brannon raised his arms then the Followers all raised theirs simultaneously. The Guardians lifted their weapons and the crowd fell into silence. Flames shot into the air from Followers' fingertips and onlookers cheered in amazement. The horses on the bridge began to move forward, clomping on the stone. Jace stood back and let go of Cathlyn's horse.

They were gone. For most, life returned to normal, without magic. People settled back into their daily routines, although talk of magic ran through the town like a wildfire in dry brush. Children also played magic with renewed vigor, hoping one day to take the test and belong to the future school.

Jace wandered through the town aimlessly watching them play. Thoughts of the Soulkind strayed through his mind and he kicked the rocks along the street. He pulled the hood tightly over his head to block out any sounds but it didn't help. Everything he heard just reminded him how much he couldn't use the magic.

Straeten's family stables appeared around the corner with a small stand out front holding riding equipment for sale. Among the many customers, a small girl stood off to the side of the stand trying to not be noticed. He knew what she was trying to do. He had done it many times before. When she crept closer to the wares and slid her wiry arm through the patrons Jace stopped where he was.

He shook his head and quickly pulled out his whistle and blew a sharp warning blast out to her. Upon hearing it, the little girl pulled her hand back and looked around. Her eyes settled on Jace across the way, arms folded across his chest. The crowd didn't even notice her as she was absorbed into the milling mass. She was good, Evvy.

The customers at the booth slowly cleared away and Jace cringed when he saw Straeten working. His mother, a wide lady with a hard face smiled briefly at him before returning to helping a customer with a bridle. Jace walked up in front of the stand.

"I thought they kept you out back."

"Well, they thought I needed a little experience here." Straeten motioned for Jace to follow him back to the stables. "I'll be taking over business someday."

"Well, putting you up front is going to scare away that—"

"Are you going to tell me what that was all about?" Straeten said suddenly turning around and grabbing Jace by the arm.

Jace stood silently for a moment then pulled off his hood. "What do you mean?"

"I'm not stupid, Jace. I was watching that kid the whole time and then suddenly I hear a whistle. One of the ones you used to have. And then you show up."

"And?"

Straeten let go of his sleeve and kept walking.

"Yeah, so I went back. Just for a little bit. Until I get something else I can do."

"I thought you were going to work here with me?"

Jace laughed. Straeten slowed his step and then continued. "I think I'd kill myself within a week. No offense."

"I can't believe it. That's not who you are."

"I don't know who you think I am, Straet. Anything I wanted to be left when I couldn't touch that stupid magic. There's nothing left."

"And so you're going to take from people like my parents? Why did you blow that whistle then? And don't tell me it's because she was doing something wrong."

"You don't know anything."

"I guess I don't." Straeten walked into one of the stables. "Your bird is all better now. I didn't know why you've been asking me to watch him during the daytime until now. You should probably let him go."

He came out of the stable with Valor on his arm. Although the hawk could fly again, he never tried to escape, yet Jace could sense his desire to go into the wild again. The long feared day had come for Jace to say goodbye to yet another friend.

"Here he is," Straeten said and thrust him onto Jace's arm.

Jace looked into Valor's dark eyes and took a deep breath. "I think I should bring him up to the cave and let him go there. Near where we found him. I could also check on the cave."

"Why? I thought you wanted to let all your friends down? Why should Turic be any different?"

"You're not going to let this go, are you?" Jace said with a laugh.

Straeten tried to look stern but a small smile appeared on his face. He did punch Jace in the arm though.

"Ow!" Jace said and rubbed where it landed. "Are you coming with me, or what?"

Climbing the hill, Jace felt Valor creep from his forearm to perch upon his shoulder. He eyed his friend while the hawk peered out at every movement in the trees.

"Goodbye, Valor," he said when they reached the waterfall. The crashing water sprayed a fine mist into the air, cooling his sweating forehead.

"Take care in this valley, you've seen how dangerous it can be."

Testing out his wings, Valor began to step in excitement when Jace put him on the ground.

"Are you sure you don't want to keep him?" Straeten asked.

"Want to?" Jace said. "I want to, but I can't. Go on, Valor."

The hawk turned his head from the open valley to the two boys and in the next instant flapped his wings and was airborne. He let out a loud cry that Jace answered with an equally loud call. Valor circled in the air above the cave while the two boys waved and finally headed east and caught some updrafts. The two watched the hawk until they had to strain their eyes then headed into the cave.

"You know, you really got pretty good at talking to that bird," Straeten said.

"Thanks. Next you're going to encourage me to go into business with…" Jace stopped and stared at the cave walls.

Once again, they had changed.

In the middle of the carving, a large group of people stood, undoubtedly the Guardians and Followers. They appeared to have entered a town, and from the air and ground, winged creatures attacked them.

Straeten walked over to the wall. "It looks like the creatures are taking the Soulkind away."

A robed person led the creatures off with a cart and some prisoners.

"What's happening?" Jace said. "Is this the future? The past?"

"I don't know. But they're in danger, and we'd better do something about it."

Jace began to copy down the drawings. "Like what?"

"Let's go to the Hall and tell someone there. The Council might listen to us," Straeten said and tried to hurry Jace's copying.

"'Tilbury,' this says here. The town?"

"I can't read that.... Where did you learn that language?" Straeten asked as he traced the symbols with his forefinger.

"I just know it. Turic must've shown me."

Jace hastily sketched the picture into his book.

"All right, let's move. Back to Beldan."

They packed their pouches and started a fast hike down the mountain path to their horses. Jace glanced up on occasion, looking for Valor. Once on the horses, they rode them through the woods on a mission to reach the Hall.

Across NorBridge, they raced to the Tower of Law where the Council resided. The people waiting in line for the Council representative turned to face the boys who rushed in and demanded to speak to the Council. Several people laughed. The lady in red robes holding the golden winged scepter rose to stop them as they raced passed to the door behind her.

"Halt!" she said and two of the Hall Guards blocked the stairs to the Council chambers.

"For what purpose do you seek the Council?"

"We're sorry to interrupt," Jace said and swept a bow to her. "This may sound crazy, but we have reason to believe the Followers and Guardians are in danger."

"What proof do you have?"

"There is no time to waste," Jace said as he unrolled his manuscript. He paused for a second. "Turic Bander, the Follower sent us on a mission before he left. We just came back from a cave in the mountains, whose walls have changed, and not by humans. We think the carvings on the walls may speak of the past or future. Please, we're serious about this."

The line of townspeople started to yell for the lady in red. She looked back and forth between the boys and the line.

"Turic, you say? Let me speak to the Council. I will return shortly."

She then went through the massive door to the interior of the Tower. In the several minutes that passed, neither said a word, although

Jace slowly twirled his whistle between his fingers. Finally, the lady in red returned.

"You may see the Council," she said, and pointed to the stairs.

The guards stood aside from the door and let them proceed and the lady returned to her tall chair. They guided them up massive stone steps that circled upwards and around the Tower. Jace and Straeten reached the Council chamber and walked in. At a half-circular table facing the door, nine men and women, including Mathes Spier, waited. In the middle sat Talhar Co'lere, father of Brannon Co'lere and head of the Council.

"What is it that you bring? You had best not lie to us," Talhar said.

Great, just like his son. Taking a deep breath, Jace opened the manuscript and proceeded to tell the Council about all the happenings at the cave.

"...so you should send troops to this town of Tilbury to rescue the Followers," Jace concluded.

He let out a big sigh, but held another breath while he watched the Council take their time discussing the issue.

"That's preposterous," one lady said.

"Who would attack them?" said another.

"Even if they were attacked, the Guardians would be more than enough to handle common thieves," said another.

Some members laughed and shook their heads.

Mathes silenced the group with his hand. "These creatures don't appear to be common. I think we should examine this cave Turic discovered. I will go see it myself...if the boys will direct me?"

Jace and Straeten nodded. "A path leads up to the waterfall behind the Hall Library. We'll tell you...but we have to hurry."

Talhar Co'lere knocked on the table with a mallet.

"We shall send an emissary to the town of Tilbury to find out if a problem exists."

"But..." Jace said.

The Council arose as one and Talhar dismissed them without another word. When the door shut behind them, Straeten and Jace shook their heads.

"I can't believe they didn't send help," Straeten said.

"Try to see it their way. We show up with a story of magical carvings and expect the head of the Council to send out an entire army. Come on, let's go."

Straeten slapped Jace's shoulder. "I'll get all of our supplies ready and the horses prepped. Do you want Blue? Or should we take...?"

"Blue, of course," Jace said. "And I won't tell her you suggested otherwise. I'll head to Turic's and get the maps to plan our route. This is it, Straet. I'll meet you at my house in an hour."

"An hour. Got it."

"Wait!"

Mathes ran down the stairs after them. Hearts still pounding, the boys waited for Mathes to catch up. The tall, brown haired man walked down the steps to where they stood.

"Please, could you to tell me how to get up to that cave?"

After detailing the trip to him, making sure to point out the large crows that might be around, they told him their plan.

"You're more than welcome to come along with us," Jace said. "I know you would want to make sure Karanne is okay, too. Plus, we could use your help."

Mathes scratched his chin for a moment. "I need to think about that."

"Well, don't take too long, we're leaving within the hour." Jace said and started to walk down the stairs. "If you want to follow, we'll be at the Citadel by nightfall and then northward from there tomorrow."

Mathes stood on the steps as the two boys ran from the Hall.

Jace sat in Turic's room sorting through different maps to find the best way to Tilbury. He knew Tilbury was a small farming town that lay northeast of the valley, but he needed clearer directions. He hurriedly scrawled out a map on a roll of parchment from Beldan to Tilbury, which included some of the neighboring towns and mountain ranges, just to be safe. He threw sand on the page and after the ink dried enough, he rolled up the map, and headed home to grab his gear.

He stuffed a change of clothes and gray riding cloak into his pack. Feeling his arms, waist, and legs, he reassured himself that he had more than enough daggers along for the trip. And rope; he learned from an old story that you should always bring rope on a journey. Finally, he unlocked the chest containing his precious stones and sorted out several, including those with memories of his friends. Opening the drawstrings on the small pouch at his side, he dropped them in upon the smooth green stone he always carried. All set to go. Pretty soon, he heard the trod of horse's hooves on the earthen floor outside the cottage.

84

"Blue!"

"Nice to see you, too," Straeten said.

He sat atop his horse, a black horse as solid as he. An oak staff hung from his saddle.

"You know how to use that thing?"

"You never see any of your thief friends looting inside our stables, do you?"

"I've never seen thieves have a need for horse dung."

"Nice. I've got some food, but I know I can forage some more along the way."

Jace threw his packs on Blue, slapping her flanks and putting his head beside hers.

"One more adventure, eh Blue?"

She threw back her dark head in a whinny. He stepped into the stirrups and mounted the saddle, feeling his heart beat strongly within his chest.

"Your parents?"

"They'll be fine. Any sign of Mathes?"

"I'm afraid not," Jace replied, glancing into the hills where Mathes would be climbing to examine the cave.

"Don't you have to check out with your old friends?"

Jace clasped the whistle in his fist and shook his head.

"Well, then, let's go!" Straeten said.

And with that, the two nudged their horses and headed northward beyond the town and beside the Crescent River to begin the pursuit.

Chapter 9: Encounters

Towards the end of the first day out of Beldan, Karanne and the other Followers reached the Citadel and the calmer waters at the valley entrance. As difficult as it was for her to leave Mathes behind, she felt even worse about leaving Jace. The boy would be fine, as long as he stayed with Straeten, and away from the suffering guild.

The tower of the Citadel guarded the gateway into the valley and could be seen for miles. The journey from the town had been uneventful, and trying to speak with the Guardians proved even less so. They sent scouts off in all directions at constant intervals, always leaving a strong force behind with the Followers. Perhaps they might encounter a brigand or two, but she could fend for herself if that time ever arose.

The Citadel guarded the valley with towering stone walls on either side of the Crescent River. Only a few guards manned the Fortress. In times of war, more than this small number strengthened the defenses, of course; however, war had not entered this valley for centuries. A bridge of stone and wood stretched across the river connecting the two towers, nearly fifty feet across the water. Karanne gaped at the bridge. How could someone build something like that?

Approaching the gateway to pass through the Citadel, Karanne rode beside the scribe who had brought her in to test.

"How is your son?"

Shrugging her shoulders Karanne answered, "He has his good days and his bad ones. Why is it that some are turned away from a power they could use for good, and others are given this great gift to use for…whatever? It doesn't make any sense. Already the Soulkind has chosen people who will abuse magic."

She looked over at Jervis Redferr, who was bowing and pawing to get a few words in with Brannon Co'lere.

"What would you suggest be done about this…injustice?"

"Do you suppose the testing could be more selective? Learn more about people before allowing them to test? That way, the teacher could be sure of the students' intentions."

She nodded her head a few seconds later.

"You should present that idea to Brannon," Kal said.

Karanne's eyes widened. "Me? Oh, no. Perhaps Turic, or maybe you. You could be more persuasive, I bet."

"He wouldn't listen to me. He doesn't listen to people who are 'below' him…and I never passed the test—"

Karanne looked at him as he faltered but he soon regained his composure.

"—but I convinced Brannon to let me travel with the Followers to record their deeds; to make sure future generations know about the many adventures you will surely go on, and possibly lead."

"Adventures? I don't think I'm up for adventures anymore. A lot of traveling, perhaps, a lot of training others; but I lost track of adventure long ago and I'm sure whatever you write will, unfortunately, be trite. Make sure to spice up my 'deeds' a little so we don't bore future readers, all right?"

"I'll do my best. But perhaps the Soulkind awakening will provide what the world has lost."

"Well, I'll have to watch out then, won't I?"

The Followers passed through the gate out of the valley of Beldan heading towards Myraton.

For several days, the party followed the Crescent River northward. Many had never before seen the lands outside their peaceful valley. The river took a much different turn further as they headed downstream; previously narrow and rough, the now wide river meandered through the countryside. The dense trees that had lined the sharp mountain valley behind them now gave way to open fields and wandering hills.

A few looked behind, seeing the tall, jagged peaks of the Khalad Mountains guarding their town vigilantly, and waved goodbye to their homeland. Some of the younger Followers slowed ever so slightly, but the surrounding Guardians urged them forward.

Turic Bander; however, smiled all day long. Even speaking with Brannon about the Soulkind seemed pleasant now.

"What have you done with the Flame as of late, Brannon? You must be quite excited to have this creative power at your fingertips."

Brannon eyed the old man. "If you are trying to get me to teach you more spells, I will tell you what I told the others who have asked: we will wait until we are set up in Myraton before any more are passed on.

As for new spells, I haven't quite had the time to experiment. I have heard that the power of the Flame is very strong, perhaps the strongest among the Soulkind."

Turic scoffed.

"Strongest? Perhaps in rumor, but from what I read, each Soulkind was kept in balance by the powers of the others, so no one magic would rule. And as for fighting, Marathas was meant for more divine purposes, I am sure. For instance—"

"When we begin the training, perhaps I shall consult with you, but for now, Turic, my student, we will wait." Brannon booted his horse.

Turic caught up to him. "With each new Master, the Soulkind adapts somehow. Why look at your amulet! The wings are beginning to cover up the ruby ...."

"I think you're seeing things, old man."

"I think otherwise, young one. Your pride will cover the true power of the Flame and soon the only magic left in it will be your little tricks. You had better grow up soon, Brannon Co'lere. This is a big world, and unfortunately, you are responsible for teaching others the beginnings of magic."

He kicked his horse off into another direction to try to find Cathlyn among the other Followers. He whispered an apology to his horse for kicking her harder than normal.

In the distance, Brannon looked down at his amulet. He turned it over in silence and then slipped it back under his robes.

Cathlyn spoke in hushed tones with Aeril, the woman she met at the test, several hundred feet behind Turic.

"There are times I wish I had told my friends the truth about the test. I feel horrible about lying to them. They are my best friends."

"You did the right thing." Aeril, her dark hood pulled close over her face, rode without looking at anyone, not even Cathlyn.

"My dream is to help the world with magic. I've always felt that way. Now that I can't be a Follower...."

"You are better than a Follower. You've told me you cannot stand to watch the world go by and do nothing. And I've told you I will help you; you must wait."

"And that. I still don't know how you can say that. How can you help me when even you did not pass the test?"

Aeril continued to stare ahead.

"There is more to the Soulkind than you know, Cathlyn. Brannon Co'lere is quite unaware of what he 'awakened,' and I doubt he will ever realize it fully. Remember, do not tell anyone of our visits. Your participation here could be compromised."

Cathlyn watched Aeril disappear into the band of other horses as Turic approached. The woman was obviously very important to the Followers; she took orders from no one and spoke to none about her actions.

As Turic rode up alongside her horse, Cathlyn smiled and waved. She could count on him not to judge her recent decisions.

"Hail, Cathlyn! Tonight we arrive in the farming town of Tilbury, about our halfway point to Myraton. That leaves us with just about a week left to travel."

"I'll be glad to have a warm bath. That is, if they have an inn in the town," Cathlyn said.

She was happy to get her mind off her previous conversation. The sooner she could begin learning whatever Aeril could teach her the better. May this last week before Myraton speed by.

The group realized they were approaching Tilbury when the sparse farms along the way became more frequent. Children stood with their pets staring at the Guardians and Followers passing by. Those toiling in the fields harvesting their crops ran to their houses. A few of the braver ones grabbed scythes or axes from sheds and stood guard on their porches.

Cathlyn watched as one of the Soulkind Guardians in front of the procession darted faster down the road, perhaps to announce their arrival. She looked for her brother amongst the Followers' cloaked escort and tried to catch his attention when she spotted him. Along the trip to Tilbury, they had not talked much, although she sensed him watching her at all times. From what she gathered, the Guardians would camp outside the town to watch for danger, but the Followers would stay at an inn, if possible. The townsfolk should appreciate their business since not many people traversed the road that ran into Beldan's valley, and fewer still stopped in Tilbury.

After a few more miles on the road, the procession entered the village. Most of the Followers were surprised at the quaintness of the small town, having lived in a much bigger city all their lives. In the middle of town a young boy frantically sounded a bell, alerting the town to the approaching band. The Guardian who rode ahead earlier stood beside the boy waiting for the Followers to enter. The little boy, who had been gaping at the cloaked rider, now dropped his jaw at the horses entering the town. A man and woman stood beside the bell, also waiting. The troupe stopped in front of them, whereupon Brannon Co'lere dismounted and began to speak with the two townsfolk.

Cathlyn watched as their faces turned from disbelief to astonishment. A bright flame shot into the air from Brannon's upturned hand, startling and amazing the onlookers. The little boy who had been ringing the bell tore off, no doubt seeking his friends. After several minutes of conversing with Brannon, the man and woman turned to look at the Followers. Cathlyn wondered if they thought the Followers posed any danger to the town. With a deep bow, however, the lady approached them.

"Welcome to Tilbury. We are honored to have you among us."

The man beside her also bowed and said, "I am Honus Achemy, and this is my wife, Ciladrel. We are the leaders of this town and are pleased to announce there is an inn for you to stay at tonight. There are rooms for all of the...Followers. Master Co'lere?"

Brannon waved and walked to the leader of the Soulkind Guardians. The tall man stood silently with his hood pulled close around his face. Cathlyn hadn't noticed him before, but she knew she would not forget him now. His dark eyes took in everything and his hawk-like nose jutted out from the depths of his hood. The man's hand never strayed too far from the hilt of his sword and he seldom talked to anyone, save to bark an order. Cathlyn heard Brannon call the man Stroud. Everyone seemed to avoid looking directly into his eyes. Even Brannon.

While Cathlyn looked on as Stroud instructed the bodyguards, Allar walked to her side. Smiling proudly, he told her he was being sent into town to get supplies. She nodded and asked about his silent leader.

"He is the leader of the Guard in Myraton and they say he never talks to anyone."

"And why would that be?"

"His former Captain was betrayed and murdered a few years ago."

Cathlyn looked at him with disbelief.

"Right."

"What do you mean? That's what I heard, anyway."

"You'd better hurry up, he's looking at you right now," Cathlyn said, pointing away.

90

Snapping to attention, Allar whirled around only to see Stroud facing the other direction.

"Very funny, Cath I think I'll get those supplies now, if you're finished badgering me."

She waved him goodbye with a laugh and followed the rest of her companions to the inn, joining with Turic and Karanne along the way. Townsfolk began to come out from behind their porches and front windows. Two young girls, about Cathlyn's age, looked around at the crowd and stepped behind Cathlyn.

"Who are you all? What are you doing in our town?"

"There's nothing to worry about," Cathlyn said. "We are on our way to Myraton—"

"Maybe you did not hear the first time," Brannon said. "There is to be no interaction with the public. They will learn soon enough."

He nodded to Cathlyn and left. The two girls sighed as the group walked away.

Cathlyn looked over at Brannon as she walked towards the inn. He appeared to be having a conversation with himself, and not for the first time. She overheard something about "villagers," and "unenlightened," but could not hear anything else..

The inn was a long stone building nestled amongst the other buildings, hardly differing from them except for its small hanging wooden sign above the front door that read "Inn." Catchy name. Cathlyn smirked at it on her way in, but soon forgot as the smells from the kitchen reminded her of her hunger. The bottom level opened out into a hall with wide tables and benches along either side. Before she could sit down, several small boys gathered up the Followers' belongings.

The Followers sat along several tables quietly until the barmaids began to bring in food and drink. Cathlyn looked down the line of Followers and saw a man who appeared to be a blacksmith; he had a large build and soot covering his hands. A small woman with slender fingers, whom Cathlyn overheard discussing her sewing, sat talking to a pretty-looking man with slanted features and hands adorned with fine rings.

"Is anyone sitting here?" Cathlyn asked a woman sitting by herself, who was not speaking or looking at anyone.

The lady eyed Cathlyn up and down.

"Can you believe that they are serving *us* in this room? And what is this, 'food?'"

She poked at her plate with her long fingernails and wrinkled her nose.

"I'll take that as a 'no'," Cathlyn said under her breath and walked to a bench where Karanne had just sat down.

Cathlyn ate silently while she watched the sun set and darkness settle through the windows. Voices rose as songs from a small band filled the air and pipe smoke hung at the ceiling. Soon, the townsfolk dared to come into the inn, as well, seeking their dinner and also wanting to find out more about the strange visitors.

Cathlyn looked out the window and saw the Guardians helping the Tilbury guards – ten aged men wearing work clothes and singing songs – keep an eye out for any sign of trouble. Two Guardians were posted outside the door of the inn and kept a careful watch inside.

Cathlyn yawned and glanced around the room as she heard Jervis and a couple of his new rowdy friends singing. They sat at their bench where several empty pitchers adorned the tabletop. A barmaid walked quickly to the table to remove them while the boys drained their cups. Before the young lady could leave, Jervis grabbed her by the wrist.

"Not so fast," he said, nearly falling over. "Sit and stay with us for awhile."

The girl struggled vainly in his grasp, but eventually sat down.

"That's better," Jervis said. "We can help keep you warm."

And with a leer, he turned his palm upward and a spout of flame flew into the air. The girl screamed outright and the entire hall went silent. She dumped what was left in one of the pitchers she was carrying onto Jervis's arm and then bolted from the hall into the kitchen. Jervis looked around the room to see everyone staring at him.

"This evening is over," Brannon yelled out and stood up to find the inn master.

As the Followers got up, Cathlyn could see Brannon handing the inn master, a tall and wide man, a bag of coins and apologizing. The rest of the kitchen staff peeked out into the hall through windows, their whispers no doubt full of talk about the mysterious magic they had just witnessed. But soon, all seemed to be forgotten and the Followers fell asleep in their beds, unaware of the danger closing in on them.

The peace that the night brought forth was short lived.

"Wake up, Karanne! There's something outside."

Karanne sat straight up and ran to the window to look out below. Her face turned white. Shaking, Cathlyn hurried to the window to see what caused Karanne to be so afraid.

When Cathlyn gazed out upon the square, she saw a scene out of her darkest nightmares. The buildings across the street were ablaze and people ran screaming out of the doors only to encounter.... What were they? She could not see their features, they moved too quickly. Hundreds of black, scaly creatures swarmed the streets, striking down townsfolk and Guardians with ease. And above all the panic and dying, she heard a sound...a strange animal scream that emanated from the throats of the vile, attacking creatures. Cathlyn covered her ears in a futile attempt to block out their howls.

Stroud, the leader of the Guardians, stood in the center of the town, one of the creatures dead at his feet. He looked around at the Guardians, panic wild on their faces.

"To me!"

His clear, strong voice seemed to snap the Guardians out of their shock and they gathered beside their leader.

"They're everywhere!" a Guardian shouted.

Like a wave of black water, the creatures flooded into the town, all converging on the inn. Karanne and Cathlyn watched as they set fire to the building. Without a thought, they ran down the stairs. The inn master, bearing a gash on the side of his head, waved the Followers out the back.

"This way! Your friends are this way!"

Some brave or foolish Followers, however, ran to the front door, flames beginning to crackle from their fingertips. The Followers unleashed their magic onto the black beasts. Fire leapt from their hands in chaotic blasts. Bolts of light and fire broke into the mass of darkness, exploding with fiery sparks. The fire knocked the beings down, but failed to burn through their scaly, black skin and they just stood back up. Amidst their animal screams, hundreds of raspy voices spoke in harsh, mocking tones. Cathlyn heard those voices and froze, and it wasn't until the blacksmith Follower grabbed her wrist that she was able to run out the back of the inn into the black woods.

Several of the winged creatures swooped from the sky and divided the group, which scattered throughout the trees. A young Guardian screamed as the sharp talons of a creature raked across his arm and chest. The Followers fled, shooting bolts of fiery magic in all directions; some torching buildings, trees, and even people. Cathlyn ran into the woods away from the shrieks echoing in her ears. She could vaguely hear Karanne calling for her.

She stumbled several times, falling onto her face, but kept getting up to run away, away from the madness. Tears streamed down her cheeks as the horrid sounds almost faded away, but the bloody images remained sharp in her eyes and the evil voices, loud in her ears. How could this be happening? Monsters do not exist... As she ran, sobbing, she entered a clearing where a lone person stood motionless. The person was cloaked in darkness, yet Cathlyn could sense him staring at her. When her eyes met his, she blacked out.

Chapter 10: Chase

"Do you really think they're in trouble?" Straeten said.

Jace looked at the open road before them and glanced into the Crescent River rushing past.

"It doesn't seem like they would be. But I feel like someone or something is trying to warn us."

"Could you be a little more vague?"

"Well," Jace said with a laugh, "even if nothing happens, this sure beats shoveling your stables out."

He patted his horse's neck and then nodded to the few guards who stood atop the Citadel's rooftops. The horses' steps echoed loudly against the silence that followed.

As the day progressed, the country began to change, and fairly quickly. On this side of the valley, most everything looked different; green rolling hills and lush forests replaced the stark, sheer cliffs of the mountains near their home.

Straeten bounded from his horse's back and carefully took a sample. He placed it in a notebook from his pack, only to drop to his knees and pick a mushroom.

"This looks similar to the ones in our forest back home." He brought it to his mouth.

"Probably not a good idea, Straet," Jace said.

Straeten paused for a moment, then nodded his head and placed it in his saddlebag. He pulled out his journal and scribbled a few notes.

The road appeared lightly traversed with no house or person in sight. Jace kept his eyes open for any sign of danger, scanning the road both ahead and behind at all times, occasionally looking down at the map laid out across Blue's neck.

"We should catch up to them in a few days, at this pace. And it's going to be flat, too. Mostly flood plains here, according to the map. Look at how the river widens out up here."

The hills rolled past, the Crescent River wound through the wide, low, valley, and time crept in silence. After what seemed like hours, Straeten finally spoke.

"Don't you think we've pushed the horses far enough today?"

"I think they want to get to the town as quickly as we do," Jace said. "But you're right, I guess I was thinking of something else."

"Just now? Or for the last six leagues?"

"Funny." Jace said. "Let's set up camp here and give them a rest. We'll get to Tilbury, but not today."

On the fifth day after leaving the Citadel, Jace saw a horse approaching from the north and urged Blue to go forward to meet it. As the animal came closer, he could see that no rider sat in the saddle.

"What is it, Jace?"

Jace squinted and looked at the horse. A lone shield bumped against the saddle with each stride.

"It's a Guardian's horse."

The horse plodded along the road. Dried saliva congealed around his face and his head hung down.

"Must have been scared by something to make him run to near death."

Jace jumped off Blue and ran closer, speaking in soft, low tones. At first, the horse widened his eyes and took a shaking step backwards. Jace placed his hand over the beast's eyes. Luckily, a running stream babbled not far from the road. The horse's legs wobbled while he attempted to bend his head and take a drink, and in an instant, he toppled over into the stream. Straeten and Jace scrambled in and tried to keep his head above water. Soon, they had him standing again and fed him some oats they brought along for their own steeds.

"I don't think this one is going any further today. We'd better camp here."

Jace walked to Blue and began to unload their equipment. He checked his daggers and pulled the bow off the other horse.

"I can handle this all right," he said in response when Straeten raised his eyebrow at that weapon.

"Okay, okay," Straeten said. "I never said you couldn't, it's just that I trust you more with your knives."

Straeten pulled his pack off his horse while Jace collected some wood for a fire.

"I'll take first watch tonight," Straeten yawned.

Jace nodded and laid his head upon a springy patch of grass.

The stars shone brightly overhead that night. Sitting on a rock by the fire, Straeten whittled several leaves and vines into the end of his staff. When his watch ended, he awakened Jace with another yawn.

"Your turn. It's quiet out here, but there's still about five hours left until dawn. You going to be okay?"

Jace squinted at him through one open eye and said, "I've never liked this idea about shifts."

Forcing himself to get up, he said goodnight to Straeten and went to the stream to splash some water on his face. The freezing water did the job. Soon, Jace could hear nothing but the crackling fire and Straeten's rhythmic snoring. Straeten was right— the night was quiet. He did not even hear the usually loud crickets. He stood by the fire with an arrow ready to be drawn, watching every direction.

As he stared at the woods, something triggered his dreams from earlier in the evening. He had been dreaming of being under the water ten years ago. This time, the part before going under water blurred and his time inside the cave seemed easier to remember, somehow clearer. He could plainly see his hands, severely wrinkled by the cold water, and when he clenched them into fists, they ached with a numbing pain. He could actually remember feeling the pain.

The torches around the pool reflected off the water in mesmerizing shimmers, and the blackness of the person's robe was as deep as night. Fortunately, Straeten woke him out of the memory before the man shoved him under the water again; that part of the memory was taking longer to happen now that he remembered and focused more. He drew in the cold, crisp air and continued his watch.

The stars continued their path along the heavens and the waning crescent moon rose above the horizon. With just an hour left before dawn, an animal let forth a piercing call into the still air. If any weariness was left in him that cry drove it out and he pulled the arrow in his bow fully back.

"Straeten…get up!"

Straeten, usually slow to awake, arose quickly. Before he stood to grasp his staff, he slapped his face a couple times. Standing beside his friend, he held his simple, yet solid, staff at the ready.

"I heard a cry from that direction," Jace gestured across the stream to the north. "It almost sounded like a…almost like a warning."

He watched the wooded entrance from the campsite clearing about a hundred feet away. Several minutes passed in silence. His arms began to shake from holding the bowstring taut, but he stayed at the ready. The horses whinnied.

Under the pale light of the coming dawn, a black, scaled creature stormed out of the trees at a surreal speed towards the campsite. Wearing a ragged cloth and carrying a jagged edged sword, the beast screamed as it bounded towards them in a near crouching run. Jace and Straeten paused and gaped for a second before attacking.

The arrow set in Jace's bow launched towards the demon, sailing wide into the water. In a second, he had another drawn and launched, this time with a steadier arm. The arrow whined and struck the attacker in the arm, but failed to even slow it down. The creature leapt in the stream and crossed it in three strides. In the gray morning light, they saw its slightly tapered, black scaled head and elongated jaw filled with yellow, pointed teeth. One of its deep-set, black eyes was missing, replaced by a long, fresh scar. Jace's third arrow struck the beast in the shoulder and it finally slowed a step.

The creature's eye kept straying to the horses, awake and stamping. The horse who arrived yesterday yanked at the rope around its neck, drawing blood. The scaled beast sneered at the horse and raised its jagged, black bladed sword to strike at Jace and Straeten. The site of blood drove it into a deeper frenzy and it leapt towards them into the air.

Jace pulled back another arrow, but before he could launch it, Straeten bellowed a deep cry and ran in front of him, getting into a defensive stance with his staff. A guttural sound, almost a laugh, escaped the creature's throat as it landed and swung its blade. Jace threw his bow aside, and in an instant, ran to the demon, twin daggers flashing in his hands.

Straeten blocked the swing, but recoiled, stunned by the strength of the blow. Quickly he planted himself firmly on the ground and returned the attack with a flurry of his own. The demon easily repelled the blows with its blade and its clawed forearm. The one black eye glared into Straeten's, but the boy continued to fight.

Straeten swung wildly with the staff and the beast caught the weapon with its left hand, razor sharp claws digging into the wood. The demon raised its blade, but before it could strike, Jace, who had maneuvered around the beast unseen, stuck a dagger between its shoulders. Black blood spilled out onto his hand. A scream erupted while the creature spun around to see what hit it, spittle flying from its mouth. It looked square into Jace's eyes and made to strike, but not before Straeten cracked his heavy staff into its face with a full swing.

The beast dropped to the ground, clutching its bleeding eye and growling and hissing. It jumped upon its clawed feet again, speeding away to the west alongside the stream. It turned around and looked at them with its good eye and then at the horse from the north. Still staring, it pulled one of Jace's arrows out of its arm and then the other out of its shoulder. Jace ran and picked up his bow.

Before he could draw the string back, the creature said something unintelligible in a harsh voice and they stopped. It reached back with a clawed fist and yanked out Jace's dagger, wincing slightly. It pointed the blade at Jace, who returned the gesture with his drawn bow. The demon sprung away through the trees, narrowly avoiding the incoming arrow.

An hour passed before Jace and Straeten relaxed their weapons and stopped staring into the woods. Not until the sun came up fully did the two breathe a little easier in the morning light, but they were still edgy and jumping at every sound from the woods. They walked back to the center of their camp, still shaking from the attack.

"I would've run the same as you did," Jace said to the new horse. "We'll call you 'Chase,' all right?"

The horse, blood hardened around its throat from the chafing rope, neighed his response.

"Straet, what out of the darkness was that?"

Straeten, sitting down at the burnt out campfire with his face in his hands shook his head.

"All I know is that I'm glad there were two of us and just one of him."

Standing up, he walked to the river and scanned the ground to get a good look at any tracks. Jace walked beside him and looked at the claw marks in the wet riverbank. He shook his head and glanced back at the horses.

"I don't know whether to take Chase with us, or send him south. Seems like that thing was chasing him, and now it'll be after us, too. Maybe more than one next time."

He knelt down and finished cleaning the black blood off his hands at the stream. When he stood up, he bumped into the horse's neck. He looked the horse in the eyes.

"No, we're not going to leave you, Chase."

Chase nodded his head and Jace smiled.

"Besides," Straeten said, "it probably wants us both dead even more than the horse now, thanks to your dagger and arrows and the tiny pat I gave him."

"True," Jace said. "Let's get going and try to lose it before we get to Tilbury today. Or maybe we'll meet him there."

The two packed up their camp, ate a small breakfast, and headed a bit more warily along the road to the north.

Chapter 11: What Remains

According to Jace's map, the main road to Myraton was about to branch away from the Crescent River and head due east towards the great city. Only a few hours of traveling upon this road and he and Straeten would reach the small town of Tilbury nestled among the smooth, rolling hills to the north. Tucking the map away into his saddle, he looked up at the dark mountain range climbing sharply into the western skies. Several streams cascaded from the gray cliffs and wound their way to the larger river beside the travelers. He urged Blue onward, although still wary of another encounter with their strange attacker, or even swarms of the scaly creatures storming down from the mountains. He glanced at Straeten who was also scanning the towering hills.

After the road turned abruptly east away from the river, they saw smoke rising on the horizon, yet neither spoke of their fears. They kept a careful eye on the woods and hills, weapons in hand. Small, seemingly abandoned, farms appeared along the road more frequently as they came closer to Tilbury. At this time of day, farmers should be out tending their crops or animals...yet all was quiet. Even the forest creatures made no sounds, as if any noise would draw danger towards them. The horses' hooves clomped on the sun-baked road, kicking up clouds of dust in their wake and obscuring Jace's and Straeten's vision. The two quickened their pace.

When they finally entered the town of Tilbury, they saw buildings smoldering with thick smoke and dark birds circling, as the late afternoon sun bore down. The birds eyed what Jace had feared he would encounter. He and Straeten attempted to scatter the persistent carrion hunters, but when they frightened one group, another only took its place.

Mainly Guardians littered the ground, their gray cloaks torn asunder and expressions of fear etched on their faces. A few bore claw marks that stretched across their bodies, and some were mutilated, seemingly after they were killed. A few of the brown robed Followers also lay about randomly. Jace scrambled off of his horse and vomited. He had never seen anything like this. Sure, the thieves ended up in a bad spot sometimes, sometimes had to kill someone, but Jace had never seen it before. He looked up at Straeten still on his horse and saw the fear in his face. He had a bit of cloth across his mouth to block the smell.

Jace ran to the bodies and, forgetting about the death that surrounded him, knelt down beside them and turned them face up. He went through bodies as quickly as he could, wanting to identify them all, yet dreading what he might find. He found an older man and a young woman close to Cathlyn's age, yet no one he knew.

"Jace?"

Jace stopped and slowly turned when he heard the tone of Straeten's voice. Straeten stood at the base of a small hill looking at a body lying face down. Long red hair streamed down the person's back. Jace rushed to her side.

"Karanne!" he said, grabbing her lifeless shoulders.

He turned her over and looked upon her blood-covered face. With a sigh, he slowly let her rest back on the ground.

"It's not her."

"We should bury them."

Closing his eyes, Jace grimaced and clenched his fists repeatedly. When he opened them again, he stared past the town, looking for any sign of the attackers.

"Right. No way to end up," he said, motioning to the birds circling above.

After tying their horses, he and Straeten searched throughout the farm town for shovels. On their way to a farmhouse, a familiar face appeared from behind a still smoking building.

It was Allar, leading a horse and a cart carrying some of the fallen. Surprise and perhaps relief appeared, however slightly, on Allar's face when he saw them. He walked slowly, however, and his eyes returned to the ground as he trudged. Soot covered his body, and black streams of tears crossed his cheeks. Giving the two a blank look, he walked his horse over to another group of bodies.

"Come to steal from the dead?"

He stared at the bodies of the Guardians as he leaned over to load them onto the cart.

"Allar! What out of darkness happened around here? Have you found anyone, Karanne, Turic…? Cathlyn?"

Jace ran to Allar, who had fallen forward onto his cart. Jace and Straeten helped lift the older boy and carried him somewhere where the smoke was thinner.

Straeten and Jace took turns watching over Allar as he rested; while one watched, the other carted bodies to the gruesome pit Allar began. The next few hours stretched on, but luckily, help arrived later in the afternoon. Townsfolk and farmers with ash-covered faces silently joined the two and helped to bury their own friends and family. They worked late into the evening and when the stars shone upon them, all the bodies were covered. The villagers' torches cast eerie shadows on the burial mound and surrounding faces.

"Did you see where they headed?" Jace asked a villager.

Burgis, as he introduced himself to Jace, responded, "It was a nightmare; they swarmed around everyone, from the air. I tried to follow them with a couple friends this morning, but they left no trail. We headed west towards the mountains where we thought they went, but they didn't disturb anything...only...."

Bowing his head and swinging the club clenched in his fist, he took a deep, shuddering breath.

"We found bodies, or what was left of them, along the way. They were people we knew, and some were ...eaten. We turned back."

Allar awoke later that evening to an old woman dripping water on his forehead.

"You need rest," she said, but he attempted to stand nonetheless.

"It's all done," Straeten said, holding him down with a strong hand on his shoulder. This calmed him a little, but he struggled against the grip anyway.

"I must go after Cathlyn," he spoke in a raspy voice, after finally laying his full weight back down.

"It's night," Straeten said. "We'll go in the morning; we all need to rest tonight. But first tell us what happened."

The old lady caring for Allar stood up from his side. "You've exhausted yourself. You need food and more rest."

She lifted a flask of some liquid to his lips, which made him recoil, but he drank it.

Allar closed his eyes and began. "I was sent on an errand last night that took me out of town. I watched the skies when I returned and it was as if the air were alive...dark masses of...I don't know what...all over. I ran faster when I saw flashes of light burst up in the air, and when I came into town, there were hundreds of these creatures around, killing people I knew. I...."

The old woman looked at Jace and Straeten.

"He needs rest now, you all need rest."

Although still wanting answers to their questions, Jace and Straeten agreed to leave the small room and find shelter elsewhere. Once out on the streets, Jace looked up at the stars.

"We knew something was going to happen, but...."

Straeten walked out ahead. "I know."

Nodding, Jace began to plan how to find their friends. Out of the corner of his eye, he caught sight of some movement in the shadows. In one quick motion of his wrist, a dagger appeared in his hand and he called to Straeten in a hushed voice. Straeten took a defensive stance as he and Jace walked towards a smoldering building.

"Where did you see it?"

Jace motioned with his knife towards a pile of what used to be the inn.

"I can't see anything," Straeten said.

Jace motioned to Straeten to be silent and to follow. A dark shape intertwined with the shadows crawled through the wreckage of the inn. Jace and Straeten crept up, although Straeten's size forced him to work at it. Once at the remains of the inn, they saw a human-sized shape pawing over rubble under the light of the stars. Jace raised his knife to hurl at the creature, but suddenly stopped.

"The suffering!" a whiny voice uttered.

"I should throw it anyway," Jace said as he sheathed his knife.

Straeten laughed. The being stood up and yelped, a light bursting forth from its hand and crackling through the air. The flame flew way off course.

"Jervis Redferr."

"Jace? What are you doing here?"

"We're looking for friends, but found you," Jace said. "What are *you* doing here?"

Standing straighter, but still shaking, Jervis said, "After those beasts attacked...and I chased them, I realized I left some things behind."

"Looks like everything in here burnt down. Did you see what happened to the rest of the Followers? Where they went?"

Stepping over the wreckage, Jervis said, "Those things, whatever they are, those...those demons, they only seemed to kill the Followers that attacked them. Stupid magic, it didn't even hurt the beasts. Knocked a couple over, but they got right back up. They certainly went through the Guardians quickly, too. Some help they were.

"I know they took Brannon; I saw him running around yelling to himself, probably gone crazy. They took the amulet off his neck and put it with the rest of the Soulkind. They took those, too, and carted the remaining Followers off with them."

"Did you see what happened to Karanne and the others?"

"Well, I didn't see them killed, if that's what you're wondering," Jervis added. "They all headed west, but who knows where."

"You saw quite a bit of what happened," Straeten said. "How did you manage to stay alive?"

"If you're thinking I hid, then you're right. I'm no coward, though. I've certain skills, as Jace knows, that help me out when I need it. Sometimes it's better not to fight. Plus, like I said, the fire Brannon taught us was practically useless against them."

Jace wondered what he would have done in the situation. He and Straeten would have rushed headlong into the fray knowing their friends were in danger, and then they would have both been killed.

"Did any of the Guardians survive?"

"I don't know. One made it alive, barely. Stroud, the leader.... He woke the next morning with a gash on his forehead when I...well, anyway...."

He looked at the ground.

"Robbing your own Guardians," Jace said. He could see it in Jervis' eyes as the red-haired boy continued to speak. Jervis was probably looking around the wreckage of this building for a lockbox full of money. "Can't shake old habits, huh?"

"You'll see about that."

Jace flinched slightly.

"Anyway, he searched for trails left behind and must've found something, because he got on a horse and tore off into the hills. I followed for a little while, but came back here."

Straeten looked up at the sky and said, "It's getting late. Come on, Jace."

Jace nodded. "Goodbye, Jervis."

"Are you sure you don't want any company?"

The two continued without turning around.

The next morning, Allar awoke to find Straeten and Jace waiting for him outside. Jace sat petting a skinny gray dog with black patches on his chest and back. There were three horses saddled and ready to go—one of them Chase.

"You better not slow me down. And we better not take that mutt."

"No one else will take him, he'll be fine. Plus, he'll be a great watchdog for us, right Ash?"

The soot-covered dog's appearance transformed from scrawny to fierce in a second.

"Sure," Allar said when the dog growled. The dog returned to Jace, who resumed petting him.

As the three mounted their horses, three townsfolk—including Burgis, the villager they met the day before—rode towards them on their own horses.

"We're going with you," Burgis stated.

Straeten whispered to Jace, "They probably know the area well enough, and by the looks of it, they hunt with those bows."

Jace looked over at the three and saw their longbows strapped to the sides of their saddles and quivers, each bristling with arrows.

"We'd be glad to have you join," Jace said.

As the sun rose over the eastern hills, the six of them rode out of the still smoldering town of Tilbury. A few townspeople came to wave them on, but the Tilbury of the past no longer existed. The only sound on the western road out of town was the solemn stamping of the horses on the baked, dusty surface. Jace looked back to see the townsfolk slowly wandering around the streets, apparently lost in what to do next. He looked forward again and gripped his reins tightly. The travelers spoke few words to each other, not wanting to break the silence. Ash stayed about a hundred feet in front of everyone, his ears up and eyes darting.

"This is Tare, my brother," Burgis said.

Tare sat silently and tall atop a gray horse.

"Our parents were killed two nights ago. We'll find these devils that did this and kill them." Tare nodded his head. "He can't talk at all, but he can track anything. And that's Ranelle." Burgis motioned to the other traveler.

Ranelle sat straight in her saddle with her long black hair pulled back into a ponytail. Soot covered her face and she wore a large cloak in the cool early morning air. She appeared to be a few years older than Jace. She kept one hand on the reins and another on her long hunting knife at her waist. Her sharp eyes scanned the woods along either side of the road.

Allar spoke this time saying, "What happened to her?"

Ranelle looked at Allar expressionless. "You can ask me. My husband also was killed two nights ago defending our town."

She urged her horse into a gallop, leaving them behind. Allar opened his mouth to speak, but closed it as she rode ahead.

"We all lost someone," Burgis said. He looked over at Tare who stared ahead in silence.

When the sun stood directly overhead, they reached the Crescent River. Ranelle rode back from her scouting to report she spotted a lone man camped beside the river. The party approached the river on foot, weapons drawn. As Jace peered though the dense trees of the forest, he almost laughed to see Mathes Spier camped out and eating a meal beside the water's edge. So he did make the journey, after all. Ash looked back at Jace who spoke, "Friend," and the dog returned to his side. Mathes stood up to greet the newcomers when they walked out from the cover of the trees.

"I wondered when I would find you," he said as Jace and Straeten approached.

He clasped their arms in greeting and then motioned for them to sit beside him while he finished his meal. Jace introduced the others as they dismounted.

"It happened, Mathes," Jace said. "Just like in the cave."

"I feared you were correct," Mathes replied and closed his eyes and took a deep breath. "That's why I came. Did you find out what happened to anyone? Karanne?"

"She wasn't among the dead, nor was Cathlyn or Turic," Allar said. He sat tall in his saddle, the wind blowing his hair over his face as he looked westward to the distant mountains.

Mathes, breathing a sigh of relief, shook his head. "What happened?"

Allar and Burgis took turns telling the story of the massacre at Tilbury, while Ranelle stood beside her horse, her head resting on her horse's neck.

Jace took this time to scout the area and find someplace to cross the rapidly flowing river, someplace shallow. Straeten nodded to him as he left. Ash followed him downriver northward, leaving the party behind. As his eyes scanned the waters, his hand strayed into the small pouch where he kept his stones. He felt the edges of the first one and immediately saw Karanne, as clear as when he last saw her, walking along the bridge the morning the Followers departed. Dropping the one in his hand back into the pouch, his fingers clasped upon the green stone from his fall. His vision passed through his mind, jarring and real.

Slow down, concentrate.

Instead of racing across the rooftop, he stood atop the Hall Library. He felt tall and powerful as he stepped assuredly to the edge of the roof and gazed out across the shining city of Beldan.

Ash barked a warning, causing Jace to drop the stone.

"What is it?"

Dazed, he realized he had wandered out of his friends' sight. Ash pointed his nose to the trees to the east and Jace ran there to take cover.

Luckily, the dog was smart enough to follow Jace quietly behind a tree. Jace peered into the dense woods with a dagger in his hands, but could neither hear nor see any shape among the trees. Seconds passed and nothing moved. Suddenly, an animal's cry pierced the air, much like the cry the other night that warned Jace about the attack from that strange creature.

Then Jace saw him. The red-haired, freckled boy ran from behind a tree. With a deep sigh, Jace stood up from behind the tree and sheathed his dagger. Waving his arms in the air, he got Jervis' attention.

"Jervis!"

Ash growled, but Jace put his hand on his head to calm him. Jervis ran towards the river, leading his horse. His free hand glowed red as if he were about to cast a fireball at anything that moved.

"Jervis, relax!"

"This forest!" Jervis said. "It's haunted."

He turned around and looked into the woods, hands on his sides as he panted.

"Hey dog," Jervis said in a short breath, and walked over to pet him. Ash backed away staring at him, a low growl in his throat.

"What are you doing here?"

Jace and Ash began to walk back to the camp and Jervis followed several feet behind.

"Well, I was in Tilbury thinking that I wasn't headed anywhere." Jervis laughed. "So, when you agreed to let me come along...."

"I agreed to that?" Jace asked with one eyebrow cocked.

108

"Well, whatever," Jervis said. "I thought I could help out somehow."

"I doubt that," Jace said under his breath, but was cut short by a sharp bark from Ash.

On the ground in front of him, he found a scrap of brown cloth, stuck to a rock. Must be part of a Follower's cloak. Looking out, he tried to see across the waters. The river appeared to run deep at this part, but when he threw a rock in frustration, he heard it strike a hard surface and bounce upwards.

"Did you see that?"

"All I see is this mutt looking at me like I'm lunch."

Jace looked closely at the water. He put his hand in, then smiled. Jervis' jaw dropped as he watched Jace run across the surface of the river.

"I'm going back to tell the others," Jace said, walking back onto dry land.

With a satisfied look at Jervis' perplexed expression, he trotted upstream with Ash, scrawling something upon the map he began at Turic's cottage.

As those around Mathes' fire heard Jace approaching, they rose to greet him. All except Allar, that is.

"Great," he said, crossing his arms. "Another thief."

"Hey, I'm not *just* a thief now," Jervis said, pointing to his robes. "I'm a Follower."

He cast a fiery globe into the water, where it hissed and bubbled straight to the bottom.

"We know what you are, and we don't need you 'accompanying' us anymore." Allar reached for his sword, and Jervis squinted his eyes.

Mathes stood between the two. "Enough!" Pacing in front of his supplies, he said, "Allar, we can use his...help."

Straeten and Jace exchanged looks with each other and then with Mathes. Mathes nodded at them and said, "Now, Jervis, I bet you would like nothing better than to go back to Beldan right now, yes?"

Jervis looked at Mathes with a glare of anger still in his eyes. "All right...."

"Good. Now I have a letter that needs to be delivered to the head of the Council in the Hall." Mathes scrawled words down onto a parchment laid out across a flat board he carried for writing upon. "This informs them of the battle at Tilbury and will ask for reinforcements while we investigate...."

109

"You know, Mathes," Allar said, "you're not fit for a journey like this. You're just a teacher."

"Yes, and in my training as a teacher," Mathes produced a rapier from inside his cloak with lightning speed, "I learned many things."

Standing upright, he saluted Allar with the hilt to his brow, and then, as quickly as he took it out, slid the blade back under his robes. He sat down and continued to write the letter while Allar shrugged his shoulders and smiled.

Jervis squinted his eyes and asked, "Why would anyone listen to what I had to say?"

Mathes kept writing in a flowing script as he spoke, "Because you are not *just* a thief, remember? Plus, this is my handwriting and seal."

He looked around for something to melt the wax.

Jervis reached forward and cast a ball of fire onto a piece of river wood. He smiled as Mathes recoiled from the magic.

"What? You afraid of this?"

Mathes held his piece of wax as far from the flame as he could to melt it, when Jervis sent another bolt near the log. He pulled back, but not before the hot wax dripped on his hand. Jervis laughed until Jace cuffed him upside his head.

"Enough, Jervis!"

The red haired boy turned around and glared, raising his tattooed hand towards Jace. Straeten raised his fist and Allar grabbed the hilt of his sword. Mathes forced a laugh as he pressed his signet ring into the pool of melted wax on the parchment.

"It's fine, Jace. I appreciate a good joke now and then."

After a few words under his breath, he tied a small string around the rolled up note and held it out for Jervis to take.

The Follower scowled at everyone staring at him. Seeing their weapons still drawn, he grabbed the parchment and ran to his horse, who skipped about and turned southward.

"Those reinforcements won't show up in time to save you!"

He kicked his steed in the side and bolted along the river towards the southern road until he was gone from sight.

"Can we really trust him to bring the letter to the Council?" Straeten asked.

Mathes began to pack up his small lunch site, putting away his extra parchments first.

110

"You know as well as I that we couldn't trust him to do anything, other than to slit our throats and take our money. At least we got him out of our way."

Jace nodded his head. "I suppose you're right, Mathes."

"I spoke to the Council when I left after visiting the cave, so hopefully, they'll investigate without the letter," he said. "Besides, we couldn't count on very much help anyway, since there is little to give from Beldan. Now, describe those creatures to me again."

He listened when the party told him more about the black, lizard-like beasts. Jace even sketched one of them upon the yellowing parchment. After hearing their stories and looking at Jace's drawing, Mathes closed his eyes and a silence fell over the group. A few moments passed before he spoke.

"If my memory does not deceive me, I recall reading similar descriptions of creatures created through the use of a Dark Soulkind many thousands of years past, a race of demons called 'Darrak.' If they are once again roaming the land, evil must also have awoken with the accursed Soulkind to bring them forth. But to what purpose…."

He stared into the rushing waters beside the bank of the river. "With those beasts out there, I don't see how we even stand a chance."

Ranelle straightened her neck, staring up at the dark mountains to the west. "I'm going, with or without you."

Jace believed her. Looking around at the others, he nodded. Everyone, including Mathes bore an expression of grim determination.

"A small party is hard to notice, especially when some of us have certain skills that can help us remain unseen."

With a wink, Jace jumped onto Blue and lead the others northward towards the ford in the Crescent.

Chapter 12: Trapped

Karanne sat with her back up against a cold stone wall, her head resting on her knees, and her hands bound tightly behind her back. The only light was what managed to find its way under the crack of the door and flickered like a dying candle. Time seemed to stop, the rising and setting of the sun forgotten to her. Her only company was the sound of incessant dripping water, echoing faintly in the hall, the moans of other Followers captured and separated in their prisons, and the beasts pacing outside her cell.

The night in Tilbury now seemed a like a nightmare. Images of her companions flashed through her mind as she relived the attack. Over and over, she told herself this could not be possible, that demons like that did not exist in her world. She forced a laugh. Just a few weeks ago, magic did not exist.

And now she was trapped in this prison.

The beasts would never hold her for long, she swore; she had special…skills.

Outside the locked door, the constant movement of someone guarding her cell reminded her she was not entirely alone. The thing seemed to wait and hope for any sign of resistance. She had been captured before in her life, stupidly, when she was young. Very young. She did find a way out then, but the prison was smaller and not as heavily guarded. Still, this was just a prison, and she always found a way out.

Others had tried to use their magic to escape, but that was almost as useless as when they tried to fight back in Tilbury. Any use of magic was quickly met with a tramp of the clawed feet. The lights under her doorway stopped flashing and just before they killed the Follower, the creatures spoke again, this time in words Karanne could understand. They made the Follower say his name, almost squeezing the words from his throat. Later, as they carried his head past every doorway, the Followers knew the name Gradus, as well as the fate of anyone who used magic. All that power, and she could not hurt them or use it to escape.

She had to get out of here.

In the few weeks after becoming a Follower, Karanne learned a small trick, something that began the night she tried to hide the magic from Jace's eyes. With a picture of a tiny spark in her mind, she managed to conjure up the smallest of flames, its weak light barely flickering in the darkness. The Followers were told they could not learn new spells on their own, that only the Master Follower could create and teach them, but she discovered the intensity of her flame could be drastically altered. Although she wanted answers for what happened, she felt it best not to tell anyone. With this new skill, she explored her cell.

Under the magical light, she felt around the floor. A foul stench arose from some corner of the room. As she felt about with her hands chained together behind her back, she brushed past the remains of some rotting carcass. Biting back an urge to vomit, she pulled her hands back in reflex and cringed. There had to be some way out.

She moved the small spark of magic in darting motions around the room, barely lighting the grim prison. She tried to move, but could not stray far since her hands were bound in chains behind her back and to the wall. She stayed away from the food and water she had in her prison, as much as she could. The smell seemed to be of rotting meat (not unlike the smell of the carcass in the corner), and the water they gave her had more texture to it than she remembered water ever having. Only by telling herself she needed to conserve her strength for escape, did she manage to keep the "food" down.

Yanking on the chains, she groaned. The locks seemed old and rusty, yet strong and well made. She ran her fingers over the bindings on her wrist to see if she could recognize the style, but it was well beyond her age and experience. However, she hadn't yet run into a lock she couldn't pick.

Because she could not separate her hands from each other or bring them in front of her, she had to crawl backwards as much as the chain let her to search for some sort of tool. The creatures took all the supplies within her pouch and belt that could have helped. Wrenching her neck to see into the corners of the cell, she spied the little spark she summoned sitting upon a skeleton, roughly human-sized. Certainly one of those bones could be used to pick the lock.... With renewed spirit, she spun around and kicked out with her legs trying to pull the bones closer. "Come on!"

The metal cuffs dug into her wrists and as blood trickled onto her palm, her mind wound with anger and she cursed with every kick.

Down the corridor outside her cell, she heard doors opening and the deep raspy voices of the beasts mocking the prisoners. She froze when she realized her peril: the spark she conjured now formed a sphere a foot in diameter and emitted a blazing light! Trying to calm herself as the voices grew louder outside, she concentrated on letting go of the spell.

"Suffering!"

Her one weakness was releasing the magic.

Another door crashed open, likely the one next to hers, she guessed. She tried to calm herself by closing her eyes and concentrating on a single point. She peeked at the sphere, yet still, no change. Another door crashed open, this time across the hall, and she knew hers was next. A key clicked harshly in her cell door. As she focused, the sphere began to decrease in size and intensity. She released a deep, long held breath. Smaller and smaller it shrunk until she heard the key grate upon the metal door as it turned.

Turning away from the door, she saw the flame, now the size of her finger, and edged over as much as she could to try to cover it. As if alive, the spark of fire darted into her waiting palm as the door crashed open, spilling wavering light into the room. She clasped her hand shut over the spark and bit back the pain of the searing flame as two of her captors pushed their way in.

She clenched her teeth while one of the black, scaly creatures prodded her with the butt of his spear. She would not let them know of her pain. The other dumped some water on her face. She stared at the creatures with a mixture of fear and awe. This was her first time getting a good look at one of them.

They stood hunched over with their forearms nearly touching the ground. They would've been a good six or seven feet tall, if they stood up straight. Their reptilian heads tapered to a jaw full of yellowed teeth. But it wasn't the fangs that made Karanne shudder. What should've been a blank stare coming out of a snake's head, was cold and hateful.

"Not long before you teach us your fire," the one with the spear sneered and spoke in a harsh voice.

A stench like rotted flesh blew from its mouth to her face and she practically vomited. The pain in her hand suddenly subsided and she felt relieved, although the company prevented her from relaxing.

The demons wore nothing but rags upon their midsections; their scales must have offered protection enough, though, especially a magical one. They had startlingly human-like hands, but with smooth black scales and hooked claws that flexed as the beasts moved. A sickly yellow claw protruded from each of their elbows. Karanne watched in grim

114

fascination as the claws retracted when the creatures relaxed their arms. They exited and locked the door, once again leaving the room in darkness.

She felt her hand for a scar, but felt nothing but her smooth palm. With a thought, she conjured up the spark again, but when she did so, it felt different somehow. She twisted her neck to see her hands. From her palm, first came a glow and then a flame the size of her finger. The surface of her palm appeared to bear a scar, but as she looked closer under her spell's light, she saw a red line in a perfect circle on her skin.

She made the flame dart faster than she had before and with much greater control. The flame twisted around and around in a bright, but confined, glow as it hovered in the air. As she thought of the bones sitting on the floor, the light darted over to them with pinpoint precision, and in an instant, she smelled them burning. She glanced over at the door, thinking she heard a sound, and the flame darted over and began to bore a hole in the metal.

"No!"

She opened her palm and called the flame to her, which flew to her hand. She winced, thinking it would burn again when it touched her, but she felt nothing and it disappeared, leaving a brief glow that illuminated the rest of the scar: an intricate flame inscribed in a circle. She smiled. Twisting her fingers about, she located the lock entrance on her wrists....

"Why won't the magic affect them?" Turic wondered aloud, as he sat in the dank, dark, cell.

These were Darrak, cruel beasts controlled by a Dark Soulkind. Somehow, that Soulkind was once again being used to create or awaken this past evil; a power that had to have awoken even before the awakening of Marathas.

Turic's mind ached, and not only from his thoughts. He had struggled painfully along the road from Tilbury to this dark cell. Turic had feared the Darrak would kill him if he fell behind, as they did several of the others.

Kill and eat.

In Tilbury, the Darrak split the Followers into two groups and Turic never found out if Karanne or Cathlyn survived. He felt fairly certain both were too intelligent to put up a fight. The odds were too far out of Karanne's favor and Cathlyn...Cathlyn could not even use magic to begin with.

Poor Brannon. That man, Turic feared, had gone insane after his capture. He spoke incessantly to himself; he pleaded for help, to be released, for anything. But after the Darrak stripped the Soulkind from around his neck and threw it into the chests with the others, all he said, or in fact whimpered, was, "Marathas." Turic pitied the man. He also feared for the rest of the Soulkind; their destination unknown after the Darrak took the cart away from his group of Followers. Turic had little time to think about what would happen to Brannon; somehow he escaped soon after the flight from Tilbury. However he did it, it did not please the Darrak.

Cold Darrak laughter and a door slamming outside his cell broke him out of his thoughts and he began to wonder if he was so lucky to make it out of Tilbury alive.

Those eyes. Cathlyn shuddered and closed her eyes, but images of people dying, running, and screaming continued to spin through her mind.

When next she awoke from her nightmares, she found she was in a cart along a bumpy road. Her eyes slowly opened to the gray of an early morning sunrise and the creatures surrounding her. She tried to stand up, but bumped her head on the metal cage trapping her within the cart.

Not only were Cathlyn's friends nowhere to be seen, but no other human lay in sight, either; only those scaly demons hauling the cart steadily uphill and prodding her with their weapons accompanied her. She marveled at the strange creatures; they seemed to roughly mimic a human form. She couldn't quite tell if they were supposed to have two or four legs because some walked hunched over like a person and others tread upon the rocks like a beast. Whichever way they walked she could sense their strength and speed in every movement.

She did not recognize the landscape outside; it was different from anything she had ever seen or read about. Small and twisted trees randomly grew along a rock-covered ground with an oozing look, although the ground below proved solid. Many of the taller trees appeared dead or dying and only smaller plants and gnarled bushes seemed to thrive in the soil. Brown moss and lichen clung to every surface, as if trying to survive in the unforgiving environment. A strange, white flowering plant also grew in great numbers. Cathlyn wondered how, while everything looked so desolate, a beautiful flower continued to live on.

116

For days, they dragged her in her small cage atop the cart, and only the beautiful white flowers throughout the countryside brought her any cheer. But soon, even the flowers faded as the path rose higher into the approaching mountains.

Cathlyn noticed packed crates filled the cart alongside her cage. Each one bore a strange mark she recognized from the doomed journey to Myraton: an old symbol meaning "Soulkind." These creatures now took the Soulkind for themselves, or someone else.

She strained to reach a crate and one of the monsters battered her hand with the flat of its sword. Another grabbed the attacker's sinewy arm and shouted something unintelligible. The first creature looked at Cathlyn, spat, and continued onward along the path. Although the creature shot back glares, it never came near her again.

"What are you?" she asked one of them on the second day.

Several of the scaled creatures walked past her with their strange gait and dragged their weapons along the bars.

"Chekra, talk to her!"

A horrible sound Cathlyn could only guess was laughter erupted from the army around her. A taller creature walked towards the cart. He bore an evil sneer from a wide jaw, exposing sharp teeth and emitting a foul smell. In one lightning quick motion, hidden skin-like wings opened and he leapt upward. Landing on the top of the cage, his clawed feet gripped the bars and his wings slowly moved up and down. Cathlyn clutched herself, shrinking away from the demon, but continued to look Chekra in his deathly black eyes. He shoved his spear down into the cage and the point stopped only inches from her face. As the cart bounced upon the road, she swallowed, but Chekra did not move, nor did the spear.

"You are lucky someone doesn't want you dead…." Hisses and laughs arose from the creatures around the cart. "But don't think this won't be fun for us." With another flying jump, the black creature leapt off the cage onto the ground. "Now, speak no more…."

The cart jarred as it hit a hole in the road, causing Cathlyn to hit her head on the bars above her. Her escorts laughed again hideously, some threw rocks at her, and she buried herself under her arms, crying softly.

"Marathas! Marathas?" Brannon looked around.

Stroud thought once again about putting the gag back around Brannon's mouth. Co'lere's ramblings put them in great danger. The demons were still searching for them and would have no problem finding and capturing both of them. Well, at least Co'lere.

"We need to go back and get my Soulkind."

"They will kill you if they find you; they're searching for us right now."

Stroud readied his pack to leave in the middle of the night, hoping to depart under the cover of darkness. His sword lay unbuckled and ready at his hip.

"All the more reason why we need to go and get it, Marathas?" Brannon looked across the fire beside Stroud with glazed eyes.

Stroud looked beside himself at the small fire, then looked back at Brannon with pity. He had to keep him alive, but he also had to get the Soulkind. First, he would bring Co'lere to safety, then go back and retrieve the amulet.

Brannon looked across the fire at Marathas, who sat in his red robes with his hands folded across his lap. Only he could see this man, someone whose soul was a part of the Soulkind. He looked so cold and regal, and held Brannon's gaze without question.

"I think we're going back to find it, now," Brannon said.

Marathas replied in a calm yet sharp voice, "If he decides not to come with us, then we'll leave together, tonight. You must get your Soulkind back no matter what; no one else must use it. When we do find it, I promise to teach you more magic. You will be the most powerful Master ever."

Brannon smiled, looked at Stroud still packing his horse for the trip, and sighed. He was glad to have Marathas back with him. He had disappeared several times before, but never for this long. Marathas was right, he had to leave and retrieve his amulet tonight, and Stroud was not coming along.

A day passed after Jace and his companions crossed the hidden bridge over the Crescent River. Every hundred feet or so Jace looked over his shoulder expecting to see a tailing Jervis. Luckily, Ash proved an excellent watchdog and would also alert him to anything out of the ordinary, which in this land were most things.

The terrain around them changed as they headed westward. Trees became sparse and rolling hills turned to craggy outcrops of gray rock. At some parts, the rock looked like it had formed from solidifying liquid. It retained the hardness of rock, but appeared oozy and rippled. The animals also changed. Jace could still hear birds, but less than in the woods. Dark rats with glowing red eyes replaced the squirrels and foxes. As the group walked closer, the rat creatures jumped back into their caves, but when Jace turned around, he could see them peering out at him leaving their territory.

The rocky, craggy ground soon became littered with massive pits. Dark holes marked the entrance to unknown depths, and cool, damp wind emanated from within. That night, they camped within a deep, rocky depression in the ground to attain shelter from the growing wind. Jace talked each of the horses down, caressing their noses and speaking gently as they attempted the steep path. Ash paced silently around the top of the pit's border and did not relent from his watch until Jace walked up the steep hill to feed him.

"This road we're following seems well traveled," Jace said. "There might be company pretty soon."

Straeten nodded. "Let's get off the road for a while. We can try to stay close, but in the trees or hills."

"What trees?" Allar asked. "The few here are dead or dying. This is a wasteland. And did you see those creatures? I've never seen anything like them before."

"There are some trees, although the soil isn't quite right for them to grow in," Straeten said. "The plants that survive here are amazing."

He drew a picture of a delicate white flower in a small book.

"There should be enough cover for us to run to, if we need it." Mathes shivered and pulled a blanket around his shoulders. "Lucky we came across this hole, the wind is freezing."

A gust howled over their encampment.

"I'm not cold," Straeten said, and the others looked at him as they shivered. Straeten looked back and laughed. "I'd share some if I could, but this is all muscle."

Across from Straeten on the other side of the fire, Burgis, Ranelle, and Tare sat huddled together, talking amongst themselves. Burgis spoke up.

"Jace, where are we heading?"

All eyes turned to Jace. All eyes, that is, except Allar's, which stared into the fire in front of him.

"I studied several maps of the land before we left, and brought this one, although it's not very thorough. We crossed the Crescent River here," Jace said as he traced his finger across from Tilbury.

"And we are heading directly towards this mountain range, with this high mountain in the middle."

Mathes spoke up. "That mountain is called Retzlaff, and behind it is a smaller one, Rabiroff. The story of their naming dates back many thousands of years. Retzlaff and Rabiroff were evil sorcerers, or so they say in the legends. The mountains, I believe, are named for their volcanic distemper."

"I remember reading a story that involved these mountains," Jace said and looked off for a moment. "The story was about two brothers. Marlec, the brother of the king Lu'Calen, led his corrupted Followers to claim all the Soulkind. Before the attack, Marlec, who none knew to be a betrayer, convinced the Followers guarding the castle to leave the city on an important mission. The Followers returned in time to rescue the city from the attack; however, not quickly enough to save the king from his brother."

He prodded the fire with a stick and his eyes focused again on something far away. "When Marlec saw his Followers were defeated, he retreated with them into these very mountains: Retzlaff and Rabiroff."

The wind howled overhead and everyone sat a little closer to the fire.

"What happened to Marlec?" Straeten asked.

"I don't remember what the book said," Jace answered, blinking his eyes.

After a minute of nothing but the crackle of the fire, Mathes said, "I've never heard that story before."

"I know I read it somewhere in the Library," Jace said. "Or maybe Turic told me. All I know is that there was a fortress up there somewhere over a thousand years ago, and if it's still here, that might be where we're heading."

After several minutes, Ranelle spoke up. "Jace, how did you learn to share a bond with the animals? I've never seen such a trainer."

"I don't train them, I just always have gotten along with them." Jace turned around and saw Ash sitting right behind him.

Burgis laughed. "Well, Ranelle has been training animals for years, and she is the best in Tilbury. A compliment from her goes a long way, Jace."

Tare smiled when his brother spoke. He sat quietly at the fire, whittling a piece of wood with a hunting knife. He peered at his tiny carving and made vigorous, yet delicate, cuts.

Ranelle looked into the fire. "It wasn't only my husband they killed that night. I trained the best tracker I've ever known; raised him from a pup. He, too, was killed by one of those nightwalkers."

"I'm sorry, Ranelle," Jace said.

He hated these situations where he knew there was something he should say or do, but locked up instead. He looked at Ash, who walked around the fire to Ranelle and nuzzled her arm.

She smiled. Ash placed his nose on her leg and she put her hand on his head. Looking up at Jace, she said, "Thank you."

Everyone looked at Jace, who shrugged his shoulders. "But I didn't do anything!"

Tare smiled and handed his carving to Ranelle. It was a tiny, black dog.

Ranelle's eyes widened. "This looks exactly like my Faraz, Tare!" She kept the carving on her knee and she stroked Ash's head with her left hand.

"What do you know of these creatures, the 'nightwalkers' as you called them?" Allar said.

"Stories are passed down by those my husband tracked with, legends not written down but told to the next generation. In them they spoke of the Nightwalkers. When I first heard the stories, I thought the creatures were made up. Now, they are much worse than I could have imagined."

She would say no more on the subject.

Allar was the first to lie down to sleep, and soon thereafter, everyone settled in. The fire dwindled down to the barest of embers. Ash looked over at Jace as if asking permission to stay by Ranelle's side. Jace nodded and the dog lay down beside her.

That night, Jace sat up on watch near the top of the depression and tried to listen to the animals around him. At first, nothing seemed to be nearby, but soon, strange animal sounds like screams came from above his head and away towards the trees and hills. Jace sensed a touch of fear in their calls. Their distress seemed to grow the farther they walked from the Crescent River into this land.

From the east, he heard the crack of a fallen branch and crouched down while trying to see through the thick darkness. The frigid night was clear, yet there were no stars in the sky. In the blackness, he could barely see right in front of him, much less fifty or so feet into the trees. The woods remained silent, except for the strained animal calls. In this darkness, he could do nothing but wait.

121

Chapter 13: Unexpected Help

The sun rose the next morning as always, although Jace and his companions did not see it. When the party climbed out of their camp with the horses, the countryside looked even more dismal than the day before. The sky and landscape seemed to blend into one overhanging cloud. The rough gray rocks they tread upon and the dead trees lining their way matched perfectly with the bleakness of the gray sky. Straeten managed to find edible plants in the desolate landscape and offered the others some plant and fungal life.

"These are actually good. They resemble a species I've seen before. Here," he said and pointed to a pile of cleaned mushrooms sitting on the ground.

Tare slowly reached out and took the food, and even more slowly, placed it on his tongue.

"No, wait!" Straeten yelled. "That's a poison one!"

Tare spat it out and wiped his tongue. He looked up in horror, but stopped when he saw Straeten doubled over. Burgis, too, joined in the laughter. The silent boy glared at Straeten and then, smiling, picked another mushroom up and placed it in his mouth.

Allar stood beside his horse, Chase, and kept a straight face, although he let Straeten have his fun. He stroked Chase's mane and started to walk away when the horse nuzzled him back. With a sigh, he spoke to the others.

"The terrain is getting much too rocky as we go further into these mountains. As much as I hate it, I think before too long, we'll have to leave our horses behind."

"I don't know if we should," Jace said. "I've heard something, or someone following us."

"Are you sure?" Mathes asked as he tied his books onto his horse.

"He's sure," Ranelle said.

"It's too dangerous to send someone to scout for our pursuer," Mathes said. "It might be a Darrak."

Jace pulled his bow off Blue's saddle and looped the string around, making it taut. "It's no Darrak, although he may happen to lead them to us. Jervis. Maybe we should've taken him with us."

He sighed and looked at Allar. "I guess you're right about the horses. We should send them back somewhere safer. Plus, we'll be less visible on foot and harder to track."

He patted Blue's nose as he took off what gear he could carry and spoke into her ear.

"Now Blue, we have to send you to safety."

Blue whinnied and shook her head.

Allar laughed. "'Horse Boy', we ought to call you!"

"A compliment, where I am from," Ranelle said, silencing Allar.

Jace continued, "You must bring these other horses back to Tilbury, alright?"

Ranelle led her horse beside Blue and said, "Don't worry. They are smart animals, and my mount will know the way. They'll be all right."

As soon as the animals were ready to go, she slapped hers on the rump sending her speeding off. The others felt the excitement and were on their way, as well, galloping out of sight through the bleak landscape. The travelers covered up their fire, hefted their packs, and headed towards the snow-capped mountains in the distance.

The road seemed the easiest way to travel, but was in plain view and the party was forced to trudge over unforgiving terrain under the cover of the sparse trees. They all tried to keep an eye on the road to watch for approaching enemies, but when they looked away from the rocky ground, even Jace ended up stumbling. The path later became even harder to traverse because of the steady rise in slope and the cold, steady rain soaking them through.

The mountaintop loomed before them, dark and ominous. Looking back at the group he led, Jace saw their hoods sticking to their heads and water running down their faces. Mathes looked to the side, his brow furrowed. Allar kept an eye on Jace, but looked at the ground when he met his gaze. The three from Tilbury held their bowstrings away from the water, but to little avail. Straeten, bringing up the rear, poked the ground with his staff, probably looking for plant life. He smiled and gave a small wave. Ash, in the lead with Jace, stepped swiftly and kept watch for any movement. The rain did not seem to affect him—in fact, he lapped at the air to catch some.

After marching upward for an hour Jace saw something.

"Get down! Everyone!"

The party all dropped to the ground and craned their necks towards where Jace looked. He called them in closer and pointed towards the road.

"There's a building about a quarter of a mile that way."

Through the rain, they could just barely make out a stone structure, a guardhouse of some sort. Ash growled while the rest stared in silence at the dark shapes moving about the building and perching on the rooftop. A Darrak sentry. The rain began to pour harder.

"Let's try to move around them," he said. "I'm sure they haven't seen us, yet. Come on!"

"Around?" Allar said. "Looks like that's a sheer cliff to me."

Jace slowly nodded. They faced a nearly vertical wall beyond the sparse patch of trees they stood within.

"I'll go ahead up there and scout a way for us."

"I'll come with you." Straeten took a few steps towards Jace.

"The fewer there are of us to get spotted, the better. Thanks, Straet."

Straeten frowned for a moment, but let him go. He and the others knelt in the rain to wait for Jace's return, looking down the mountain from the edge of the trees, weapons drawn.

Ash followed Jace closely up into the cliffs. Jace saw the sentry post not far away and knew the Darrak would easily see them climbing along the rocks, if they happened to look this way. He drew his gray cloak around his shoulders for camouflage. The path to the fortress was certainly well protected. With each rock he clambered over, another steeper one blocked his way. Even Ash missed some of his jumps and slid back.

After climbing for awhile, Jace felt the sharp edges of the mountainside bite into his hand. Blood mixed with the rain covered rocks. Ash, thoroughly soaked, licked Jace's wounds. Jace pet the dog and looked back the way they came. They had not climbed more than several hundred feet, and still, the mountain's peak lay miles away. Apparently, no easy way around the mountain existed, except back on the road and through the Darrak encampment. Well protected, indeed. Several large birds circled in the air and he could almost sense their intent to pick his bones if he fell now.

With a sigh, he decided they had no choice but to venture up the mountain and began to climb back down to where he left the others. Ash panted heavily, yet kept up on the way down.

Closer to his friends, the hillside grew easier to climb and he quickened his pace. "Almost there...." Ash froze in place, blending in with the gray rocks. Jace looked down the hill to see a group of...six, seven, eight Darrak encircling his friends. He stepped behind a tree.

Burgis lay flat on the ground, but Jace could not tell if he was alive. A Darrak, limping because of an arrow pierced through his calf, stood yelling down at him. Tare tore away from his captor and tackled the Darrak who had begun to kick his brother. Soon, though, he joined Burgis on the ground when a Darrak's spear cracked him across the forehead. The rain poured even harder.

Ranelle and Mathes stood with Darrak behind them, spears pointed at the bases of their necks. Straeten kneeled, holding his ear; blood covered his hand. Two Darrak held Straeten down, their black, clawed hands pressed into his shoulder.

Another two yanked up the Burgis and Tare and carried them while the rest led the others away, prodding them with spears and claws. As they departed, a few Darrak stayed behind and shouted, pointing upwards at the mountain in Jace's direction. Jace muttered a curse under his breath and moved back behind the tree. After a moment he peered around the tree and saw the remaining Darrak had joined the others and headed towards the sentry building.

Shaking, Jace waited many minutes before heading down the hill. He looked into the middle of the clearing where his friends had stood and saw their gear. Ash sniffed the air as Jace crept in front of him down to the clearing. The rain slowed to a cold mist and Jace stopped in his tracks and looked around; the animals he had been hearing before the downpour were silent. He took the bow from around his shoulders, knocked an arrow, and pulled the string back. Another minute passed and the shadows around him did not move. He relaxed slightly and put the arrow away.

Still with an eye watching the few trees and boulders, he shoved the weapons and gear he thought they would need, and that he could carry, into a large sack. Ash stood at the edge of the grove of trees, facing the sentry and the group being herded downward about a mile away. Taking a deep breath and exhaling sharply, Jace hefted the pack of weapons and walked towards Ash, who abruptly looked up into the sky.

The next few moments spun in Jace's mind. His instincts screamed at him to jump away. Time slowed as a bird's piercing call cried out. He dropped his pack and dove to the right, but not before he heard the sound of a blade flying through the air. He rolled to the rocky ground and a burning pain shot through his arm. Shouting, he looked around and saw a familiar knife sticking out of his left shoulder: one of his own. The knife did not hold his attention for long; when he turned around, he saw a black-scaled Darrak leaping into the small clearing thirty feet away—a Darrak with a great scar over one of his eyes.

The beast made a sort of gurgling laugh in its throat. Jace reached back with his good arm and pulled out the blade with a grunt. He paused for the slightest moment to ponder the irony, but the moment passed and his eyes fell upon his attacker. The Darrak swiftly moved towards him swinging its jagged-edged sword.

From the sky, a blurred shape screeched, diving and striking the Darrak in the face with outstretched talons. The Darrak howled in pain, dropped its sword, and tried to claw at the attacker clinging to his head.

"Valor!"

With renewed spirit, Jace raised his dagger to throw, but even before he could release it, Ash flew past him like a gray shadow and leaped into the demon. Before the scaly beast could react, Ash's jaws locked around its throat and it fell backwards. Ash shook his head while still gripping, but with a swing of a clawed arm, the creature sent him flying away with a yelp. Valor still clung onto the beast's face with his claws as it scrambled to its feet again.

Jace hurled his dagger. It flipped through the air and planted itself in the Darrak's scaly chest. The demon screamed again and Valor leapt off, avoiding its swinging claws. Black blood dripped from the deep scratches on the creature's face and neck and it plunged to its knees. It stared at Jace with its good eye through a haze of black blood, wobbled and spat blood at him.

With another cry piercing the skies, Valor swooped into the back of the creature's head and knocked it forward onto its chest with a thud. The force of the fall drove the dagger through the Darrak's back. The creature shuddered for a moment, then lay motionless. Valor landed on a tree branch and scanned the clearing.

Breathing heavily and shaking, Jace smiled up at the bird and laughed. He started to rush over but noticed Ash lying on the ground, nursing a painful wound on his front leg.

126

"Hold on, Valor. I need to help him out first."

Jace knelt to examine Ash's wounds. The dog lay on his stomach, licking his paw. Jace cleaned the cut and rolled it up in a bandage, soothing Ash's soft whining as best he could.

"That was pretty brave, and it's going to stay with you for awhile."

Once Jace finished, Ash stood up, but whined again when he put his paw down to walk. He then plopped back onto the ground, panting. Jace cradled his arm and took off his shirt exposing a bloody wound that gaped open on the fleshy part of his left shoulder. It was pretty close to the base of his neck. If not for Valor....

He poured water over the cut to clean it out and put pressure on the still bleeding injury with his right hand. As he looked for a bandage, he flexed his left hand and winced.

Among Mathes' belongings, he found a small jar with a salve.

"This should work—ow!"

He closed his eyes for a moment until he could once again stand to make a fist. Holding a shirt with one hand, he used his teeth to tear off a long strip. He tied it tightly around the wound, then rotated his arm. So much for carrying all the gear. He packed as much as he thought he could handle into the sack and hefted it over his good shoulder.

He held out his right arm and watched as Valor flew to it.

"You've been helping us out all along, haven't you?"

Valor turned to look in Jace's eyes and cocked his head before he took to the air again. As he watched Valor circle overhead, other birds circled closer to the clearing. Vultures eyed the corpse of the Darrak lying on his face. Jace kicked the dead creature over, exposing the handle of his dagger. After he pulled out the blade, he wiped off the thick, black blood with a piece of cloth.

The knife wasn't a plain blade anymore. The creature had engraved tiny shapes and words upon it, but it was almost as if it were telling a story. The carvings were intricate and he thought them possibly the finest quality he had ever seen; and he had seen some high quality artwork in his jaunts with Caspan Dral around Beldan—seen and stolen. The cawing of birds overhead broke his thoughts and he spun the dagger in his palm. Better leave them to their meal.

The first living thing he had ever killed. A sudden pang of guilt went through him. Surely, the creature would have finished him, but he sensed there was something more to these creatures than just their killing instinct. Breathing heavily, he looked again at the dagger before sheathing it beneath his cloak. Now, his friends needed him.

As he turned, he caught a glimpse of the fallen Darrak moving! He wrinkled his nose in disgust; the Darrak was dead, but its entire body crawled with insects. The red-eyed rat creatures they had seen earlier scampered towards the body to contend for their share. They paid no attention to Jace.

He stepped backwards and stared in amazement when two tiny, lizard-like creatures half crawled, half slithered from the safety of their caves towards the dead Darrak. Clawed legs and long tails propelled the creatures along the ground. A pair of short, curved horns protruded from the flat pointed heads of the gold-colored animals. Forked tongues flicked in and out of their mouths.

Jace had never heard of such beasts...or had he? With a start, he remembered one of the statues back in Beldan looking similar to these creatures. The statue was much bigger, but still held similarities. What was happening? The slithering, crawling creatures frightened away the smaller rat beasts with hissing and then settled upon the Darrak, tearing at its flesh and breaking Jace out of his thoughts. He continued to back away, his mouth hanging open. Soon, the body would be completely gone.

Ash followed Jace as he began his descent to the sentry building where the Darrak undoubtedly held his friends. The gray dog limped as he trotted, all the while watching Jace and the hawk circling high overhead. Vultures' harsh calls pierced the air as they descended on the body to finish what remained. Nothing would last too long lying around here in the wilderness.

Once Jace got within a quarter mile of the sentry building, he stopped. From there, he could find out how many he was up against. On the ground, as many as ten paced back and forth. Half as many winged Darrak perched on the rooftop of the large, stone building, looking almost like the gargoyles he had seen at the Hall and on NorBridge.

"Great. They can fly."

If he stayed there much longer, the Darrak would easily spot him if they even looked in his direction. He had to find some sort of cover to wait out the hours until nightfall, in hopes that a patrol would not stumble upon him. Where, though?

Valor flew over him and began to ascend high into the air, circling on the updrafts. Jace's heart soared with him; he always wished he could fly like that! He shook his head and concentrated on sneaking along the gray rocky ground to a boulder. Ash limped alongside him and sat down. Luckily, he had his own camouflage in this stark countryside.

This would do for now. Jace glanced up into the sky to see where Valor had gone. Soon, he found him perched in a dead tree closer to the building that stood only several hundred feet away. Valor seemed to be looking straight at him.

Does he want me to come over there?

Jace looked along the ground and tried to figure out how to get by without being noticed.

Suddenly, Valor leapt off the branch with a cry and flew towards the right side of the rock where Jace and Ash hid.

What are you thinking?

Surely, the Darrak would spot them now. He soon had an answer to that question; three Darrak patrolled where Valor was now flying. They would have been upon him in a few minutes, but were now after the hawk. They smiled, eager for target practice. Arrows shot into the air, followed by raucous shouts when each one missed its mark. Valor was no easy target. He flew at the Darrak's heads, leaving them only cursing and swinging their claws uselessly. The black creatures followed him when he veered away northward away from Jace and the guardhouse.

Jace and Ash crept from tree to tree towards the tree Valor had perched on earlier. Slowly and painstakingly, Jace continued making his way there. Right below the decaying trunk, a barely seen cave entrance gaped into the earth. He tried to hurry Ash into the cave, but the dog sniffed at the entrance before limping inside.

"Come on, Ash! They're going to see us!"

After he turned his head sideways, Jace saw no one looked their way yet, luckily. Ash crept into the cave and Jace scrambled in after him. Some of the gray light made its way in and Jace could see the peculiar, rounded stone walls, which had a pattern much like tree bark. But when he tried to see more he hit his head trying to straighten his back. He sat at the lip of the cave and looked out directly at the sentry building. *Perfect!*

Soon thereafter, the three Darrak who went after Valor returned empty handed. They walked to the front gate of the stone building to taunts and jeers from the others. Once Jace got a better look at the guardhouse, he tried to make a plan to get inside. Fortunately, he had some prior experience breaking into buildings. What did Karanne mean he would never need what he learned from the thieves?

The large, stone guardhouse set between two steep outcrops of rock and thus blocked the way to the road on the other side. On the left side of the building, several Darrak dragged a carcass towards a large wooden door. Large crows and vultures made swooping dives towards the animal. Jace could not see it since a crowd of Darrak stood right in his way, but could tell that whatever it was, it was huge. The Darrak swung their spears at the birds as they pulled the beast inside. Soon, their loud cawing was all Jace could hear.

Two entrances stood out on this side of the building: one was a huge portcullis blocking the tunnel to the mountain path beyond, and the other, a wooden gate leading inside the prison through which the Darrak had taken their prize. A Darrak sat atop the roof; perhaps an entrance lay on the flat rooftop, which was over thirty feet high.

With his left arm in its condition, he might not be able to make the climb. He unwrapped the makeshift bandage and examined the wound. He winced as he flexed his arm, but the medicine he applied seemed to have lessened the pain. He cleaned the wound, added more of Mathes' salve and wrapped another bandage around it.

The plan would work. It had to.

Under the cover of night, he would rescue his friends.

He watched the sun through the gray haze as it crept towards the horizon. His legs were numb with being cramped in the cave. Finally, he decided to risk stretching them, but heard a noise outside. His heart pounded in his throat and Ash stood upright. The slow, steady sound of footsteps approached and Jace and Ash scurried further back into the cave. Jace dragged the supply bag along, his heart pounding in his ears. When he heard the footsteps near the entrance, he turned around and froze, putting his hand on Ash to stop him, as well.

The darkness of the cool cave covered them as they sat nearly twenty feet inside. Jace heard the sound of rocks being kicked outside the cave. Just when he thought the danger had passed, the Darrak kicked another rock, this time into the cave. The noise of the rock bouncing along the walls echoed loudly. Jace saw a pair of black, scaled legs walk to the cave entrance and stop.

The Darrak stood facing the entryway and bent its legs into a kneeling position. Jace felt Ash leave his side and reached for him, but felt nothing. *Another branch of the tunnel!* Quickly, he rolled away into the side passage, but without the bag. He cursed to himself as he drew his daggers out. *The Darrak will at least get a few scars....*

130

Seconds dragged on and Jace's heart continued thudding in his chest. Although he tried to remain still and quiet, he was sure the Darrak could hear his very heartbeat. He held his breath and waited for something, anything, to happen.

Many minutes later, he finally worked up the courage to peek around the corner. Nothing. Slowly, he crept to the edge of the branch and stuck his head out to look down the tunnel at the sunlit entrance. Nothing. There was nothing there. Letting out a breath he had been holding for what felt like hours, he called to Ash and they crept back through the tunnel. The bag sat unnoticed on the ground, looking like a rock under the pale light.

The grayness of the day disappeared as the sun finally sank into the west. The dark gloom of night covered the land when Jace woke to Ash's gentle nipping on his leg.

"Didn't realize I fell asleep, pal. Hey, you want something to eat?"

He blindly searched through the supply bag to find some food. Ash turned his head aside.

"Come on, Ash. You should really—"

Four sets of red eyes, barely glowing and motionless, lay on the ground behind him. Ash gnawed on the bones.

"Thanks, Ash."

His eyes adjusted slightly to the darkness of the cave as he prepared to leave. At the lip of the cave, he looked towards the guardhouse. Torches lined the building outside the gates and on top of the roof. Only a few Darrak remained outside, but they were laughing and stumbling over each other as they passed around a large bottle.

"The best way to break into a place, as Caspan Dral, used to say, is to 'observe, observe, observe.' Find out the patterns of the people living there; find out when they wake up, go to sleep, eat; when they do everything. I don't think we have enough time to do all that, huh?"

Valor then flew onto a branch right outside of the cave. Jace could not quite see the bird, but heard the sound of talons scratching on the dead wood. Continuing to observe the building, he now counted twenty guards walking around, but could not be certain. The guards out in front randomly went in and out of the building, and he tried hard to identify bits of each to get an accurate count. After an hour, he hoped he counted a total of twenty-five Darrak, several more than he had thought upon arrival at the sentry. He was pretty sure the Darrak all took turns watching the prisoners and then coming outside to drink.

"Ash," Jace spoke into the cave. "I'm going to do some climbing and I don't think you'll be able to follow. You're going to have to stay somewhere close by."

As he began to walk towards the rocks surrounding the building, Ash followed closely by his side.

"No, Ash," he whispered, "Wait here until I call. There are rocks... Great, I'm trying to reason with a dog."

Staying low, they crept towards the south side of the building where the steep cliff met the stone wall and the portcullis came into view. Jace wanted to slip through the bars and pass to the other side, but the passage beyond was so heavily guarded that he reverted to his original plan, which was up to the roof. When they reached the cliff, Ash lay down behind a stone without a word from Jace.

"I'll come back for you before we move on, I promise, all right Ash?" Ash put his face down between his front paws.

Jace found out shortly that his arm worked pretty well climbing the steep rock. His shoulder ached dully each time he reached out for a handhold, but he forgot about the pain while concentrating on the mission before him. He was the only hope for his friends.

Only forty more feet to the top of the sheer cliff and Jace could climb down onto the roof. The darkness made the climb even more difficult, but Jace relied on his other senses and the sturdy footholds to quietly struggle his way to the top. When he pulled himself over the cliff, he looked down to the torch-lit rooftop, which lay about ten feet down and appeared to be built right into the cliff itself. The way down had no handholds. He rubbed his throbbing shoulder, and then ducked while he looked for signs of life.

A single Darrak sat on the roof with its legs dangling over the edge. A strange sound came from the Darrak, a sound Jace almost thought might be singing. Clenching a round flask in its clawed fist, the Darrak took turns "singing" and swigging. Jace heard the creature's comrades about forty feet below on the ground, pointing and laughing.

He's very close to the edge.... If he fell somehow, they would all think he was just clumsy from his drunkenness, and there would be one less.... Jace looked at the perched Darrak and tried to see if it had wings, but could not tell. While he weighed his options, he pulled out a dagger, the marked dagger, and he felt a pit in his stomach. No matter how evil and full of malice this creature seemed, Jace knew he could not force himself to kill another, unless he had to, unless there was no other way. Something

132

about how he knew the Darrak to be intelligent creatures made it feel…wrong. They were pawns of something greater, but they were not mindless.

He sheathed the dagger and sighed. Tying off his rope securely to a rock protruding from the cliff, he began to descend to the roof. He kept his eyes on the back of the Darrak still swinging his legs over the edge of the roof, but the creature made no attempt to get up. When his feet touched the surface, he tried to pull his rope down, but it was too well attached to the stone above. *Well, hopefully no one will see this.* He ducked and headed for the trapdoor. *I wouldn't be much of a thief if he heard me.* He pulled the trapdoor closed behind him and slid the bolt through the lock. Barring him up here was fine.

He crept down the steep flight of wooden steps leading into a large main room filled with ten Darrak, drinking and laughing. *There's Purple Helm, Limp, Boots…* He went through the list again in his mind to keep track. *There's a new one; you're twenty-six, Trophy.* Jace watched from his vantage point on the steps as a Darrak much bigger than the others stood by a golden-scaled beast hanging from a small support. The Darrak wore a golden claw on a chain around his neck.

Jace gasped at the hanging golden creature. It was huge! Indeed it was like the statue back in Beldan. Two cages stood beside the dead beast containing smaller versions of the same animal. The tiny, golden lizard creatures snapped at the Darrak, who poked at them through the bars. Jace reconsidered feeling guilty for killing a Darrak.

A pounding from above startled him. Luckily, the noise from the other Darrak below would cover the commotion for a while, but soon, somebody would hear it. Jace knew he had to leave, and fast. On the other side of the room, he saw a door he suspected led into the tunnel through to the other side and up the mountain. He also spotted the two main doors: one in the front and the other at the back of the building. At the bottom of the stairs, a hall branched off from the main room, hopefully leading to the prisoner holding area.

As the Darrak yelled and cursed from the other side of the trapdoor, Jace crawled down the steps as quickly as he could. Torchlight flickered and cast shadows of the Darrak onto the walls. At the bottom, he crept from shadow to shadow and behind supports to reach the hallway.

The Darrak who Jace named Trophy, suddenly yelled out an order for someone to check out the noise. Jace froze underneath a table about ten feet from the hall. A Darrak on the stairs shouted out something that sounded like "locked," and soon roaring laughter echoed in the hall.

"Leave him up there!" Trophy hollered.

With the small distraction, Jace snuck to the hallway. He turned around at the entrance and stood in the shadows to see if anyone looked in his direction, yet the Darrak still did not notice him. What worried him even more, however, was how he was going to escape the building with his five friends. *Always have a plan to get out*, he remembered Caspan saying.

"Suffering."

He walked down the hall, which seemed to slant downwards after a short time and grew colder. He saw that the halls themselves were carved out of the rock. The number of torches lessened as he walked further down and the sparse light cast eerie shadows on the wall. The first door he came to was nearly fifty paces into the earth on his left. A torch stood right inside the door, and another at the far side of the room. Two Darrak, sitting at a table, had their backs to the doorway and were deep in discussion.

Twenty-eight total… so far. Three wooden tables also stood inside. A pile of papers caught his attention and he slunk into the room. Maps. His leather boots did not make a sound as he walked upon the cold, stone floor. The Darrak, sitting less than ten feet away, continued to talk. The torch at the room's entrance sputtered and popped and they looked back to the door. Jace froze in his crouched position next to the table and held his breath. In a second, the Darrak turned back around and resumed their conversation. Jace slowly let his breath out.

He reached up and carefully took two maps off the top of the table then crept backwards out of the room. Exhaling another long-held breath, he tucked the maps away in his belt and continued on down the hall. *Even Caspan Dral would be impressed. Maybe even Karanne.*

No, probably not her.

The next few rooms he looked into were lined with bunks. He passed all of them, taking the time to count the Darrak. Their snoring sounded like a combination of hissing and growling. Jace recognized all fifteen sleeping Darrak, which left fourteen awake to contend with.

The next room down the hall held a few boxes and Jace walked in to see what was inside. As he peered around the back of the boxes he saw someone he did not expect.

"Jace! What are you doing here?"

Jace put one finger up to his mouth and motioned Jervis out and into the hall. A hood covered his face, but Jace saw it was covered with filth and blood. "What am I doing here? Are you alright?"

"Yeah. Thanks," Jervis said. "I just got out of a cage back there."

Jace stopped and stood in a shadow beside the wall. "Did you see anyone else?"

"I think I saw your friends there, but...." Jervis stopped for a second then said. "Maybe I should go back to the entrance to keep an eye out, okay?" He walked back up the passageway.

Jace nodded. "Just watch out for the two Darrak in the room down on your right. And hide back here if you see anyone coming." Jervis nodded and then was gone. *Well, Jervis' help is better than no help.*

I hope.

Finally, after passing many empty rooms and thinking his friends might not be there, Jace came across a large cell at the end of the tunnel. A solitary torch sputtered on the wall and barely illuminated the room and his companions' long faces.

Jace's fingers moved quickly within the metal door, and soon, the lock popped open with a satisfying *click*. He opened the door with a bow and said, "This way, if you please." Straeten helped Tare and Burgis to their feet. "Are you all okay? Anyone need this?" he asked, holding Mathes' salve. He administered some to the gaping cut on Allar's scalp.

"Thanks," Allar said with effort. "Thanks for getting us out."

"Well, don't thank me yet. We've still got the Darrak army camped out up there to get through. There should be fourteen of them—that is if most of them stay asleep."

Ranelle said, "I don't think we're ready to take on one of those Darrak in our condition, much less fourteen. Plus, we have no weapons."

"I got in here, didn't I?" Jace said. "Plus, I saw Jervis earlier. He'll be able to help us too." They exchanged looks and rolled their eyes. "Come on, he may be a miserable thief, but he can't get any lower, can he?"

The group quickly walked up the sloping passageway. Straeten gripped Jace's shoulder and gave him a nod of thanks. Jace kept looking for any sign of Jervis, but he was nowhere in the tunnel. The snoring continued to emanate from the room with the bunks as they crept up the stretch of hallway past the resting creatures. Only a little farther to the main room. Only a little longer to think of a way to get out. The time quickly passed and soon they were looking at the Darrak carousing in the main hall. Jervis was still nowhere to be found. He probably tried to free himself.

"If Jervis gets caught...," Allar started, "the whole camp will be on us, and fast. Do you have a plan for getting us out, Jace?"

Backing into the tunnel out of the light, everyone looked to Jace, who held up one finger and crawled to the tunnel entrance to look in again. First, he looked up to the staircase leading to the roof. *Good.* He could still hear the pounding of the enraged Darrak. *That's still one less we have to worry about.* He glanced around and counted the Darrak in the main room. Of the seven that remained inside most were passed out at the long tables around the room, and the others not far from it. With one on the roof, that left six outside. Jace eyed the way out of the building that would lead them up the mountain. The door was propped halfway open, enticing him as a means of escape. He might be able to sneak to the doorway, but he could not picture everyone else doing the same.

What we need is some sort of distraction. Something that would bring them all out of the building. He looked at the young, golden-scaled lizards making high pitched whines while they stared up at their mother, whose carcass still hung from the rafters. He could set the lizard creatures free and maybe the Darrak would chase them outside.... No, the little beasts would probably stay and fight, or maybe even go out the way Jace wanted to leave. *The suffering!*

The sounds of the pounding on the roof abruptly ceased. Perhaps the excluded Darrak finally gave up his useless attempts. Suddenly, a great shout from the front of the building arose and all the Darrak made a great clamor to head out the front gate. He wasn't certain what roused the Darrak, but scrambled to his feet.

"Come on," he whispered back to his friends, "we're leaving!"

They all crept to the entrance and watched while the last Darrak left the room. Jace pointed to the half-opened door and everyone started to run for it. He watched from behind as Mathes first went out, followed by Ranelle, and then Burgis. Ranelle scrounged around for some weapons on her sprint towards the door, claiming several bows and a couple quivers of arrows. When they all had gone through the door, Jace followed, but slowed when he heard the cries of the lizards. He made a dash for the two cages.

Straeten looked back through the door and waved to get Jace's attention. "Are you crazy? Hurry up!"

136

Jace reached the cages and looked at the simple locks while trying to calm the squirming animals. They snapped at his fingers with sharp beaks when he reached for the doors. "I'm here to help." He pulled the pins holding the cages shut and the doors sprung open. The two lizards swung their tails, pulled forward with their arms, and scurried out of their prisons. Jace sprinted to the back door where Straeten waited. Then, he stopped abruptly, turned, and headed straight for the doorway leading to the portcullis.

"Ash!"

Straeten waved to the rest of the group to continue onward and then turned around to follow Jace. He saw the two lizard creatures for the first time and paused. They slid around the room sniffing the ground and walls. He then ran as fast as he could after Jace and into a long tunnel.

Jace was leading something through the narrow gate, something scrawny and gray. "Good boy, Ash!" he was repeating. "Hey Straet, don't worry; I see all fourteen of them out there." Outside, the Darrak gathered around a shape lying on the ground. "Looks like he didn't need my help falling off after all."

"All right," Straeten said, "can we leave now?" He turned around and saw the other end of the tunnel that led up the mountain about one hundred feet away. Jace nodded and they ran.

Without warning, a bolt of spinning flame shot over their heads, striking the wall of the tunnel in front of them and exploding in an arc of light. Jace ran for the end of the tunnel, Straeten and Ash close behind. In the next instant, the sound of chain against chain echoed as the other portcullis closed on their escape.

Jace cursed as he watched the gate shut. That final Darrak was manning the portcullis.

Behind them, they could hear more cranking noises as the other gate opened to let the Darrak in. They turned around to find Jervis standing at the opening gate with a bolt of magic burning in his hand and fire smoldering in his eyes. He smiled at them as he called the Darrak into the tunnel.

"Go wake the others and retrieve the rest of them."

The Darrak Jace named Trophy nodded and ordered another to wake the rest of the guards. A shorter Darrak ran through the tunnel and into the main building to carry out his command. Jervis and the remaining Darrak advanced upon Jace and Straeten.

"What are you doing?"

"Didn't I tell you about my new friends?" Jervis said with a smile that faded suddenly. A darkness covering his face flickered with the pale torchlight.

Before Jace could continue, another bolt of magic erupted into the air from behind him this time. With an ear-shattering crack, the bolt flew overhead towards Jervis and the approaching Darrak. Instead of hitting them, the blast careened into the ceiling, shaking the building and bringing exploding rock down upon them. Jace and Straeten sprinted inside the guardhouse while the building began to collapse.

Outside the tunnel, they heard the stone crack and felt the building shake again as the rooftop buckled onto the Darrak beneath it. "We've got to stop the Darrak from waking the oth—" Jace stopped when he saw the two gold lizard creatures feeding upon the Darrak that had attempted to run through to the barracks. "Never mind...."

"Let's go now," Straeten said in a shaky voice and pulled Jace out the back door into the open night air. Jace stumbled out and looked back into the building.

"But who saved us? There's got to be another Follower still trapped in there," Jace said. "We've got to go back and—"

"Look out!" Straeten said and pointed to the Darrak manning the portcullis crank on the top of the building. The Darrak held a bow and arrow pointed straight at them. From Straeten's hand, a bolt of light arced upwards and struck the Darrak square in its chest. The Darrak stumbled off balance and plummeted off the roof, breaking its neck with a *crack* as it hit the rocks below. Jace stared with his jaw open at Straeten.

"Come on!" Straeten yelled, practically dragging Jace. "Come on!" Soon, they were running up the road while Jace stammered.

Chapter 14: A New Magic

From behind a stone support, Karanne spied a patrol bringing several Followers out of their cells and up a flight of stairs. She had escaped from her cell an hour earlier and still, no one spotted her, but she expected no less of herself. Not with her experience.

Now to get out of this place.

The little flame from Karanne's palm worked well on her manacles. The mere thought of the key entrance caused the little white flame to enter the lock and spin, melting the locking mechanism. She laughed. Could have used this trick a few years back.

The spark also made short work of the lock on the cell door. She looked inside the keyhole as the spark spun faster and faster, soon melting its innards. *Great, why don't I just leave a sign for them.* With a slight push, she opened the door just enough to look into the hall.

With a deep breath, she stepped into the corridor, but then stopped and felt around her neck in a panic. With a sigh, she pulled a chain from underneath her shirt. They didn't take her necklace. Before heading into the hall, she clasped the white stone at the end of the chain and nodded her head.

From behind the pillar, she continued watching the other Followers being herded like cattle. The darkness of the building tried to swallow up the meager light emitted from the few torches upon the walls. She counted twelve Followers being led up a huge, spiraling staircase from another level below. Thirty Followers had left Beldan, but some had died in the battle at Tilbury and on the way to this foul prison. She estimated, at most, twenty Followers in this prison, but even with her good sight, she could not identify them through the darkness and the distance. With the Followers being occupied here, she felt now was as good time as any to try to escape.

Before she continued to look for a way out, her eyes were drawn to a figure wearing a long, purple cloak followed the group, barking out orders and addressing the creatures as "Darrak." A helmet covered the figure's head and the lighting was poor, but she could tell he was a man.

She melted into the shadows and snuck up closer, creeping from pillar to pillar. Anything she could overhear might help, but the man walked out of the room the opposite way from her cell. Darrak patrols passed through the hall, scanning the darkness for anything. She took a breath and held it for a moment. She knew what to do. She had been trained by the best thieves. This was in her blood.

She slipped through the hall unnoticed, and followed the cloaked man. The hall opened up into a great room, and she could see the entrance to the fortress wide open. Beyond the gates she could see those creatures, those Darrak, gathering among campfires. She could make it. Night was coming soon and she could sneak past them all. She had counted the steps here from Tilbury, she remembered the directions they had gone.

All she had to do was hide and wait for the right moment. Hiding even in plain sight for her would be no problem, and this room had plenty of spots for her to remain undetected.

An hour passed and she knew it was time to go. She crept to the gate, still wide open, and she smiled. Freedom. The word echoed in her head. It was as if all the years of thievery were training her for this moment. She stepped outside.

What about the others?

She hesitated for a moment and looked back inside. "But they don't even know I left yet. Any minute and the alarms will go off and they'll double the patrols." She took two more steps outside.

Always thinking about yourself.

She reached up and touched the white stone at the end of her necklace.

How am I going to free the others? And even if I did, what would I do with them? They're not getting out like I can.

The voice inside her mind was silent. She cursed and snuck off into the night.

As the Darrak herded them out of the dank dungeon and up a long, stone stairway, Turic's legs ached from lack of movement over the past hours. He shuddered as he thought about what he was about to do: give these creatures even more power. When his eyes adjusted to the dimly lit staircase, he looked around at the others and frowned. He counted only eleven.

Karanne was not in this group, but Turic did not fear for her safety. Instead, he looked around for Cathlyn and Kal. If the Darrak found out they were not Followers, what use would they have? At that moment, a bell clanged from somewhere deep in the fortress. It sounded like an alarm. Half of the Darrak leading them turned around and ran towards the sound of the bell but the others keep forcing the Followers up the stairs. Maybe he was being rescued? Not likely.

At last, they reached the top. A large, windowless hall with high vaulted ceilings awaited them, as well as hordes of Darrak. Turic wondered who controlled this army. He glanced around the room, but at first, saw none besides the Darrak and his companions. Squinting his eyes, he thought he saw a man at the end of the procession into the hall. He appeared to be giving out orders to the Darrak, but before he could look closer, two Darrak behind him snarled and pushed him forward.

A thought passed through his mind as he and the others walked up a short flight of steps at the far end of the hall: once the Darrak learned the magic, they could pass it on to others and the Followers would then be expendable. A slim amount of hope remained in his heart, though. If Brannon Co'lere were still alive, Marathas would be useless.

Turic shook his head. With the magic of the Soulkind finally coursing through his body, he had thought his dreams had at last awakened. He had always hoped he would one day become a Soulkind Master. But now, instead of using magic himself, others would control magic through him and he would be a mere puppet. He looked down upon the lines of Darrak in the hall. The old Healer shook his head again as his first "student" walked up the stairs.

Cathlyn woke from a sleep that had taken her when the cart finally stopped and the beasts threw her in a cell. Her head pounded. Unfortunately, the nightmare she slept with did not disappear. What did they want with her? *They must know I cannot use the Soulkind.* When her eyes opened, they fell upon a familiar face. Aeril lay passed out in a cell adjacent to hers. Cathlyn stood up and walked to the bars separating the two cells.

"Aeril!"

The woman's blood-shot eyes fluttered open. Aeril pointed up at Cathlyn's head. "You must have been hit pretty hard. I'm glad you awoke; I was starting to worry."

Cathlyn reached up through her long brown hair, grimacing in pain as she touched a large bump on the top of her skull. The memory of having rocks thrown at her flooded into her mind. She shook her head.

"Those Darrak will pay for this," Aeril said.

Cathlyn stood with her hands on the metal bars. "Where are we?"

"I don't know. We rode west for days and up into the mountains. We're in some sort of prison. Go ahead, see for yourself." She gestured with her gloved hands to the small window in Cathlyn's cell.

Cathlyn walked to the barred window and gazed upon the grim view outside. A swarm of snow filled her vision as she looked upon the gray and oppressive sky. The sky, however, was not what held her attention. The prison sat nestled high in the peak of a foreboding, snow capped mountain. The frigid air turned her breath to mist as she exhaled. Memories of summer were lost in this icy world. Through her misting breath, she saw another building, a massive fortress, nearly a mile away. Steep, craggy cliffs protected the ominous castle from anyone entering the valley, and narrow bridges heavily guarded by Darrak spanned a gap at the base of the fortress. A gust of icy wind blew into the cell forcing her to look away for a moment.

Beyond the fortress and through the window, she saw hordes of encamped enemy soldiers. The mountainside seemed to roil in a black sea of Darrak. As she again stared at the nearby fortress, the clouds broke in the wind, revealing an enormous mountain looming overhead. She had never seen such magnificence and she almost forgot her fear.

"Somebody's coming...." Aeril said, interrupting her daze.

Before Cathlyn could turn around, the door to her cell flung open and two Darrak walked in. She slid down against the wall and covered her face, while the Darrak approached.

"Don't hurt her again!" Aeril shouted from her cell.

Cathlyn uncovered her eyes and saw Aeril pointing through the metal bars at the Darrak. She winced, wondering when the blow would land, but none came. Instead, the Darrak grabbed her underneath her arms and jerked her to her feet. She had no more tears to shed. She half-walked and was half-dragged through the doorway, barely having enough energy to look back at Aeril. The woman stood solemnly at the barrier between the cells, gripping the bars.

The Darrak led her through a darkened hallway decorated with a few paintings in dire need of dusting. Torches randomly illuminated the long corridor; at times, she walked in the light, and at others, in utter darkness. She looked up ahead for the next torch, for the bit of light that would bring her out of the blackness. The Darrak's scratching claws and her shuffling feet echoed in the hall.

She glanced up into her escorts' faces when she built up enough courage. They did not return her look, but stared straight ahead with their pure black eyes. During the darkest parts of the march, she toyed with the idea of attempting escape. The Darrak were not holding her, they merely expected her to follow. But where would she run? This fortress was high in the freezing mountains; she had no supplies and very little sense of direction.

At times like these, she turned to fantasies of magic. If only she were like the great sorcerers and sorceresses from legends…like Sarissa. The walls would erupt, the Darrak would fall, and a dragon would come and bear her away from this evil place. She scoffed, as she could not even conjure a mere spark.

The Darrak stopped in front of a large wooden door and motioned her to enter. She reached slowly for the handle and pushed it open. Looking in, she saw a small, dark room with a figure sitting in a tall chair at the end. On the table in front of the robed person, a single candle flickered in the silent breeze that swept into the room.

"Sit down where I can see you."

Cathlyn's skin shivered and crawled at the voice that seemed to originate from nowhere in the room. There was no emotion to the voice, but its command alone drew her feet into the room against her will. The door slammed behind her, leaving only the light from the lone candle. As she walked around the table, her eyes were drawn to the hood covering the man's head and she remembered their first meeting in the woods beyond Tilbury. The man sat with both hands placed on the edge of the table. On each, he wore a thick, elaborately carved, black, metal gauntlet. Cathlyn sat down in the chair opposite the man.

The candlelight flickered unevenly as they sat in silence. Cathlyn's hands shook against her will. The light fell upon something glittering in a coiled pile on the table, and her breath caught as she recognized Brannon's Soulkind. The man reached over with his gloved hands to touch the amulet. As he twisted it in the dim light, Cathlyn thought the Soulkind looked different than she remembered. Indeed, the three golden wings now completely covered the red gemstone in the middle.

Cathlyn's mind raced with questions, but no words came out. She knew that with Brannon still alive, the Soulkind was useless to this man. She also knew that someone who mastered a Soulkind could not learn spells from a different one, but instead are the most powerful in their own. Did this man control a Soulkind of his own? The dim light and his robes prevented her from seeing if he bore a mark, and before she could think further, the man spoke.

144

"If you prove to be totally useless to us, you will die, Cathlyn Dunwell."

Cathlyn looked uneasily into the man's face.

"Yes, I know more than you could guess. Now, as I said, if you prove worthless...." The man closed his fists.

Cathlyn knew what she faced and started to shake; she had no magical power whatsoever. "What about Aeril?"

The man paused slightly and then laughed. "Your friend? I will deal with her." The derisive laughter faded from his voice. "Now go...."

Cathlyn could not leave fast enough. She was not even supposed to be here! As she ran to the door, she thought of Jace and Straeten. They were better off for not passing the test. She would die for her lies.

Chapter 15: Through the Mountains

After Jace and the others escaped from the guardhouse, the night was free from any encounters. For the first hour afterwards, they ran up the mountain path, looking behind them almost constantly.

Ash kept the lead and ran ahead smelling the ground. The party, still in awe, kept thanking Jace for their rescue. Even Allar thanked him and made no thief comments. But none were so amazed at what happened as Jace himself.

"So all this time you should have been with the Followers?"

"I suppose so, but look where that would have gotten me, eh?" Straeten said.

Jace laughed, then let out a deep breath. "Why didn't you go with them, Straet?"

Straeten paused before continuing. "I never really wanted to go off and study magic like that. That's not for me."

"Straet, that's a lie," Jace said. "Why did they let you stay back in Beldan? I thought they needed to train everyone who passed to prevent any 'accidents?'"

"I lied to them," Straeten said.

"But why didn't you use magic before? Like when we were first attacked?"

Straeten looked down at the ground. "I've been fighting the urge to use magic ever since I learned it. But do you remember how easily the campfires have been starting up?"

Jace smiled and Straeten continued. "When you and I were attacked, I didn't even think of using magic. I just charged in at that demon with my staff." He swung a heavy spiked staff he took from the Darrak prison. "Then yesterday when we were captured, I figured using magic wouldn't even help, based on what Jervis and Allar said what happened to the Followers at Tilbury."

"Jervis..." Jace muttered. "I guess he could sink lower."

"Hopefully, he died when the building fell," Straeten said.

"Not likely. Jervis is a thief, after all. He always seems to get himself out of some kind of trouble, and someone else into it. Something was different about him, though. I knew he could act like he wanted to kill me, but I never thought he'd actually do it." After several minutes of silence, he looked to his friend. "You must've wanted to burn me up for working with the guild again."

"I came pretty close," Straeten said with a smile.

Morning came, once again bringing its gray blanket to the sky. Jace looked up and saw Valor wheeling overhead and smiled. When they stopped for a small rest, Valor sat close to Ash and the two remained side by side in silence, guarding the camp.

"So, he was following us all along?" Straeten said.

Jace nodded. "Warned us, too, several times. Don't know if he knows what he's got himself into, though."

He looked up at the road ahead. The twin mountains, Retzlaff and Rabiroff, loomed on the western horizon, but still stood miles away. Their snow-capped peaks brought a chill to everyone's hearts. With each step, the summer warmth faded under the blasts of a damp, icy wind. With the sentry building only a few miles behind, the party knew that around any corner, past any hill, and beyond any dead or dying tree, Darrak could be waiting to ambush. Although Jace did not think his luck would last for another rescue like his previous one, they began again.

Burgis broke the silence of their morning march. "I still don't understand why all those Darrak cleared out of the building like that."

"Yeah, you didn't smell *that* bad Allar," Straeten said.

Allar stared at Straeten for a second, but made no response.

"Come on, Allar," Straeten said clapping twice in front of his face. "You've got to be quicker than that. You've got to come back with something, like—"

"I didn't think they got a good look at your face, but apparently, they did," Allar interrupted. "How's that?"

Straeten paused for a second and said, "Hey...."

Despite Straeten's joking around, Jace knew he was worried, too. They both often tried to make light of bad situations, a trait that enraged some people at rather serious times. People like Cathlyn. *They had to be alive.* Cathlyn and Turic were his best friends besides Straeten, and Karanne was like a mother to him. He never let the thought of their deaths cross his mind; the belief that they were alive drove him onward.

Jace noticed Mathes staring straight ahead, ignoring the bantering going on between the other party members. Ever since the rescue, Mathes remained silent and would not even acknowledge Straeten.

They walked onward the whole day, stopping only for food and water when they desperately needed it. Jace had only brought what he could carry into the guardhouse, which was not very much, and now they were quickly running out of supplies. They found some small streams running off the side of the mountains to replenish their water, but food was harder to come by. Straeten found some more mushrooms and small plants, which would help them for a while, and Burgis went to hunt with the few arrows they took from the prison. Game was sparse, and no one really wanted to find out what the lizards or rats tasted like. They soon might have to, though.

The party had stayed off the road as much as possible, in hopes of avoiding any troops on patrol, but the rocks were so treacherous that they had to return. Even though Burgis and Tare could walk again unaided, a small slip on any of the loose rocks or steep cliffs would be disastrous in their state. The cliff grew steeper beside the road as the group continued along upward.

Straeten looked over the edge at the dizzying view below. Allar stood beside him and pushed him slightly forward, keeping a good grip on his back. "Watch out below, Straeten...."

Straeten stumbled quickly to regain his balance, looked back and said, "All right, Allar, good one." He let out a breath when he thought no one was looking. Jace laughed under his breath.

After many hours of trudging along, the group finally decided to rest for lunch. Collectively, they determined that stopping on the road would be dangerous, so they opted to find a place somewhere in the hills. The trees had ceased to exist this far up in the mountains, but some shorter plants still remained. The party huddled close within a small circle of boulders and began their meal.

Mathes spoke first. "By now, those Darrak are looking for us. They will definitely follow us up the mountain."

"Not necessarily," Allar replied. "For all we know, they might think we headed back down the mountain."

"They probably don't see us as a threat, but they don't like anything to get away from them," Jace said, remembering Chase's experience.

"Who knows we're even up here?" Straeten said.

Jace shrugged. "Well, whatever happens, I think for certain Jervis will follow us, and the Darrak will at least send news up here about what Straeten did to the building." Straeten acknowledged the comment with a slow nod of his head.

148

"That isn't right," Straeten said. "What he's doing. Did you see his eyes?"

Jace nodded and remembered the fire that burned in them. Valor's cry echoing out from above broke the afternoon quiet. Jace said, "I think something's coming." Well hidden behind the rocks, the party watched silently and eventually heard the pounding of horses galloping. Ash growled deep in his throat. Jace peered over the top of the rock and saw two Darrak riding hard and fast up the path from the direction of the guardhouse. The air filled with dust as the horses sped along the trail.

Burgis said, "Let's jump them. We'll be able to push them over the cliff."

Allar agreed. "If we don't stop them now, they might alert others, many others, further up the mountain."

"But what about the horses? We can't just kill them," Jace added.

"We can't risk them getting ahead," Allar said. "They're almost here. The horses won't necessarily go over the side with them."

Jace reluctantly nodded. Ranelle, Tare, and Burgis drew their bows and positioned themselves so they had a clear shot at the Darrak. Ranelle looked over at Jace and said, "Don't worry. We're all good shots. We won't hit the horses." The riders were almost beside the party; if they were to act, now was the time.

"They're riding too fast; you'll never hit them." Straeten stood up suddenly and pointed his arm at a huge boulder on the side of the trail. The air seemed to shake around everyone's ears when a bolt of light leapt forth from his fist and struck the boulder, causing it to dislodge and start rolling. The boulder slammed down right in front of the two riders on the road below.

Chaos broke loose on the trail below. Jace held his hand up in front of the three archers, holding them off for a few more seconds.

If only they'd throw them off! Jace screamed inside his head. The horses, spooked by the crashing rock, spun around and began to kick. The Darrak did not appear to notice the group up above. The steeds, still out of control, flung the Darrak off, causing one to land close to the edge of the cliff, then bolted back down the road.

Jace closed his fist, and in an instant, three arrows whined through the air towards the bewildered Darrak. One struck the Darrak near the edge of the road and sent him plummeting over the cliff with a howl. The other two arrows hit the remaining Darrak in the chest. The demon fell to his knees.

"We've got to stop those horses from reaching the guardhouse, or they'll know for sure we're up here!" Jace yelled.

Ash leapt up and nearly slid down the path to the road, speeding past the fallen Darrak towards the runaways. The Darrak, however, was not dead yet. After ripping the arrows from its chest, it leapt to its feet with only a slight falter and sprung up the hill onto all of its limbs and began to pull itself along the ground towards the party. Mathes picked up a rock and hurled it at the approaching Darrak. Jace and Allar, too, pelted the creature with heavy stones, but the hits barely slowed it. By this time, the archers reloaded and hit the Darrak again, and it finally stumbled back a few steps.

Straeten summoned another bolt and sent it crackling down the mountainside into the Darrak's chest. The blast sent the Darrak rolling down the hill and finally off the other side of the road into the chasm. Jace watched as the black beast spun downwards with a dying howl. The whole ambush lasted only a few moments, but Jace's heart pounded in his ears.

"You're getting pretty good with that, Straet," Jace said. He felt happy for Straeten about his magic, or at least he tried to be. With a start, he remembered the horses and scrambled down the hill to follow Ash.

He reached the road with a stumble, but did not have to go further. Up from the mountain path came Ash, herding the two frightened animals. When they looked back at the dog to challenge him, he growled, barked, or snapped at their feet, and they obeyed.

"Good boy!" Jace called while gathering the reins and calming the horses, "Shh. You're all right now."

"Look!" Straeten said. "There are some supplies in these saddlebags. That should help us for a while...."

The horses allowed the party to take them along. As they traveled, Jace and the others continually looked for a separate path away from the frequently used road; the Darrak would send another messenger before long or an army would march down upon them. Right before sunset, they found what they were looking for.

To the south of the winding mountain road, a statue stood defaced. Jace looked at the deep scratches on the white stone. "Two guesses who made these. Can't even tell what it's supposed to be." The group ventured off the main road towards the mountain. The path appeared to be less treacherous than their previous, although still quite rocky.

150

Not far from the path, Jace spotted several other damaged statues. The pure, white stone was defiled with what seemed to be dark blood, but he could now make out the shape of the creatures; they had curled claws, winding tails, and furled wings.

"These are Dragons. Just like the ones outside the Library. This way is safe."

He stepped over the broken pieces lying about. "Look, these are warding symbols here, although they didn't seem to do much good," he said, pointing to strange markings on the ground. Straeten shrugged his shoulders to the others.

On the other side of the clearing, another path began winding up the side of the mountain. Two fallen statues bearing similar markings blocked the entrance to the path. The circle of crumpled stones they walked through looked like the aftermath of a great battle. Bodies of fallen, stone creatures lay strewn about everywhere. The party progressed in silence. Even Ash and the horses treaded carefully upon the ground.

Soon after climbing onto the path, Jace looked back the way they came. Jace felt Retzlaff, the imperious mountain, look down upon the insignificant party. He led onwards. "I know this path seems to be going up rather than westward, but I have a strong feeling about this," he said and his eyes turned up to the skies where Valor circled.

The weather worsened as they ascended the new path. Snow began to fall in sheets of icy rain and wind. Everyone pulled their hoods close over their faces while the rain soaked right through their cloaks. Ash appeared even scrawnier when the water matted down his coat. Even Valor landed and hunched over on the soaking wet horses. Night began to fall, but the snowy rain continued and finding shelter filled Jace's mind. As darkness crept and icy winds blew, the path still wound up the mountain without a cave in sight, so they kept marching onward.

An hour past sunset, Mathes wobbled on his tired legs. Most of the others were not far from doing the same way. Although a slight glow remained in the sky, the gusting sheets of snow made seeing more than five feet ahead nearly impossible. Suddenly, Ash darted and disappeared from sight.

"What is it, Ash?" Jace said through chattering teeth. "Ash?"

The dog reappeared after a minute, barked, and then disappeared again. Jace waved for the others to follow him. Leaning forward into the wind while trying to duck through the gusts of sleet, he arrived in front of a ten-foot tall cave entrance. Jace reached down and pet Ash. "In here.

Hurry!" The tunnel was pitch black and he felt around with his hands. *If only we had some light.*

Before Jace could say his thought aloud, Straeten cast a fire bolt onto the end of a stick he had picked up. "I thought we might need wood, so I grabbed some earlier." He stuck the torch into the darkness before leading the way in. The rest followed quickly.

The cavern they walked into was only a small tunnel leading further into the mountainside. The howling of the storm faded away and the cave opened up into a much larger area. Straeten dumped the small pile of wood he had managed to carry up the mountain into the middle of the room and cast another flame into its center. Even though the logs were soaking wet, the magic took and burned intensely. He let out a sigh and relaxed his shoulders. Burgis stripped off his soaked and frozen boots, Ranelle wrung out her cloak, and Ash shook, spraying Allar next to him.

Burgis sat down on a rock next to Straeten and asked, "What does it feel like, to cast magic?" All, except Mathes, stopped what they were doing and listened. Straeten sat for a while with his eyes closed before answering.

"I first feel the need to cast the spell, as if I don't always choose to call forth the magic myself. Then, the magic comes out with a rush of...of life. I needed to start the fire just now, but I don't know how I controlled it to do that. Same thing when I used the fire to bring the building down."

"Well maybe you shouldn't try that one out here, all right, Straet?" Jace said.

Straeten smiled. Everyone was still looking at him, so he continued. "I know I received magic through the Soulkind, but it's now a part of me. The magic seems *almost* alive, but...."

"But what?" Ranelle asked as Tare looked on, perhaps wanting to ask the same question.

Straeten closed his eyes. "The flame doesn't seem quite...*right*. When I cast the spell, I feel exhausted, like it takes something away from me. Yet, I feel like there could be more to this fire. I don't know how to explain it, but I can feel it." He scanned everyone's faces for any skeptical looks, but found none. "I felt like Brannon never really knew what was happening with the Soulkind. The magic seemed...out of his control, I guess."

152

By now, they were all dry and their eyes heavy from the long journey. The two horses stood silently in the tunnel while everyone else bedded down to sleep. Or almost everyone. Jace held his green stone in one hand and practiced flipping his daggers with the other, while two thoughts battled in his mind: one of respect for Straeten's skill with the fire, and the other of envy over the fact that now all his friends had been chosen by the Soulkind, and he had not. But his friend had stayed by his side. Why? He'd have gone with the Followers. Right? He threw a dagger into a small pile of snow, and then rubbed the cool, water-smoothed stone with his left hand. His other hand reached into the pouch for another of the stones he brought along on the journey. In a second he was back in Beldan.

A sharp cry in an alley drew his attention. He turned around and slunk down the shadows towards the sound. The smell of horses filled his nose. In one of the stalls, a boy in fine clothing stood over a chubby boy about Jace's age; probably eight. The older, well-dressed boy kicked the stable boy with his black leather boots.

"How dare you talk to my sister?"

"I'm sorry." The younger boy rolled on the ground to avoid the blows.

"Just feed our horses."

The older boy reared back to take another kick, but paused slightly as the whisper of something spun past followed by a solid *thunk*. He turned to see what landed behind him, but the fine woolen material of his cloak ripped when he moved. It was stuck to a wooden beam behind him by a blade. He looked around, and laughed, seeing only Jace. He reached over to pull out the knife, but another spun through the air, and this time pinned his sleeve to the beam.

The boy on the ground sat up. Before the older boy could yank the blade from the wood, he saw Jace casually flipping another in the air. With a yell, he ripped both his cloak and sleeve and ran away.

The little boy jumped up, but then doubled over. Jace ran to him. "You all right?"

The boy nodded.

"I'm Jace." He extended his hand, then remembered he still held a knife. With a sudden flick of his wrist, the blade disappeared.

"Rin Ver Straeten, but call me Straeten. How did you learn to do that?"

Jace paused for a second. "My mother taught me."

"Your mother? I wish my ma did that."

Jace squatted down next to Straeten and a knife appeared in his hands. Straeten grinned.

"It's not hard, you just have to—"

"Straeten!" a voice called out from the stables. "Where are you?"

"Comin'!" Straeten stood up and brushed off the straw sticking to his back. "I got to get back. Could you show me some of that later?"

"Sure," Jace said, smiling as the boy ran off.

Jace walked over to the knives, still stuck in the stall door, and grasped their hilts.

"Your *mother* taught you?"

Karanne vaulted silently over the gate behind him, her long red hair trailing.

"It was all I could think of," Jace said.

"If I were your real mother, I would have taught you better. No Lorefeld would ever throw like this." She walked beside him and picked up Jace's two knives out of the stall where his throws had gone wide.

"Did you have to throw these so hard?" Jace yanked on Karanne's blades and pulled them loose, landing flat on his back.

"I wouldn't have to if you practiced more. And who is that? You know you're not allowed to talk to anyone outside the Guild."

"I don't have any friends. Don't tell, please?"

She silently worked her knives out of the beam. "Why this one?"

"Don't you ever just know something?"

All she did was smile. That was good enough for Jace. He grabbed a stone off the ground and ran back to the guild, practicing his knife tricks for Straeten.

The next morning, Jace opened his eyes to see Tare and Straeten collecting snow from outside. Tare held the snow lightly in his hands over his water flask while Straeten called forth his magic.

"Don't worry, Tare. I've done this...."

The flame vaporized the ice instantly. Tare jumped up and down and then cuffed Straeten upside his head. Tare ran out of the cave to put his hands into the cooling snow to the sound of Straeten apologizing behind him. Burgis laughed at his brother running, but stopped when Straeten put his hand on his shoulder.

"Your turn."

Jace walked to the entrance of the cave. The snow had stopped falling sometime last night, leaving a few inches in some areas and drifts of several feet in others. At least yesterday's tracks would be covered. The path continuing up the mountain still appeared passable.

Tare knelt down right outside the entrance, his hands buried in the snow. He shook his head and mouthed words in his silence, but all the while a half-smile shown on his face watching his brother go through the same process.

Ranelle had taken her long black hair out of her usual ponytail and was playing with Ash outside in the snow. She threw a stick, but when he returned, he dropped it and jumped up, trying to bite her hair. When Ash saw Jace walk outside, he ran over to greet him and rolled onto his back. After a short morning hello, he jumped up and returned to playing with Ranelle. Jace waved to her and she smiled back before resuming play.

The sun almost looked like it would show itself through the gray covering overhead. Valor, sitting atop a ledge, cried out when he saw Jace and the boy returned the hawk's hello with a wave as he walked. He came upon Allar sitting on a rock, not far from the entrance. The older boy motioned for Jace to sit down and offered him some of the food left from the Darrak. The two sat in silence for several minutes, eating and looking around at the mountain. Allar spoke first.

"I'm scared about what might happen to my sister. I always promised I would protect her, no matter what happened. I...."

"We'll find her and the others," Jace said. Words never came easily when he talked to Allar—*kind* words, anyway.

"A lot of people owe you something big, Jace," Allar said. "Straeten told me how you two became friends. I guess that was my fault, huh?"

Jace laughed. "well, I guess I owe you for something."

"You've rescued me several times already, and now you're on your way to help my sister. I'm—"

"Hey, don't worry about it." Jace shifted and looked away. He smiled though. "We're a team, now, and we've got a lot to do today."

He saluted Allar in a manner he had read about somewhere in the Library, holding his hand palm forward and pointing his first two fingers up. Allar returned the salute with a slight nod of his head.

Standing up, Jace began to walk back to the cave to prepare the horses. "Oh, and Allar, watch out for Straeten this morning."

"Why is that?"

"Just trust me." Jace smiled and walked to the entrance of the cave where Burgis knelt with his hands in the snow.

Soon after, they resumed their trek up the mountain. Occasionally, the party came across flat, broken stones sticking up through the snow that looked like paving stones of an ancient road. From this point, they could still see the Darrak road, and the fear of being spotted felt real and close.

"Why do you suppose the Darrak don't use this trail?" Burgis asked.

Jace shrugged his shoulders. "They still might be up here."

Although the snow had ceased for the day, the wind still howled across the stark mountainside, causing the temperature to plummet. After many hours of walking and plodding, when the bright gray circle they assumed was the sun reached its peak, the path opened up into a clearing. A structure made of white stone lay waiting for them. Toppled walls and broken steps lay strewn about. The once smooth, white stone now bore a pitted and worn façade, shorn by the elements after many forgotten years. Valor flew around the clearing as the party walked around the ruins.

"I don't see any tracks, no food or fire pits," Allar said while he searched among the fallen stones.

"Everything must have been plundered a long time ago," Mathes said, speaking for the first time in many hours. "The ruins look like they could have been a temple or shrine, perhaps."

The main structure still had some intact walls, but not many. Jace looked up at what remained and agreed. The curved arches resembled those in the Hall in Beldan.

The party regrouped after their search of the outlying area and prepared to climb the shattered steps leading into the ruins. Suddenly, Ash's nose perked up and he stood alert, giving a sharp bark. Everyone drew their weapons. Jace looked up to see Valor circling above. Ash ran ahead and began sniffing the ground.

"This way!" he shouted and led everyone up the stairs. "Be careful; some of these walls may collapse even more."

"Should we go in there? The Darrak would have an advantage...." Mathes said.

"I don't think they're here," Jace whispered.

"Then why are you whispering?"

156

Jace opened his mouth to answer but only shook his head and continued. The gray and white remains loomed over their heads as they walked through the silent hallways. Only their footsteps crunching on the eroded rocks and the occasional falling piece of wall somewhere in the distance broke the silence. Straeten walked in back, ready to swing his spiked metal staff at anything that moved.

Ash led them further within the damaged walls. With the crash of falling rock, something sped across their path a stone's throw ahead and blurred down an adjoining hallway to the right. The sudden movement caused Ash to bark and dart forward, but Jace called him back and motioned for the others to split up down another hallway intersecting the path. Tare and Burgis went to the right while Allar and Ranelle went left, moving quickly and keeping silent. Straeten, Jace, and Mathes continued straight ahead past where they saw the figure run and turned down the crumbled hallway.

They reached the path and saw that it led to a large room with an altar at the other end. Jace, looking up and seeing Valor circling right above the altar through the crumbled roof, motioned Straeten and Mathes to spread out and surround whomever, or whatever, lay ahead. As they approached, Burgis and Tare entered the room from the right with their bows pulled taut and nodded at Jace. Crouched side by side, they then advanced.

When they were but ten feet from the altar with weapons poised for attack, the figure darted again. Mathes dropped his rapier and ran forward, motioning to Tare and Burgis to hold their attack. The brothers looked to Jace who nodded for them to stand down and lowered their weapons.

"I hope he knows what he's doing," Straeten said.

Mathes ducked his head as he ran through a small entrance in the tunnel. Fallen stones blocked some of the way through, but Mathes scrambled along and over the debris. Jace and the others waited with their weapons drawn.

"Did anyone see what it was?" Straeten said.

Jace motioned with his hand for him to stop talking. "He's talking to someone."

A minute dragged on until Mathes came back to the group. Behind him was a ragged image of the once regal looking Brannon Co'lere. Jace sheathed his daggers quickly.

"All right, some good news finally."

By this time, Allar and Ranelle had joined the rest. Brannon held himself like a king—a proud and arrogant king. His countenance seemed almost comical with his tattered appearance, but he still received everyone's respect immediately. Jace and Straeten knew him as the man who awakened the Soulkind, and they gathered around to ask questions. The rest were introduced and Brannon nodded his head.

"A Soulkind Master could create new magic to use against the Darrak," Jace said.

Brannon cleared his throat. "Actually, without the Soulkind, I discovered I cannot create new spells. That is why you will help me retrieve Marathas from the enemy."

"We're on our way to rescue our friends that were captured," Jace said. "We believe they are with the enemy now, somewhere, and the rest of the Soulkind are probably with them, as well." He looked around at the others before consenting, and they all nodded in agreement. "We'd be honored to help you."

Brannon nodded and began to pack his meager belongings. "In order for us to do this, we all need to have an edge. Now, I can try to pass on the magic to anyone who would like to try. I'm not promising anything, though."

The reaction from the party did not seem to impress him. "I'm talking about the magic of Marathas! Now, who will be first?"

"Well, I've already tried to teach them," Straeten said, pointing to the villagers from Tilbury, "but they can't learn."

Jace glanced at Straeten as they walked out into the open, shaking his head. Straeten winced. Brannon snapped his attention to Straeten.

"How could *you* teach anyone? You're not a Follower…."

Straeten first tried to ignore the comment, but then took a deep breath and explained his story to Brannon. Brannon's eyes widened, hearing about such lies, astonished as to why anyone would do such a thing.

"Yes, now I remember you both," Brannon said. "You were among the first, right? I remember almost not believing you that day, boy. I thought I felt you learn, but I figured no one would actually lie about it."

"I had my reasons," Straeten said.

Brannon laughed once and then stopped to look into Straeten's eyes. "Do not lie to me again. You are *my* Follower. And the Followers must abide by the rules, or else chaos will reign. Isn't that what you keep saying, Mathes?"

He strode out of the ruins and pulled his tattered purple robes around his sides and Mathes nodded his head slowly. Brannon mounted one of the two horses waiting there without pause.

"First rule: if you teach anyone, it will be because *I* say you can. Do you understand?" Brannon looked down at Straeten as the horse darted from side to side. "Get my things and let's go," he commanded, swinging back his head revealing the mark of fire around his throat.

Jace looked around at his companions. Brannon called again, telling them to hurry, and then urged his horse onward. Shrugging at Straeten, Jace glanced back at the building, looking for Ash.

"Come on, Ash! Let's go!" He heard a bark somewhere within the ruins.

"We have no time, come on!" Brannon ordered from up ahead, he licked his lips and looked back and forth from the path to the group.

Jace started to walk into the ruins, sensing the dog's distress, but Brannon called again. "Come on, boy!" Jace frowned and called Ash one last time before obeying.

On the other side of the ruins, Ash stood barking in a collapsed room as Jace called. Ash finally heeded his master's beckoning. Left behind under a collapsed portion of the ruins, a man with burns covering his face and body lay bound and gagged. Tight leather straps held his arms and legs. Only a muffled sound escaped through Stroud's gag, remaining with him in his prison.

Chapter 16: The Soulkind Master

Past the ruins, the road branched into two directions. One path led down a gentle slope to the west, while the other, steeper path followed a southern route to the peak of the mountain, obscured by clouds. Brannon steered his mount to the downward path. The others looked to Jace who contemplated the choices while they waited. The steeper way called to him, even though it appeared more dangerous. He looked to his animal companions. Valor sat atop a rock on the southern route and Ash paced in circles beside him. The choice became clear in his mind. Brannon tapped his fingers on the horse's saddle.

"I have a good feeling about this southern path," Jace said pointing up the mountain. "I suggest we go that way." His companions began to walk towards the incline. Brannon, however, shook his head.

"This way is the logical choice. See how it heads downward?" Brannon asked. "I am certain the way will lead us directly to the enemy encampment where my Soulkind awaits."

Straeten, his staff already set upon the southern trail, looked back at Brannon. "I think we've decided to go this way. If you want company, I suggest you do the same."

Jace smiled at his friend and noticed Ranelle whispering to Tare. The silent boy nodded his head and walked to the southern path followed by Burgis, Ranelle, Allar, and Mathes. Brannon clenched his horse's reins. His face appeared a mix of emotions battling each other. In resolution, he kicked his horse into a gallop ahead of the others up the southern pathway.

Mathes put his hand on Jace's shoulder for a moment and then hurried ahead to speak to Brannon. Jace watched as Mathes stood on the ground next to Brannon's horse and the two spent several minutes in discussion. When the two finished speaking, Brannon returned without a word or a glance to anyone and took the lead on the path Jace chose. Straeten started to say something, but Jace held up a hand and shook his head. He did not think it wise to damage the man's pride any further. Mathes gave a nod to Jace.

The hours left in the day passed without further surprise or encounter, although Jace still sensed something was wrong with Ash. The dog trailed far behind everyone with his head hung close to the ground and his tail drooped between his legs. Jace halted the group, knelt down, and reached out towards Ash's injured paw.

"You're healing up just fine. But there's something else, isn't there?" Ash looked back down the mountain and whined softly.

"Come on, the day is going to leave us while you tend the pack." Brannon began again up the trail.

Jace frowned at Ash. He had the nagging feeling that they needed to turn around. "We have to go back."

Brannon laughed. "Did the dog tell you that?"

For the first time, Jace looked up at his companions and he saw the doubt in their minds. Despite the burning in his head about the issue, he also knew that they had to continue. He breathed a soft apology to Ash and walked on.

Brannon continued to ride the horse for the remainder of the sunlit day, leading the group continually upwards. The path became less of a path as the day wore on, but Jace kept looking to the sky at his flying companion for direction. Valor, unfailingly, gave the group guidance from atop rocks or his circling in the sky. Unfortunately, Jace's attempts at consoling Ash were still in vain and he continued to slink behind. Jace, too, marched behind, watching Ash and his other companions. The amount of snow increased as they walked up the mountain and the flat stones they tread upon eventually disappeared. Snow and the growing slope slowed the march considerably.

Burgis slipped on the steep path, but Allar quickly reached over and caught him before he could hit the ground. Jace saw something pass between them after Burgis stood; a motion of their hands that looked like the salute Jace had given Allar earlier.

Brannon and Mathes kept the pace up and stayed nearly twenty paces ahead as they talked quietly. The extra horse remained beside Brannon's horse. Perhaps the beast was scared about what happened and needed a familiar companion, Jace thought. It certainly wasn't there for Brannon's personality.

Brannon headed towards Jace. "I suppose you should lead from here."

Before Jace asked, Burgis and Tare volunteered to scout ahead. Jace sat on a rock and tried to pet Ash's head as he waited for the two scouts to return, but the dog slipped away from everyone, even refusing offers of food.

"That dog is diseased," Brannon said. "Does he have any injuries?"

Jace looked over at Ash. "He did get cut by a Darrak recently, but the wound—"

Brannon jumped off his horse. "I was a Healer, let me take a look at him." He walked over to Ash, who was still lying down. He knelt down to examine the dog, but Ash growled, barring his teeth. Brannon stood up abruptly, walked back, and gripped his horse's reins. "Just as I thought. That dog is sick. He is becoming a danger to us all. I've seen this sort of behavior in animals around Beldan that were bitten. Unfortunately, there is but one cure...."

"I think we'll wait this one out," Jace said and stood between the man and the dog with his arms crossed. Brannon cleared his throat, expecting Jace to give him attention.

"Nonetheless, if I see that dog getting worse...or if he attacks me—"

"If you ever touch this dog...."

Brannon climbed onto his horse and looked down upon Jace with near amusement, but also a glint of anger. A fiery globe appeared above Brannon's outstretched hand as if to counter Jace's words. "Without a Soulkind? You wouldn't stand a chance, boy."

Ash jumped in front of Jace, growling at Brannon. Straeten walked beside them. Brannon laughed at the three, but his smile faded when he saw the others all staring at him, as well. A sharp cry rang out as Valor indicated his return with Burgis and Tare. Mathes walked over to Brannon and said something. Brannon's magic flame disappeared and Jace let out his breath and nodded to Mathes.

"Everything is clear up ahead, but you need to come see this," Burgis said. He looked at Jace and Brannon. "What did we miss?"

"Nothing of importance," Brannon said. "Now, follow me." He kicked his horse and proceeded to the clearing.

Jace shook his head as Brannon left. "Everything is fine. Now what did you find? Something dangerous, I hope," he said, watching Brannon ride up the road.

Burgis frowned, but replied, "Well, there's definitely a place to camp tonight, and maybe a place to swim, too."

Allar looked at Burgis and raised his eyebrows. "Swim?" Tare just looked back with a smile and waved for them to follow as he ran along the path. Allar and Ranelle looked back at Jace, but he waved them on.

Straeten stayed at his side. "Don't worry about Brannon; he is up on his little cloud above us all, too good for anyone."

"I'm not worried about Brannon," Jace replied. "Ash won't even let me touch him anymore." He reached over to pet Ash, but the dog recoiled and whined. "Maybe he is sick. Maybe that Darrak had something on its claws, a poison…" Somehow, even as he spoke the words, he knew they weren't true. He tried to let Ash know he wanted to help, but he felt only confusion in return.

Straeten looked at Ash and then at Jace. "He'll come out of whatever he's under. I'm sure of it." He walked ahead a few steps but then turned around. "And forget what he said, Jace. You don't need what he has. Come on. Let's go see what they found."

Jace nodded and followed, but he had felt a twist of a knife in his side after Brannon's words of magic. He had actually almost forgotten.

With a look back at Ash, Jace followed Straeten up the rocky path. The snow and ice gave way to clear stones, which seemed much less slippery to walk upon. The path leveled out just slightly and Jace saw his companions standing alongside several indentations in the ground filled with what should have been ice. Steam emitted from the water in the pools and a faint odor of rotten eggs filled the air. Ash's nose perked up.

Tare stood beside one of the pools with his toes dangling over the water. Everyone else, except for Brannon, who still sat atop his horse, removed their cloaks and stripped down to under clothes. The silent boy slid his sore feet into the hot water, wincing.

"How do you suppose these got so hot?" Burgis asked, already halfway in.

Mathes, also joining in said, "Well, these mountains are volcanic, and it appears they are still active." He looked around and saw some questioning looks. "Fiery, liquid rock sits under this mountain, waiting to erupt, and heats this whole area. That's why there is no ice or snow at this elevation." He eased himself into one of the pools. "And that is what is heating this lovely water so we can take this…bath…."

Soon, Straeten was in the water, splashing around and laughing. Jace smiled, he could definitely use this. Even Valor was settling in; the hawk caught one of the red eyed rats and was feeding as he perched above the pools.

Brannon watched Jace from a distance. Jace waved at him and then stripped down to join the others in the steamy waters. The heat seeped into his weary bones as he immersed himself. Even the pain in his shoulder seemed to disappear in the steaming bath. Ash sat close to the water's edge, but not within Jace's reach.

"The poor dog is probably just exhausted," Allar said. "He'll be fine in the morning after some rest."

Jace nodded his head slowly. He looked around at everyone, splashing about in the separate pools, and tried to enjoy this time of temporary peace with his friends. He saw Ash facing down the path they had just walked up. With a flurry of feathers, Valor landed beside Ash and dropped the rat he caught on the ground. The dog was slow to react to the offer of food, but eventually began to eat.

The sight of even a little life returning to the dog, as well as the friendly offer from Valor, made Jace smile. Brannon, watching Ash from the cave entrance, gave him an unsettling feeling, though, and he vowed to keep a close eye on that man. The cave did not look as spacious as last night's, but fortunately, there would be shelter above them. *A nice place to rest.*

That night, Jace had vivid dreams. He gazed out at the world again from atop the Library. Valor and Blue stood beside him, but there was no sign of Ash. Looking to the sky, he called for Valor to begin searching for his missing companion, but the hawk remained on top of Blue's saddle.

In a rage, he leapt from the rooftop and ran through the woods; bounding over fallen trees, gliding over ravines to find any sign of Ash. He ran across a vast field of tall grass only to be met by a wall of swirling darkness, abruptly stopping him from going any further. Behind him, another wall sprung up, and then two others to his sides sealed him into a cage of shadows.

A tall, robed figure walked towards him through the walls. A cry rang out from above, and Jace saw Valor wheeling in the sky. With a leap, he spun into the sky himself, flying like a hawk away from the trap. Arms as dark as night reached up to grab him, clutching at his heels as he tried to escape....

Jace awoke to a gloomy, gray morning. Stretching, he glanced around at the others, who still slept. With a start, he ran outside to look for Ash. The sounds he usually heard from the animals were absent and he looked around frantically. Ash was nowhere in sight.

Jace whistled and called Ash's name and woke the others in the process. Slowly, they emerged from the cave. Soon, Jace's friends joined him and spread out across the area. Brannon, however, crossed his arms and bore a half-smile as he stood at the cave entrance watching the search. Jace stormed up to him and his hand inched closer to one of the daggers beneath his cloak..

"What did you do?"

"I had nothing to do with it," Brannon said, straight-faced. "I told you your dog was ill. I knew he would run away to die."

Jace paused a moment. "I *know* Ash wasn't sick. But I also know you're telling the truth." Although he believed the man, Brannon's attitude did not have to be so heartless. He turned away, looking again for Ash.

"This day waits for no one. I suggest we continue onward, and soon," Brannon said as the others spread out.

"We'll leave when we're ready to," Straeten said.

Ranelle and Tare mounted the two horses and waved a salute as they raced away. Tare sped up the path while Ranelle headed back down the way they came yesterday. Allar and Straeten ran off the path calling Ash's name, and even Mathes resumed searching. He apparently had grown fond of their gray companion, as well. Only Brannon remained behind, sitting by the pools.

Jace looked up in the sky for Valor, but the hawk was resting on a boulder near the trail's edge. "He's our friend, Valor. I need your help," he pleaded, but the bird only cocked his head sideways.

An hour passed, and the group met back at the pools without having seen any trace of the dog. No one spoke a word to Jace. Even Brannon was wise enough not to speak his thoughts. With a deep sigh, Jace resolved to continue forward. Closing his eyes and placing one knee on the ground, he thought about Ash and his faithful personality and courage. Jace still felt Ash's presence. Suddenly, a sharp pain drove into his knee as he leaned forward. When he opened his eyes, he saw he was kneeling on a black, glassy rock. He held the stone in his palm and burned the dog's memory into its glossy surface.

Ranelle stood over Jace and placed her hand on his shoulder. "His spirit was strong, Seeker. You form deep ties to your companions. Ash will live in our hearts, as he will in yours."

A quiver to her voice spoke of her own loss and pain. Jace looked at her and saw she clenched something small and black in her other hand. The black stone slipped into his pouch and he stood up and nodded at her. Wiping his eyes, he walked to the cave to gather his supplies. The others silently joined him and prepared to continue their journey.

Few words were spoken on the trail. Brannon took the lead upon one of the horses yet again, but Jace did not care about that, or much else. The frigid wind blew against them as they plodded up the still snow-free road. Jace did not feel the wind, though; he focused only on the path ahead. Where was this path taking them? Brannon's disapproving looks undoubtedly signified similar thoughts.

The low riding clouds above their heads flitted away for a moment and showed them the height they had climbed. Jace stood still for a moment to look around off the edge of the mountain path, speechless. Hills and broken forests stretched past even Jace's vision, but still no sign of the enemy encampment. He removed the map from his pack and sat down to locate where they were atop the mountains. He shook his head and rolled up the map. Brannon sat with a small smile and his eyebrows raised.

"You've lost us haven't you?"

The clouds covered them all and a fine cold mist soaked through to Jace's skin. He just stared at Brannon and didn't respond. A sudden cry from Valor drew his gaze upwards. The hawk was struggling to fly straight, so he held out his arm to call him in. *He'll freeze in this weather!* Valor flew down to him, but instead of landing on his outstretched arm he chose to land on his right shoulder. The bird nipped at his ear and curly hair until the boy began to laugh despite himself.

Ranelle walked a few paces in front of him. "What was that name you called me back there, Ranelle?"

"'Seeker?' Near Tilbury, a group of people we call 'Spirit Seekers' often pass through the wilderness. They believe we are all tied to an animal spirit. Some feel it more than others and seek out their animal companions. They travel in groups, searching for and training animals for the towns they pass in exchange for food and supplies. When they find their bond, only then are they complete." She paused.

"My...husband...was a Seeker...."

After a few more steps in silence, Jace said, "How did you meet?"

"I happened upon Alid when I got lost in the woods once when I was young. He helped me back to my home, but then disappeared without a trace. I knew then that I would follow him into those woods and spend my life with him." She smiled. "I searched and searched, but

166

could find no sign of him. Some years later, after traveling through the woods and mountains countless times for any trace of the man who helped me, I finally found him. He laughed when I came upon him and the other Seekers that night. No one had ever tracked them down like that before, he told me. We were bonded as husband and wife soon after."

"Did you live as a Seeker then?"

"We mixed our lives together," she answered. "I could not bear to leave Tilbury, and he would not leave his company. The bonds they shared were stronger than iron. You would have fit in well with them." She nodded her head and smiled at Valor sitting on Jace's shoulder.

'Seeker.' 'Thief.' At least my options are growing.

A sudden, warm wind gusted from the north and their sound of footsteps on the white, stone walkway ceased. Trails of clouds parted from the road and Jace looked up from his thoughts to see everyone gazing upwards with wide eyes at the structure before them.

Massive, white stone steps led up from the path into the side of the mountain. Fifty feet above, a stone temple almost glowed at the top. A vast expanse, big enough for twenty people to walk side by side, led within. From that point on, the building seemed to burrow its way back into the mountain.

Valor alighted on top of a high pillar of the temple and kept watch from his vantage point. Jace, amazed that something so ancient and beautiful could have gone unnoticed in the records of the Hall Library, wished he had the time to draw a sketch for Turic. He knew that the first thing Turic would tell him when he was rescued wouldn't be, "It was terrifying," or "Thanks!" it would be, "Well, why didn't you draw it?" He continued admiring the outside of the temple while Brannon walked up the steps past him. The others followed close behind, and when they came close enough to pass him, Brannon put his hand back to stop them.

Brannon walked up the steep steps to the entrance, pausing only to look up at the enormous building waiting at the top. No one questioned whether or not they would search the inside of this building. When the party reached the top of the stairs, a wide, flat platform stood before them preceding the entrance. They tied the horses off here to a couple of scraggly trees. Looking up, Jace saw foreign symbols carved into the temple: "Graebyrn Du Harl." The architecture and the words touched his memory from years ago.

When Jace looked down again, Brannon had already walked into the pitch black, enormous tunnel with the others close behind. Hurrying to catch up, he looked up at Valor above him. The hawk was watching him pass through the temple entrance.

"You coming?"

The hawk just sat atop the carvings and twitched his head back and forth.

"Be good, then, and watch after the horses," Jace said.

Once past the entryway, a warm, white glow seemed to emanate from the walls, illuminating their path. Unlike the formality of the temple entrance outside, the inside was just the bare rock of the mountain, which spanned nearly thirty feet above. The staircase sloped downwards, but continued straight into the mountain without any curves.

The cave around them maintained the same height and width as they descended slowly. After a while, Jace looked back and could no longer see the light of the entrance.

"This is the perfect place for an ambush," Allar said.

Burgis and Tare drew their weapons.

"I don't think the enemy is here," Jace said. "The horses would have sensed something, I am sure."

Jace thought about Ash and how the dog saved him from those red-eyed creatures back in the tree-shaped cave. He turned the black stone of Ash's memory over in his palm. He carried it now instead of leaving it in his pouch.

Silence bore down on them. They all stepped lightly, but their boots echoed sharply. After hundreds of steps downward, the tunnel widened and a dim light could be seen some steps ahead. The light grew brighter as they approached and cast a warm, bluish-white glow on the rocks and their faces and finally upon the vast room that opened before them.

Jace gasped at the huge, round cavern as they entered. The blue glow seemed to originate from this room, but he saw no visible holes in the ceiling or walls to let in the light. A dozen pools lay around the cave, filled with softly glowing, blue water. In the center of the immense chamber, a wondrously detailed statue of a dragon sat atop a massive platform.

A feeling of peace seeped into their bodies while they basked in the blue glow. They sheathed their weapons and walked inside. Only Mathes remained near the entrance. Instead, he sat down and pulled out his papers to draw and write. Brannon stood beside him and held his hands in the air.

168

"I sense a great good here. We will be safe," Brannon said.

Straeten turned his head to Jace.

"Really?"

The two laughed and continued to explore the cavern. Allar, Ranelle, Burgis, and Tare knelt to look into the glowing waters. Burgis reached down to cup some to drink, but Tare held out his hand to stop him.

"He's right," Ranelle said. "These are sacred waters." Burgis nodded and stood up.

Straeten spoke to Jace as they walked towards the statue's platform. "Don't these pools look familiar?"

Indeed, they did. An elaborately carved rim ran around each of the pools' edges, several feet in height. Jace remembered the same wall around the pool beneath the Hall Library. He nodded at Straeten and they continued to walk to the dragon statue. By now, Brannon had caught up to them and rushed to be the first up the steps to the platform.

Allar and Tare stood near the base of the statue. When Jace reached them, he saw a gilded tomb built into the stone floor.

"What is this place?"

"I will tell you," a low voice, unlike any they had ever heard, boomed from above them.

Above, the magnificent face of a very much living dragon stared down upon them. Gray scales reflected the blue light of the room, and two silvery horns protruded off of the fantastical creature's head. Everyone scrambled and fell over each other in a panic—everyone except Jace. He stared up at the grand creature with a broad smile on his lips. The chaos caused by his companions was only a slight buzz in his mind. This was his dream in the flesh.

"Fear not, I will not hurt you," the dragon said, slowly holding his clawed fist up, palm outward. Despite the dragon's words, several minutes passed in silence and fear spread throughout the party. Mathes stood at the mouth of the chamber entrance watching the dragon, his drawings neglected. Finally, after seeing the dragon wasn't going to kill them, or even move, for that matter, everyone relaxed slightly and stood as calm as they could before the magnificent creature.

The dragon sniffed at the air in Mathes' direction. "Come down, friend." His voice carried itself clearly to Jace's ears, as if the sound went directly into his mind. Mathes slowly walked forward to join everyone else. "Welcome to my lair. I am Graebyrn."

This was too much for Jace. It could all end now and he wouldn't mind.

"The one who Masters the Soulkind, step forward, I have been calling you."

Brannon Co'lere began to walk up the steps before the great dragon. He bowed then stood up straight to look him in the eyes.

"No, not you. You have awoken something, but not the true power of a Soulkind. There is someone else amongst you who is a Master."

Chapter 17: The Plan

Several days passed and still Turic continued to train the Darrak how to use the flame of Marathas. How every Darrak could learn magic, he could not fathom. In Beldan, only about thirty people total acquired the skill of the Soulkind, but here.... He laid his hands upon hundreds of Darrak and cringed each time he felt the power of the fire surge into their bodies. Amidst all this chaos and fear, he did find one small comfort: he and the other Followers were not expendable after all.

The Darrak could not pass the magic on to another.

On the second day of teaching, after standing for hours, Turic fell from exhaustion. A Follower stooped to hold him up, but Turic still collapsed onto the floor. Strong hands gripped him from behind and carried him to the side of the large hall. When he opened his eyes through the pain, he looked upon the man in the mask who always stood in the back of the room, watching. He could only see his mouth. "Who are you?" Turic asked in a raspy voice. Days went by with barely any water for him and his companions.

The man sneered through his mask. "Come now, Turic. We have met before. I am Huron Caldre, from the court of Myraton." He smiled. "A scholar informed me that you were unworthy of magic, that you were a bumbling old fool. He was certainly correct about the latter." He opened a water flask and poured it onto Turic's face. "Now hurry, old man. There are many to train, and soon you and this group will be moved to the Darrak breeding grounds, *if* you live past this day."

Of course, Turic remembered him now. This was the man who chose Brannon over him to study the Soulkind. But who could have convinced him to deny Turic the research position, though? Later, he would think on this matter, but now, there were other pressing concerns. He took a deep breath.

"*You* cannot possibly be the one who is in control here, *Guard Master*," he said. Caldre was Stroud's former leader, and up until now, presumed killed.

The man paused and his smile faltered. "I am no longer Guard Master," he said. "But soon, I will be in control of Marathas, once it has been properly awakened. Now, this has been entertaining, but..." He grasped Turic's worn cloak at the neck and yanked him to his feet. He pushed Turic back through the crowd of Darrak to continue his lessons.

"Where are the other Followers?"

Caldre laughed. "You are in no position to ask questions." He thrust Turic up onto the top of the stairs where the other worn out Followers stood. The old man stumbled, falling back upon the steps. His anger crested and he thought about lashing out with his magic. He never thought much about using the flame for destruction, but this man was almost begging him to.

Caldre shook his head. "You would be killed instantly."

Turic squinted his eyes. "And you." He turned to face the next Darrak.

Karanne peered out from her hiding place high in the stone rafters overlooking the Darrak patrols searching for her below. She cursed herself many times since turning around and coming back into the fortress. Narrowly avoiding capture on several occasions, she learned to stay put above everyone, where they fortunately decided not to look. They probably did not think anyone could actually make the climb.

Her luck was running out. The time to free everyone had better show itself soon. Getting just herself out would've been nearly impossible, but getting all the Followers out there with the Darrak on alert was another thing entirely. When she was outside, she saw another fortress; an immense tower extending above seemingly impregnable castle walls. Her heart sank. She shook her head in disbelief at the size of the army amassed on the valley floor, but still maintained a flame of hope in her heart. She knew she couldn't leave without the others.

Ten Followers and three others, Kal and two guardians, had been captured. She crept down the rafters and highly ornate support beams back to the cell block where the others were being held. She felt the burden of freeing them fully upon her.

She knelt down and peered under the space beneath the cell door of the first Follower and whispered, "I'm a Follower, like you, and I'm here to help." .

"I remember you," a small voice said through the door. "I'm Mitaya. How did you get out?"

Karanne smiled. She remembered Mitaya from the trip to Tilbury, remembered hearing her say she used to be a beggar. "With this!" The white flame shot from Karanne's palm under the door into the cell.

"With what?"

"What do you mean? It should be floating right there on the ground...." Karanne furrowed her brow and concentrated until she felt the spell explode in the air. Karanne heard a yelp and something fall onto the ground.

"What was that?" Mitaya asked. "I can see it spinning around the room now!"

A soft, clicking sound came from down the hall and Karanne's instincts took over. Whenever she came to any room, she thought of at least three ways out, or at least one good place to hide.

"I'll be back," she said, and called the spell back to her hand.

In two long strides, she crossed the distance to her old cell. With a smile she reached for the handle, only to find her cell bolted shut. Her smile fell. Then, she heard the Darrak footsteps coming from both directions in the hall.

"Don't panic," she told herself. "If I got out of my cell once, I can get back in." She summoned the white flame and in it went, quickly tearing up the inside of the lock. *They just better not look at it again.* Her skill seemed to be improving; the flame made short work of the barrier. She slid the door shut as quietly as she could behind her and then remained motionless on the ground, facing the hall. Her heart thudded in her ears.

Soon, the clicking grew louder and louder until she sensed two Darrak meet from both directions right in front of her room. They stopped and so did her breath. *Don't look at the door, don't look at the door...*

"The Master is mad that we let that one escape," a raspy Darrak voice uttered.

"It wasn't me, I was on break," the other replied.

"You'll be on the spit if we don't get her back, break or no. There can't be too many places she could be. And she's not outside, she'd be dead already. Get your crew back to work—and move it or we're finished." The shadows of the two Darrak shifted and soon they departed from the block.

Karanne let out her breath when the clicking of their claws was no longer heard and rolled onto her back. Her old cell was helpful, but she didn't miss it yet. She walked back out into the hall to Mitaya's cell.

At first when she tried to show the spell, she doubted Mitaya's eyesight. When she created this spell, however, she hadn't wanted the Darrak to see it; perhaps it was invisible to others. *She* created it.... she didn't learn the magic from Brannon, but perhaps she could still pass it on.

"Mitaya?"

"Are you all right?"

"I just had a little run in with some of the locals. Let me see your hand, under the door." The sound of chains scraping against the stone floor cut into her ears, but soon Mitaya backed up to the entrance and slipped her hands under the door to grasp Karanne's.

"I've never tried this; it probably won't work. This might burn for a second...."

The white flame shot downwards into Mitaya's hand and disappeared. Like a growing vine, an elaborate glowing pattern branched over her palm, just like the one on Karanne's. Well, not exactly; a slight addition to the circle appeared: a tiny, eight-pointed star just below the original pattern. She looked at her own hand, and the change was there, as well. "Now, concentrate on the magic I just gave you and cast it into—"

"I already have!" Mitaya said. "Can't you see it under the door?" Luckily, Karanne put her hands up in anticipation. The white flame exploded in the air and Mitaya apologized as Karanne tried to rub the blue patterns floating in front of her eyes.

"But I thought we couldn't create new magic. I thought only the Master could do that."

Karanne shrugged her shoulders in response. "I don't know why or how, the Fireflash just happened." She smiled at the name she gave it. "I have to go now and teach this to the others, but I'll be back when I figure out what to do next."

She set off to pass on the magic to the rest of the Followers through the base of the doors. She told the prisoners to wait for some sort of distraction in the next few hours, signaling the rescue. Unfortunately, not all the Followers were rational, however.

"Tell them to let me out of here. I will pay them anything!" one Follower said.

"You're going to bring the entire army in here if you don't quiet down," Karanne said. She hesitated before putting her hand through the hole under the door. "What is your name?"

She heard only sobs for a moment. "I am Lady Danelia."

174

The noblewoman from Beldan. *Great.* "Danelia, I am going to give you something, a new spell; it will help, but be careful. It could melt through the door, and we can't let that happen."

"It is 'Lady Danelia,'" she whimpered. After a minute, her hand reached Karanne's under the door. When the spell was passed on, only soft crying came through.

"I'll be back," Karanne said and finished with the Followers in the block. After returning to her hiding place above the entrance hall, she watched the Darrak patrols more carefully. When several of them began to fight, or even argue, bolts of flame invariably crashed into the walls, often catching the building on fire and forcing Karanne to duck. Would the armies of Myraton be able to stop them? She returned her focus to the task at hand.

Always *observe, observe, observe,* she used to lecture to Caspan Dral. She would need to be especially careful if she planned to rescue the three non-Followers at once. But where to bring them? She doubted they could make it up the rafters as she did. She looked down at the hall below and heard Darrak calling out into adjoining hallways for her to, "show her ugly face," as they uttered occasionally. Eventually, maybe they would think she actually escaped. *Suffering! There must be another place somewhere in the building to hide.*

Eventually, she found a staircase leading deeper into the bowels of the fortress. Down, the steps took her, away from any trace of light. She felt as if the earth were swallowing her alive. In the lowest levels, she saw several grates along the floor. Then the smell hit her and she knew the route they would take. The sewer. *It must lead outside the building somewhere.*

On her way back up the stairs, she heard more noise than normal coming from the hallways further into the building as Darrak shouted orders. She sprinted into the huge entry room and to her refuge, the stone archway. As soon she scrambled halfway up, a robed figure carrying a large, bright torch entered the dimly lit room. Darrak looked away from the light as he passed. The man barked an order to the Darrak and they ran out the way he came. She could not understand the order from so high, but when the massive gate opened leading outside, she figured they were planning to leave.

Daylight streamed into the dusty air and the Darrak covered their eyes with their hands until they could adjust to it. Twelve chained Followers were led into the main entry room, including Turic. She wanted to shout out and swoop down to save them all right then, but her heart settled and her mind took back control. Where were they going? A thirteenth robed person walked behind the rest, guided ahead by the Darrak. With her sharp eyesight, she saw greasy, red hair. *Jervis.* That was one more person still alive, one more person to rescue. What did she get herself into?

The group passed beneath her into the snowy wasteland as the gray haze of day faded into the dark of night. She watched as they headed east and away from the fortress. As the massive door shut, leaving the room below quite empty except for a few Darrak and the robed man, she crept, once again, down the stone arch.

A pit grew in her stomach. Perhaps now the Followers in her cellblock were going to be used to train the Darrak. If so, she had to hurry and free Kal and the Guardians, or else they would soon be dead. Her mind raced as she headed to the cellblock.

Cathlyn sat in the room again with the Soulkind. *Why am I here?* The man in the cloak brought her there daily, never saying what to do, never asking if anything happened. All that were in the Hall when she was tested, plus sixteen more, lay before her. She recognized most of them from her research with Turic in the Hall Library. All those years, she had only sketches and notes, but now, in the fortress of an enemy, she beheld them in their true forms. And not just the Light Soulkind.

She had only heard of the Dark Soulkind in stories from Turic; there didn't seem to be any other record of them, at least in the Library. A cold and icy sensation passed through her body as she reached towards them and she withdrew her hands. The Dark Soulkind had been perverted from their original intent and used for destructive and evil purposes. Since the Soulkind were receptive to their bearer's intentions, different uses of magic altered their overall effects; "Passed down family values," Turic used to tell her.

Cathlyn glanced through the pile in front of her and saw a dangerous, weapon-like Soulkind, which was vaguely similar to the noble-looking shield next to it. It had a short, but vicious-looking, blade protruding from the front and spikes sticking out alongside the wrist. The weapon, like the shield, looked like it wrapped onto a person's arm; however, like a claw or fangs. Unlike the opal set near the shield's wrist piece, a dark, clouded gem was embedded in the weapon near the base of the wicked blade.

176

A circlet, a spiked staff, and a crystal ring with four icy looking prongs projecting from the band were but some of the Soulkind she figured to be Dark. If she could awaken any one of these, she'd be able to escape and...

No. Cathlyn resisted her urge to touch any of the objects before her, even when it nearly overwhelmed her. When she returned to her prison she told Aeril she thought the man was trying to use them to unleash even more power.

"But that's where you're wrong!" she said. "We could use the power ourselves to get out of here. Imagine what we could do if we could use any one of those Soulkind!"

Cathlyn shook her head slowly, resting her back against the cage between her and Aeril. "I know I cannot control them. Trying to would just make that known to the Darrak, as well. And then..."

Aeril sighed. "Well, I don't picture us escaping anytime too soon unless you try *something*."

Chapter 18: A Path through Darkness

Trying to get out the sewers by herself was one thing, to move an entire cellblock out of a heavily guarded prison.... Karanne just shook her head. This would be the greatest act of thievery she had ever attempted. She almost laughed at the thought. When she reached the first cell, she looked at the keyhole. She could pick the lock easily, if she only had the right tools. Leaving any visible signs of escape was not an option, and a big melted hole through the door would be a little too obvious. *Well, maybe I do have what I need....* She had been able to change the size of her flame; maybe she could alter the temperature to melt only the locking mechanism. She held her hand forward with her palm facing upwards. With a thought, the circle on her palm glowed with a soft red light and the white spark shot out, hovering in front of her face.

"Now I want you to be cooler, much cooler," she whispered to the magic. She laughed, but quickly began to concentrate on making the heat dissipate. She had to melt only the tumblers. *Concentrate!* As the flame spun, it turned from bright white to blue to red, and began to throb slower. Finally, the fire turned orange-yellow as its pulse slowed to the speed of a thudding heart. *This will have to do.* Next, she focused on the lock and sent the magic inside.

She was used to feeling around the innards of locks like this with a pick and knew she could have had it open in no time if she only.... *No. I have to work with what I have.* She looked down, and with a start, saw that her flame was once again a bright white. Returning her focus to the fire, she made it shift once more to the cooler yellow. *No mistakes.*

The lock, luckily, did not start to glow, and she continued to think about moving the flame inside and touching only the inner mechanisms. *I can do this.* The light from the magic began to show through the door and she concentrated even harder. *I can't afford to have another melted lock.* Without warning, she heard a sharp *click.*

Mitaya's door opened, and as the pale light poured in, a mix of emotions flashed across her face: fear, excitement, joy. After she made short work of the manacles, she clasped Karanne's hand and nodded with determination shining in her eyes. With a sharp rap on the cell doors, the two women instructed the others to use Fireflash to release their bonds and open the doors. Karanne worked on one side of the hall, while Mitaya minded the other.

"These doors need to look as if nothing has happened," Karanne said. "We don't want the Darrak to notice when they walk by. Just concentrate and you can control the flame." *I'd do it myself if I had any more time…*

A few Followers were quick and could open both their manacles and cell doors before Karanne or any others assisted them, but most were slow to even release their hands. The Followers emerged from their cells with mixed feelings. Some seemed excited about their chance to escape, while others cowered in the safety of their cells. They knew what awaited them: the jaws of a Darrak, or an unforgiving, unknown land. Karanne practically dragged a few out who refused to walk.

Mitaya and Karanne continued to work to release everyone as fast as they could. Kal and the two Guardians waited as the magic spun within their bindings. The locks clicked open and they jumped to their feet, ready to leave their vile prison. Once in the corridor, the two Guardians began to pace.

"Looking for something?" Karanne asked and produced two Darrak swords.

"You've been busy," one of them said. He hefted the sword and tried to get a feel for the oddly weighted blade.

Karanne smiled. "Mitaya, we've got to get everyone down the central staircase soon. I can get through these last few doors myself. Just keep climbing down. You will know the place by its smell, I'm afraid."

Mitaya nodded and gathered everyone together to follow her. Karanne watched them creep out of sight. All the doors of the freed prisoners were closed and the locks intact. *Not bad. We'll make it yet.*

Hissing and pounding arose from down the hall, interrupting her thoughts. The sound was coming from inside one of the cells. Abandoning the lock she had started on, she ran to the door and tried to whisper, but her voice rose, "Wait…wait!"

But she was too late. The last door in the tunnel glowed red and smoke poured from the keyhole. When Karanne reached the door, she heard the Follower inside pounding and sobbing. "What about me? You forgot me!" The entire door had turned a white-hot, melting and spattering mess. The woman inside, still frantic, jumped over the pile that was the door and ran out into Karanne.

Karanne looked into Lady Danelia's eyes and shook her head. She bit back harsh words and gripped her hand over the hysterical woman's mouth. There was no hiding their escape now. The acrid smell of smoke hung in the air.

"Wait here, now. I am going to free the others. We're all going *together*, Danelia," Karanne whispered and left to work on the few remaining doors. The damage was done; there was nothing she could do now to fix the door. *She'll get us all killed!* She shook herself as she noticed her Fireflash spun too hotly. She tried to concentrate, realizing she could make the danger that much greater if she repeated Lady Danelia's mistake.

Inside the next cell, she met a young man fumbling with his manacles. When the metal clinked to the floor, he stood up and hugged her. She smiled, but tried to calm him. "We're not out of this yet."

Lady Danelia stood in the hall and looked crossly at Karanne when she emerged with the Follower. "Where are the others?" she asked, barring the way.

Karanne shook her head again and pushed past the astonished lady to the other cells. "They are on their way out of this place to the sewers. We're going, too, as soon as I free the others here."

The man whom she just freed stayed by her side. "Can I help?" Karanne nodded and motioned to the other cells.

Lady Danelia crossed her arms and glared. "The sewers? For the suffering! I am not going in there." Her face contorted. "I could have turned you in. They offered to make the situation here much better for me if I did. Anything would be better than…the sewers."

Karanne looked at the Follower beside her. He returned her questioning look with a slow nod. "They did ask about you.…"

Karanne wondered what Lady Danelia told the Darrak, or the cloaked man. She was sure the woman said something, but how much? She released the door lock for the last Follower to escape.

"There's a narrow staircase beyond this hall. The Darrak are going to be here shortly, so we need to hurry," she whispered as they crept throughout the tunnel. "We'll meet the other Followers there and continue downward to the sewer system running underneath the prison."

The Followers wrinkled their noses only briefly except for Lady Danelia, who crossed her arms and looked at Karanne and scoffed loudly. At the end of the hallway, Karanne stopped and motioned for the others to do the same. Across an intersecting hall, she saw the entrance to the narrow staircase and looked both ways. The area was quiet, perhaps because Turic and the other group of Followers had left not too long ago. She motioned the others to run to the stairs one at a time while she kept watch. Silently, they made their way, even the Lady Danelia. Finally, when Karanne scurried across the hall, they all began to descend the unlit spiraling stairs.

"Use your Fireflash to light the way," Karanne said. As she took her first steps downward, she heard voices from behind in the intersecting hallway. "Keep moving! You'll see the rest shortly, just keep going. I'll be there soon." She turned around and dropped to the floor at the top of the staircase as those four went on to the sewers.

Three figures approached the cellblock: two Darrak scraping and clicking their clawed feet on the stone, and also the soft steps of one with booted feet. Straining to listen, she heard a man giving orders.

"...and you will continue to gather your troops outside the fortress and await the Master's signal. Once the prisoners are at the spawning pits tomorrow...." She shuffled backwards as they approached, missing some of what was said. "We shall bring in the next group of Darrak in an hour. Our Lord will have what he wants soon enough."

The utter blackness of the staircase settled on her as she descended and she called Fireflash to light the way. She held her hand up and the spinning light burst forth and spun in wide circles around her as she hurried down the long, spiral staircase. She finally came upon the bottom where her thirteen companions awaited. The stench in the hall caused her to stumble before she could cover her nose.

"They are coming for us in the cells soon. I just overheard them before I came down," she whispered. "Very soon." The other escapees looked at each other with furrowed brows and then to her. "We can do this."

Mitaya stood at the entrance of the lower tunnels leading to the sewers and beckoned to Karanne. A rusty metal gate barred their way. The gate was not locked the last time she had been here. The Fireflash circled her and she sensed it now like a part of her own body. Sometimes, she felt the magic did not respond as well as she liked, however. To echo her thoughts, it spun rapidly in front of her face when she commanded it to enter the lock.

Shaking her head, she concentrated to melt the lock and the flame darted to the gate. Karanne closed her eyes, easily cooled off the flame, and began to work on the lock. In a few seconds, it opened and she pushed the gate sideways. A shout from behind startled her out of her concentration. "Someone's coming!" said one of the Guardians. Her flame darted in long orbits around her head.

Sharp clicking noises on the stone staircase increased in speed and intensity. A Darrak with its black face covered in red paint turned the corner and jumped into the center of the Followers. The Followers retreated to the side walls while the Guardians stood unwavering with their swords raised. The Darrak raised its arm and a fire bolt leaped from the extended claws and barreled into a crouching Follower.

How can it see us so well in the dark? Before Karanne could think further, she sent a fire bolt, which exploded in a burst of light, at the Darrak's eyes. The creature dropped to the ground, clutching at its face and screaming in a raspy hiss. The party paused, staring at the creature. The Darrak soon stopped wailing and stood back up on wobbly legs, rubbing its eyes.

"It's wearing off!" Karanne shouted. Not waiting another second, the two Guardians drove their swords into the blinded beast. The Followers breathed out a collective sigh as the Guardians wiped their swords. Kal walked to the Darrak and picked up its weapon. He held the blade lightly and turned it over in his hands.

Karanne ran to the Follower struck down by the flame. He was a young man, not much older than Jace. Before she could inspect him for injury, he stood up, much to everyone's surprise. Not a thread of his clothing was burnt, but he massaged his shoulder and bore a grimace of discomfort.

"I didn't feel the fire at all for some reason," he said. "But it sure knocked me down hard."

"How did you two see the Darrak? I'm pretty sure it's pitch dark in here..." a Follower said to the Guardians.

The two looked at each other and shrugged their shoulders. "This is as clear as day to us." Kal nodded his head, as well. "Mitaya 'showed' us her spell earlier."

Karanne smiled. "It works on the Darrak, too; but much better." The others nodded and looked down the hallway for any other Darrak.

Before she headed towards the sewer entrance, Karanne turned around and said, "We better hide this body before—"

"Disgusting!" Lady Danelia moaned as insects poured from the walls onto the carcass. Karanne could not disagree with her as she watched the surreal, rapid decomposition. Although she urged the others to proceed through the gate, she could not keep her eyes from the decreasing bulk of what was once a Darrak. *So much for having to hide it.*

With her companions through the entrance to the reeking sewers, Karanne followed closely behind. She knew they would be chased. Any time now, the alarms would sound. *Best to seal the gate behind us.* Her Fireflash spun into the lock and melted it shut. As she continued on, she tore off a piece of her cloak and covered her nose. Up ahead, she saw several of the Followers retching. Soon, everyone tied rags over their faces, following her example.

The party moved quickly through the tunnels. "Look out from above," Karanne said. Chutes from the ceiling dripped a rank substance to the slimy floor. Her boots sloshed through a thick liquid she did not want to think about. Apparently, neither did Lady Danelia.

The haughty woman sobbed as she tiptoed through the murky tunnel and foul liquid trickled onto her hair. Karanne actually began to feel sorry for the lady, but did not have time to think about her pity when a loud, low bell sounded in the distance. Lady Danelia's sobbing stopped as she listened.

"It's my fault!" she whimpered.

No one said anything, yet they all remembered her hasty escape from her cell. Altogether, the party ran with the echoes of the tolling bell ringing behind them.

The tunnel sloped downwards towards a large room with grates surrounding the edges. When Mitaya entered the room first, she met four Darrak waiting for them in ambush. From the rear of the party, arcing fire bolts streamed into the corridor and screams followed. Lady Danelia covered her ears and cowered behind as Karanne ran past to help her friends.

When Karanne entered, the room was alive with fire. Mitaya lay crumpled in a ball near the entrance. The other Followers were caught in a fire fight with the three standing Darrak. All of these Darrak, too, had red paint on their heads. One of the scaled creatures had apparently been knocked to the other wall by a blast before Karanne reached the room. A huge dent in the living rock was carved out by the skull of the Darrak. Several balls of flame careened into the walls, blasting chips of rock in all directions.

"Blind them! Quickly!" Karanne shouted.

The Followers were slow to react, and a Darrak threaded its way like lightning across the floor and struck a Follower next to Karanne in her chest with a black bladed sword. The Darrak looked up at Karanne with a spike-toothed scowl as the body dropped to the floor. It raised its bloody sword to strike her next. Before it could complete the slash, the creature screamed, clawing at its eyes.

Karanne glanced down at Mitaya and saw the girl weakly pointing her hand at the Darrak. Karanne concentrated and extended her hand towards the two standing enemies. Her Fireflash darted ahead and the remaining Darrak crumpled in a painful explosion of light. The Guardians and Kal made short work of the blinded creatures.

Karanne let out a huge breath and knelt down to examine her friend. The girl was breathing, barely. In the background, she heard Kal ordering the Followers to pry open a grate in the center of the room. Holding Mitaya's hand, she forced a smile through her tears and looked into the injured girl's eyes.

"You saved my life." She touched the young girl's face with shaking hands. "We'll get you out of here, don't worry." She did not believe her own words, though.

"I can't move. I can't feel my legs." She looked Karanne in the eyes and held the stare. A spasm of pain crossed her face. Karanne hushed the girl and glanced to see how they were proceeding.

A loud crash resounded when the grate dropped to the stone floor. "We've got it! Everybody, come on!" Kal shouted. Suddenly, he looked around and put out his arms. "What's going on, I can't see a thing!" The two Guardians stumbled.

Karanne closed her eyes before looking back at Mitaya. With a thought, she allowed her Fireflash to be seen by the three. Confusion turned to understanding and they bowed their heads. She ran her hands over Mitaya's lifeless eyes to close them. She looked around the room at two other fallen Followers.

Lady Danelia walked into the room and looked down at her companions without expression. She watched as the flood of insects poured over the Darrak bodies, but did not touch the deceased humans. "We can't just leave them here like this...."

Karanne nodded. "Does anyone know these Followers?"

Kal walked over to the bodies. "I know them, but just their names."

The complete circle mark in Mitaya's hand glowed slightly. Placing her own palm over the mark, Karanne closed her eyes. "I'm sorry...." When she looked down at Mitaya's hand, she saw that the mark was gone! There was a new mark on her hand, as well. Quickly, she took the hands of the other two Followers and watched their marks disappear, as well, only to reappear on her own hand.

Memories of the people flitted along the borders of her own memory, like remembrances of dreams. Now, she would be able to help Kal write down their deeds and inform their families of what happened here. If *I ever make it back to Beldan.*

Nodding to Kal, she stood over the bodies, waiting for everyone to pass below into the sewers. Lady Danelia walked past the Guardians and Kal and looked back before climbing below.

"Farewell." With her eyes closed, Karanne sent flames towards the bodies and headed further into the sewer behind the last Guardian. Before pulling the grate shut, she looked at the bodies of the Darrak; at least what was left of them. A swirling mass of ravenous insects covered them, as with the other they killed. Ashes were all that remained of the fallen Followers.

The narrow stairs down into the stench were just big enough for Karanne and a Guardian to stand upon and yank the grate back into place. "What's your name?"

"I'm Rayin." He stood nearly as tall as Karanne and appeared several years older than Jace. His straight black hair swung past the rag wrapped around his forehead.

"Wait," Karanne said. Pointing her finger at the grate, she commanded the white dart of fire to melt the metal. The flame spun in rapid circles around the base of the opening, turning the bars red hot. She looked at her handiwork when she was through. "With any luck, they'll never know we went through here. If they do, this will stall them, if only a little."

She hurried to the front of the party and looked at the Followers' faces as she passed them. A few looked up at her, but most held their heads down as she passed by them. "We were surprised back there. If we stay to the shadows and know what to expect when we encounter the Darrak again—and we *will* encounter them again—we'll be alright." The Followers nodded their heads and she continued. "These are our Guardians, Rayin, and—"

"Gerant…" the other Guardian said.

"Yes, Gerant," Karanne said. "Rayin, Gerant, and Kal will be our swords, and we'll fight from behind with fire." She continued instructing the others on what to do in their next confrontation, all the while making sure to ask for everyone's names.

"Now, let's get out of this stinking hole."

Several other tunnels branched out of the rounded one they walked through, but Karanne felt they needed to stay on this one since it continued to slope downwards. *There needs to be an exit around here somewhere.* Nausea crept through her body. Escape from the Darrak kept her focused, but she wondered for how long.

Eventually, the Lady Danelia walked up to Karanne, head held high, even though her robes and long blonde hair were covered in filth. In a hushed voice, she asked, "What was it that you did to the bodies, back there?"

Karanne looked at the younger woman, who was now looking at the ground. "I made certain the Darrak would not find them."

"But you did something to them before that, too...."

The memories. The spirits, or at least imprints, of Mitaya and the other two Followers resided inside Karanne's mind.

"I could feel... Let me try something. Give me your hand."

Lady Danelia held up her palm to Karanne, who then clasped it within her own and willed the memories to continue into the other woman's mind. She nodded when Lady Danelia's eyes widened. "I...I can see them in my mind," Lady Danelia whispered. "I know what they felt..." Her face turned again to the ground.

"The others should know, as well."

Lady Danelia nodded. "Do you think we will make it out of here?"

"Only if we work together." Karanne noticed Lady Danelia was no longer beside her. She looked back and saw the young noblewoman looking down, her brows furrowed. Slowly, the woman turned to the other Followers and held up her hand. Karanne turned around and kept trudging.

After what seemed like hours, the company finally reached a part of the tunnel with a breeze of cold, fresh air. "Be careful!" Karanne said to several Followers who darted forward. Slowing only briefly, the Followers went on ahead.

Nighttime greeted them at the tall metal gate at the end of the sewer. They rushed to the bars and took deep breaths of the air gusting in. Luckily, no Darrak awaited them, but all exits would be checked, and this was a probable escape route. The ringing of the alarm bell still echoed in the thin, mountain air. Down below, Karanne saw the waste flowing from the tunnel into a large hole in the snow-covered earth. To their right, many hundred yards away, fires and tents of the Darrak army shrouded the mountainside.

"There is a war starting here," she said, shuddering.

The Followers, sensing the freedom of the open air before them, began to shake on the gateway. Karanne could see the hinges of the gate glow as Followers commanded their flame to melt through. In seconds, they sent it crashing to the snow and rocks below.

"We're not free, yet," Karanne said.

"We don't have any food or water!"

"Which direction do we go?"

"How are we going to get out of here?"

"Let's just go!"

Karanne tried to lead them out of view of the campfires in the distance. "We need to stay together! Listen!" She unwrapped the rag from around her face. "When I said we're not free yet, I meant there are still other Followers to rescue."

"I'm not going back in there!" a man shouted. Several others agreed.

"We won't have to. They've been taken out already and are being led by the Darrak...somewhere. We *must* rescue them."

"*Somewhere?*" someone said. Other frantic voices rose up in disagreement at the idea. The Guardians and Kal, however, stood by Karanne's side.

"Think of how you would feel if you were one of them," Karanne said.

The Lady Danelia looked up into Karanne's face and then at the marks on her palm. Clenching her fist, she slowly stepped forward beside Karanne and looked back at the other Followers. Karanne smiled at the woman while the others stood silently.

One at a time, the Followers fell in line beside her. With a deep breath, Karanne smiled her thanks and headed in what she hoped was the direction of the still imprisoned Followers.

Turic stumbled to the snowy ground, pulling down the Follower connected to him by a thick chain. The darkness of night made his aged eyes even worse. He felt certain his usefulness would come to an end before long.

"I am sorry," he said to the person in front of him. The Follower he downed first looked back and frowned, but then forced a smile and helped him to his feet. After several similar incidences, a Darrak with red paint on its face and a red strap across its shoulder held aloft an unlit torch and pointed a clawed finger at the piece of wood. A bolt of fire careened into it, sending sparks and burning embers into the air.

The Darrak marched them throughout the frigid night. Some of them had the red straps and paint, and Turic reasoned those were the ones he and the others had taught to use the power of the Soulkind. Both Followers and Darrak walked doubled over from the iciness. Brief snatches of their conversation floated through the air, their foul, hissing voices grating in his ears. Several spat on the Followers.

Turic could see only five feet in front of him. He was surprised to see Jervis Redferr, unchained. He called to the boy, but the Darrak hissed at him and raised their spears.

After an hour of trudging uphill, the group reached the top of a knoll leading into a shallow valley. Walking downhill came as little comfort to Turic; his bones ached so from all the marching. Here in this small shelter from the wind, the Darrak allowed them to rest for what he hoped would be the remainder of the night.

The snow did not stick to the ground here. There was little firewood in the region, but the Darrak threw what they found into the middle of the dale. A Darrak cast a bolt of fire that crackled into the wood and burned greedily. They huddled around the warmth, yet a few kept their black eyes on the chained Followers. Turic and the others sat in a line behind the Darrak with their backs against a steep cliff.

Turic glanced around and saw Jervis sitting alone and called out for him to join the others. The greasy-haired boy stood up, receiving glares from the Darrak beside the fire, and sat down beside the old man. Turic nodded his head at the boy, who only stared at the ground in silence.

"Have you come from the other group of Followers in the prison?" Turic asked. "I did not see you during the training."

Jervis nodded his head. "Looks like they ran out of chain for me, though, eh?"

Turic rubbed his hands together in front of the meager heat blocked by the Darrak. "Do you know how far it is to these 'breeding areas'?"

Jervis paused. "I'm sure it's not too far, old man."

Stuck in the freezing wilderness on my way to someplace worse and I get to sit and talk with Jervis. Lovely.

Turic saw fifteen Darrak around the fire—more than he counted previously. Despite being chained and nearly starved, he could think of nothing but escape. He watched as ten Darrak sprawled out on the hard earth to sleep. *I must escape…*

Then what? He would either starve, freeze, be recaptured, or end up as food for some wild animal. As if in response to his thoughts, a strange wailing noise called from a short distance away. *Perhaps staying by the fire would not be such a bad idea after all.*

He attempted to close his eyes, but the surrounding noises kept him from dropping off into a much-needed slumber. As if the sounds were not enough, the local insects tried to make a meal out of him, even in this freezing weather. Turic tried to swat at a brightly glowing firefly attempting to land on his hands. The irritating creature avoided his swats with ease.

"Go on! Shoo!" Blowing at the annoying bug, Turic almost started yelling. He could feel himself on the verge of laughing hysterically.

"What are you doing, old man?" Jervis asked, watching Turic waving the chains in the air.

Turic's waving dragged another Follower's hand in the air. "You'll wake them! Please don't wake them!" the Follower said.

The firefly stood still for a moment in front of Turic's blurry vision. Turic blew as hard as he could, but the insect still didn't move. "Look at this!"

"Let me sleep," Jervis said through the long hair covering his face.

The Darrak started to stir as Turic continued to swat. One of the scaly creatures knelt in front of Turic and pointed a claw into his shoulder. The firefly zipped from sight. Hissing in its raspy voice, the Darrak said, "You want breakfast?"

"I think you meant to say, 'Do you want to be breakfast,' but maybe I shouldn't point things out like that." The other Darrak beside the fire looked back during their raucous laughter. Turic glanced into the solid black eyes of the creature in front of him and knew the beast was not joking. The Darrak walked back to his companions, glaring at Turic before he sat once again.

The moment Turic stopped moving, the brightly lit insect jumped into his manacles. Before he could shake it out, the chains binding his hands together dropped to the ground. Shouts of pain, coupled with the sound of sizzling erupted from the line of Followers beside him. He saw liquid metal flying into the air as shackles burst apart and several Followers dropped to the ground howling. Jervis shot up and opened his mouth, but before he could speak, the Darrak around the fire drew their weapons and fluidly advanced upon the Followers.

The air filled with intermittent bursts of blinding lights. Through the bright blue spots burning his eyes, Turic saw the approaching Darrak drop to the ground, clawing at their faces. He was being rescued; but by whom? Lifting his hands, he unleashed a blast he had been holding back directly into the confused circle of Darrak. An explosion echoed in the small valley as his bolt struck the stunned creatures. The force of the blast knocked many of them into nearby walls of rock, causing their bones to crack from the impact. Although two Darrak would not stand again, the others arose, glaring and hissing warnings to their companions awakening from the noise.

The sleeping Darrak jumped up, but before they could react, blinding lights crumpled them to the ground. Turic's companions, at least those who could stand on their own now without panic, hurled fire at their captors. The magic, although still slightly out of reach, throbbed within Turic's body.

Out of the chaos, winged Darrak leapt into the air, flying at the prisoners and slashing with their claws. Curdling screams rang out and Followers dropped to the valley floor. Turic launched more fire at the beasts, knocking them off-balance, but also fueling their rage.

Another group of lights flashed in the air, but the Darrak did not fall to the ground as before; they only slowed to blink for a moment. Turic knew his friends would not last much longer. He looked for Jervis, yet the boy was nowhere to be seen. Turic cried out as a winged Darrak jumped into the air and headed straight for him. From the opposite side of the valley, a searing bolt of fire tore through the air, striking the leaping Darrak in mid-flight. The Darrak careened into the cliff behind Turic and fell, his head turned at an awkward angle.

Turic looked up at the hill and saw figures standing and hurling fire downward. Most began to walk into the valley, but a few stood at the top, perhaps to hinder an escape. A Darrak stood before Turic, but in an instant, his head fell to the ground and rolled past Turic's feet. When the rest of the body collapsed, Turic saw three men wielding swords, hacking at the surprised captors.

Four Darrak remained on foot, now backing away from the attackers. They lashed out with their claws to break free of the circle of swords and blasts of fire and made for the valley exit. The Followers on the ridge above, however, drove them back down into the shallow pit with bursts of light. The swordsmen chased the Darrak, crippling the scaly beasts by slashing at the backs of their legs. One remaining winged Darrak took drunkenly to the skies, followed by a score of fiery blasts from the ground. A bolt erupted from the valley top, slamming into the Darrak with such power that the beast's wings crumpled, sending it twirling to the awaiting swords below.

In the following silence, Turic surveyed the damage. None of the Followers escaped without a mark, and several lay unmoving. Jervis crawled out from behind a bush and sat down on a flat rock, looking dumbfounded.

"What happened?"

"Not to worry, Jervis. You've just been rescued." The boy buried his face in his hands.

The formerly imprisoned Followers looked around to see who had rescued them. Turic walked to the edge of the clearing and looked up the hill as Karanne came towards him. She was speaking to a blond haired woman with her hand on her shoulder. The woman beamed under the apparent praise and adjusted her hair. Karanne then looked up to see Turic, bruised and barely standing. Turic laughed as they clasped arms. The other Followers cheered for their rescuers, despite their pressing injuries. Those coming down the hill smiled and patted each other on the shoulders.

"Brannon Co'lere must be with you?" Turic looked around for the Master Follower as he ran to his companions, doing what he could for their wounds.

Karanne furrowed her brows. "No, why?"

"Well, he must have passed on this new spell to you...."

Karanne smiled and took Turic's hand. "I have a lot to tell you."

Turic's eyes widened as he watched the blossoming pattern on his hand and the spell filled his mind. She yelled out to the other Followers, "Pass on your Fireflash and mind the injuries from the shackles."

"How did you do this? How did you find us?"

She looked back at Turic. "It'll take awhile to tell. There is something else I must do first." She walked to each of the fallen Followers and held their hands. Before she finished, the sky from the east began to glow with the coming of the dawn.

"Now let's go home," Karanne said, and the Followers nodded.

Turic looked up with a start. "We cannot leave now. Cathlyn is not with us, and the enemy has the Soulkind. We *must* not leave."

Chapter 19: The Truth of the Past

"You are mistaken, surely...."

Brannon waited a moment and laughed uncomfortably. The dragon did not respond and Brannon's laugh died. He cocked his head, his cheek twitched, and he reached slowly for his throat. In the next instant, he twisted around to face the onlookers.

Jace's expression turned to shock as he looked down the line of his friends. *Someone else?* He looked up at Graebyrn who was staring at him.

No.

Surely, he was mistaken. The Flame of Marathas refused to burn within his body and the other Soulkind he handled sat cold and lifeless in his hands.

"That's impossible."

"Be seated," Graebyrn said. "You have many questions to ask, and very little time." The dragon looked down on the humans while they slowly sat. Both the thrill and fear of being in the presence of a dragon battled across their faces. Brannon sat on the lowest step, glaring at Jace.

Jace looked up into the dragon's face and saw emerald green eyes staring straight back into his. Only in his dreams had he envisioned such a creature. He instinctively began searching the steps for a stone to remember this experience. He found one and clasped it tightly.

"How can *I* be a Soulkind Master?"

What could have been a smile crossed Graebyrn's reptilian face. "This is a long story, and you have much to do, so I must speak quickly."

The party listened to the story with many astonished glances at Jace.

"Two brothers lived a thousand years ago: one a venerable king and my friend, the other, a man twisted by the shadows of an evil magic. Both were Soulkind Masters, although few knew of the dark brother's secret until it was too late. Even I did not know of his treachery."

A memory flitted into Jace's mind. "Marlec. Was the brother's name Marlec?"

Graebyrn nodded. "And the king was Lu'Calen. Marlec, with the Dark Followers behind him, led an attack upon his brother's castle. I watched, through these magic pools, as he drowned his brother until the evil of the murder clouded the waters." He closed his eyes and breathed on Jace.

Jace looked down at his wrinkled hands; wrinkled from age, he knew now, not from water. Strange markings he once thought bruises were in fact elaborate symbols covering his fingers. The pool around his body glowed with a dying blue light. The radiance from the water shone on the walls and upon the other man in the room, who knelt, searching. Screaming, he kicked a small chest by the pool into the wall.

"Where did you hide your Soulkind, brother?"

Lu'Calen tried to lift himself out of the pool, and sputtered out swallowed water. Marlec twirled around. A deep flame burned in his eyes. Grabbing hold of Lu'Calen's hair with a black-gloved fist, he knelt down. Jace felt the hate, the malice bearing down upon him, even though the eyes he looked through were not his own.

"Where is it hidden?"

"So you are 'the Shadow,' my brother," Lu'Calen whispered. "You cannot control the Light from the shadows."

"Who said I wanted any part of the Light? There needs to be Light to have a Shadow, yes, but not to have eternal darkness!"

"How could this happen to you?"

"There is power in the Dark Soulkind you will never understand." The anger in his eyes flickered briefly.

"You are not strong enough to control it, and soon all will be over. Through these waters, you have been uncovered; your ways are known to everyone now."

Marlec looked into the waters and saw the eyes of a dragon watching him through the pool. Lu'Calen barely held himself above the water with a trembling hand. The fire in Marlec's eyes rekindled and burned even brighter.

"Not strong enough? If only your Light were not ending, you could see how strong I've actually become."

"Mine will not end," Lu'Calen said. "Never touch these waters, Marlec. I will be waiting." Marlec stepped on Lu'Calen's fingers, which gripped in vain at the edge of the pool until he could resist no more.

Jace looked out through Lu'Calen's fading vision and felt the freezing waters swallow him. In his outstretched hand, Lu'Calen held a green stone. The cold enveloped him as he sank further downward. Before he finally closed his eyes, he watched the green stone tumble over and over as it slipped through the water. Jace saw the stone fade slowly

194

away to the point of disappearing, and then come closer and grow clearer. The rock settled into the dirt and he reached out. This time, his hand was his own.

Opening his eyes and fist, he stared disbelieving at the green stone he always carried.

"This can't be."

"These pools were formed through magic, allowing people to speak to each other, no matter the distance in time or space. Lu'Calen used this Soulkind to find you."

Jace turned the stone over in his palm, and shook his head. Not only was he able to use magic, but he was a Master of a Soulkind.

"Shouldn't he bear a mark then?" Brannon said and crossed his arms over his chest. "If he really is a *Master*?"

"That is true," Graebyrn said. Lifting his huge forearm, he reached behind Jace's head, and with one claw, lifted his curly hair.

When Jace turned around to look at his friends, Straeten said, "There is a mark, right at the base of your neck! Let me see that again." He walked behind Jace and lifted up his hair.

"What does it look like?" Jace asked.

"There is a set of wings...." Graebyrn unfurled his large wings. Pointing to the dragon over Jace's shoulder, Straeten said, "...and they look like those."

"A mark is born when you create magic through your abilities as a Soulkind Master," Graebyrn said. "You have developed skills I have never before seen; similar to Lu'Calen's, yet not so. His was a peaceful Soulkind, and he used its powers to help him rule wisely. The powers of each Soulkind may change according to the will of the Master—sometimes, as in Marlec's Soulkind, for evil." He glanced over at Brannon Co'lere. "You have taken in some knowledge from the Soulkind, however. Marathas has not yet fully awakened and your magic is not strong enough to call forth the full power trapped within."

Jace turned the plain stone over in his hands. He could learn much from Graebyrn, if not for his friends in danger.

Graebyrn settled down upon the dais. "These past few weeks, I have been calling to you. There is magic in this world, if one knows how to find it."

"The stone walls in the cave!" Straeten said.

Graebyrn nodded. "The time has come for magic to return to the land, for good or evil. I wanted to make sure that you knew who you were. For all of us doubt ourselves at times and it is the decisions we make that define us."

Jace felt the dragon's eyes peering into his mind, sensing his doubt. He shifted uncomfortably and glanced around the chamber. "Who is buried there?"

Graebyrn waved a clawed hand to the tomb, urging them to walk to it. Mathes already stood there, staring at the markings on the ground.

The stone cover of the tomb was lined with intricate, archaic symbols. A small, engraved plaque sat upon the tomb. Jace read the word, "Sarissa," aloud for everyone to hear.

"Who was she?" Burgis asked.

Mathes opened his mouth to answer, but Allar interrupted, "I've heard my sister say that name before. She used to talk about a great sorceress who lived long ago. Is this the same Sarissa?"

"She is the one," Graebyrn said. "Sarissa ruled alongside Lu'Calen one thousand years ago before the Soulkind were trapped. I have only known a few souls who could touch magic without a Soulkind…Sarissa was one of them. Magic flowed strongly in the world then; creatures you have only read of in stories walked the land and flew in the skies. But as humans grew in the ways of the Soulkind, so, too, were the powers used for evil purposes.

"A dark faction, led by Marlec, rose in the shadows. Perhaps I should say the faction was led by the evil inside Marlec's Soulkind, for generations of malice and deception were infused within his foul gauntlets, and he was as much a slave as a master. Many attempts were made to recapture the Dark Soulkind, for there was always the chance they could be returned to the Light.

"After her husband was killed, Sarissa swore vengeance on Marlec. She devised a spell she hoped would silence the powers of the Dark Soulkind, locking their magic away from the rest of the world.

Graebyrn closed his eyes then looked down. "Sarissa led the Followers of the Light Soulkind against Marlec and his Dark Followers, not far from this mountain. When the two armies of the Soulkind met in Marlec's Shadow Vale, she cast her spell. But instead of only silencing the Dark Soulkind, she locked both the Dark Soulkind and also the Light. And worse, she trapped the souls of her friends within them.

"When I arrived at the battle, I found the two armies of Soulkind Followers staring at their Masters, who had collapsed on the earth, and at

196

Sarissa, who knelt facing the heavens. Those who could, fled, their only weapons, that of magic, closed to the world.

"Sarissa bore a white metal lock that held the souls and magic within the Soulkind, twisted upon her arm. I could feel the magic leaving, my strength fading. In her weakened state, Sarissa could not reverse the spell, and died upon my back as I flew to this lair above the chaos of the battlefield."

"Where is the lock now?" Straeten asked.

"It is here, buried with Sarissa. And I fear that Marlec is searching for it."

"But wasn't his magic trapped?" Jace said.

"Marlec avoided the locking, or at least resisted as much as he could—his power being elusive in nature. And perhaps, also, because the two Soulkind are linked. He hid his Soulkind using a powerful magic, and although he died, his spirit remained within the gauntlets, waiting for a time when the right person would find them. Waiting to use its corruptive powers again."

"How could he have hid them?" Mathes said.

"In one of these, I bet," Jace said, and pulled out the black box he found under the Library.

The box lifted from Jace's hands and spun slowly in the air before Graebyrn's face, and a raspy sound escaped his lips; Jace thought it might be a laugh. "I had been wondering where this went. In it is a gemstone that controls the power of the magic pools. After Marlec killed Lu'Calen, he sought out the different pools across the land to silence them, fearing the prophecy of which Lu'Calen spoke. This box contains one of the lost gemstones to reconnect the magic."

"How can I open it?" Jace said. "I don't even see a lid"

"It was sealed by Marlec. I might have been able to open it for you, but my waking unto this world is a slow one and I'm afraid my magic is somewhat, limited."

"Why would he just leave this lying around?" Straeten said. "Wouldn't it be better if he just held onto it?"

Graebyrn smiled.

"The magic is a curse to him, as Lu'Calen warned, so he had to keep them away from himself. I'm sure he protected it somehow after hiding it."

Jace nodded and looked at his wrist. The two cuts there had healed, but the scars, he felt, would remain.

"I will guard this carefully."

"Now, don't you want to know more about your Soulkind? And what you can do with it?"

Jace smiled but he cocked his head and strained to hear something: A call he thought he caught echoing into the room. "Did you hear that?"

Everyone else just shook their heads. Jace held up his hand.

"We have visitors," the dragon whispered.

The sounds of claws scratching on the rock broke through the silence, and the echoes of what had to be a group of Darrak making their way to the burial chamber.

"And I led them right to you," Jace said under his breath, and swore. He quickly unsheathed a couple of daggers and the others drew their weapons as well.

"Those will do you no good," Graebyrn hissed as he slowly entered a battle stance, his bones cracking into place. "And the fires you can produce from Marathas will only anger them. There is a secret exit through the back of the cave behind that dais."

"But I want to help you," Jace said.

"You can take this," Graebyrn said.

A strange white object lifted up from Sarissa's tomb. It looked like an odd white snake.

"The Lock!" Jace said.

Brannon, who had remained quiet, reached out and pulled the lock into the folds of his cloak. "No time to wait around, let's get out of here!"

The cries of the Darrak grew louder, and Straeten led them to the secret passageway.

The dragon sighed and faced the wave of Darrak that burst into the chamber. "Run!"

Jace ran into the dimly lit hallway and turned around to see several of the black lizard creatures jump onto the dragon and tear into his wing. Before he could shout, the dragon's tail lashed out and smashed the entrance to the passage. Stones collapsed to the ground, and a great cloud of dust filled his eyes. A deep roar resonated through the stones at his feet and darkness filled his eyes.

They ran through the tunnel blindly, waving their hands before them trying to feel their way out. A loud crash reverberated through the rocks, and Jace could only imagine what Graebyrn was doing. A flash from Straeten lighting a torch blinded them as it shone through the tunnel. Jace looked amongst his companions and saw them scrambling into each other, but soon they slowed their steps as the tunnel became clear in their eyes. Brannon was nearly running at the lead, well ahead of the rest, staring at something in his hands.

Jace glanced again at his Soulkind. The stone looked ordinary enough. Why was it a plain stone, when many of other Soulkind were so elaborate? And what could he do with it? Was he really a Master? So many questions he still had for Graebyrn.

The dragon had to survive the attack.

"I can't believe we left him there," Jace said.

"What would we have done?" Straeten asked. "We'd be dead. I'm sure he can handle them."

"But I've got this," he said and held up his Soulkind. "I could've done something."

"But you don't know what it even does, if it can do anything at all," Brannon called back before disappearing around a corner.

"Hey, stay close," Jace called, but Brannon didn't respond.

Another crash sounded through the stone and Jace put his hand on the wall. He could imagine the dragon, weak but fighting until his last breath. Suddenly, the crashing stopped. "I think the Darrak left. They must've been looking for the Lock."

"So they'll be coming after us now," Straeten said. "Great."

Ranelle walked close by Jace and whispered to him. "What are we going to do? Our horses and most of our gear are lost now."

"I don't know, I only hope Valor heard them coming and flew off." He didn't voice his fears about how to find him again. "Let's just get out of here first."

The tunnel wound through the mountain. They crawled at some points where the ceiling was too low and climbed steep walls when the path seemingly ended. They gradually made their way along in silence and only by the light of Straeten's torch. After a mile or so of this they climbed up one last wall, and Jace saw a dim glow up ahead as the tunnel started to open up a bit.

"We've got to be getting close," Jace said. "Where's Brannon?"

They all looked around to see if he fell behind, but no one remembered seeing him last. Jace strained his eyes to look ahead and thought he saw some movement up ahead.

"Brannon! Come back!"

Jace shouted out through the tunnel as they turned a corner to see the bright snow outside. Brannon stood there looking back at them with his head cocked to the side. In a heartbeat a winged Darrak swept Brannon up into the air and then the air crackled with energy.

"Run!" Jace shouted.

A blast of fire filled the tunnel and raced towards them as they all scrambled backwards as fast as they could. As the fireball rumbled up the tunnel, Jace shoved his companions down the cliff wall they had just clambered over. Quickly he swung over the edge and called up to Straeten, still up top.

Straeten started to climb down when the fire rolling down the tunnel struck him in the back and flung him off the edge. A huge crash erupted in their ears as Jace guessed the tunnel entrance collapsed in a fiery explosion. He ran over to Straeten who lay dazed on the ground.

"You weren't even touched by the fire," Jace said as he sat his friend up, dusting him off.

"At least it works both ways for the magic when its cast on me, huh?" he said, rubbing his head.

"This whole mountain is coming down," Jace said as the earth around them shook. Bits of the ceiling fell to the ground. Burgis lifted his brother up and started to climb back up the rock wall.

"We're not going out that way. Not with the Darrak waiting for us. We need to find another way out of here."

Under other circumstances, Jace would've been talking nonstop about seeing a dragon. But now, with the mountain surrounding them like a tomb with no clear way out, he could only try to force his mind to stay focused on the task at hand. The rest of the party, too, remained silent as they backtracked into the mountain.

Soon their hands bled from the constant scrambling over fallen rocks. They once went back to the exit, but heard the Darrak lifting and throwing debris to come into the caves after them. They quickly turned around and resumed their search.

For an hour they scoured the mountain for another exit, and went down several paths that at first seemed to be their way out, but only ended with a dead end. The torches they used were burning down fast. Finally, when another tremor shook the rock and brought down several huge boulders just behind them, a new path revealed itself.

This tunnel was shorter than the other one, and also climbed upward much more steeply. Before long, they could see sunlight ahead creeping into the mountain. With a collective sigh, they all reached the end and shoved a few boulders from the entrance. Still wary of the

200

Darrak, they slunk outside and peered around the mountaintop. Nothing. The sun shone brightly through a cloud break upon a stark mountain side. There was little cover up here, mainly some scrub brush that could survive this high up. In the distance to the north, they could see the smaller mountains that awaited them.

Somewhere in a valley ahead lay their friends. Jace looked up into the sky, half expecting to see Valor looking out for them. The sun fell behind dark clouds and a light snow began to fall.

"Everyone ok?" Jace asked.

"I'm all right," Straeten said. "But if another mountain falls on me, I'm heading home."

Mathes, Allar, Ranelle, Tare, Burgis and Straeten all checked their remaining gear and followed Jace down the mountain side.

After being under the brightness of day for awhile, everyone started to talk at once. Burgis clapped his brother on the back, who gestured how large the dragon was that they just witnessed. Ranelle and Allar laughed about who appeared more frightened when the dragon first spoke to them.

"I can't believe it, Jace." Straeten said. "You're actually a Master. How come you hid it from us so well? You sure could have saved us a lot of trouble back in Beldan."

Jace held up the stone and laughed. "I'm sure it would have if I knew. I'm glad you stayed behind—"

"Don't worry about it; I wouldn't have missed this for anything." Straeten smiled and asked, "What can you do with that thing?"

"I have no idea," Jace said, rubbing the stone in his fingers. The memories falling into the water seemed to be gone when he touched it now. "Graebyrn said he's never seen anything like it yet though. Says I've already created something, but I don't know what it is."

It felt suddenly strange to think about himself in this way: was something he was capable of doing only possible because of the magic in the Soulkind? He didn't like to think that anything he did was caused by that, he felt like he worked hard to be who he was and it almost made him feel like a weaker person. When was it created? If it was taken away, what would be left of himself?

Mathes interrupted his thoughts. "What about Brannon? He's got the Lock."

"This just keeps getting worse all the time," Allar said. He had been quiet this whole time in the mountain, Jace noticed. In fact everyone was looking at him differently.

"Come on, don't look at me like that. It's just me."

Allar gestured with the salute Jace had made jokingly days ago. When the others joined in, Jace shook his head and laughed. He stopped laughing, however, when he noticed Mathes standing off to the side watching him and writing in a journal. He knew the teacher disapproved of using magic. Mathes also had not spoken much since leaving the lair.

"Come on," Jace said. "Brannon is with the Darrak now, and that's where we're going anyway. We've just got to try to beat him to their fortress out here."

Jace looked up into the sky again and strained to see something, anything in the sky that might be Valor but no luck. He pulled out the stone he associated with Ash's memory and turned the black rock over in his fingers, dropped it back into his pouch, and drew the drawstrings tight.

A day passed as they marched downward along the mountain path and still no sign of Brannon. There was little chance of catching him: they had no idea where they were going unlike the Darrak. Their food ran in short supply, but Straeten managed to find edible things in the wasteland to help sustain them and water was plentiful since he successfully learned to melt the snow. Many fingers were burned, but in the end, they had water.

Jace thought about Brannon and how he taught others his power. He wanted to pass something to Straeten, but could not quite figure out how, or what exactly, to teach, since he did not even know what he possessed. He held the Soulkind in his hand. *Just a simple green stone.*

He was happy he was able to suppress Lu'Calen's memories; perhaps because he now understood their meaning. But how was he supposed to make the magic work? He tried projecting his thoughts into the Soulkind, tried to feel anything "magical," but nothing happened. Maybe the magic was not in the stone; maybe his mind held the answer. But he did not even know where to begin to find magic within himself. He just felt what he felt every day, nothing special in his consciousness.

The day wore on as the path curved alongside the mountain. Before long, another mountain peak rose in the distance. Jace assumed the mountain was Rabiroff, the shorter counterpart of the mountain they were descending. The path began to drop dangerously where they walked, and Allar loosened a rock that flew spinning past Straeten's head.

"Still sore about the snow thing?" Straeten said as the rock bounced off of the steep path.

"Sorry," Allar said.

Night began to fall soon after they left the cliff. The path still descended along the mountain, but leveled slightly. The party sought out shelter to camp as the night dropped to freezing and bits of ice whipped against their faces.

Jace led the party towards some towering gray rocks off the path as the gray glow of day gave way to the bitter night. Straeten, used to the normal nightly routine now, started the fire with his magic while the rest huddled around. After they ate their meal, their eyes closed almost by themselves.

"I wouldn't mind sleeping on grass again," Straeten said through a yawn. "Even dirt would be better than this rock and snow all the time."

Jace nodded at his friend. "We're getting close, Straet. What are we going to do when we get there anyway?"

"We always figure something out, right?"

Jace stretched his arms and rubbed his legs. "I sure hope so."

"Anyway, I'm more worried about getting back home *from* the fortress," Straeten said.

"Thanks for the reminder."

"Anything to keep us going. See you in the morning then."

The radiating warmth of Straeten's fire soaked through Jace's frozen limbs, numbed his mind, and brought a peaceful slumber. Almost immediately, dreams sprung through his head: images of Graebyrn and hundreds of swirling voices. Valor flew past his eyes, as did Ash and Blue. His sleep did not last long enough.

"There's something out there," Ranelle said, waking everyone.

"I heard it, too." Burgis pointed with his bow and arrow.

"We would be dead already if it were Darrak," Allar said, poised at the edge of the campsite.

"What are we going to do if we actually ever find Brannon?" Straeten whispered. "He seemed a little unstable."

"I'd rather put some miles between us," Jace said, "but someone has to protect him until his Soulkind is safe."

The sound of footsteps clicked at irregular intervals on the rocky ground and Jace squinted into the darkness to look for any movement.

The footsteps were getting closer. A cloaked figure walked into the light of Straeten's fire and three bowstrings pulled taut.

"Brannon?" Jace said, unable to see the man's face since it was wrapped in cloths.

A muffled voice spoke from under the hood, "No, but I, too, am seeking that man."

Jace looked at the man's raiment, and recognized the cloak, much like the one Allar wore. Allar rushed to the man. "Stroud!"

Stroud stumbled and reached out, catching Allar's shoulder before he toppled. Horrible burns lined his skin.

"We've got to help him!" Allar shouted. "Mathes!"

The others put away their weapons and brought Stroud beside the fire. Mathes rushed to Stroud's side and placed his hand on the man's forehead.

"He needs some water."

Straeten left with Burgis to find some while Mathes dressed the burns. The man's clothes were in shambles.

Stroud's eyes closed as he passed out from the shock of the fire and cold wind. "He was tied up somewhere," Mathes said, pointing to the abrasions on Stroud's wrists.

After Straeten returned with the water, Mathes finished applying salve to Stroud's injuries. "There's nothing more we can do for him tonight. We can only wait," Mathes said and left the man to rest beside the fire.

"You did a good job with him," Allar said.

Mathes nodded his head, but said, "We will see."

Jace walked to the edge of the firelight and peered off into the surrounding darkness. Straeten followed and watched him as he stared into the night.

"You better get some sleep, Jace," he said, stifling a yawn.

"No, you go ahead," Jace answered. "There's something out there tonight. I think I'll stay on watch now."

Straeten spoke through another yawn, "All right, if you insist. Wake me when you need to switch." He patted Jace on the shoulder and lay down beside the others on the rock.

The night enveloped Jace's mind as he stared out into the blankness. The only sounds he heard were the slow and regular breaths of his friends. A strange feeling, something familiar he could not quite place, filled his body, and he continued to peer out into the night for an answer.

Jace looked over at Stroud. *What could have caused those burns? Or who? Perhaps they were given to him in Tilbury...no, that was too long ago, the burns are too fresh. Jervis?* His heart chilled with the possibility of Brannon being behind this, and as the cold seeped into his bones, he welcomed the sensation. For the next few hours, he stared at his Soulkind.

As light returned to the gray world, Jace sat watching his companions awake. He allowed them to sleep through the night so he could ponder their next step and await the magic within his stone. Mathes woke first and walked over to Stroud. He glanced over at Jace without speaking then continued with his patient.

Stroud sat up and saw who rescued him from the night. Jace recalled seeing him before the Followers departed on their journey back in Beldan. The man made him uneasy, with his solid countenance and determined eyes. The fresh scar running across his face and burns across his arms didn't help.

Shortly after, the others awoke, stretched out their sore backs, and rubbed their tired eyes. Stroud nodded to Allar. "I'm glad others made it out of Tilbury alive."

Allar motioned to the others. "Thanks to my friends."

He told of their reasons for coming this far. When Allar mentioned the dragon, Stroud's eyes widened slightly. And even more so when Allar mentioned Jace's Soulkind.

"I've seen too much lately to doubt that story," he said. "Now for mine." Allar offered the man a bit of breakfast before he continued. Stroud nodded and reached for the food.

"Before this all happened in Tilbury, I spoke to a Follower named Turic," Stroud said. "He told me what would happen if Brannon died and someone else got hold of his Soulkind. I rescued Brannon from those creatures, but he was set on finding his amulet, even if it meant going alone into this wilderness. He tricked me and escaped, but I began to track him down again. You are lucky you were headed in the same direction—"

"What do you mean?"

Stroud looked at Jace and shook his head. "I found Co'lere again five days ago, in the ruins we just left. This time, he met me with fire. Then he bound me and left me to die. When your dog—"

"You saw Ash?" Jace asked, kneeling beside the injured man.

"Ash? Yes. On that day when you left with Co'lere, he ran up to me, barking to get your attention. It took many calls for that dog to leave me there, but he did. When he left and I heard you heading up the mountain, I gave up."

Jace looked down at the ground, remembering how many times he called Ash that day.

"But the next day, I opened my eyes to see him gnawing at my bonds."

Jace jumped up. "What? Is he still alive? Where is he?"

"He's not here? He led me most of the way."

Jace whistled and called out, "Ash! Ash!" He ran, leaving the circle of people and tripped over a protruding stone. He got up again and ran while scanning the rocky ground and calling Ash's name.

He ran for several hundred yards and then stopped when he saw a gray circle under a bed of feathers. Valor lay outstretched on the dog's back. Jace touched the hawk, who started and hopped off the dog. Jace smiled at him but then he looked down upon Ash's still form. Jace sensed Ranelle standing over his shoulders. He reached down,

"Ash. Ash?" Ash's fur was barely warm. He shook him, but to no avail.

Chapter 20: The Shadow Vale

Jace buried his face in Ash's short gray fur. Ranelle placed her hand on his shoulder. He could sense some of the others had joined her. Just when he began to lift his head, he felt something wet brush his cheek.

"Ash!" Jace laughed and hugged the dog for several minutes. After covering Jace's face with licking, Ash slowly got up and nudged each of the others, then lay back down.

Jace smiled when he saw bones sitting on the ground where the dog had collapsed. He looked up and silently thanked Valor for taking care of Ash, who stood again and returned to Jace's side. Soon, though, he began sniffing the air. Jace, with Valor on his shoulder, slowly guided the dog up to their camp. Ash placed his nose on Stroud's side, gently licking the burns on his hands. Stroud opened his eyes and stroked his back.

"And that's your bird?" Stroud asked. "Your dog seemed to be following it when it appeared yesterday."

Jace just smiled and looked into Valor's eyes.

"You sure have a way with animals."

The hawk stared back, unflinching. Jace saw himself reflected in the bird's wide eyes and wondered how Valor could've found them in the wilderness. Why would he have tracked and lead Ash to them?

Graebyrn's voice filled his mind: *There is magic in this world, if one knows how to find it.*

Jace held the Soulkind in his palm and looked back into Valor's eyes. He closed his mind and focused on the bird, nothing else. For a minute he stared.

Nothing.

With a sigh he lifted his arm upward and Valor flew up into the sky. He wheeled around and around, further up into the sky until Jace had to strain his eyes to see him. He concentrated on the bird. In an instant, Jace's knees buckled and he reached out for something to hold onto.

"We're there!" Jace shouted out as he knelt on the ground.

"What do you mean?" Straeten asked, walking over to him and helped him stand.

"Take a look for yourself," Jace said and pointed to a group of boulders to the north.

Straeten and Jace walked several hundred paces up the mountain towards the boulders. "Are you all right?" Straeten asked.

"You wouldn't believe me if I told you," Jace said and looked up at Valor with a smile. He carefully placed his Soulkind into the pouch on his belt.

They climbed upon the rocks and peered over the ledge upon the darkened vale below. The entire ground surface from this distance roiled, as if it were a thick, black liquid. A dark army amassed in the valley. Looming in the distance on the side of the other mountain, two fortresses commanded the valley.

"For the suffering," Straeten whispered.

"What are we doing here?" Jace asked himself aloud, sinking to the ground and facing the others. They followed them and climbed up the boulders to view the scene. Stroud even forced himself up to the ledge, but had no reaction to the sea of enemies below. The army blocked the way to the fortress and stark cliffs protected all other routes, except through one break on the valley floor.

"They're leaving soon," Stroud said.

"How do you know?" Mathes asked as he stared at the fortress.

"An army this large is not intended to stay in one place too long."

"In that case, we should wait until they're gone," Straeten said. "Then we'll have a clear path to the prison."

Jace shook his head. "It may be days before they finally leave," he said, "and we aren't going to survive much longer if we stay in these mountains. I hope we're safe on this trail. If not...."

The trail continued down into the valley, twisting amongst the massive boulders strewn across the surface like some giant had tossed them about. Statues of dragons lined the sides of the path, as they did at the beginning of the trail on the other side of the mountain. These, too, were defaced.

"Where are they marching?" Mathes asked.

"Wherever they're headed, I can't hold much hope for the people there," Jace said.

"They are probably going to attack Myraton, the center of the kingdom." Stroud stood up and limped over to his supply pack where he had slept the night before. The others pulled themselves away from the macabre scene below to join him.

"We have to find Co'lere before those creatures," Stroud said, hoisting his pack over his shoulders and wincing slightly.

"They've already got him," Jace said. "Just yesterday."

Stroud's shoulders sank a bit. "Well, let's get him before he decides to do something stupid."

"Right," Straeten responded, "because burning and abandoning his companions isn't stupid." Straeten smiled when his friends snickered and Stroud's expression softened.

Jace sat on a rock, waiting for the others to finish preparing for this last march into the enemies' territory, into the Shadow Vale. Ash sat by his side, looking up at him. Jace rested his hand on the dog's soft gray head and whispered, "You did the right thing, Ash, going back to save him."

When his companions were ready to depart, Jace stood. "A narrow ridge leads around the valley, coming to the back side of those," he said, pointing around the mountain towards the fortresses.

"That should be easy enough," Straeten said and rolled his eyes. "The ridge appears to be eroding quickly." As if in answer, a boulder dropped off the edge and rolled downward.

Valor cried out and leapt from the boulder, flying down the path they had been following to where the ridge around the valley began. Ash jumped to his feet and trotted down the road, with Jace following behind. "So this is the way we should go," Jace said and looked to Stroud for support.

The Guardian nodded solemnly. The rest of the group also nodded in acceptance, also with little excitement. Straeten said, "Those cliffs make the first part of the trip seem easy."

The fortress still lay miles away. The cliffs between their camp and the Darrak stronghold dropped sharply to either side and formed a near circle around the valley. The ridge, if followed to its end, passed the back side of the fortress and then around the valley again to the gap where the Darrak undoubtedly planned to leave. Jace saw no way down and his head reeled with the incomplete plan. He wanted to hand the responsibility over to Stroud, but the Guardian deferred to him for leadership.

The ridge was in the Darrak's view, although Jace counted on the dark cloaks they wore to blend in with the rocky terrain. With a sigh, he led his friends off the cracked, stone-paved road they had followed down the mountain and towards the spine of stone winding its way to the fortress.

Allar avoided the worn rock piles as he walked along the path; a wrong step might send him down to the bottom of the ravine. "What will we do when we find Brannon?"

Stroud tread carefully, but assuredly, staying low and close to the jutting rocks along the way. "I am sure he will try to finish what he started."

Allar nodded. "Do we really want to find him again?"

Straeten laughed. "Maybe we should just get his Soulkind back, if he doesn't want our protection."

Stroud paused and shook his head. "I have a sworn duty to protect him. My first instructions were to bring him to Myraton safely." He nodded to Straeten before continuing. "Like you said, Ver Straeten, he might not want protection, but I will make certain he leaves this valley alive."

Straeten started to respond when he stepped on a loose rock. A quick grab from Tare stopped him from sliding off from the dizzying height. The rock plummeted to the valley floor, spinning as it careened off the cliff side. Straeten thanked Tare repeatedly, while staring down into the valley. The silent boy tried to pry Straeten's fingers from his sleeve.

"Careful, or you'll bring the whole mountain down with you." Jace watched the rock spin towards the Darrak. "They'll be looking up here now. Everyone down, *carefully*..." To his surprise, Valor turned and circled downwards towards the army below.

"What is he doing?" Allar said.

"Don't worry, they'll think it was just him." Jace smiled at Valor. He caught his breath when an image of the valley floor passed through his mind like the briefest memory of a dream.

They stayed in their crouched positions for many minutes, so long that Jace's legs cramped. Straeten looked over at him and smiled his usual, "This is great," expression. Jace took this time to look upon the opposite ridge on the other side of the valley. *This must be the same valley Sarissa came to when she silenced and trapped the souls of her enemies, and friends.* He placed his hand on top of the cold, gray bedrock protruding from the cliff top and imagined the wrathful sorceress calling out her enemies from atop this very stone to engage in battle....

210

Jace saw Sarissa with all the Master Followers behind her and the enemy coming forth across the Shadow Vale to greet her. Her enemies dropped to the ground in a crumpled pile, their Soulkind useless. Her spell had worked, only too well. The flow of magic stopped, and when she looked at her own companions, also dead, she buried her face in her hands and screamed.

Straeten shook Jace by the shoulders, snapping him out of his daydream. "Come on, I think we can go now," he said. Jace clutched his green stone in one hand and the valley rock in the other.

Jace looked at the Soulkind, not having noticed he had taken it out of his pouch. His knuckles were white. He wanted more. The closer he came to magic, the more he wanted to do nothing but explore the possibilities. He could almost understand Brannon's nearly maddening desire. Almost.

Hours passed as they nearly crawled along the ridge. Winged Darrak flew high enough to see the band out from behind their scant cover. No more boulders lined the ridge, and only a few feet of walking area kept them from falling into the valley on one side or down an even steeper cliff on the other. Fierce wind filled their ears with howling and threatened to push them off the precipice. They had to nearly scream to hear each other.

Jace wanted to sprint across the ridge to get over the suspense. He wished he were Valor at times like this. The hawk glided upon the updrafts on the opposite side of the ridge spiraling on the wild currents.

The main fortress sat directly below them now. Its dark spires reached upward like black claws. From this distance, Jace saw a deep fissure surrounding the castle, acting as a moat, but without water. Bridges, like spindly spider legs, arched across the gap, leading into the castle at its four corners. The main tower in the center of the fortress vaguely reminded him of the Tower of Law, which was a disturbing image. He preferred not to picture this army in his home city. The fact that he and his friends were at the same level as the tower was disconcerting, as well. A thick veil of darkness hung upon the tower like fog.

Another smaller, but no less imposing, building jutted out of the ground, lower in the valley than the main stronghold. The way down from their point on the ridge was nearly a straight shot of several hundred feet. Many Darrak campfires still burned and the acrid smell of their meals wafted up to the party.

"What are we thinking?" Allar said. "If we go down here, or anywhere, we'll be dead. They're everywhere!"

His words seemed to ring true with the party. They sat on the ground and most buried their faces in their arms.

"Let me try something," Jace said and looked up at Valor still wheeling in the smoky sky. Concentrating once again on seeing through the bird's eyes, Jace slowly felt the image creep again into his sight. He saw the sky reel as the bird spun overhead and he nearly fell, so he grabbed the nearest rock for support and let the sight take over his mind.

His sight was much sharper than before: he could discern shapes down on the valley floor he didn't know were there. The Darrak were sharpening their weapons and stuffing gear into packs. Why were some groups painted in red? Possibly a different division. The path that wound around the cliff walls crept like a snake and when he saw himself he nearly laughed. Further around the bird wheeled and he could spy the end of the path.

Abruptly he reverted his sight back to his own. "There is a way up ahead. Come on!"

"How do you know?" Mathes said.

"What's that on your hand?" Straeten said and Jace looked down.

Strange black marks were forming like snakes crawling on the back of his right hand. Everyone stared at them as they formed into some strange symbols and an eye.

"I think I've just made something with my Soulkind," Jace said and took the green stone from his pouch. "I could see through Valor's eyes."

"Nice work, Master!" Straeten said and soon everyone was back scrambling along the path. Soon after, it began to widen up and large boulders provided much needed cover. As they walked, watching the backside of the castle, an enormous tunnel, seemingly carved into the gray stone, passed under the valley wall. Darrak marching through the tunnel covered the roadway leading to the castle.

Taking cover to rest for a moment, the party gazed back upon the ridge from which they came. They stood now on a narrow path with one side sheer to the valley below, while the mountain stood at their backside. They walked closely by the mountain, no longer walking along a seemingly endless, thin spine.

"Stay low," Straeten said.

212

Jace looked out from behind his cover to see why. Over the northern ridge, a flight of four winged Darrak raced towards the castle. They soared around the tower, circled its peak, and disappeared from sight. Within a few short minutes, the same four Darrak leapt from the tower and then flew to different spots on the valley floor.

From his perch upon a large rock, Valor leapt into the air and soared along the ridge. Jace's eyes were drawn from the bird to the sound erupting from the valley below. A horn, the likes of which Jace had never heard, blasted from within the castle. Shouts and yells from the Darrak rose up to the ridge in a hideous frenzy. Loud drums echoed off the steep cliff sides. Soon, the entire army moved like a black wave as the march began. The army of Darrak began to thread their way out the eastern end of the Shadow Vale on a wide road between two cliffs.

"Not many can march side-by-side out of that valley," Jace said. "It's going to take hours, maybe days, for this place to empty."

A sudden call from Valor caused Jace to shout, "Someone's coming!"

The party ducked behind the nearest boulders. Ash sat by Jace's knee, growling, and Valor landed on Jace's shoulder. Straeten readied a fist of fire while Allar and the three from Tilbury drew the strings back on their bows. Jace exhaled sharply and twirled a throwing knife.

He spotted movement from behind the boulders in the distance. Whatever the creatures were, they blended in well with the gray background; he would not have noticed them if he were not on the lookout. They slipped from rock to rock, creeping almost as stealthily as Jace and his companions. He stifled a cheer.

Ten Followers came into clear view, and Jace crouched to run over and greet them. He scanned their surprised faces when they saw him and his friends approaching. Turic, Karanne, and Cathlyn were not among them. Jace sighed and hung his head briefly, but then looked up and approached the blond haired woman in the front.

"What are you doing out here?" both Jace and the woman asked simultaneously. Jace answered first by explaining they were there to rescue the Followers and then to find the stolen Soulkind.

"We're also looking for Brannon Co'lere."

"Brannon? We haven't seen him since Tilbury."

"Have you seen any other Followers?" Jace asked.

The woman nodded her head. "We left them last night. Eight others like us. We all escaped together. They are attempting to do the same as you—to rescue the Soulkind." Jace, Allar, and Mathes started to speak at once.

"Was there a tall, red-haired woman?"

"…a girl with long brown hair, and blue eyes?"

"…a frazzled old man?"

The woman began to answer hurriedly. "Karanne Lorefeld? Yes, she was with them. She bravely lead our escape from that foul prison," she said pointing to the smaller of the two strongholds in the valley below.

"And the old man…Turic? He, too, was there. He wanted to lead us into the castle to find the Soulkind, insisting it was too dangerous to leave them in enemy hands. And this girl…I can only guess you're referring to Cathlyn."

Allar and Jace held their breath as the woman spoke.

"She was not with us, nor had anyone seen her, but Turic and Karanne mentioned her several times and made certain to go look for her in the fortress. Half of us went this way, and half with them. They took a few Guardians, a red-haired boy—"

Jace's eyes widened and his stomach lurched. "Jervis?"

"I seem to remember someone calling him that. You know him?"

Jace and the others hung their heads. "He is a traitor," Jace said. "The second he has a chance, he'll turn them over to the Darrak…or kill them."

"Where were the other Followers headed when you left them?"

"Jervis…" The woman turned around and looked at the fortress then back at Jace. "We assumed the Soulkind were held in that castle. The other Followers went to find a way in, which might be easier now with the armies leaving. They're hiding in a cave on the far side of this ridge. Please help her, she saved our lives…That ridge behind us is a dead end; is there a way out of this cursed valley?"

Their expedition could not make it through the mountains alone—not without knowing the way nor having the supplies to survive. Ranelle spoke up.

"The ridge is narrow, and the winds will knock you over if you stand, but there is a path through the mountains that the Darrak seem to avoid; we came that way." She looked at Jace and asked, "What if I helped these people to Myraton?"

Jace smiled. "You show great honor and bravery."

Burgis and Tare held their hands palm forward to her in Jace's salute, and Straeten wished her good luck. Allar, still dazed since the Followers told him of his sister, barely seemed to notice Ranelle leave, but she turned to him before going, placed her hand on his shoulder, and nodded. Allar stared straight ahead in silence.

Ranelle knelt down beside Ash, who sat looking at her. Laying her hand on his soft, gray head, she spoke words only the dog heard. After scratching Ash's back, she stood and looked at Jace.

Jace clasped her arm in his. "May the spirits guide you."

"I shall miss journeying with you, Seeker," Ranelle said, saluting him. "You will be welcome in the hills of Tilbury when you make it out of this Shadow Vale." She walked to the group of Followers then looked back upon her companions with a big smile. She saluted again and led the Followers behind the cover of the boulders. Jace watched for a moment as she conversed with their leader. The group crept away, disappearing from sight.

Jace looked over at Allar and said, "We won't leave until we find her." Allar's blank expression did not change.

"Hurry," Mathes said. "We must find Karanne on the other side of the ridge."

"And stay low," Jace said.

Fresh rockslides lined the path; the Followers were lucky to have made it this far. The party saw the end of the ridge and started to move faster, but Jace slowed their pace. They had come too far to end up on the canyon floor. Jace continued to hold back the pace until they came to a path far less steep than the cliffs.

The Followers must have traveled through the tunnel below. They would also have to make their way through that hole to get back to the fortress. The drums echoed across the Shadow Vale. Perhaps the route would be clear. That is, unless Jervis Redferr alerted the enemy to the Followers' whereabouts.

Once they were out of immediate sight and off the narrow ridge, Jace let their speed increase in their downward climb. The Follower had told Jace to look for a cave. Would Karanne be waiting there for nightfall? Would Jervis offer to scout a way, only to seek out the Darrak? Jace's eyes darted to every stone, hoping to find a sign of their hiding place. Following Jace's lead, Valor and Ash searched the hillside, fanning out to cover a wider area.

A short bark from Ash warned Jace, and he held up his hand to stop his companions just before a party of Darrak wound into view in the valley below. His first instinct was to look for prisoners, but the Darrak returned alone. He held his breath, hoping their search would continue to be unsuccessful as they drew closer. Moments later, a winged Darrak flew overhead scanning the rocky cliffs. Jace watched with hawk-like eyes as the beast looked towards their position on the rocks. The marching Darrak disappeared from sight below them into the tunnel under the ridge. Jace heard his companions expel their breaths, but continued to hold his as the lone flying Darrak flew up the ridge.

It'll see us for sure. Ducking his head down, showing only his gray hood to the sky, he almost felt like standing up to face the Darrak. The sound of flapping wings beat down upon his ears. Instead of the sound of Darrak's claws gripping the stones or his throat, the flapping continued until it was so faint that he knew the Darrak had crossed the ridge.

"They're gone."

"I don't know how those things didn't see us," Straeten said, looking back over the ridge top, expecting the creatures to return.

Jace shrugged his shoulders. "They must've been in a hurry."

Mathes, who usually walked near the rear of the group, stayed close to Jace's side. Jace glanced at the older man, his gray traveling clothes worn and his face nearing the same condition. His eyes had been more alert and anxious ever since their meeting with Graebyrn and now even more with the news of Karanne alive and close by. "We'll find her, Mathes. She knows what she's doing." Mathes only nodded and sighed.

Valor, who had been circling the hillside, dove to the rocky ground.

"There it is!" Jace said. Valor landed upon the top of a narrow cave entrance.

"That can't be it," Burgis said.

Jace knew better. Kneeling, he looked inside, but Ash darted in first, determined to scout the area. In only a few seconds, Ash stuck his nose back out and scooted aside for Jace to enter. When Jace crawled forward into the cave, Mathes peered inside.

From outside, the group heard Jace call out Karanne's name repeatedly. The calls continued for only a short while, and soon Jace crawled out to the others. Jace confirmed their worries with a sad shake of his head. "They can't be too far ahead." He arose to dust himself off.

"That patrol we just saw going through the tunnel is probably going to run into them eventually," Straeten said.

216

Wasting no more time, Jace motioned for the others to press onward, but noticed Straeten was halfway into the cave already. He sighed and shook his head. But when Straeten emerged seconds later with a face covered in dirt and presented brown mushrooms to his friends, Jace said, "It was worth the wait."

Straeten smiled and said, "At least this land isn't totally barren." He handed pieces of the cave fungus to everyone. His companions gave up doubting his food offerings; whatever they were, they consistently proved edible (and sometimes delicious), even though they often looked slightly unappetizing…or as in this case, more than slightly.

"This may be our last meal for a while," Jace said, while he ate the chewy brown mushroom. He looked for Valor and saw him tearing apart a small rodent next to Ash in a pile of snow. Somehow, the hawk always managed to find food and to share it with Ash. Jace felt revived and eager to begin the last part of the journey into this land. But how they were going to get out was beyond him.

At least the snow barely covered the ground in this part of the valley. That would keep the Darrak from easily seeing tracks. Despite the lack of snow, a massive wall of ice stood to the north. As for the temperature, the air was slightly less frigid than before, probably from the valley walls blocking the wind. The remaining chill, though, caused everybody to keep their cloaks tightly wrapped.

They crept downwards toward the tunnel, stopping at rocks along the way for cover. Jace and Straeten led the way, although Valor flew ahead, scouting for danger. Jace had to hold Ash back when the dog saw the hawk soar. "One is enough for now, Ash."

He glanced over at Straeten and waved his hand in front of Straeten's gaze. "Are you there, Straet?"

"I'm all right. I was just wondering what would've happened if I had joined the Followers. I'd be right in that fortress now or worse, I bet."

"I wouldn't have made it this far without you," Jace said. Straeten nodded and let out a deep breath.

Jace looked to Valor down below and knew the path was clear. With a quick signal to Straeten, he stood and ran to the next group of boulders closer to the tunnel where Valor awaited. The dark tunnel entered the wall of stone no more than fifty paces ahead. The path to the entrance sloped downward steeply, and small ice patches warned them to walk carefully or else slide into the back of an unwitting Darrak, if any remained inside. With a knot in his chest, Jace proceeded with Valor settled on his shoulder.

Ash wagged his tail. Jace nodded to the dog, who tore ahead through the cave, into the darkness. From what Jace could see from the sparse lighting, the tunnel looked similar to the entrance of Graebyrn's lair, having an unnatural roundness like worm holes he saw as a child while digging in the earth.

Soon, darkness covered Jace's eyes as the light from behind faded. The path still sloped downward, but his grip was sure and he soon forgot about the threat of slipping. Only the sound of his companions' boots and the clicking of Ash's claws reached his ears. No one heard his footsteps.

Jace kept listening for the sound of claws other than Ash's, although he did not know what he would do if he heard them. They would be trapped.

Ash imprinted a wet nose on the back of Jace's hand every couple of minutes and then was off again to scout ahead. Jace's eyes began to adjust to the ever-present shadow just enough to see the outline of his fingers. Soon, a dim glow appeared in the distance straightway to what must have been the end of the tunnel.

When the exit appeared like a bright star in the night sky, Jace squinted to adjust again. Ash's silhouette within the brightness ahead told him the way was safe, so he crept along the side wall, whispering back to make certain all were following. Valor kneaded his claws into Jace's shoulder.

When he reached the end, he changed his mind. The march of the army had continued for several hours now, but still, the valley floor was littered with Darrak. Here, at the far end of the valley, they stood beside hundreds of carts. Most were hauled by horses, but strange creatures Jace had never seen before were also harnessed. From this distance, they appeared almost like horses, but with horns on their heads and shoulders. The Darrak repeatedly lashed them to stop their dissent. A burning arose within Jace's chest.

He looked at the Darrak preparing to march, wondering again about their intent. There was something there. Something intangible about their thoughts. He sensed something controlling them, commanding them to do what they did.

Before long, the party's eyes were pulled upwards to the structure before them. The castle tower climbed to the sky, even higher than the

Tower of Law. The spires seen from the ridge hundreds of feet above stabbed the sky with their pointed, black peaks. Bridges spanned the chasm-like moat at the corners of the fortress, wide enough for only one person to cross at a time. The bridges had no supports.

Behind the stronghold, only a few Darrak walked or flew, and those hurried to join the others marching from the valley. Straeten spoke to Jace when his jaw finally closed. "There could be others coming through this tunnel behind us. If we're going to that castle, we better get moving!" He clutched his quarterstaff in his fists.

Jace glanced at his companions, who were looking to him for their next move. He took a deep breath and looked for a way to run. He motioned to travel around the back side of the valley and enter the fortress by way of one of the narrow bridges. Valor stayed on his shoulder and they began their trek around the base of the cliff.

All Jace's energy was spent on remaining hidden. He flashed back to his study with Caspan Dral. The thief had a game for the novices to practice: Dral sat in an abandoned building and the new recruits had to sneak around him without getting caught. When a thief was spotted, he or she was beaten and then locked in a cage. Dral looked for any reason to beat one of his thieves. He considered such punishment "good training." In this thief game, like all others Dral concocted, Jace was never caught. Another reason why Jervis hated him. The stakes were much higher here, but thinking of this danger more like a game put Jace's mind at ease, if only slightly.

A rock falling from the steep valley walls brought his mind back to the Shadow Vale. Just when the winged Darrak flew overhead on the valley side, Jace concentrated on remaining unseen and started the race to the arching bridge. Ash darted and stopped whenever Jace did, mimicking his every move. Drums and shouts of the waiting troops reverberated in everyone's ears and bones. Jace's party sped hundreds of feet away, unnoticed.

The chasm surrounding the castle appeared around fifty feet wide as they approached the black, glass-like bridge leading from the building to the ground—fifty feet wide, but the depth, unfathomable. A foul smell arose from the abyss amidst black smoke, and Jace's eyes began to water. Glancing over his shoulder, he saw Straeten raise his eyebrows slightly. "Aw, come on, Straet. This is easy." Straeten glared back at him.

Each of the slender bridges led to one of the shorter spires, which appeared to be watchtowers. The bridge held his initial steps, and so he began the ascent with the others close behind. Valor continued to cling to his shoulder, held back so as not to alert the Darrak. Jace was not worried about the bird's safety since he could fly, but Ash's…. One look at the dog, and he smiled. Ash walked along the bridge without slowing or wobbling.

The wind returned as the party climbed across the chasm making their balance even more of a challenge. Straeten crawled along the bridge, bringing up the end of the party. He shook his head when Jace looked back, as if to say he would kill Jace if they ever made it out alive. Halfway across the bridge, Jace looked back again and saw Straeten motioning for him to look up ahead. On the parapet, a Darrak watched the army leaving the valley. Ash loosed a small growl and Valor prepared to attack.

Burgis and Tare saw the danger, drew forth their bows, and knocked dark arrows. Before they could shoot, a thin bolt of flame crackled from Straeten's fist and flew towards the unsuspecting Darrak. The flame struck the creature from behind with a spray of sparks, knocking it off balance and into the pit below. The Darrak flailed its arms for a moment and Jace sighed as the chasm consumed the body.

Before the party could fully relax, the Darrak flew out of the depths straight towards them. With a short *twang* of bowstrings, Burgis and Tare's arrows whistled through the air—one tearing right through the scaly flesh on the left wing and the other burying itself deep into the Darrak's chest. The crippled wing folded and the creature screamed in pain, but the momentum of the Darrak was great and the bulk of the demon slammed into the bridge in front of Straeten.

The Darrak held onto the bridge, scraping and scrambling for anything to grip. Before Straeten could react, one of the swinging claws latched onto his leg, yanked him over the edge, and sent his staff twirling as it fell. His strong hands grasped onto the slick stone, but his muscles strained under the weight.

Tare dropped to his stomach in a heartbeat and seized Straeten's forearm. Straddling the bridge with his knees, he gripped as strong as iron. Burgis attempted to shoot arrows at the crippled, swinging Darrak, but could not get a clear shot over the narrow ledge. Allar gripped Burgis' back, allowing him to lean over the edge a bit more to get a better shot.

Jace yelled in frustration, as he could not get any closer to Straeten without jumping over the rest of his companions. Valor leapt off his shoulder, and tucking his wings back, flew into the chasm.

"Watch out for Valor!" Jace shouted.

Burgis nodded, releasing an arrow into the Darrak's side. The beast's tail lashed out, and its free arm swung at the dark blur that made several passes, clawing at the demon's black eyes.

Nearly pushing Mathes to get to Straeten, Jace flicked his wrist, produced a dagger, and waited for the moment to strike. The Darrak below flailed about like a pendulum, tearing at Straeten's legs. Tare strained to hold onto Straeten's arms, but Jace knew he could not last much longer. Straeten's face turned a dark red as he tried to free himself from the claws in his legs. The howl of the wind covered the hissing shouts of the Darrak, but its cries still threatened to draw unwanted attention this way.

The Darrak swung once more into view, and with one swift motion, Jace launched the dagger. As the beast opened his fang-filled maw to bite onto Straeten's leg, the dagger buried itself deep into the back of its throat, silencing it forever. With a kick, Straeten released the grip on his legs and sent the demon to the unknown depths.

Tare strained his muscles to pull Straeten back up to the relative safety of the narrow bridge. Straeten's leg bled through the gaping holes in his tall leather boots. Valor landed on Jace's shoulder and the boy reached over with a shaking hand to thank the hawk, stroking his head.

After catching his breath, Straeten looked up. "Now can we get off this bridge?"

Jace smiled and turned around to continue. Luck was with them, for no other guards remained in the tower at the end of the bridge. Past the midway point, the arch on the bridge began to level out towards the castle. Everyone's pace quickened to reach cover, aware that more Darrak could come into view. Tare and Burgis walked to the doorway with bows drawn behind Jace and the two animals. Dagger in hand, Jace looked into the small guardroom.

Empty. Just a cask of liquor, a chest, and a weapon rack. Straeten limped immediately to the rack, looking for something to replace his lost staff. Crossbows and a variety of swords decorated the wall, but Straeten ignored the more common weapons and opted for a staff with a curved, barbed blade at its peak. Spinning it around, he smiled as Mathes took a step backwards.

"Now have a seat, and mind where you swing that." Mathes prepared a bandage for the injury. Straeten set the bladed staff against the wall, removed his bloodied boot, and picked off a black claw the Darrak left behind.

"Something to remember this place by." Straeten winced as Mathes cleaned and bandaged the wound. He placed the claw in a pouch.

Jace looked at the four exits from the room. One headed to the bridge. Two other doorways led to posts where guards could watch the valley below. The fourth opened to a stone stairway leading down into the castle, the way they must head next.

The archers restocked their arrows from a bucket and grabbed short swords. Burgis tossed Allar a sword and offered one to Mathes, who shook his head. Mathes turned to go, then picked up a rapier. He smiled as he checked the weight of the blackened blade and gave the air a few sharp stabs. Jace looked down at the elaborate carvings on his dagger made by the Darrak and nodded to the others, ready to depart.

He took the lead again with Valor and Ash, walking silently down the spiraling stairs. The only noise came from the great pounding of drums filtering in from outside. He strained to hear a Darrak coming around the corner, but none came. Ash sniffed occasionally at the musty air.

A round, quiet room opened at the bottom of the stairs. Jace held the others back with a raised hand. He handed Valor over to Straeten while the others waited. He thought he heard some movement below as he crept down the stone steps. Dagger ready to strike, he reached the bottom and headed towards the large hallway entrance at the side of the room. He took only two steps on the stone floor when an arm grabbed him from behind and placed a cold steel blade up to his throat.

"Welcome, my fellow thief."

Chapter 21: Unlocked

Cathlyn awoke to the sound of Aeril's cries coming from outside the cell door. Two Darrak pushed her into the wall and then, again, into her cell. She fell flat on the floor, her body bruised and shaking, and began to sob.

"Every day, I try to use the Soulkind. I can feel them calling to me, but I don't know what to do.... I know we're being used, but magic may be our only way out of here."

Cathlyn leaned up against the bars and sighed. "We'll find a way out, somehow."

Aeril's body convulsed with her sobbing and she shook her head. "This morning, they told me I was useless, that I showed no progress with the Soulkind...."

"They say that to us everyday."

"But today, they told me they will kill me if I don't make one work, and I know they're not lying!" A wail erupted from her lips. "They brought me in here to say goodbye to you. They said they would take me to the center of the Darrak encampment at breakfast...." She buried her face in her hands.

One of the Darrak who had led Aeril in unlocked Cathlyn's cage door.

"Get out."

Cathlyn stood slowly and followed the dark creature into the hallway. As she turned back, she saw Aeril being dragged out of the cell and taken in the opposite direction. The Darrak pulling her smiled through its sharp fangs.

Cathlyn sat once again amongst the Soulkind, as she did every day, trying to avoid the temptation of trying to awaken their ancient powers. She did not want to face rejection again. Even after what felt like a month of returning to this room, her captors never told her what to do. She put her head down on the table.

Just recently, there was something new on the table. A white spiraling bracelet that she was told belonged to Sarissa. Once she found out it belonged to that ancient sorceress, she could not keep it out of her mind. The walls of avoidance were breaking. Something had to be done. Despite herself, excitement began to rise within her with every thought of reaching for the bracelet.

She grasped the white object from the table and turned it over on her palm, wondering if the material was stone or metal. The loop felt cool and warm at the same time; she could not quite determine which sensation was real to her touch. With great reverence, she placed the bent loop on her forearm.

Nothing. She watched the bracelet, wanting to sense magic flooding into her body, to feel Sarissa's powers. Instead, the loop dangled off her arm and she gave up on the tiny bit of hope she had held onto. Her heart felt as if crushed in a vice. There was no way out. This prison would be her home until she was deemed useless and killed, as would Aeril.

The odd bracelet hung loosely on her arm for a few more minutes, yet before she took it off the metal warmed ever so slightly. The solid material started to melt inward like dripping wax, bending towards her skin. Her eyes widened as the loop formed perfectly and snugly to her arm. Different colors shone forth deep within the bracelet then faded, swallowed by a pure white cloud. She could feel the other Soulkind upon the table pulsating energy towards her.

Somehow, Sarissa was helping her. What did she want her to do? Her mind soared, but she forced herself to focus on the situation before her.

She closed her eyes tight and wished for the power to help her friend, to get them both away from the confines of this prison. The Soulkind on the table glittered in the light emanating from the pure whiteness of the bracelet. Thoughts of freedom throbbed deep inside her and she envisioned cage doors unlocking. A whirlwind of emotions swept through her followed by a strong, cool wind that blew into the room. The locked door swung open against the stone wall.

With this power, she could soar! The pulse of freedom beat in her mind. Wind gusted again through the doorway, blowing her hair across her face, and her resolve hardened. She held an artifact owned by the greatest sorceress the world had ever known. She ran from the room.

The guards who usually manned the door were missing. She walked to the window across the hall and peered down to the valley below. Thousands of Darrak camped on the ground. A cold, steady wind continued to sweep her hair back. Her blood boiled inside her. Looking both ways along the hall, she almost wished for a Darrak to attack. Power surrounded her, pressed in on her from all directions, making her feel like she could defeat anything standing in her way.

As Cathlyn drew a deep, shaky breath, Aeril's pained cries rang in her ears. A blast of power wracked her body, as if lightning coursed through her bones, and she clung to the magic before her. Alive with power, she ran headlong down the abandoned hallways, drawn inexplicably towards a distant source, which she knew to be Aeril.

The hall curved on her way around the building. She hardly noticed when closed doors opened before her and slammed shut in her wake. She let the thoughts of magic stoke her desire to reach and rescue Aeril, let the power run her faster than she ever ran before. Eventually, the hall led her to the middle of a spiraling staircase. She knew escape lay downwards, but the voice called her upwards.

The stairs spiraled, and she leapt two steps per stride, barely noticing the stairwell widen as she progressed. The ground seen outside the window, hundreds of feet below, circled dizzyingly in her eyes as she climbed faster towards the cries in her mind. She saw nothing but the next step, her mind focused on one thought only: rescue.

When she reached the top of the tower, an open area greeted her. A dim light filtering through crevices in the ceiling filled her eyes. She looked around, taking in the massive stairs leading up to an ominous throne, empty except for shadows. The room weighed down upon her like a heavy fog. Wisps of darkness flitted past the light and threatened to cover it completely. She was drawn to a pool in the middle of the chamber filled with an opaque, glass-like liquid. In the reflection, she saw Aeril's body contorted in chains.

She looked up and ran to Aeril's side, examining the shackles around her arms, legs, and throat. Aeril's eyes were shut. Stains of tears ran down her cheeks. Cathlyn called out her name and tried to open the bindings. The chains remained securely fastened to the walls, despite Cathlyn's newfound power. Aeril's eyes fluttered and she gazed upon Cathlyn with relief and thanks.

"I knew you'd come..." Aeril whispered, blood caked onto her cracked lips. Her head slumped forward.

Cathlyn's body shook. *I must remove these bonds!* Nearly screaming, she yanked on the chains, but only tore the flesh on Aeril's palms in the process. Something snapped and she closed her eyes. Like water creeping up a levee in the springtime flood, some power welled up somewhere within her and she stood up, willing Aeril's chains to burst apart. The burning pulsated throughout her body and she basked in the pain. Freedom shouted out in her mind, overpowering any other thoughts or feelings.

A wave of energy burst out of her body and the shockwave pulsed through the room. With a brilliant flash, the bindings surrounding Aeril shattered and blew apart. Cathlyn covered her face, feeling hot shards stream past her body. The wave struck the walls and the darkness covering the openings in the ceiling flittered away. The blast subsided and total silence filled the room. With a start, she felt for Sarissa's bracelet. She gaped at her bare arm, unaware of when or how the bracelet came off. She scanned the floor and noticed a white, snake-like form slithering up the shadowy stairs.

The shadows surrounding the throne swirled like black smoke and swept through the room. A shadowy hand reached through the darkness, leaving a wispy trail of night, and beckoned to the creeping white shape. Coldness gripped her heart. More shadowy body parts began to coalesce upon the throne until she could see the darkened form of the hooded man. A shadow seemed to precede each movement the man made. The scene mesmerized Cathlyn and she watched with morbid curiosity as the man held his gloved fist to the floor, awaiting the bracelet. Although the rod crawled into his hand, it hesitated, as if coerced into submission by the powers this man wielded.

The hooded man sat back upon the throne and held up his right hand with the white rod twisted around his black gauntlet in a tight spiral, no longer a continuous loop. The spiral's brilliant white color seemed to fade. The man clenched his hand into a fist, turning it back and forth in front of his hidden face. All the while, a dark, low laugh escaped from deep within the cowls of his hood.

Cathlyn, terrified and shaking, tore her eyes away, looking to see what happened to Aeril. A small table, covered with shadow-enveloped shapes, lay where Aeril once stood. Cathlyn crawled over in confusion and her eyes widened with recognition. They were the Soulkind. *But how? And why?*

More laughter erupted into the cavernous room from behind her; this time, the laugh belonged to a woman. Slowly, she turned her head to look at the pool in the center of the room, afraid of what might be awaiting her. Aeril, free of bruises, cuts, and blood, stood upon the surface of the water. For a moment, the woman adjusted her petite, white gloves. In the next instant, the gloves swirled in shadows, replaced by thick, metal gauntlets. Aeril's face, too, began to swirl in shadows, and then the rest of her disappeared in a suffocating darkness.

226

Two blood-red eyes burned out of Aeril's shadowy face. She hid her face in her hands...

"Thank you, my servant, you have finally removed the lock," a voice boomed down upon Cathlyn's ears. She uncovered her face to look again and saw the shadowy form of a man where Aeril had been. Trying to face the eyes made her shake uncontrollably.

"I am Marlec...." The shadowy form of Marlec drifted towards the hooded man, who sat silent and motionless, on the throne. "He cannot hear or see me. He was a Follower of mine who is now but a shell for my power. Thank you for putting an end to Sarissa's spell. No, this is not a Soulkind, just a tool that will bind the magic of these Soulkind to me—with your help, of course."

The darkness and the man merged, and red eyes burned within the hood. Cathlyn could barely breathe. She tried to make sense of all that had happened in the past few seconds. Turic spoke a few times of Marlec before: a merciless and evil sorcerer, but that man lived a thousand years ago! Her mind reeled. *The Soulkind are unlocked.* But how did she do it? If Sarissa's bracelet was not a Soulkind, where had her magic come from? And what of Aeril?

"Now, you have a choice to make." Marlec, in his new form, arose from his throne and walked along the shadows towards where Cathlyn sat, still eyeing the table. "You will make a fine student, and I will teach you all you could possibly desire of magic, or...I will consume your soul."

He finished with a quick clench of his fist, the Gauntlet glinting darkly in the pale light. With that motion, shadowy bars formed a tight cage surrounding Cathlyn. The bars were not quite solid; she placed her hand around one and her fingers slipped through. The space between was deathly cold and she pulled her hand back. Perhaps if she ran fast enough through the shadows....

"Your body would survive," Marlec spoke, answering her thoughts once more. "But your heart, your mind, and your Soul would be frozen. You may try if you want...."

Cathlyn sat down and avoided the bars while Marlec walked towards his throne. *Was that really magic?* The whole thing seemed like a dream to her now. When she ran up the steps to this room; she felt an unbridled storm within. Was that her or Sarissa? Tentatively, she reached for that power again.

Marlec turned around to face her with a wry smile. "Your efforts will be in vain; those bars will contain magic, I assure you. It would a shame for this world to lose you now. I will give you time to decide."

Magic had to come from a Soulkind! Sarissa was the only person to use magic without— Cathlyn's heart stopped for an instant and then resumed pounding in her ears. *No. Impossible.* She nearly yelled out in excitement. She had to do something! Although Marlec warned her not to, she once again reached for her magic.

The cage started to shrink. She let go of her thoughts, but the shadowy bars continued to creep closer and closer. She curled herself into a ball to avoid their coldness. She cried out as they touched her skin, causing her to convulse.

"I'm sorry! I'm sorry!" she said and wept.

Marlec waited, watching from his throne. "Are you really? You do not seem to understand the importance of your life." He stared at her for a few more seconds before allowing the bars to back away. She let out another sob and pounded her fist onto the floor.

Brannon sat curled up in a small room with a securely barred door. He tumbled to the ground and stayed there alone, curled up on the floor. The only sounds that broke the silence were the clicking of Darrak claws and the incessant beating of drums from the valley. Each beat drove fear further into his soul. For the first time since awakening the Soulkind, he felt powerless, and afraid.

He thought back to *his* Followers. *Ingrates! I teach them the ways of magic and this is how they repay me: by abandoning my cause!* Marathas also disappeared from his side just before they came. Betrayal surrounded him.

Although some light found its way to his cell, a sudden darkness swept through the bars. A moment later, the door opened. A man walked in, or at least it looked like a man; shadows swirled and moved before each movement he made. Moments passed and all Brannon heard was his own breath and heart pounding in his ears. Finally, the man spoke.

"You will be given a choice. The Soulkind have all been released now, but the one you follow is still partially dormant and attached to your soul. There are two ways of correcting this: you may willingly pass on your bond with Marathas or we will take it from you by death. You must decide now, for your successor will arrive shortly from the frontlines of my army and will not give you the choice I do." The shadow arose, once again moving before the body, and said, "Here's an old friend of mine who said he would like to keep you company…and perhaps assist you in your dilemma."

In the weak light, Brannon saw a familiar face smiling down upon him. Marathas. Why would the man who accompanied him all the way through this dark land now side with the enemy? He started to speak, but all that came out of his mouth incoherent muttering as his world collapsed and he stared at Marathas in disbelief.

Chapter 22: The Shadow

"Welcome, my fellow thief. Now be quiet, or you'll call the whole army in after us."

Jace turned around and wrapped his arms around Karanne. She hid her dagger in her sleeve with a flick of her wrist before returning the hug. "How did you get here?" she said.

Her words were met with Jace's smile. He sensed she was alive all along, but looking at her now, realized how great his fears had been. "With that smell? Anyone could find you." He walked with her away from the door back to the staircase and wrinkled his nose.

She shrugged her shoulders and shook her head, "I'll tell you that story later. What are you doing here? How did…" she sputtered out several questions, but after one more embrace, returned to her vigilance. She almost yelled out, though, when she saw Jace's companions walking down the stairs.

"You're alive!"

Mathes shoved his way ahead of the others and embraced her. Karanne returned the affection, but pulled away, remembering danger still surrounded them. After squeezing Mathes' hand, she motioned for all to be quiet and to follow her underneath the stairs. She smiled at Straeten and patted him on the back as he passed.

"There are others with me—"

"Where's Jervis?" Jace whispered. He brandished his blade and peered past several large casks. "He's a traitor!"

From behind the casks, five others stood up, but Jervis was not among them. Three appeared to be Guardians, and two others to be Followers. He could not make out the sixth.

One of the men bearing a sword said, "He was just here behind me! He must have run down this hall…." Everyone peered into the darkness of the narrow tunnel, and the man looked back at Karanne.

Karanne nodded her head. "He's like a snake, that boy. Rayin, take one of the Followers with you, and be careful. We'll be heading towards the stairs by then."

A shorter, young man in the brown Follower robes joined Rayin and the two hurried into the darkness. Karanne shook her head.

"I should have known. For the suffering! We're not going to find him, are we? He's been trained as a thief, and there's something else." She looked at Jace and he nodded. "Turic, we'd better hurry now. They'll find us soon enough if we don't get moving."

"Turic?" Jace said.

The sixth Follower stood up and came out from his resting place in the darkness. Jace and Straeten both ran to his side, helped him stand, and gripped his shoulders. All three were beyond words. Jace thought his old teacher looked much older than he had upon leaving Beldan, and more gaunt.

"You boys look like you have much to tell me of your journey." Straeten and Jace exchanged looks and Turic smiled. "Come now, let's get on with this, shall we? The Soulkind and Brannon Co'lere await us somewhere in the bowels of this fortress. I might be old, but, you know...."

Stroud walked to Turic and clasped his arm. Turic looked at the burns on the Guardian's face and hands and shook his head. "I have some news you may not wish to hear," Turic said, placing his hand on Stroud's shoulder.

Jace watched as the two of them turned away from the others and talked in low voices. At that moment, a surge of energy, like a wave, pulsed through the room, knocking everyone to the floor. Barrels fell over and opened, spilling their contents. A chest on the floor in front of Jace suddenly sprung open. Everyone slowly got up and looked around, unable to speak. Jace felt something shift inside his pack as he stood.

He stuck his hand in the pouch to see what it was. The black box he had been carrying was now open for some reason. Inside, lay a single black unpolished gemstone.

"Straet, look at this," he said and showed his friend the box and the stone.

Straeten backed up quickly. "There may be another one of those things in there."

Jace looked carefully into the box.

Jace shrugged his shoulders. "Nothing else. Whatever that blast was, let's just hope it doesn't happen again."

The black gem felt deathly cold as he turned it over in his hand before closing it tightly into his pouch. Behind him, Turic stood watching Stroud walk slowly back to the others with confusion and anger crossing his face. Karanne motioned for everyone to follow her to the doorway leading into the central building. Mathes hung back a ways as she directed the party. Jace rushed past the others to her side.

"Have you seen Cathlyn?"

Allar stopped and turned to see Karanne shake her head. "We've been here for at least an hour now and haven't seen any other prisoners. Two of these hallways lead around the perimeter of the building, while this one leads through many rooms to a staircase, which goes up to the central tower and down to the main floor. We hope any other prisoners will be on this level, but haven't found them yet."

"And what about guards?"

"That's the strange part," Karanne said. "They've almost all disappeared out of the castle. Other than the Darrak that walked past us to the catwalk above, we've seen no one."

She looked at Jace, and nodded when he made a quick motion across his throat indicating the creature's demise.

"We ran into the other Followers leaving this valley," Jace said.

Karanne sighed. "They need to get through the mountains *and* stay in front of that army. I don't know how they'll be able to—"

"They should be all right; I sent one of my group with them. She's been through these hills and will find a way," Jace said. "Now, we should split up to cover this floor."

Karanne nodded slowly and they separated into three groups to search the area for Brannon, the Soulkind, and any other prisoners. Jace motioned for Allar and Straeten to follow him down the center hallway, and he turned around to see Karanne and Mathes walking down another with Kal and the remaining Guardian.

Stroud stood close to Turic and drew his sword. He asked for either Burgis or Tare to come with him and the tall silent boy walked to his side, as did the other Follower, a young man with dark hair. Burgis looked back at his brother, but joined Jace without a word.

As Jace led his friends down the hallway, Ash walked beside him and Valor returned to his shoulder. He drew two daggers from within his cloak and saw the others ready themselves, as well. Straeten could wield magic, but felt more comfortable with a weapon in his hands, so he held the bladed staff in front of him. Burgis, now as silent as his brother, walked behind with Allar.

The hall headed straight in the same direction, and although many smaller passages branched off from the main one, Jace felt compelled to continue ahead, as if guided. Up ahead, he saw the large

232

circular wall surrounded by a spiral staircase of which Karanne spoke. He crawled to the edge to look down the stairs.

A score of Darrak troops crawled like ants in the opposite direction. Jervis must not have made his way down to them…yet. Again, a voice echoed in his mind, beckoning him up the stairs, and he obeyed.

The building was too quiet for his liking, and he was sure the others felt the same; their eyes darted around, expecting danger to jump out from where the light failed to shine. The shadows cast from the few torches throughout the stairwell seemed almost alive, almost to bite at their feet. The further they climbed, the more consuming the shadows became, and the darkness nearly swallowed the torchlight. Eventually, they were blanketed by the shade of night.

After what felt like hours of utter blackness, the stairs ended in a deathly cold room. The room appeared empty, except for the shadowy, thick air. Then he recognized the structure in the center of the room—a raised pool like the one below the Library and in his memory. The edge of the pool was demolished, the carvings smashed. He couldn't see where the gem had been taken out. He ran to the pool's side, dropped to his knees, and peered over the cracked ledge, seeing cloudy, black waters. In the reflection, he saw four jagged holes in the tower above, appearing as the snarling visage of a demon. Valor skittishly flew off his shoulder up to the light above to perch on one of the openings. Deep in the waters, a faint glimmer of blue light began to shine, but the darkness fought to contain it.

"I don't like this," Straeten said, backing towards Jace and holding out his spear. "This darkness isn't right…." Burgis drew upon his bowstring and pointed the arrow into the shadows.

"Jace, watch out!"

Cathlyn! Following his instinct, Jace dropped to the cold floor just as a bolt of flame screamed past his head, piercing the shadows and exploding upon the rounded walls with a flurry of sparks. In the glare that lingered after the explosion, he rolled behind the cover of the pool and looked around the room to spot his attacker and Cathlyn. Burgis, Allar, and Straeten also scrambled for cover.

Upon a small set of stairs in the middle of the room, Jervis stood with his arms outstretched and a smile on his face, his eyes burning brightly with a strange light. Ash growled, but stayed by Jace's side. Jace ducked his head as another bolt filled the room with fire, this time striking the surface of the pool. Sizzling water splashed up, searing Jace's face. Ash yelped as the boiling water hit his fur. Jervis laughed, but his laughter turned to howling as Valor dove from above, ripping at his face with talons.

"Don't shoot!" Jace cried out as he saw Burgis draw the bowstring back. With a thought, he willed Valor to fly away to give his friends a clear shot. Almost instantly, the hawk cried out and flew away from Jervis' swinging arms. Burgis released the bowstring, and darkness fell, concealing Jervis. The sound of the arrow clattering off the steps rang into the air.

Straeten waited no longer and released his own fireball upward to the ceiling. The bolt penetrated the dark and illuminated the entire room, exposing Jervis at the top of the stairs next to a throne. Fire rippled at the end of Straeten's hand as he prepared to throw another blast.

Under the glare of Straeten's magic, Allar could see for a moment.

"Cathlyn?"

He ducked and ran across to his sister, trapped behind bars of darkness.

Jace looked over to the darkened cage and saw Cathlyn's delicate hands reaching out trying hard not to touch the shadowy cage.

"Allar, no!" Jace said.

Jervis pointed his hand at the Guardian and the flames leapt downward. Straeten watched the magic hurled at Allar and sent his own crackling ball of fire through the air. With a jarring explosion, his blast struck and deflected Jervis', causing it to careen towards the wall and burst in a brilliant shower of light. The impact threw Allar across the ground and knocked his sword aside. He arose but staggered momentarily before continuing to run to Cathlyn, all the while looking for his weapon.

Burgis then drew back another arrow and loosed it at Jervis. Jervis glanced towards the sound and disappeared in a shadow. The arrow passed through where Jervis' throat should have been and imbedded itself with a *thud* into the darkened throne. Burgis swore and drew back another arrow.

Jace looked around for any movement from Jervis. A second later, Jervis reappeared and cast a bolt of flame. The bolt caught Straeten off guard and struck him in the chest, knocking him backward against the wall. He grunted in an effort to stand, but fell down again, dazed. Jervis laughed and faded away into the shadows before Burgis could launch his arrow.

"Jervis!" Jace yelled out. "Why are you doing this?"

"You always thought you were better than me!" Jervis' voice emanated from somewhere in the room. "Not anymore."

Ash barked and Jace looked towards where the dog stared. He could also sense Valor watching from above. Nothing moved, but Jace concentrated and tried to use Ash's sight this time. The symbol on his hand glowed slightly and almost instantly the connection between them grew. A strong smell of sweat, and...*hate?* entered his nose; Jervis, he was sure of it. As he focused on the direction of the smell, his vision leapt to Valor's, and he saw a shape within the darkness, the black outline of a human only a few feet from Burgis.

"Burgis! In front of you!" Before Burgis could release an arrow, Jervis appeared out of the folds of shadow. Burgis' bow suddenly burst into white flames, crumbling to ashes in an instant. He yelled out in pain, but swung out nonetheless. Jervis caught the backhand blow on his chin, and spun hard to the floor. When he landed, he sneered up at Burgis. Before he could raise his hands, a spiral of fire spun from Straeten's hand and he slipped away under the cover of the folding shadow, disappearing from sight. Burgis fell to his knees, clenching his burned fists to his stomach, and grimaced in pain. Jace looked over at Straeten, who still stumbled in his attempts to stand.

Allar reached Cathlyn in her cage, and started to reach for her hands. "Don't touch them," Cathlyn said. "They'll kill you."

Allar nodded and stood up, watching behind him for any sign of the moving shadow. "Jace, do you see him?" He continued looking around on the floor for his weapon.

Jace tried to see within the depths of the darkness. His new senses opened again in his mind and the traitor's smell filled his nose. He concentrated on Jervis' scent and saw the outline of his shadowy form at the top of the stairs, standing next to the throne. Jace flipped his dagger and hurled it. The dagger spun, end over end, and, with a sickening thud, planted itself into the throne, and something else. Jervis screamed and began releasing fire at anything that moved, all the while trying to free his pinned hand.

Allar jumped away from a blast into a table and sent its contents crashing to the floor. In a panic, he reached around for something to use as a weapon. Jervis paused from his chaotic blasts to yank at the blade and blood spilled to the floor and he screamed, unable to pull out the knife. "Your friend will die in her cage!" With that, Jervis pointed his burning hand at Cathlyn in her dark prison and sent a bolt in her direction.

With a shout, Allar jumped from behind the table he upended with a strange gleaming shield attached to his forearm. He dove in front of Cathlyn's cage before the fire struck and held up his arm. The flame crashed into the shield. The fire burned in Jervis' eyes in satisfaction.

His eyes widened, however, when he released the spell and saw Allar and Cathlyn alive. The smoking shield dropped from Allar's arm. Jervis tore the dagger in his hand free from the throne with a grunt through his clenched teeth. Fire dripped alongside blood and the dagger clinked onto the floor. Before anyone could make a move, a wind, beginning inside the room, whirled the surrounding shadows like dark smoke in a storm.

Icy fingers from within the shadows clenched Jace's body, dragging him to the floor and pinning him to the wall. Jace looked outside the black bars that now held him to see his companions trapped the same way; even Ash was encased in a shadowy, iron cage. A look of fear crossed Jervis' face as the thief backed away from the throne with his head pointed to the floor and his injured right hand cradled under his arm. Jace's eyes returned to the top of the steps.

A shadow, darker than his nightmares grew from the throne and a body began to appear. He looked around at his companions, all staring at the forbidding spectacle. On the floor lay the shield Allar used, unscathed from Jervis' fires.

Jervis knelt at the foot of the steps while the figure materialized and held up a black, gloved hand. "Enough," a voice Jace recognized boomed. "Even with all those powers I gave you, you still are worthless."

The fire in Jervis' eyes left and the thief slumped to the floor. He looked over at Jace with a strange expression, but before Jace could read it, he saw two eyes shine forth a bloody, red glow from within the hooded figure.

Turic shook his head as Stroud finished recounting his tale of the journey with Brannon. Clearly the man had reached the limits of sanity. Turic mused momentarily on what types of magic a lunatic might create with the Soulkind. He continued searching the cells for the man to bring him back from the reaches of his madness.

Turic knew Stroud was a man of honor, but he had been betrayed by both Huron Caldre and Brannon and almost killed in the process. He looked at Stroud's face to ascertain his intentions and yet could not make out anything from the man's blank stare.

Tare and a Follower named Barsal walked closely behind Turic and Stroud. All four walked to the end of the passage until they reached the next corner of the building, where again, the path branched off. Stroud opened every door they passed, but found no trace of a living being or the Soulkind.

When Turic saw blood on the ground in front of a half-opened door, he motioned to Stroud, who then rushed forward, sword at the ready. Stroud pushed open the wooden door, peered into the room, and lowered his weapon. Turic glanced inside and saw the Guardian and Follower who had chased Jervis. Their bodies had been dragged and thrown in the corner, throats slit. Jervis was apparently more dangerous than they realized.

Turic said a few words for the safety of their souls and then followed Stroud into the hall. The rest of the corridor was barren, except for the bones of someone long-departed. Eventually, they reached the end of the passage and continued on their way down the next when they met up with Kal and Gerant. Turic looked behind the two for Mathes and Karanne.

"Mathes insisted he go up the tower," Kal said, "and Karanne went with him. We stayed back to keep looking on this level."

Turic waved for the newcomers to follow them through the hallway leading to the central staircase. They had not walked long when Turic saw movement in the darkness ahead. He recognized the armored man immediately: Huron Caldre. He waved the others into silence as he watched the man unlocking a door. Stroud's eyes tightened. With a rush of adrenaline, Turic rushed forward as quietly as he could, followed closely by the others.

As he approached the door Caldre had entered, he slowed to listen. Whining and pleading emanated from inside. Brannon.

Turic looked to Stroud who nodded and pushed open the door. Brannon kneeled behind a caged wall, clasping onto the metal bars. Caldre stood over him with his hands on his waist and shook his head. Brannon turned his eyes towards Turic and Caldre whipped his head around. Marathas dangled from Caldre's neck. With a start, Caldre swept out his sword and reached through the cage for Brannon's throat, but Brannon backed away. He reached into a pouch for the key to open the cell.

Stroud forced himself past Turic into the room. His sword flashed in the light streaming through the window. Caldre fumbled with the keys, then brought his own sword up as Stroud's came down hard. His eyes widened in recognition of his attacker, and then he laughed and returned the blows.

"Why, Stroud, it is so good to see you again," Caldre gloated.

Stroud said nothing, but winced as he swung his sword.

Turic ran towards the cell seeing Brannon inside. Brannon looked up from his shaking hands. Caldre's sword barely missed Turic's head while fighting. With each swing, Stroud parried the man's blow and forced him away from the cage. Fury blazed in his eyes.

"We thought you were dead, Caldre."

"I was tired of such a powerless system. Darkness is where the true power lies."

Stroud was an adept warrior, but the burns he sustained clearly slowed his steps. Eventually he was herded into a corner. Turic turned to Brannon, who was arguing with someone he could not see. A shout, accompanied by a clang of metal, drew Turic from the cage; Caldre had knocked Stroud's sword from his hand.

"I cannot accept this responsibility any further," Brannon uttered. "I pass it to you, Turic…"

"No!" Another voice called out of the cell to Turic. Turic looked inside and now saw two people. Brannon lay cowering on the floor, and a tall man in elegant robes stood beside him, eyes wide. Suddenly, visions of glory and riches flitted past Turic's eyes: he held the highest position on the Hall Council, he was the advisor to the king of Myraton, and finally, the king himself. He could be all these, he could have all the power he wanted…. if only he listened to Marathas. Turic sensed something else: a true magic, the real nature of the Soulkind, like a fiery ember encased in burnt out wood. He stretched past Marathas' voice deep into the heart of the Soulkind.

The Soulkind around Caldre's neck was no longer a shiny gold bauble. Now, it glittered bright as the sun.

"Finally, it is mine!" Caldre said and stared at the amulet. He reached his hand up to clasp it in triumph, but screamed as the burning gemstone seared his hand.

"You will never have the Soulkind, Guard Master."

Caldre turned around and saw Turic with a burning mark of flames encircling his neck

"How...?"

Caldre shuddered as Stroud drove a sword through his heart.

"Lie in darkness, Caldre."

The Soulkind burned brightly upon Caldre's throat. Stroud lifted it over the dead man's head, offering it to the new Master. Turic received the gemstone necklace with reverence. The glowing lines around his neck faded into thin, intricate black lines in the shape of tiny flames.

Brannon's mouth gaped open when he saw the Soulkind, as did Marathas'. The golden wings that once enveloped the burning gemstone unfurled until they were barely visible from behind the fiery red gem. The ancient Master's soul faded slightly into the shadows, as if his grip on the Soulkind had slipped. Turic ignored Marathas for now; he had more important issues to confront. As he held up his right hand, the lock on Brannon's cell door began to glow, first a bright orange, then a fierce white. Drops of molten metal spattered onto the floor and dripped down the bars until nothing remained of the lock except a gaping hole.

The cell door opened on its own, leaving a bewildered Brannon. Stroud walked to the door, blood-covered sword still drawn and at the ready, and scowled at Co'lere. The Guardian appeared more intimidating with the burns covering his face. Brannon took a step backwards, placed one hand upon the stone wall of the cell, and held the other in front of him, as if to ward off Stroud. He stared at the man, pleading in silence.

Turic held his hand out and said, "His soul is not completely lost. We cannot leave him here amongst this evil. Barsal, Tare...escort our friend."

"Turic!" Barsal called from the hall. "We're not alone!"

Jace watched as Marlec walked towards his friends through an ever-present shadowy shroud. The man's boots clicked upon the stone floor with each menacing step. At the foot of the stairs, he turned and looked at all the cages then walked towards Allar.

The man kicked the smoking shield and sent it skidding and jumping across the floor. Allar looked away as Marlec held up his gloved hand in a fist in front of the dark cage but then grabbed his chest, his eyes bulging. Marlec held up his other jet-black gauntlet, drawing Allar's eyes towards his.

"You are a problem which I shall soon solve." Then to everyone, he said, "Get used to your cages, they're yours forever."

He walked past Allar's cage and stopped in front of Jace. The glowing red eyes made him turn away. *Those eyes.* Memories stirred of

Lu'Calen's death at his brother's hand. Marlec's icy grip clenched him around the neck, lifting his chin upwards. In the instant that Jace gazed upon the eyes, they narrowed, and the shadowy bars around his body faded.

"I know you," Marlec began. "Somehow, I know you...."

How could he? Before Jace could think further, he reached to his chest and gasped as if his heart was trapped in a vice. Through clouded vision, he saw the man's hand clasping into a fist. Compelled to walk forward, he stumbled to the pool's edge, dropping to his knees and grasping the carved stone. The glassy surface of the water seemed to glow, like a gray, winter sky.

He positioned himself so the pool lay between him and Jace. Jace's neck jerked forward, bent by the darkness of Marlec's will, until his hair fell into the water. Marlec stared quietly at the mark on his hand.

"Do you have it with you?"

Pain clouded Jace's mind and he could barely lift his head to nod. The man motioned with a gauntlet-clad fist and Jace, once again forced beyond his will, reached into the pouch by his side. Memories slipped past his eyes as he brushed his fingers across the stones until he settled on the flat, rounded, green stone. When he drew forth the Soulkind, Marlec's eyes glowed brighter. The hooded man beckoned with his gauntlets and a shadow enveloped Jace's palm, calling the stone from his hand through the air.

When the stone reappeared within Marlec's hand, he clenched it and said, "At last, I have you. And now, to finish what I started."

Jace felt a shove into his back and toppled headfirst into the frigid waters, shattering the surface. The water brought forth the memories of his fall from the Library roof and Lu'Calen's past mixed in an icy swirl. An invisible hand kept him struggling below the water and he kicked to reach the air his lungs screamed for. The top of the water distorted his vision, but he could see Marlec's eyes a foot from the edge of the pool, watching.

Visions swirled in Jace's head like a whirlwind. At first, he was Lu'Calen, surprised at his brother's treachery. Then, he was himself, only eight years ago, struggling below the waters of the Soulwash. Finally, he entered the chaotic reality of the present, where Marlec stood above him, resting his hands and Jace's Soulkind on the pool's edge. Nearing the end of his struggles, he saw the shadows underneath Marlec's hood disappear through the glowing of the water, leaving behind a young man's face, filled with anger and satisfaction. Jace could barely resist succumbing to the waters.

Then another vision flew into his eyes, this time from above Marlec. He was watching through the eyes of something else diving straight down towards the hooded man. Suddenly, the dark force holding Jace down released him and he broke the surface of the water, reaching upwards with his arms and drawing the blessed air into his empty lungs. The man with Marlec's eyes backed away from the splashing water as Valor swept off his hood. The bloody red eyes stood out against the man's pale, exposed face as he struggled for control, waving at the ripping talons of the hawk. Bleeding claw marks lined the man's face. A bolt of flame seared through the room and Valor flew upwards out of the tower. The flame burst into the throne past Marlec, causing him to stumble.

With his remaining energy, Jace grasped the stone edge of the pool and looked behind him to see Karanne and Mathes facing the darkness. Karanne hurled bolts of fire towards Marlec, but the shadows surrounding the man snuffed the flames as if extinguishing candles. The darkness of shadowy cages quickly encircled both Mathes and Karanne, trapping them like the others. Marlec returned his stare to Jace, still breathing heavily in the icy pool. His red eyes glanced upwards to where Valor flew, and with a wave of his hands, he clouded the exits from the room with a wall darker than night. Darkness settled and only the soft glow of the pool attempted to penetrate the shadows.

"That's a clever trick," he said. "Any others I should know about?"

Marlec's grasp once again clenched Jace's throat and constricted his lungs. Before Marlec could push him into the waters, Jace lifted his hand to show what he held.

"Just this one."

It was his Soulkind.

"How did you…" Marlec's eyes flared as he looked in disbelief. By changing the wispy shadows holding Jace down to a gust of wind, Marlec lifted his hand for Jace to come out of the waters. Surprising both Marlec and himself, Jace didn't move. Marlec's eyes swelled and bore down upon Jace like a great weight. The man lifted again with his gauntlets.

Jace responded with a smirk.

The waters pulsed with a brighter glow. Marlec stepped closer to the pool and raised his fist, motioning to clench Jace's heart again.

Instead of the iciness closing in on his body, the water now surrounded Jace with warmth and support.

"If you kill me now, I will take this Soulkind with me to the bottom of these waters." He gripped the green stone in his hand.

Marlec, now at the edge of the pool, looked down upon him and said, "I will retrieve the stone when you fall...."

"I don't think so." Jace tread water in the center of the pool and as the words left his lips, a distant boom of thunder shook the room and Marlec's eyes dimmed. Jace felt something pulse within his mind, like the lighting of a great fire. Marlec then returned his focus, his red eyes burning once again.

"We have taken Marathas from you," Jace said.

The shadow lessened under the hood and Jace saw the man beneath the darkness, no longer just the red eyes. He lunged forward and grabbed Jace around the throat. Jace lifted his hand to show the man he dropped the stone into the pool. The water rippled as it swallowed the rock.

Marlec thrust his arm into the now brightly glowing pool with a sound like breaking glass. After making contact with the water, his red eyes blazed again as he realized his folly.

"I told you never to touch these waters," a voice called out. Jace knew the words came from him, but they were not his own.

The water swirled, as a rippling arm extended from the surface. Before Marlec could move, the liquid pierced his chest with a burst of light and the hand clasped around his heart, withdrawing a shadow Jace knew was Marlec's soul. The translucent arm dragged the struggling darkness into the waters below and left the used body to slump onto the floor.

Jace breathed easier now and felt the warmth of the waters surrounding him, almost inviting him to follow. He started to close his eyes just as rough hands grabbed him by the shoulders, shaking him and pulling him up. The next thing he knew, he was resting soaked on the cold floor and Straeten was looking on with concern. Jace's other friends stood above him, as well, and helped him to his feet. Karanne held him by the shoulder with a smile.

Jace, feeling his strength return, looked at the water, and for an instant, saw a figure forming on the surface. The water glowed with a bright blue light and filled the shadowy tower with its warmth. He smiled when he recognized the man's face. In his hand he held the black gemstone that Jace had dropped into the pool. Lu'Calen smiled once at Jace and then disappeared, leaving only the glowing water behind. The darkness left through the ceiling like trails of smoke and light cleansed the room from outside.

Jace ran over to Cathlyn and wrapped his arms around her before she could say anything. He looked at her face and, without thinking, kissed her. His heart beat loudly in his head as she returned the kiss, but then the thudding began to falter. It was the drums in the Shadow Vale; the once incessant drumming pushing the march onward changed into a rhythmic pattern.

The Darrak voices lifted in screams and shouts, terrifying to Jace's ears and he looked away from Cathlyn to the window. The Darrak had regained control of their own wills, their souls now free from Marlec's grasp. Abruptly, another thought entered his mind.

"Jervis!"

Jace's companions spun around, looking for the thief, expecting his shadow to appear at any moment, yet it never came. Jace tried sensing Jervis, calling upon his Soulkind to see through the shadows, but there was no darkness in which to hide. He was gone.

Burgis leaned against the wall with a sword in hand. He held the blade tentatively and glanced around the room.

"We've got to leave before the Darrak get here," Cathlyn said and looked out the window at winged creatures filling the skies. "Quickly! Gather the Soulkind!"

They rushed to the Soulkind and began gently picking up the relics. Allar held the long, white shield that saved Cathlyn and strapped it onto his arm.

Straeten stood beside Jace. "How did you get your Soulkind away from him? I can't believe you just threw it away."

Jace smirked. "You have to have fast hands to be a thief." He produced the smooth green stone with a quick gesture of his wrist. "It was the stone from the box. I switched them." He reached down and pet Ash's head. Straeten laughed and continued collecting the Soulkind.

"*Your* Soulkind?" Cathlyn said.

"I'll tell you later," Jace said with a smile.

"Some are missing," Cathlyn said suddenly, making certain as she counted them again and searched through everyone's packs.

Jace looked up as he heard someone's blade quickly being drawn. Mathes was on the other side of the pool, standing beside the body that

Marlec left behind with his sword pointed at the man's throat. "He's still alive."

Jace rushed over with a knife held tightly in his fist.

"What are you waiting for?" Allar called. "Kill him!"

Jace pushed Mathes aside and bent to inspect the man in the black robes, holding his blade to his throat. The man was out cold. He knelt silently for several seconds until he heard the others behind him, waiting for his decision. He gripped the knife tighter for a moment.

He could end it.

"Who is he?" someone said, Jace didn't really know who.

"I...don't know," he said, and slid his knife back into his sleeve. "But he's coming with us."

"What?" Burgis said. "Are you crazy? After what he did?"

"It wasn't him. It was these."

Jace took the black gloves off the man's hands. The metal burned him with deathly coldness. Marlec's soul had been removed, but the darkness remained, and Jace could feel it. He wrapped the gloves in thick cloth and stowed them carefully in his pack.

"Is Sarissa's lock on him?" Cathlyn shouted, searching the body.

"I only saw those gauntlets on him," Mathes replied.

Cathlyn clenched her fist and pounded the ground.

"Jervis," Straeten said.

Jace walked to the window again to gaze upon the Darrak. They now covered the Shadow Vale, scrambling about like ants, and filled the skies like storm clouds, making escape by way of the valley ledge impossible.

"I hope Ranelle was able to lead the Followers to safety before this began."

They were left with only one way to depart: beyond the tunnel they came through and into the unknown.

"Tie him up, we're leaving," Jace said. The accursed weight of the gauntlets bore down against him as he shouldered his pack. Jace gave a thought to his hawk companion and Valor leapt into the air to wait outside the castle. Ash barked at the hawk, who returned the call with a cry of his own. With Ash at his side, Jace ran down the stairs. Down they spiraled, dragging the body of Marlec's puppet with them. Jace turned around and smiled at Cathlyn, who was close behind and smiled back.

Jace's mind raced faster than his feet upon the stone stairs, trying to think of a way out of the valley. He shook his head; first he had to find

Turic and get out of the fortress. As if in answer, a burst of fire, brighter than the sun, slammed into the wall in front of him. Two Darrak sped down the stairs, without a glance at Jace and the others.

Turic strode towards them with a glowing ring of flames around his throat, followed by Stroud, Tare, a Guardian, and Brannon Co'lere, who slunk behind. Jace thought for a second he saw a figure dressed in rich robes with them, but with a second look, saw only shadows cast by the fiery mark upon Turic's throat dancing on the wall.

"This is new," Jace said and smiled at Turic, knowing he must wait to hear the story of the red gemstone around his neck.

"As is your companion," Turic replied. "It seems we'll both have to wait."

Stroud, Tare, a Guardian, and Brannon followed. Burgis and Tare clasped arms and exchanged the salute. The two brothers then carried their prisoner in between them. With a wave of his hand, Jace called everyone to follow and ran down the hall towards the spidery bridge. Glancing backwards, he saw Allar running beside Cathlyn; he had never left her side since they were freed. Jace fell back to run with her and grasped her hand.

No Darrak waited for them inside the corridors, nor at the bridge spanning the chasm. Out of breath, the party walked to the narrow bridge. The Darrak had not returned to this side of the valley yet, and the tunnel through the ridge appeared empty. Jace knew they must reach that tunnel if they were to have any chance of escape. In single file, the party crept along the stone arch, fully aware of the danger of being spotted. Jace encouraged his friends along and breathed a sigh of relief when Straeten, bringing up the rear of the line, stepped safely onto the valley floor.

The tunnel across the valley beckoned to Jace. He wondered how they would ever cross the valley floor without being seen. The cries of the Darrak pierced his ears. He laughed to himself as he envisioned a line of horses awaiting, ready to carry him and his companions away from this place. *That would be nice.*

"Blue?" Straeten said. Jace blinked his eyes. Valor sat atop Blue's saddle and Jace finally realized this was no dream when his companions mounted the horses, calling for him to hurry. Even Chase had appeared, and Allar jumped onto him with a smile. With a start, Jace ran to his old friend, jumped into the saddle, and tore off across the valley, stroking Blue's mane as she ran.

If any Darrak took notice amongst the pandemonium, none followed. Blue gained the lead on the other wild horses she managed to bring with her. Darkness swallowed them when they reached the tunnel and the Darrak's cries fell silent within the walls. Only the pounding of the horses' hooves filled the party's ears until they broke through the darkness and out of the underground passage.

Once they rode through to the other side and Ash followed shortly afterward, they looked towards the top of the ridge, expecting winged Darrak to follow them in a massive wave of overcoming darkness. The tunnel exit opened like an evil mouth, threatening to spew forth the army of Darrak, but none followed. To be sure none would give chase through the cave, Straeten, Turic, and Karanne summoned great swaths of firebursts, and sent them at the opening. Huge boulders fell in front of the cliff, forbidding any entrance, or exit.

The crashing of the boulders ceased and the dust settled, but the shouts and drumming from the Darrak still filled the air and drove Jace onward. Snow began to fall as they fled. His companions breathed heavily in silence while they urged their horses to follow him into the unknown. Jace stroked the side of Blue's neck again.

"Take us home."

The End

Steve Davala is a middle school science and math teacher and maintains partial sanity by writing. The Soulkind Awakening is book one in the Soulkind Series; the second book is due in 2014. He lives in Oregon with his family.

Made in the USA
Charleston, SC
04 October 2013